Loradell Cassler

Let Us

Consider One Another

Let Us Consider One Another

BY JOSEPHINE LAWRENCE

D. APPLETON-CENTURY COMPANY
INCORPORATED • NEW YORK • LONDON

All names, characters, and events in this book are fictional, and any resemblance which may seem to exist to real persons is purely coincidental.

PRINTED IN THE UNITED STATES OF AMERICA

Let Us Consider One Another

Chapter One

TOBIAS FERRIS opened the door of his small, neat house, the third from the corner in a row of one-family houses equally small and neat. The hall smelled fragrantly of lamb-stew and he was glad that he had reached home before his daughter, Dora. She had some kind of a contraption rigged to absorb cooking smells—a bottle she opened and left standing on the table uncorked. With the scarcity of meat you'd think any woman might enjoy smelling a bit of it stewing, Tobias reflected, treading heavily toward the kitchen which was at the end of the hall.

"Quilty?" The door was ajar and the weight of his tall, angular figure pushed it open as he peered in at the colored woman standing before the gas range. "I'm back," he informed her.

"Yes, sir." Tranquility Mead shook a red tin box over an iron pot with a practised hand.

The old man sniffed; his lips under the scrubby gray clipped mustache smacked in anticipation. "Any letters or phone calls?"

He put this question as a matter of routine and it surprised him when Quilty said, "There was a phone call." She picked up a second box and airly dusted the contents of the kettle again.

"A phone call? When? Did you take it down?" Tobias' excitement was that of the man no longer active in business, to whom nothing is trivial because all his days are unimportant.

The colored woman's gentle eyes surveyed him indulgently. "It was Miss Cecilia."

"Ceil!" Tobias' inflection betrayed his astonishment. "Why, we haven't heard from her in—why, it must be almost a year." He shrugged his shoulders in an effort to keep his gray top coat from sliding to the floor. "What did she say? Did she ask for me?" he probed.

His granddaughter had asked for him, Tranquility reported. "Miss Cecilia say she coming tonight. After dinner. She wanted you should tell Miss Dora to please be home."

With a worried glance at Tobias, still in the doorway, Tranquility hinted that it might be well to close the door. "Miss Dora don't like the house smelled up," she reminded him.

Tobias grumbled. No one minded smelling a good dinner, he argued, but he shut the door and proceeded to hang his hat and coat tidily in the closet under the hall stairs. Evening-in-Paris, the beautiful black cat who occupied the living room club chair in his master's absence, reluctantly stepped down long enough for Tobas to seat himself and turn on the radio. Then, Paris in his lap, Tobias fell asleep, facing the fireplace. He had made it a rule not to light the fire before dinner, since Dora so seldom came in early enough to enjoy it.

The click of her key in the lock aroused him from his doze and he started up, an unreasoning feeling of guilt heavy on his sluggish mind. He sank back, clutching the indignant cat. "That you, Dora?"

A slender, trim woman, dark-eyed, with silver-gray hair rolled smoothly under her black hat, came into the room from the hall. She carried a large handbag and several paper-wrapped parcels, her gloves, and the evening paper telescoped into a kind of bouquet as she leaned down to kiss her father. "Hello, Father! Hi, Paris! Everything all right?"

He was all right, Tobias assured her. "Got something to tell you, too. Guess who telephoned—Ceil!"

"Cecilia!" Dora, on her way to the kitchen, turned. "Are you sure? Is anything the matter? What did she say?"

There didn't have to be anything the matter, Tobias argued querulously; Ceil just phoned, that was all. He had been down at the drugstore, buying stamps, but Quilty had taken the message.

"Said she was coming here tonight, after dinner. Wanted you to know, so's you'd be home."

Dora laughed unexpectedly, as if she had heard a joke. "I'll be home. It will be nice to see her. I'll tell Quilty we're ready for dinner, Father."

The old man heard her voice in the kitchen and Quilty's in reply. Then the door closed and the house again fell silent.

Tobias had turned the radio off as soon as he recognized a program for children. His nerves and those of Paris, he had discovered, could not endure the excitement and tension of entertainment created for the little ones. But the brief and overwhelming desire to nap had passed, and he felt animated and awake. As he stroked the purring cat it surprised him to perceive that the thought of a visit from Cecilia stimulated him. His evenings lately had been all alike. He and Dora lived too quietly, saw too few people. It was their own fault that they followed a rut.

"I couldn't come earlier, because Grandmother has dinner so late." Cecilia Warren, defying all the posture rules, still managed to look lovely in the depths of the dull red chair.

Tobias had lighted the fire which burned with a comfortable sedateness, as if keyed to the quiet room. In September it was yet too early to start the furnace, but the chill of the tomb filled the house at night, unless one supplied a little heat of some kind. He eyed his granddaughter's short-sleeved blouse with disapproval, but she appeared to be as warm as Dora who, despite her rose-colored sweater, sat almost in the fireplace.

Tobias spoke around his pipe. "Your grandmother been well, has she?"

Her Grandmother Warren, Cecilia replied in her clear young voice, was very well. So much better than usual, that she spoke of spending the winter in the city, instead of going to Florida. "She asked to be remembered to you and Aunt Dora," Cecilia said.

A slight hesitancy in her speech only served to intensify the engaging simplicity of her manner and the direct gaze of her fine dark eyes—eyes so dark that they looked black in the lamplight, although in reality they were a deep brown. Her hair looked to be as black as the wool skirt of her suit and it hung, shining and beautifully arranged, to her shoulders. She wore no make-up save a faint rose tint on her lips and fingernails; her blouse was severely plain, expensively tailored.

As she leaned forward to pat the cat on his knee Tobias reflected that her awkwardness was more attractive than another girl's studied grace. Ceil was all angles; she was as tall as he was, amazingly thin with a coltish flare to her wrists and ankles that he found endearingly stumbling and young. Dora had once told him that the precise Mrs. Warren complained that Cecilia fell over things and plunged into rooms instead of making a dignified entrance, but the old lady hadn't been able to destroy the girl's natural charm.

"We haven't seen you since—why since a year ago last July. Your nineteenth birthday." Dora smiled. "You may be twenty now, but you look about sixteen." Ridiculous, to have this feeling of constraint between the three of them, Dora thought. Cecilia was her own flesh and blood, the daughter of her dead sister. Lucy had been dead for seventeen years now; they almost never spoke of her, but that might be because they saw Cecilia so seldom. *She's more a Ferris than a Warren,* Dora told herself and promptly administered a silent rebuke. *You sound like a typical old-maid aunt.*

"I wanted to ask you—" Cecilia hesitated. She looked at Dora, then toward Tobias, but turned slightly so that she faced Dora. "You see, there's a man," she said. "I'd like to bring him to call."

A tremendous protest stirred in Dora's heart. Cecilia was too young, she was too childlike. Her Catholic grandmother had left her entirely to the convent nuns. *I don't believe she knows any more about life than a two-year-old baby,* Dora fretted. There was something in Cecilia's shining look of innocence and confidence that hurt the other woman intolerably, No one who looked like that could find what she expected, nothing as perfect as she sought could come to her on earth.

"A man?" Tobias put his pipe down on the brass smoking stand. "You got a beau, Ceil? Your old grandfather'll look him over and size him up. That's what you want, eh?"

Cecilia did not answer. She was smiling, her eyes on the fire, seeing a face in the logs' glow.

"We'd love to meet him, darling." Dora tried to be enthusiastic, but to her own ears she sounded old and cumbersome and tired. "Bring him to dinner. Quilty will put her best foot forward. Is he—special?"

"He's wonderful!" The quality of Cecilia's shining radiance seemed to have been transmuted to her hair, her eyes, the whole vibrant body that could suggest ecstasy in the movement of its small, fine bones.

She wished that she knew her grandfather better, Cecilia was thinking. By "better," she meant more intimately. The years at the convent had separated her from her mother's people and on her father's side there had been only his mother, the stately, gracious grandmother, always busy with interests of her own. Cecilia assumed that men must, by nature of their experiences in the world, be wiser than women. Old men she regarded as veritable founts of knowledge. She loved her Aunt Dora—she hoped she loved all her aunts; but she reasoned that in moments of crisis a man's advice possessed a mysterious value all women recognized. This must be so, because her Grandmother Warren had herself suggested this visit to Grandfather Ferris.

Tobias had refilled his pipe without disturbing Paris and as he lighted it the ugly black iron clock on the mantelpiece struck nine. It had a rich, mellow tone, in spite of its grotesque design, and his wife had cherished it as one of their wedding gifts. He suspected that the clock, like many other things in the house, secretly distressed Dora whose tastes were of another generation. *Dora ought to have married, like the other two girls.* Tobias blew out his match.

"I recollect your mother bringing your father home to dinner, Ceil," he said. "When he first began beauing her around. Your Aunt Sarah brought Lion to Sunday dinner once, too. But only once." He halted abruptly, for Lucy had not invited young Post Warren a second time. *He was a right nice young fellow, only he was a Catholic.* "I'm still waiting to see your Aunt Dora's young man," Tobias finished. His eyes, faded to aquamarine blue, beamed affectionately upon the family spinster.

His daughter scarcely heard him. An impression that Cecilia still had something to tell them, was inexpertly struggling to establish communication, persisted. Whatever the child had on her mind she had not yet put it into words. The lovely, awkward young creature in the old red chair had come to ask for something—sympathy, help, advice, or perhaps approval. *She's a stranger, in spite of our kinship,* Dora thought, *just as this room is still Mother's parlor, although I'm careful to call it the living room. New labels change nothing.*

Cecilia moved her long legs restlessly. She yearned to tell her grandfather about Tag and certainly she read only encouragement in the faded blue eyes that surveyed her with meditative calm. The top of his head as revealed in the light from the floor lamp reminded her somewhat of a pie, pinkish-brown in the center, a scalloped rim of white and gray hair circling it. She admired his extreme neatness—her Grandmother Warren had once complained that old men drizzled tobacco.

"This fellow of yours—I suppose he's draft age?" Tobias reached for the tongs as a log quivered, ready to break. The cat leaped down from his knees and stalked across the rug to Dora.

"He's twenty-three. He's in the Army." It was clear that Cecilia thought the Army was to be congratulated.

Perhaps if she brought in the sandwiches Quilty had left—Dora rose, slim and tall like all the Ferris women, who stayed slim if they had to diet. "Ceil, do you drink coffee? Or would you like ginger ale?" *I don't even know what she likes to eat,* Dora reflected.

Behind her her father spoke. "You haven't told us his name. Maybe your Grandmother Warren knows all about him, but we'll have to start from scratch. Where did you say you met him?"

Cecilia answered so quietly that unconsciously she created the effect of emphasis. "His name is Hyman Silverstein."

Dora would have sworn that the three chairs and the sofa in the silk-upholstered parlor "set" leaped at her. She distinctly saw tiny blue and gold flowers start convulsively, then settle into the pattern of their scarlet background. *This is it,* she found herself repeating without reason or connection. *This is it.* Yet when a car horn bleated in the street outside her mind carefully identified and registered the sound. She turned and said aloud, "Hyman Silverstein?"

To her exasperation she heard her father's voice trail hers. "Hyman Silverstein?" He added, "You mean that's his name?"

Cecilia nodded. "Yes."

"Well," Tobias floundered, "well, then, isn't he—isn't he a Jew?"

His granddaughter's beautiful shining dark eyes glanced from him to Dora who immediately realized, too late, that she must look stricken.

"Tag's mother was a Gentile," Cecilia was saying "his father was a Jew. Both are dead."

Her Grandmother Warren, she admitted, had been prejudiced at first, but Tag had charmed her, as he did everyone who met him. "His middle name is Taget and his friends call him Tag," the girl explained. "Taget is his mother's family name."

"And you want to bring him to dinner?" Dora suggested inanely.

"I want to marry him," Cecilia said.

"She can't marry him," Tobias protested, after he had taken Cecilia home to her grandmother's apartment in one of the city's most luxurious co-operatives. "Her folks won't stand for it."

Dora, watching her father eat sandwiches and drink milk at the kitchen table, observed that they were Ceil's "folks."

"Well, the Warrens brought her up," Tobias submitted. "I saw the old lady for just a minute—she had people there playing bridge. Said she'd call me in the morning." Mrs. Warren had not appeared to be upset, he reported, but then she was not the type to display her feelings. "I always did admire that woman," Tobias declared, tossing a bit of chicken to the indifferent Paris. "Even if she *is* a Catholic," he concluded magnanimously.

Her father's attitude toward the members of the Catholic Church was too familiar to Dora to hold her attention at half-past twelve in the morning. She remembered that she had planned to reach the office half an hour ahead of her usual time, to put through a batch of phone calls. She made it a rule not to bring her job home, but she did not consider it illogical to put in extra time at her desk.

"We can't judge Ceil's boy friend until we see him," Dora suggested, replacing the milk bottle in the refrigerator. "It may be a passing fancy. She's young, even for her age."

Tobias wadded his paper napkin. "We can tell a hell of a lot about him by his name. If her father was living, the thing would never have got this far."

Cupping her hand as a tray, Dora used the crumpled napkin to sweep the crumbs from the table-top. "You tried to keep Lucy from marrying Post Warren," she reminded her father. "It didn't work. You did everything to prevent Sarah's marriage to Lion—and she went right ahead and married him. I don't imagine Ceil's father would have much to say about her marriage, even if he were here to say it."

"It's all the fault of those nuns," Tobias decided, moving back to avoid the advance of the napkin-brush. "There's a crumb you missed—what do nuns know about bringing up a girl to get herself a man?"

Dora deposited the crumbs in the garbage pail under the sink, rinsed her hands. The ivory and blue kitchen, Quilty's kitchen, not hers, looked to her at night like a stage set. Pretty, precise, and strange—*I don't have time to use any of the gadgets,* Dora thought.

"What do nuns know about getting married?" Tobias persisted.

"As much as I do," said Dora. "Perhaps if you'd put me in a convent, I might have married as soon as I had finished school."

One of the sudden, secret communications they shared not too frequently, flashed between them and they smiled. The old man stood up, his shadow repeating his deliberate movements on the painted wall.

"Why didn't you marry someone, Dory?" He studied his tired, middle-aged daughter for a moment and remembered that she nust be lonely. "You were a good-looking girl," he assured her.

Her laughter deepened the parenthesis lines that bracketed her good-tempered mouth. She had never exactly fathomed the reasons for her spinsterhood, she reflected as she climbed the stairs to her own room a few moments later. Probably some fundamental defect in her temperament was responsible, but she was conscious of no emotional blockades or suppressed instincts. She honestly believed, when she thought about it at all, that for women like herself the time for love and marriage went by as swiftly as the wind and that they, struggling for economic success, scarcely noticed their failures in love. Later, too late, they might perceive what had happened; as they grew older the humiliation of their mortified families might be transferred to them, tempting them to distort the truth.

Dora had no wish as yet to pose as a sacrifice to her parents' need of her, for they had been financially and psychologically independent during her young womanhood. Neither had she experienced any desperately unhappy affairs. Her few friendships with men had jogged along desultorily until terminated by the announcements of their engagements to other girls. The patronage of married women alternately amused and angered her, but she had supposed herself to be free of envy, until the sight of Cecilia's beautiful, radiant face, the sound of rushing ecstasy in the clear voice, had shaken her tonight. For there had been a boy . . .

A fine time to develop a set of regrets! Dora reproved herself, setting her alarm for half-past six.

But the brilliant moonlight that flooded the room kept her awake and against her will she recalled the weddings of her two sisters—of Lucy who had married Post Warren and Sarah who had espoused, as the Bible said, Lionel Eustice, so many years ago. And Lucy, who had shocked her Protestant family by taking the Catholic faith of her husband, was dead and Post also, and Cecilia, their daughter, had fallen in love with a Jew. As for Sarah and Lionel, although their marriage was far from happy, they still lived under the same roof. They had three daughters, one pregnant, so Sarah had recently confided. *I suppose I feel old because my sister is to be a grandmother,* Dora concluded, watching the ripples advance and retreat on the ceiling.

Dora cooked breakfasts for herself and her father, but left the dishes for Quilty who came at eight-thirty or nine, unless detained, when she arrived at ten. If Dora found it necessary to discuss the housekeeping arrangements with her, or had special instructions to impart, she might have recourse to the telephone, or to written notes. The dinner for Cecilia and her fiancé, if he were her fiancé would have interest for Quilty as well as for the host and hostess, and so it seemed to Dora essential that she consult with Quilty in person. To achieve this direct communication, Dora had only to reach home a half-hour ahead of her regular schedule and seek out Quilty engaged in the orderly preparation of dinner.

It was characteristic of Tranquility Mead that she never minded demands upon her attention when she was working toward a definite object, like the evening dinner; but it was positively dangerous to attempt to deflect her when she was "clearing away," and indeed her method of completing her day was strikingly suggestive of a tornado, relentless, sweeping, and grim. She was a large woman, a year or two older than Dora, who was forty-five. But Tranquility had been married twice and was the mother of half a dozen children. Her café-au-lait skin and gentle brown eyes made her handsome in her middle-age and Dora often thought that as a girl she must have been beautiful.

"You want dinner early, Miss Dora?" Tranquility glanced up from the table where she was cutting celery for salad, when Dora entered the kitchen.

She had no wish to hurry dinner, Dora disclaimed; she had left the office ahead of schedule in order to talk about Miss Cecilia. "She wants to have dinner with us and bring her young man, Quilty."

"Um-m," said Tranquility, a comfortable, rich quality in her soft voice.

Dora took one of the chairs by the window. The well-lighted kitchen, competently equipped, spanned the width of the house, but was so shallow that Tobias likened it to a Pullman. The porcelain refrigerator, the sink and gas range, all pre-war models and handsome as tombstones, Tobias observed, were set against the outer wall, with a deep window beside the stove and another above the sink. Cupboards and cabinets lined the inside wall and windows at either end of the room supplied the coveted cross-ventilation. The ivory and blue color scheme was repeated in the checked gingham curtains which Tranquility kept as immaculately laundered as her own bright-colored wash frocks.

I don't sigh to get dinner every night, thought Dora, eyeing the electric mixer on the table and recollecting the fascinating array of gadgets concealed by the cupboard doors, *but I wish I had a little time to putter in this kitchen now and then.*

"Miss Cecilia got a new beau? What you want to feed him?" Tranquility began to slice an apple into her salad.

It depended on points, Dora said practically. Tranquility, who did the marketing, would have to see what could be found. "I thought we'd splurge on the table setting and perhaps we can have a fussy dessert. They're young and they'll overlook the incessant chicken, if we dazzle them with something elaborate at the end. I'd like to put our best foot forward for Miss Cecilia's sake. She'll be showing off her mother's side of the family."

"Is he nice?" Tranquility glanced up expectantly, her paring knife poised.

Dora murmured that she had not met the young man. "We only heard of him last night. I thought Wednesday, Quilty? Thursday you're off and Friday we couldn't have meat."

She had forgotten that Miss Cecilia didn't eat meat on Fridays, Tranquility's soft voice sighed. You couldn't do much with fish, that was a fact. After you'd trimmed it up and put sauce on it, it was still fish. "This young man Catholic, too, Miss Dora? What's his name?"

"His name," Dora said, "is Hyman Silverstein."

For a brief half second she heard the water boiling fiercely in one of the pots on the gas range. The house shook slightly as a heavy truck rolled past, and the smell of baked onions, her father's favorite vegetable, seemed suddenly to fill the room. Dora saw Quilty motionless, startled, half an apple in one capable brown hand, the thin, black-handled knife in the other.

Then Quilty spoke, like someone feeling her way. "Why—why that's a Jew name."

Is this to be her portion? Dora said fiercely to herself. Aloud she heard her controlled reply. "Mr. Silverstein is Jewish, naturally. At least his father was. His mother was a Gentile."

"Well, but—that is, ain't Miss Cecilia Catholic?" faltered Quilty, her troubled fixed gaze on the gray-haired woman in the yellow painted chair. "I seem to recollect your pa telling me Miss Lucy married a Catholic and turned."

Dora had been too young at the time of her sister's conversion to speculate as to probable criticism and comment. Now she wondered whether Lucy had been made unhappy by clumsy discussion of her personal and private affairs.

"Can a Catholic marry a Jew?" Quilty asked, turning to lower the flame under a bubbling pot.

Certainly a Catholic could marry a Jew, Dora assured her with some asperity. "Not that Miss Cecilia will necessarily marry this Mr. Silverstein. She's merely bringing him to dinner to meet us."

Quilty shook the oil cruet over her salad, tossed the contents of the bowl expertly with a fork. "That's the indications," she insisted. "If a girl brings her boy friend to see her relations, he's getting serious. But I'm right sorry he's a Jew. Miss Cecilia ought to marry a Catholic boy—I believe in staying in the church where you was born."

The telephone bell brought Dora to her feet. She heard her father shuffling to answer it, but the call would probably be for her.

"Something tells me Miz' Warren won't like it," Quilty mused, tossing her salad with an artist's motions. "An' what that lady don't like she lets you know about and no mistake."

Cecilia's grandmother had, according to all the family accounts, expressed herself with a vigor when her only child had announced his intention of marrying Lucy Ferris. If it had crushed her—temporarily—to discover that her son had set his heart upon a Protestant girl, what would be her reaction to the intimation that her adored grandchild planned to marry a Jew? Dora, answering her father's summons to the phone, recalled dizzily that the Ferris Protestants were also on record as having expressed themselves forcibly when they learned that they were to acquire a Catholic in-law: how ironic, she reflected, if by another turn of the wheel Fate were to unite both branches in a common disapproval of Cecilia's lover.

"My dear," said Mrs. Hubert Warren over the phone, "Cecilia tells me you have asked her and—and a friend to dine with you Wednesday night. Will you tell me honestly what you think, after you have seen him? I have the greatest confidence in your judgment."

Although startled by this statement, Dora retained sufficient presence of mind to inquire after the elderly lady's health. Mrs. Warren was quite well, it seemed, or had been until Cecilia had upset her.

"This sort of thing is so opposed to her usual behavior," the grandmother fretted. "I don't know what the Sisters at the school would think—I haven't dared mention it to them. Cecilia knows plenty of nice young men. She has no reason to become interested in—in this person."

It became evident as the conversation continued, that old Mrs. Warren could not bring herself to pronounce the name of Silverstein. Once she said "Tag" and explained its origin at length. "What makes it all so complicated," she admitted at the very end, "is his absolute charm. It's impossible not to like him, once you see him. But charm isn't exactly the foundation on which a happy marriage rests."

On what did it rest?

Dora asked herself the next day, after Cecilia had telephoned to say that Tag couldn't come for dinner Wednesday night. He had to keep late office hours with his lieutenant, but he would pick her up after dinner and take her out to dance.

"So you and Grandfather will meet him," Cecilia's happy voice said. "And I'll love to dine with you, if it doesn't upset your plans."

Dora had notified Quilty first, then Tobias who had already disturbed the colored woman's peace of mind by persistently questioning her on her knowledge of the Jewish dietary laws. Tobias had only the vaguest impression of the rules observed by the orthodox and Quilty had never heard of the subject at all. Finally, in desperation, she directed her tormentor to "Call Miss Cecilia and ask what do her boy friend eat." The question had first bewildered, then irritated, Cecilia, who assured her grandfather that Tag ate anything except milk chocolate, which he loathed.

In the office of the *Bulletin,* where she had been society editor for twenty years, Dora could be grateful for the intervals that allowed her to withdraw into her own thoughts. The dinner plan revised and Quilty notified, Dora tried again to deny the compulsion that lay heavy upon her to pity Cecilia. Neither did she wish to examine her reasons, although, of course, she had no reasons, she argued silently as she leafed through her mail. Or, if she had a reason to feel depressed in connection with Cecilia, it was only that the sight of the child inevitably recalled old family griefs.

Lucy, Cecilia's mother, had been so pretty, they had all taken it so hard when she married Post Warren. Dora, then a young girl, had noticed much that she had not understood until after Lucy's death. There had been so many deaths—first Lucy, then her husband, within two weeks of each other, when Cecilia had been not quite three years old. There had been other children before Cecilia, but they had died at birth. *Mother died soon after Lucy,* Dora remembered. Was it any wonder that she felt old and tired this morning, when the unhappy years kept crowding her mind?

"Good morning, Miss Ferris." Trudy Spinelli, her pretty, efficient assistant and secretary, stood in the open doorway.

Dora extracted the clippings she had tucked under her blotter for safe-keeping. "Good morning, Trudy. You can check on these and paste them in the 'to come' book."

The girl bent her smartly-piled head of dark hair above the papers, her lashes black against the ivory of her cheeks. She was thirty years old, Dora knew, with a husband but no children, and the conservative element in the office liked to say that she was "radical." No one ever specified in Dora's hearing the tenets to which Trudy was supposed to subscribe, but she clearly belonged to no clique and apparently desired no close friends on the staff.

"I can't seem to get started," Dora apologized. She removed her reading glasses and passed her hand wearily over her forehead, a characteristic gesture of which she was only partially conscious.

Trudy's extraordinarily clear gray eyes surveyed her boss critically. "You look as if you didn't sleep any too well."

She had slept well enough, Dora attested; the difficulty had been to fall asleep. "My kid niece is talking about being in love. I suppose that is really what delayed the sandman."

They smiled at each other, their comfortable relationship of several years standing based on mutual respect and an absence of pretense on either side.

"Is she too young and is it another war marriage? You can't do anything about it, except give her your blessing and a two-column cut." Trudy settled her smart white cuffs contentedly as became a satisfied matron.

Cecilia was barely twenty, Dora admitted, and the boy friend was a staff sergeant in the Army. "It's likely they don't know their own minds, but we'd be glad if that was the only problem. The more I think of it, the more jittery I feel—Trudy, she's a Catholic and the man's a Jew."

Trudy's gray eyes turned toward the window, pierced by a sharp, geometric angle of September sunlight. Still staring at the pale gleam, she said, "Well?"

"Well, don't you think marriage is a risk under the most favorable circumstances?" demanded Dora. "We're worried."

Trudy hesitated. "Is he nice?"

"Mr. Silverstein? I haven't met him yet. He's coming to take Ceil to dance tomorrow night—she's dining with us."

Lots of funny combinations worked out well in marriage, Trudy volunteered. People in love were able to rise above silly obstacles, imaginary impediments. She added irrelevantly, "Funny, but I never knew you were a Catholic."

"I'm not. My sister married a Catholic and adopted his faith. Ceil, their daughter, was brought up in a convent." *Trudy must be a Catholic,* Dora thought, *her people are Italian.*

Her exquisitely cared-for hands were Trudy's one vanity. She held up her left hand now, as if to examine the plain platinum band on her third finger.

"What is there to worry about?" Her eyes had turned the cold color of gray snow clouds. "This is a democracy, you know. A new world, a melting pot. Racial and religious differences are something they have in Europe."

Dora was silent.

"One religion is as good as another," Trudy said. "There is only one God. Jews and Gentiles, Catholics and Protestants, we're all one big, happy family. In America. You've worked on a newspaper for twenty years—you ought to know."

Dora laughed, but not mirthfully. "But Trudy, even the readers who scream they're discriminated against wouldn't deny that freedom to worship is an established right in this country. At least we're all free to choose our religion."

"Legally." Trudy turned her pretty, oval face and the light from the window revealed no flaws in her make-up. "What in hell is the good of being legally free to practice your religion?" she demanded in an even tone. "Tell your niece that no law can protect her from people's tongues."

This from Trudy Spinelli, the quiet, smiling girl whose most marked characteristic hitherto had been her avoidance of personalities. Dora reflected that she really knew little of her assistant, although she had worked with her daily for five or six years. Trudy's husband worked in a defense plant, of course—all young husbands in 1943 were either in essential industries or in the service—but beyond the fact that his name was Paul Gottlieb, Dora knew nothing of *him*. Probably the girls in the business office had more information, although it was doubtful if Trudy furnished it.

Dora pulled herself up straighter in her dilapidated chair. For an instant she wondered whether Trudy's husband might not be Jewish. Certainly Trudy must be a Catholic. "Are you and your husband of the same religious faith, Trudy?" It sounded less blunt, phrased like that.

She had been brought up a Catholic, Trudy answered. Her husband was a Protestant. His first wife had been a Catholic. "He was divorced when I met him. My mother nearly died. She's only begun to speak to us, after all these years."

"What a shame for her to act like that!"

Dora was unprepared for Trudy's retort.

"Well," the girl suggested, "I imagine your mother made an

awful fuss when your sister married a Catholic man. Mothers don't seem to be any too sure that there's only one God."

The family did act as if Lucy was being buried, instead of married, Dora thought. The litter of envelopes on her desk urged her to get on with the day's work, but most of the copy for the early edition was already upstairs. A forlorn hope that through Trudy she might learn how to help Cecilia, persuaded her to ask another question.

"Your marriage has worked out all right, hasn't it, Trudy?"

She and Paul were very happy, Trudy testified, with an absence of emphasis that carried conviction. He was of German descent, she second-generation Italian, but they were conscious of no racial irritations.

"And the religious angle? Ceil is very devout." Dora wished that she knew if the Jewish and Catholic creeds had anything in common. *Except one God,* she reminded herself.

"Devout girls get along all right. I was never devout." The clear, warm color had returned to Trudy's eyes.

She had asked questions as a little girl in parochial school, she said, and the Sisters had reported her at home, asking her father to remove her. They considered her to be a bad influence on the other children. "In reality, I'm a truly religious woman. I want to know. I'm not satisfied just to be told." Her husband, Trudy continued, had no definite faith; she thought that most men left religion to their women. It was the women in her family and in her church who most bitterly condemned her marriage.

Dora protested. "But you've been married how long—nine years? And they can surely see that your marriage is happy."

"My marriage?" Trudy flashed her chaming smile. "Good Catholics don't admit that I have ever been married. So I'm living in sin and it's perfectly lovely," she concluded.

Chapter Two

TRUDY SPINELLI might have her troubles, Dora, watching the radiant Cecilia at the dinner table Wednesday night, conceded, but Paul Gottlieb wasn't Jewish. A Jewish husband posed a flock of complications of which Cecilia could be only partially aware. Dora herself had nothing more tangible than her vague impressions and faint remnants of hearsay. As for Cecilia, she continued to deny that she was engaged to Tag, but this, she was careful to explain, was due to his caution, not hers.

"He says he won't be engaged, unless the way is clear for us to marry." Cecilia in the light of Dora's festive candles was so lovely that neither Dora nor Tobias could keep their eyes from her.

An artist would have insisted on painting her, Dora thought, stealing repeated glances at the slender figure. Cecilia sat on one side of the heavy-waxed black walnut table, with Dora at the head, which had been her mother's place, Tobias at the foot. Cecilia wore her gleaming dark hair parted in the center and in a page-boy bob. Her gown, cut in a deep V at the throat was a soft black crêpe with a full skirt of lace. A wide band of deep rose silk swathed the under bodice and tied in a wide, soft bow on her breast. Lights seemed to glow behind her great dark eyes and diamond drops glittered in her love-knot gold earrings. Dora remembered that Lucy had once spoken of the Warren jewelry.

"You're too young to get married to anybody," Tobias had declared, not very brilliantly, when Quilty had served them the salad.

Millions of girls married before they were twenty-one, Cecilia assured him. Her Grandmother Warren had married at eighteen. "If I'm not married before I'm twenty-five you'll be calling me an old maid."

"Your Aunt Dora ain't married yet," Tobias pointed out.

The girl's brilliant eyes turned toward her aunt and the older woman fancied she read fear and dread under the compassion that was young and sweet and rather funny, too. *She's afraid she may come to be like me,* Dora thought, stifling an impulse to laugh.

"Now look here," she briskly interposed, "I've been the object of curiosity and pity among my own generation for long, weary years. It's a little too much, if the second generation is starting to feel sorry for me. Old maids are the happiest once they quit a-struggling, Ceil. Pin that up on your mirror."

Cecilia, with the awkwardness that managed to be more appealing than studied grace, pulled her long, slim body upright in the straight-backed chair. "Tag says he isn't sure he knows how to bring up a girl. He's like Grandfather—he doesn't believe I'm an adult."

Tobias snorted. "You don't know any more about the world than a baby," he grumbled. "From all accounts neither do those nuns who raised you. If a woman's going to live in the world, I figure she ought to have some contacts with life. You've been as sheltered as a hothouse rose."

It seemed to Dora, listening to Cecilia's defense of the convent training, that they all were evading the real issue. Just as Mrs. Warren had painfully avoided the mention of Hyman Silverstein's name, so the three of them, Cecilia, her grandfather, and her aunt, were seeking to postpone the discussion of the one question uppermost in their minds.

"For instance," Tobias was saying, "have you paid any attention as to whether this young man of yours can support you? Is he an officer? What did he do before he went into the Army?"

His granddaughter's mobile face changed. She smiled, as if she held a lovely secret safely in her heart. In that moment she seemed to have shut out the two anxious watchers and to be alone with a happiness so securely hers that she lacked nothing. It was this look of radiant confidence that made her feel aged, Dora reflected, conscious of a dull ache in her breast like the weight of an old pain. *She ought to marry him,* she mused, her eyes on the girl oblivious to everything except the sudden lovely rapture of her dream. *She will have had this, whatever else fails.* Then panic beset her lest Cecilia's love be a girl's passing fancy and no more, and all the doubt and caution of the middle-aged bade her to hold her tongue.

"I've been wondering where you met him," Tobias hinted. "I don't recollect that you told us the other night."

Cecilia had one stock answer for that stock question. No matter how many people asked it, or how many times the same persons repeated it, they would always be satisfied when, in reply to their, "How did you happen to meet him?," she said simply, "At the USO."

It was accepted that girls serving as USO hostesses should meet a variety of young men in uniform. No one took very seriously, either, the quaint ruling that girls must not date the men with whom they danced or played checkers or served at the snack bar. Just as long as you didn't actually leave the lounge arm in arm with a service man, the girls had explained to Cecilia when she first reported for duty, no fuss was made. Besides, they added, a girl could always ask her mother, or her sister, or a friend, to invite the armed forces to Sunday dinner and tea.

That may have been one reason why, when hostesses begged off from their assignments, it was more apt to be the Sunday afternoon or night trick, than on any other scheduled day. Cecilia had been filling in for Karen Small that Sunday she had first seen Tag. Karen had telephoned that she simply couldn't make it and Mary O'Brien had sent word that a heavy cold had floored her and no one knew what had happened to Mrs. Kincaid, but she also had failed to appear.

Cecilia remembered the unwashed dishes—towering peaks and crags of them—that had accumulated during a rush on the snack bar. She was washing and drying alone, for Anne Connell was serving and stout, kind Mrs. Draper had the desk in the lounge, when Anne called that Mrs. Draper was signalling for help.

The lounge was across the corridor and Cecilia slipped off her heavy, blue denim apron before she left the kitchen. Under that a trim, ruffled pinafore of pink chintz contrasted effectively with her gray crêpe frock. She suspected that Mrs. Draper was anxious to telephone the hospital about a grandchild who was seriously ill.

At the wide entrance door to the lounge, Cecilia paused. A group of service men surrounded the desk, their dark and fair heads, with the white hair of the senior hostess in the center, bent over an open book. A tall, slim figure, well at the back of the circle suddenly straightened and Cecilia had found herself looking directly into Tag's level, dark eyes.

For the space of a second his gaze held hers and then, as if drawn, she began to move slowly toward the desk. Someone had put a Strauss record on the victrola and without warning it seemed to Cecilia that now a mist enveloped all the room.

Nothing stood out clearly, except one man's intent, expectant face. It was as though a soft, dimming fog bound her body and her limbs so that only her rapidly beating heart and her eyes served her. She saw Tag's sensitive lips part in a smile, and as if far away she heard the tinkling melody, but nothing else was real.

"Bless you, Ceil!" said Mrs. Draper's brisk voice, breaking the magic spell. "I'm trying to sign these boys up for the dinner tomorrow night and that victrola is driving me mad."

Mrs. Draper, who had signed the group for the USO anniversary dinner the following evening, had promised to call the hospital at nine o'clock. She had left Cecilia to write in the individual names on the tickets and Tag's name had been at the end of the list.

"I hope you will come," Cecilia repeated with pretty, old-fashioned courtesy, as she handed his ticket to each lad.

"I hope you will come," she had said to Tag, raising her eyes for an instant as she filled in his name.

Perhaps she had been momentarily surprised. She could never be sure. At the touch of his hand on hers, again the mist filled the room and she saw only Tag's face, heard only the gay tinkle of the waltz—endlessly repeated—beating insistently in her ears.

He had asked her if she would be at the anniversary dinner and she told him she and Anne were to serve as waitresses.

"Will you wear that pink apron?" he questioned hopefully.

Cecilia thought not. "The chairman wants us all to look alike."

"You won't all look alike," Tag had said....

"So you met him in the USO," she heard her grandfather saying. "I understand that officers do pretty well for themselves," he suggested. Tobias never ate salad, but he liked the crackers and cheese that accompanied it and tonight, as usual, he was eating Dora's share.

Cecilia said, "Tag's a staff sergeant."

"Well, that's something." Tobias stopped short as Quilty, heavy-footed, deft-handed, removed the plates and let the swinging door close behind her. "But his race is against him. I'll bet even in the Army it's against him," he mumbled swiftly against Quilty's return.

A slight, almost imperceptible shade passed over Cecilia's face, a shadow so faint that perhaps, unless one happened to be watching for it, it might go unnoted. An intangible something, too vague for analysis, touched her manner as she turned to face her grandfather. *This is the way it will be,* Dora fretted. *The child has no guard.*

Quilty, beaming each time she glanced toward Cecilia, brought in the coffee and the charlotte russe she had adapted to rationing. Young folks liked a sweet dessert, she had instructed Dora. It was understood that a portion was to be set aside for Cecilia's boy friend. It would have been pleasant to serve coffee in the living room, but Tobias complained so bitterly of this innocent practice that Dora no longer made the attempt. She could fight for a principle, she told herself, but not with the added handicap of Quilty's disapproval of the extra work.

With Quilty again in the kitchen, Dora felt that she must speak. "This is a democracy, Father," she stated and was infuriated by her own smug tone.

"The Army isn't always democratic." Cecilia put down her coffee cup. "Tag told me—some things."

Her grandfather nodded. "His race is against him," he repeated.

"Oh, for heaven's sake!" Dora perceived that, like old Mrs. Warren, her father was clumsily determined to remain vague. "Suppose the man's name is Hyman Silverstein! Suppose he is Jewish! Aren't there thousands of Jews in the service? There's no discrimination. We've outgrown that." She seemed to hear Trudy Spinelli saying, "Legally."

Cecilia's dark eyes gazed straight before her. "Then why do you—why does everyone—feel so dreadfully about my wanting to marry Tag?"

It was a risk, Dora floundered, since her father was silent. It was always a risk for two different races, or two different faiths, to marry. She regretted instantly that she had mentioned the difference in faiths, but the words could not be recalled.

"No one wanted my mother to marry my father." Cecilia's quietness had an old-fashioned quality more arresting than a spirited retort. "And no one wanted my father to marry my mother. But they were happy."

Tobias cleared his throat. "They were both Americans—I mean they came from similar stock. The Ferris and the Warren families go back to the Revolution."

"Well, Tag's mother was a Gentile and maybe no one wanted her to marry his father because he was a Jew." Cecilia was not quite at ease now. "They were happy, too. Tag said so."

Still, the issue was supposed to have been settled by the blanket term of democracy, Dora thought doggedly, as the door bell rang. *The trouble starts when someone lifts the edge of the blanket and begins to look underneath democracy.* Dora heard Quilty roll through the hall to open the door. Cecilia, her face radiant, turned expectantly and—

"It's him," said Quilty, who had a magnificent simplicity of her own. She stepped aside and for a moment no one spoke.

Hyman Silverstein stood in the doorway, a lean, slim-waisted figure in khaki. Level, dark eyes looked out from a thin, handsome face; his sensitive lips were firmly closed. He was tall and poised and immaculately groomed.

"Aunt Dora!" Cecilia's voice sang, "may I present Sergeant Silverstein?"

Dora rose and went forward to meet him.

"And Grandfather, this is Tag."

Tobias pushed back his chair, stood up lean and long.

The young man shaking hands with Dora smiled. It was warm and sweet and rich with love and gaiety, that smile, as if it had roots in his heart.

"We're so glad to know you," she murmured and watched him as her father took his hand.

"Sit right down—had your dinner?" Tobias beamed, his aqua-blue eyes hospitably alight. "Here's Cecil, hardly able to eat a crumb, for thinking of you."

The girl laughed and Tag laughed, too. He took the chair beside Cecilia, when Dora and Tobias had resumed their seats, and the too-small dining room with its too-heavy furniture suddenly assumed the attributes of spaciousness and grace.

I have never known anyone to be so much in love, thought Dora. The knowledge saddened her, but she put it from her, to be examined when she should be alone.

She judged that her father recognized the inevitable, too, for he let his coffee cool while he devoted himself to the entertainment of Tag. This manifestation of personal approval was not without its embarrassing features, since the old man innocently asked questions that a service man must turn aside. Quilty brought in fresh coffee and a heaping portion of charlotte, her admiration of the guest so evident that Dora suspected she prolonged her duties in the serving pantry from which the dining room conversation could always be overheard.

"We're just going dancing, sir," said Tag in answer to a non-military query from his host.

Cecilia, her face luminous, was already dreaming of dancing, if the look in her eyes indicated her thoughts. She flashed a grateful glance toward her aunt as Dora stood up.

"Run along, children, and have fun." Dora wished suddenly that Lucy had lived to see her daughter falling in love.

Upstairs she waited while Cecilia renewed her lipstick, making that an excuse for confidential asides.

"You like him, don't you, Aunt Dora? Everyone likes Tag as soon as they meet him." Cecilia outlined her curved upper lip.

Dora, seated on the bed, nodded. "He has great charm. I think people must instinctively trust him, too."

"He's wonderful." The quiet confidence in the young voice again carried greater conviction than vehement protestations. "I tried to make Grandma understand that I know why Tag is wonderful. I've been out with other boys, Auntie—the wealthy, stupid boys who are the sons or grandsons of her friends. They're not what I want. Tag is genuine—honest and fine."

Dora found that she could say in perfect sincerity, "Darling, I believe you," and forget momentarily the persistent shadow of pity that touched her thoughts of their love.

Downstairs, as she and her father saw them off, with Quilty peeping from the dining room, Dora assured herself that if she felt sorry for two people so young, so happy, so beautifully alive, it must be because of the war. But her aching heart rejected this explanation as she lingered on the front step alone, after her father had gone into the house. Down the street the rear light of the taxi glowed vividly as the cab slowed at an intersection, winked out when it resumed its speed. A warm, damp wind blew across the house tops and the September sky, softly black, seemed to sag almost as low as the white globes of the arc lights. Somewhere on the next block a radio orchestra played "The Star Spangled Banner" and the tap of the high heels sounded as a neighbor began to descend the steps of a house across the street.

Dora drew a deep breath. *They make a lovely couple,* she sighed, turning back into her own house.

"He didn't look Jewish, did he?" Tobias had settled himself in the living room with his paper. "What did you think of him, Dory?"

She must catch Quilty before she left, Dora murmured. "I'll only be a minute, Father."

Quilty, changing her shoes for the open-toed pumps she kept for after-hours, said that she had set sponge, in case Mr. Ferris fancied yeast rolls for breakfast. "If it wasn't for his name, you wouldn't know Miss Cecilia's boy friend was a Jew at all, Miss Dora," she added.

Chapter Three

THE next morning Tobias consumed his hot rolls with a dispatch that should have wrecked the digestion of an old gentleman of seventy-eight. He, however, apparently suffered no pangs from this indulgence, nor from the three cups of coffee which, as was his custom, he swallowed scalding hot. By speeding up his nutritional routine he could be ready to walk with Dora—who devoted ten minutes to orange juice and coffee without cream—as far as the bus stop. He had planned, Tobias revealed, to call upon his married daughter, Sarah.

"Morning's a busy time for Sarah," Dora hinted, buttoning her jacket and drawing on her gloves as they went down the steps.

Her father, erect, immaculately brushed, shook his head. In his day, he hinted, a lady dressed herself in the house. "Now I see girls combing their hair as they run for the bus."

"Just so they get the bus," Dora returned, cheerfully disposed to forget her own strictures on the subject. "In your day, Father, ladies went around the house looking like wilted spinach. They may have dressed to go out, but they didn't comb their hair to stay in."

Tobias glanced in admiration at his shoes—he had polished them himself. "Sarah combs her hair," he said.

She had not said a word against her sister, Dora objected;

Sarah was as neat as wax. "Don't credit me with imaginary digs, Father."

He chuckled as if something secretly amused him, and Dora, who had stopped at the corner newsstand to buy herself a paper, lifted her chin. "I suppose you and Sarah will gossip about Cecil and Tag," she suggested, falling into step beside her father again. The mirror set into the vestibule post of the drugstore they passed, reassured her. Even in gray tweeds her figure looked slim; she had nice ankles and legs.

"Well, Sarah's married. I'd kind of like to get her viewpoint," Tobias submitted. "She has daughters; she'll be apt to have good judgment about a thing like this."

She's never shown good judgment about anything yet, Dora thought, but kept silent lest her father accuse her of jealousy. Nothing she had ever done or could do, would serve to convince him that she was mentally as well balanced as her sister. Sarah had made a hash of her own life, her hatred of men was not normal, and she spoiled her children outrageously; no matter, in her father's eyes she would always have a more successful personality than any woman who remained unmarried.

An early autumn haze, almost as heavy as smoke, filled the air, screening the sunshine and smelling vaguely of fallen leaves and dried grass. There were few trees on the uptown streets and all the grass that grew in the small back yards would not have made one meadow; strange, mused Dora irrelevantly, that the end of summer could be so poignantly suggested to the city-bred.

"If I were you," she cautioned her father hurriedly as they approached the bus stop, "I'd ask Sarah not to talk about Cecilia to the girls."

Tobias' eyebrows registered surprise. "Why, Nutmeg's married!" he remonstrated.

"Oh, for heaven's sake!" His exasperated daughter managed

to convey the effect of whirling upon him, though she continued to walk steadily forward. "Being married has nothing to do with it. Sarah and her family haven't seen Tag—they're in no position to judge. They'll tear Ceil to shreds without knowing the first thing about her love affair."

He might ask Sarah to keep mum, Tobias conceded, without enthusiasm. But as he hastily withdrew to the edge of the milling crowd, there to stand and watch his daughter storm the bus, he acknowledged that Sarah was not one to keep anything to herself.

It seemed to be his fate to be surrounded by females, Tobias reflected, backing into the gutter to avoid being run down by a frantic woman sprinter who made the bus as it got under way. Not until a man retired did he really learn the ins and outs of the feminine character and the more he learned the greater his confusion. Walking on eggs would be easy, compared to the course he had followed since the death of his wife, Tobias sometimes thought. Now as he trudged sturdily across the narrow city to the home of Sarah, his married daughter, he wondered if it might really be wiser not to mention Cecelia and the—the young man, to her. On the other hand, why was he going to see Sarah, if not to enjoy being the bringer of news?

Mrs. Lionel Eustice, the former Sarah Ferris, lived in one of a row of red brick houses with old-fashioned exteriors and fairly modern improvements within. Most of the occupants rented furnished rooms, a business that was not what it used to be, Sarah sadly informed her father, whenever she could induce him to listen.

This morning she met him at the house door as she returned from her tussle with the marketing—buying food wasn't what it used to be, either, she sighed, thrusting two tall paper bags into his arms while she searched for her key.

"I thought Nutmeg would be home—can't she open the door?" Tobias peered benevolently over the feathery tops of the bunched carrots. His scrubby gray mustache twitched, for the greenery tickled.

Sarah, a large, gaunt woman, with hair gray around her face and still blonde at the back, triumphantly fished a red ribbon from the depths of her black leather purse. A rusty, shabby purse, her father noted; one of the girls had passed it on to her, of course. Sarah never had anything new, she wore the clothes, stockings, and hats which her three daughters discarded, as well as their open-toed shoes, which hurt her feet and in which she always felt self-conscious. Ginger, she was explaining now, fitting the ribbon-tied key into the lock, was still asleep.

"She needs all the rest she can get, Father. And if you think it's funny to call her Nutmeg, I hope you can restrain yourself. She's in no condition to be teased. Anyway, what's wrong with calling herself Ginger, if she likes it?"

Nothing, except that it was a damn fool name, Tobias grunted, following Sarah through the narrow, dark hall into a bright, pleasant kitchen. The room was rather overpoweringly furnished with white porcelain equipment. Refrigerator, sink, and stove were all huge and Sarah had never ceased to give thanks that she had made her demands upon the landlord just before Pearl Harbor. She cherished the conviction that manufacture of kitchen conveniences had ceased abruptly on that memorable December seventh and she constantly blamed herself that she had failed to buy a new washing machine on the sixth.

The immaculate cleanliness of her kitchen reflected the spotlessness of her entire house. Tidy to the point of being bare, Tobias pondered, easing the bags to the white-topped table. "I don't suppose you have a drop of cold coffee left over?"

"I threw it out." Sarah never saved anything. She gave away

what she could and what remained she threw away. Her husband asserted that she stocked the neighborhood Salvation Army thrift shop and she frankly grumbled that left-overs cluttered up her icebox—she liked her shelves empty and clean.

"If you want coffee, I'll make you some fresh," she told her father cheerfully. "Let me put my ration books away first—how's Dora?"

Before Tobias could answer, the swinging door that shut off the pantry and passageway leading to the dining room opened. Sarah's weary, middle-aged face lightened—as if she had caught a glimpse of Heaven, her father thought. His granddaughter, Estelle, standing there was a pretty young piece, but not precisely his notion of an angel.

"Why, darling! You didn't have to come down—I would have been glad to bring breakfast up to you." The rasp in Sarah's voice had vanished, too, as if the sight of this beloved child smoothed out all the rough edges in the mother's life.

Tobias' old eyes crinkled in an affectionate smile. "If it ain't Nutmeg!" he teased. "You look as pretty for that husband of yours every morning and you'll start the days off right."

The girl accepted their homage as a matter of course. She was accustomed to being spoiled by her mother and a brief honeymoon with her soldier husband had only served to confirm her confidence in her attractions. At the earliest signals of pregnancy she had returned home to be the object of her mother's unflagging attention, a situation which Ginger, as she insisted on being called, was human enough to dramatize to the fullest extent. She kissed her grandfather twice, holding her peacock-blue negligée daintily clear of the floor. "One is for Junior," she smiled.

"Junior?" Tobias looked startled.

"The baby." Ginger laughed. "Your great-grandson."

Tobias felt behind him for a chair and sat down.

"I hope to heaven you never have a boy!" Sarah's voice, suddenly fierce and stern, rose above the sound of running water as she filled the teakettle. "You two go into the dining room and talk," she directed. "I'll bring your breakfast in to you, Ginger."

No, the child couldn't eat in the kitchen. Her appetite needed to be coaxed, Sarah told her father in answer to his pointed question. In her condition it was only natural that she should be a bit "peckish." Ginger trailed luxuriously out of the kitchen, but Tobias lingered to ask when the expected baby was due.

"The first week in June." Sarah lifted a tray from the wall rack.

Tobias frowned. "My good godfrey, she's starting to be an invalid too soon. And what's all this stuff about Junior? How's she know she won't have a girl?"

Sarah produced a hemstitched tray-cloth from the table drawer. "I'm praying, as I never prayed before, that she has a girl. I just couldn't stand it, if she should have a nasty, cruel, selfish creature like a boy."

"That ain't no way to talk," Tobias reproved. "Every woman I ever heard of, except you, wants a son." What annoyed him, he went on, was the attitude of the pregnant women he saw on the streets. "Women been having babies since Eve, but these young uns act as if they had just invented the whole scheme."

"It's the war." Sarah failed to amplify. Would her father please, she asked pathetically, try to be tactful and not antagonize Ginger? "Go on in and tell her a funny story. Or, if she wants to talk about the baby, just listen. It's the least any man can do, as I tell Lion."

The dining room's single window let in so little light that it was necessary to turn on the ceiling fixture whenever a meal was served. Ginger had seated herself in her mother's chair at the head of the table and was reading the morning paper. Her cinnamon-colored hair and bright brown eyes complemented an ivory skin splashed with a few golden freckles that of course distressed her. It made her so mad to read the store advertisements, she murmured, glancing up as her grandfather took a chair beside her. "Now there's toilet seats," she said.

"My good godfrey!" Tobias recollected that he had been asked to be tactful. "What about 'em?" he mumbled.

"Mother's been wanting to get one for our bathroom, but if you pay more than five dollars, you have to fill out a form." Ginger sniffed. "A toilet seat that costs more than five dollars comes under the head of house repairs and the government controls 'em." She smiled at her grandfather, revealing small, perfectly spaced teeth. "Notice anything different about me?" she challenged.

He blinked, shook his head.

"I'm letting my hair grow. I told Mama even if it does make me nervous, I'm going to let it grow."

Tobias, at a loss for the proper answer, shrugged his bony shoulders. "Has it been dormant?" he inquired.

He needn't be silly, Ginger snapped. She was planning to have a permanent as soon as her hair was long enough. "If my condition allows it. I want a real good permanent—a fifteen-dollar one this time."

"Fifteen dollars for a permanent!" Her astonished grandfather was outraged. "Why, for fifteen dollars they ought to curl your hair to last forever."

Ginger discarded the topic abruptly. "If you happen to run across any diaper advertisements, I wish you'd let me know," she said.

"Now you look here—" Tobias smelled toasting bread. "Your

breakfast will be along in a minute, Nutmeg," he encouraged. "I'll see if I can help your mother bring it in."

Something was wrong with her daughter, he informed Sarah whom he found absorbed in arranging a beautifully-poached egg on a slice of golden-brown toast. "Oh, nothing's happened to her—my Lord, you're nervous! I mean she ain't been brought up right."

Sarah's blue-gray eyes shot sparks at him. "Just what have I left undone?" She was pouring coffee and her hand trembled.

"Well, she talks about toilet seats and diapers and you know a young girl shouldn't mention those things. Not to men." Tobias sighed. "It don't sound nice."

He was a fine one to talk, Sarah snapped. "I heard what you said to the woman across the street—Dora let it out one day. You told Mrs. Kitts that you'd like to borrow her baby to water your garden. I suppose you call that a refined remark."

A man could talk like that, Tobias protested. "I'm not a young girl."

"You're not a mother, either." Bitterness tinged Sarah's tone. All men, she went on, ignoring her father's offer to take the tray, were alike. They told dirty stories with pleasure, but blushed if a woman mentioned any of the normal functions. "Ginger has an exceptionally clean mind, I'll have you know."

Tobias followed her into the dining room and watched her arrange the tray at one end of the table, bare save for the fruit bowl in the center. Sarah had trained her kids not to lift a finger for themselves, the old man mused. She seemed determined to express her love for them in terms of personal service. He perceived that he was in "the doghouse," as his grandchildren would say, with Sarah, and, in his haste to patch up a truce, he spoke unguardedly.

"Ceil came around to the house last night."

Ginger, about to take a bite of toast, put the slice back on the plate. Sarah, standing beside the buffet, dropped into a chair. Together they chorused, "Ceil?", making of the name a high-pitched duet.

"Was old Mrs. Warren with her? She wasn't? Did Ceil come alone? How'd she look? Did you tell her about Ginger?" Sarah, apparently run down, paused. "I don't think she can have heard about the baby yet," she decided. "I'll put her name on the list for the birth announcements."

A mirror hung above the buffet and Ginger glanced sideways at her reflection, patted a curl into place. "What did she wear, Grandpa? I always said she'd be lovely, if she wasn't quite so tall."

"And so awkward," Sarah amended. "If she was mine, I'd feed her milk and eggs. I don't know whether there's tuberculosis in the Warren family or not, but Ceil certainly has the build for it."

Tobias cleared his throat. "My good godfrey!" In desperation he pounded his fist on his open palm. "What ails you, anyway? Ceil looked like a million dollars and she's healthy as a young filly. She's a high-stepper, that girl." Not even to himself could he acknowledge that Cecilia's energy seemed to be mainly of the spirit, nor could he bear to recall that her mother had had no physical reserves.

"Why did she come to see you?" Ginger's round brown eyes were bright with curiosity.

Cecilia had come because she wanted to see him, Tobias asserted. "And she come to see your Aunt Dora, too, of course. Nothing strange in a girl visiting her grandfather, as far as I know."

Sarah pointed out that Cecilia had not called on her mother's relatives for a long time. "Ginger wasn't even married, the last time Ceil was here. But she did send a lovely wedding present. Sterling. A vegetable dish."

There must be some reason why Cecilia had suddenly decided to visit him, Ginger prodded her grandfather. "I'll bet she intends to get married! Mama, what do you bet that Ceil's ready to announce her engagement?"

"Of course." Sarah beamed upon her clever offspring. "Eat your egg before it's cold, darling. Did Ceil have her ring, Father?"

He was no match for them, Tobias sighed to himself, he should have known better than to mention Cecilia's name. Well, holding back now would only whet their bloodhound instincts, God alone knew what kind of a story they'd concoct unless he told them the truth.

"I guess she's thinking some of getting married," he faltered and winced as they shrieked again.

What was the man's name? Was he in the service? Did old Mrs. Warren approve? Was Cecilia planning a big announcement party? Sarah thought that the grandmother would most likely give a formal dinner, she had always been such a stickler for stately affairs.

"She might ask some of us. After all, Ceil's mother's family should be represented," Sarah declared. "I haven't anything to wear, but Dora could go and Ginger—her figure hasn't changed yet."

Ginger stirred her coffee, discontent a shadow on her pretty face. "Is he in the service, Grandpa? An officer? Of course he must be—catch Ceil Warren marrying anyone without a commission. I suppose she'll have a magnificent wedding, with a nuptial mass and all the rest of it. And Hoke and I had to be married in that makeshift chapel at camp!"

Why hadn't he remembered that Sarah was the biggest gabber in the family and that all her children took after her! Tobias mopped his face with the yellow breakfast napkin he had brought from home instead of a handkerchief. "I don't believe Ceil's figuring on having a mass," he murmured.

They fell upon him again, but Ginger's voice outrode her mother's. "Don't tell me she's engaged to a Protestant, Grandpa! After all the fuss her father's family made to force Aunt Lucy to turn Catholic—that would be too rich. Mama, you always said Ceil would end up as a nun, after spending so many years in that convent. And now she isn't going to marry a Catholic."

"What's the man's name?" Sarah glanced at the tray, noted that Ginger had disposed of the food. "Darling, how about more toast? Or another cup of coffee? You must keep up your strength." But when Ginger declined, Sarah felt free to concentrate on her earlier question. "You haven't told us the name of Ceil's fiancé, Father," she urged.

Tobias surrendered. He could endure anything, he reflected, if they wouldn't scream. "Name's Hyman Silverstein," he said.

For one stunned moment the two women stared. Tobias saw Sarah's mouth shaping words, heard Ginger draw in her breath as a preliminary to speech.

"Don't you both yell!" the old man commanded. "One at a time's all I can stand."

"Father!" Sarah plunged. "Not *Silverstein?"*

Her daughter gulped, pushed her chair back from the table as if the gesture freed her from some inhibition. "But Grandpa, that's a *Jewish* name."

"What you got against Jews?" Tobias glowered. "Tag's a sight handsomer than any man I've seen in these parts since the war began. And he's got a smile that can charm a bird right off a bush."

Ginger barely waited for him to finish. "But you said his name was Hyman," she protested. "Hyman Silverstein."

"I heard you say it," Sarah corroborated.

He had heard himself, Tobias retorted, he wasn't deaf. Hyman Silverstein had a middle name—Christians had no patents on middle names. Tobias' mounting indignation secretly surprised him. "The lad's middle name is Taget—the family name of his mother, I think Ceil told us. Folks all call him 'Tag.' Now you know all about it."

No, he didn't know how old Mrs. Warren was taking it, he admitted, when Sarah questioned him. Yes, Cecilia was apparently head over heels in love. Dora? Well, Dora hadn't said much, one way or the other.

"Dora probably figures that any marriage is better than none at all," Sarah observed. Oh, yes, she knew that Cecilia was attractive and probably had plenty of time, but the war wasn't improving any girl's chances. "There just won't be enough men to go round, Father. That's why so many young girls are rushing to the altar. They don't know what they're letting themselves in for, but no one can tell them that."

The clock in the living room across the hall struck the half-hour and Ginger's wrist watch read eleven-thirty. Sarah picked up the breakfast tray, but urged her father to stay for lunch. "The girls both come home now and you haven't seen them in ages. I must get the salads ready. Ginger, you'd better lie down in my room—it gets the sun. Take the morning paper up with you and have a good rest."

Tobias trailed after her into the kitchen. He couldn't stay for lunch; Quilty would have a snack ready for him, he said. "Does Lion come home at noon?"

Her husband had a job now which kept him downtown all day, Sarah confided. The pay was small, the work trivial—pasting labels on boxes, Sarah believed it to be—but at least it kept him out of the house. The light fell across her face as she put the tray on the sink drainboard and Tobias noticed that the front fringe of her blonde hair was white, her face lined with worry and fatigue.

"How's he been behaving lately?" Unconsciously Tobias lowered his voice, prompted by a vague impulse to protect his granddaughter, who was safely upstairs, from the knowledge of evil.

Sarah said that Lion drank as much as ever and came home every night in the week the worse for liquor. "The girls swear they'll leave home, if I don't put him out. No one would blame them."

She had been talking about divorcing her husband for twenty years, Tobias reflected, but Lion, aside from his drinking, wasn't a bad sort. A couple who had stayed together long enough to raise three children, ought to manage to stick it out till the end.

"I must be getting along," Tobias said, unwilling to encourage a discussion. "You call Dora some night and come down to see us."

Sarah, at the door, called after him. "Tell Dora all my rooms are rented. She was afraid I'd get stuck with this house."

Lunch was ready and waiting Mabel and Fern Eustice when they reached home at half-past twelve. Mabel was twenty and a stenographer, Fern three years younger, a senior in high school. They both took it for granted that their mother should serve them and wait for her own meal until after they had gone. They ate in the dining room, instead of the kitchen nook, because Mabel was fastidious and "hated" a kitchen atmosphere.

"Where's Ginger?" Fern, thin and tiny, wore her brown hair in a foaming bob that seemed to pull her head back.

Ginger was upstairs, Sarah answered. "Your grandfather was here this morning."

"When's his birthday, Mama? I want to send him a birthday card." Mabel, whose heavy eyebrows made her look chronically belligerent, salted her soup.

"I think the clock's slow," Fern said.

The Eustice girls always carried on separate conversations like this when they were together and no one expected to listen or to be listened to. Sarah, anxious to impart the news about Cecilia Warren, might have attempted to flag their attention, but Fern was already talking about the meeting of her sorority, to be held that night.

"I hope we can have the living room in peace for once," she was saying with a pout. "It's bad enough to have to rent rooms without having to introduce friends to your mother's lodgers. As soon as I get a job let's burn the 'Vacancy' sign."

Sarah interposed mildly that she had to have money coming in. "Your father can't support me. Why, Mabel—it's early, dear. And you haven't had your dessert!"

Mabel had promised to meet one of the girls from the office and do some shopping in the remainder of her noon hour. It was a good deal cheaper to come home to lunch than to eat downtown, but it was a source of irritation to her that her family did not live nearer to the center of the city.

"Mama, will you change a dress for me?" Dexterously she produced a cardboard box from under her chair, laid it in Sarah's lap. "I'm not going to Houseman's today and this dress dips in the front. Get me a refund."

Fern protested. Her mother had promised to make cake for the evening's party. She couldn't be expected to rush downtown and back, to fix up another of Mabel's mistakes. "It's a wonder you wouldn't try on a dress once in a while and make up your mind in the store," Fern grumbled.

There was plenty of time for everything, Sarah assured her

daughters. It would do her good to get a breath of air while returning the dress and the cake would be fresher if made in the late afternoon. She could buy the candy for the bridge tables, too, as well as do several errands for Ginger.

"Ginger can still walk, can't she?" Mabel, powdering her nose at the hall mirror, had overheard.

"You'd think no one else ever had a baby," commented Fern. "It's a perfectly natural development, but the way you spoil her she's begun to think she is something set apart."

All her girls were jealous of each other, Sarah frequently complained, and this in spite of her scrupulous efforts to treat them exactly alike. No one but herself, she fondly believed, ever guessed that Estelle, no, she must remember to think of her as Ginger, was the core of her heart. They shared a close communion that the two other girls could not realize.

"Ginger and I'll go to the movies tonight," Sarah assured Fern now. "You won't want any of us around until it's time to serve the refreshments."

No one had to ask if Mabel would be at home. She had the most energy of any of the three girls and her evenings were accounted for in a set schedule that left her with little or no idle time at her disposal. Her driving vitality took the form of self-improvement and she belonged to a singing class, a dancing class, a gymnastic group, a Spanish circle, and a dramatic club. She had more style than Ginger, was better looking than Fern, and had more genuine affection for her mother than either sister, although she and Sarah quarreled often and with bitterness.

"Sometimes I think the only thing that holds this family together is that none of us can bear the sight of our father," Mabel said once with a cynical penetration that irritated Sarah, who was neither cynical nor shrewd.

Mabel hurried off to her shopping and Fern, pausing only long enough to renew her make-up, rushed back to school for the afternoon session. They left Sarah with the food to put away, the dishes to wash, and eleven beds to make before she could dress to go downtown. It was her boast that each member of the family slept alone and each of the girls had a room to herself. Sarah and her husband preserved the conjugal aspect by sharing a bedroom with twin beds, and the six lodgers, all women, had single beds, two to a room.

Usually Sarah had the upstairs in order before noon, but this morning her father's visit had wrecked her schedule. Like Mabel, she was devoted to perpetual motion, even at fifty-two, and she liked to insist that she needed no help. Work, she said, agreed with her. By that she meant that she preferred to use her body, rather than her mind. She had a vast respect, not unmixed with fear, for the mentality of her youngest child. Fern, Sarah asserted, had the family brains.

It was Fern to whom she confided the news about Cecilia Warren that afternoon. Sarah had executed her shopping commissions with dispatch and had returned to make an angel-food cake, carry up tea and chicken sandwiches to Ginger, and dust the card tables for Fern who came home at four o'clock. Fern's anxiety to have everything "right" seemed pathetic to her mother, always prepared to break a lance in defense of her children's desires.

"The cake's wonderful," she greeted Fern, when the girl came into the kitchen. "It needs to cool for another hour. I got the little chocolates you like—two pounds. That ought to be enough."

Fern curled her bob with one thin hand while her bright, anxious eyes surveyed the room. The inverted cake pan, in which the angel food hung, occupied the center of the porcelain table.

Her mother at the sink was washing the pretty pink and white bon-bon dishes. Fern said, "Where's Ginger?"

"Upstairs, writing to Hoke. Wouldn't it be terrible, if he has to go overseas before the baby comes?"

Lots of men went overseas and never saw their babies, Fern remarked. It was a chance people had to take in wartime. "Hoke and Ginger are no better than anyone else."

Sarah supposed not. She was sorry for all the young people. "I didn't get a chance to tell you this noon—your cousin, Cecilia Warren's going to marry a man in the service."

"Ceil?" Fern's eyes narrowed, she stood absolutely motionless like a bird whose attention has been caught. "When?"

Well, perhaps she hadn't set the date, Sarah admitted, trying to recall what her father had said. "At least she's very much interested in a young man. The engagement hasn't been announced, but your grandfather seemed to think she had made up her mind."

Fern's hand began to twist her hair. "Is it anyone we know? How did Ceil meet him? I wonder how she looks? How did Grandpa hear about it?"

The shower of questions pleased Sarah, who sometimes was at a loss to engage Fern in conversation. Cecilia had been to see Grandpa and Aunt Dora; she had told them, Sarah explained. "I must say I don't know much about the young man, except his name. It's no one you've ever met—he's from the Middle West, I believe."

Fern tugged at her hair. "What's his name?"

"Hyman Silverstein."

Very slowly Fern opened her mouth, gulped as if she had swallowed a marble, and finally managed words. "Are you kidding?"

She certainly was not kidding, Sarah retorted. "Turn the gas lower under the beets," she interposed as a pot on the range began to hiss. "That's his name."

"But Ceil wouldn't—she can't—that is, is he a Jew?"

Grandpa had said that Hyman Silverstein was half Jewish, Sarah related: his mother had been a Gentile. "I can't help wondering how old Mrs. Warren is taking it. Maybe it's a judgment on her, she made such a fuss about her son marrying a Protestant."

"You mean Aunt Lucy? Gosh, I guess the Protestants put up just as big a fuss about her marrying a Catholic," Fern grinned. "Do you suppose Hyman Silverstein will turn Catholic?" Her thin face twinkled with curiosity.

It wasn't likely, Sarah answered. Cecilia was too young to know her own mind, but a motherless girl didn't have a fair chance to make a good match. "I always say there's no place like your own home for judging a man and his character. I hope you girls will bring your beaus home, every time, Fern."

"My God, Mama, I don't ever expect to marry, as long as I'm in my right mind!" Fern pulled a high stool toward her, climbed on the seat. "You don't think, after seeing you and Papa, and now Ginger, that I have any illusions about getting married, do you?"

Sarah said automatically, "You can't judge all men by your father." Then she must defend Ginger. "Your sister's very happily married, I'm sure. What have you got against her and Hoke Steel?"

If pregnancy affected a woman the way it did Ginger, she wanted none of it, Fern rejoined. Most of the girls in her class planned to get married, but she had seen too much ever to covet a husband. There was always something wrong with marriage. "You married a man who drinks. With Ginger it's the war—her husband may come home a wreck. And here

Ceil's had to go and fall in love with a Jew. I'm going to have a good job and a lot of clothes and not mess up my life for any man."

They had one old maid in the family already, and that was enough, Sarah argued. "Do you want people to pity you like they do your Aunt Dora?"

The argument continued desultorily while Sarah prepared dinner and even after she and the girls were at the table. As a rule they ate dinner without Lionel Eustice, husband and father. He lingered, his wife supposed, in various bars on his way homeward, and he usually slipped in abjectedly and ate what he liked while he helped with the dishes. If he was in any condition to eat, Sarah sternly pointed out to him on these occasions, he was able to dry the dishes.

Mabel heard at dinner tonight that Cecilia Warren was engaged, or about to become engaged, to a Jew. Ginger, mainly interested in studying a printed diet sheet for which she had sent to a magazine, thought that Mabel received the news with a calmness deliberately affected.

"I'm not saying that anyone should make a fuss because the man is Jewish," Ginger flared in answer to her sister's studied, "So what?" It was only natural, however, Ginger insisted, to expect the announcement to be a nine days' wonder in Cecilia's circle.

"She won't be able to wear her grandmother's wedding gown and the seed pearls, then, because she won't have a church wedding." Mabel glanced at her silverware, sighed. "I wonder what kind of a wedding she *will* have."

Mabel made no secret of her social aspirations, which included a brilliant church wedding at not too late a date. She had what her mother proudly called refined tastes, as exemplified by the single setting of sterling flatware she had bought for herself.

Sarah always arranged Mabel's place at the table after the pattern shown in the etiquette book and saw to it that she had a fresh linen napkin three times a day, although the rest of the family could be persuaded to use napkin rings. For Mabel, too, Sarah cheerfully supplied clean towels and face cloths every morning. Sometimes she said to her confidante, Ginger, that Mabel ought to live in a hotel; but it was of Mabel's comfort, not the extra work her demands entailed, that Sarah was thinking.

Fern, beginning to be excited by her responsibilities as hostess for the coming evening, said shrilly that she thought girls were too anxious to get married. "Suppose people do laugh at old maids—they wouldn't if enough of us refused to be upset about it," she suggested. "I'll bet Aunt Dora would be happy, if the pussy cats would leave her alone. I'll bet she's happier than Mama, anyway."

Ginger and Mabel studied their mother, placidly spreading margarine on her bread. She saved the butter for Ginger's condition, Fern murmured. Sarah was accustomed to being discussed by her children and was not self-conscious under their scrutiny.

"Wouldn't you rather be Aunt Dora, Mama?" Fern prodded. "With a good job and nothing to worry you? No husband coming in half shot and no daughters running you ragged—me for the life of an old maid."

Her children had made up to her for everything else she might have missed, Sarah assured them. She stirred her coffee, meeting the gaze of three pairs of eyes without flinching. "Of course, I didn't get much in the way of a husband, but marriage is a lottery, any way you take it. I'd rather be married to your father than be a lonely, single woman like your aunt."

Ginger and Mabel smoked silently for a moment. Fern, whom her sisters suspected of smoking at school, was forbidden cigarettes in the house.

"I hear Dad!" Ginger said. Her eyes turned black at night and when as now her mouth set in a thin line, she looked curiously prim.

The four women listened to the uneven footsteps shuffling in the hall. A short, loose-jointed man halted in the dining room doorway, coughed, then cleared his throat. He looked to be fifty or sixty years old, with a gentle, crumpled kind of face surmounted by fuzzy, sandy hair and light, timid eyes protected by fuzzy, sandy eyebrows. His clothes were shabby but neat, his black shoes expertly polished. When he smiled, first at his daughters and then at his wife, a certain deprecating movement of his shoulders made apology for his tardiness.

Ginger sniffed, glanced toward her mother.

Immediately Sarah stiffened. "Lion, you've been drinking again!" She frowned at her husband. "You reek with it. Fern's having a party tonight and I won't stand for you disgracing us. I tell you I won't stand for it!"

Lionel Eustice grunted. "Who says I've been drinking? Who says I'll interfere with any party? Just show me where there's a party, and I'll head the other way. Last thing I want to do is to get mixed up with a parcel of chimney-smoking women after a hard day."

"It's late, we have to clear the table now," Fern told him.

Mabel rose, ground out her cigarette, and dropped her crumpled napkin on her plate, a gesture that always irritated her father.

"It's a wonder you wouldn't fold up your napkin and save your mother a little work," he grumbled. "For all the help you give her, your mother might as well be the help in somebody's kitchen."

"And it's no thanks to you I'm not," Sarah, never able to resist an answer, retorted. "You're in no position to criticize the girls—the condition you come home in, night after night."

Her husband barred Mabel's way as she attempted to slip past him. "Not so fast, young lady. That your finery on the hall table?"

It was her new nightgown, Mabel admitted with some anxiety. "I hope you didn't paw it, Papa. That ice-blue satin soils so easily."

"Where are you going with it?"

She wasn't going anywhere, Mabel replied; she had bought it to match the ice-blue satin mules that had been a birthday gift.

"It's hotel underwear—I looked at it." Her father drew himself up. "For how long has your daughter been buying herself hotel underwear, Sadie?"

Sarah screamed at him in exasperation. "That will be about enough out of you! Aren't you ashamed to look your children in the face?"

In the four faces turned to him the shuffling little man could read no relenting. His body sagged, but he thrust his lower lip out in an effort to appear belligerent. "I guess I'd better go on up to bed and leave you free to be sweet as honey to strangers," he said. "I'm only in the way; everything I do is wrong."

No one disputed him and he started for his room at the top of the house, where he slept alone when in disgrace. Fern recollected that he was to have gone for the ice cream at ten o'clock, but Sarah insisted that she preferred to go herself.

"I thought about offering him something to eat, but it's better to have him go on to bed while he's in the mood to go," she told her daughters. "If he had his dinner, he might stay downstairs, just to torment us."

Mabel, scheduled for dancing class that evening, murmured that she must do over her hair. She did not offer to help with the after-dinner work, nor was it expected that she should. Fern cleared the table because she was anxious to arrange a centerpiece for the lace runner. That done, she could set up the card tables in the living room and set out the score pads and dishes of candy and ash trays. They were not using tallies for the duration, she informed her mother.

In the kitchen Ginger sat on a high stool to dry the dishes, and Sarah, who took a sixteen-hour day for granted, bent over her dishpan, a supremely contented woman. To be alone with Ginger, whether or not they talked, whether they were busy with some household task or idle, released all tension for Sarah, eased her body and soul. To a lesser extent Ginger experienced satisfaction, too, although her attitude was in the main quiescent, that of the idol who basks serenely in the sunlight of adoration.

"I'm so glad Fern belongs to this sorority," Sarah remarked, draining Mabel's sterling from the hot water. It was always washed separately from the family silver, to avoid the danger of scratches. She thought it lovely for girls to have such good times together, Sarah continued. "Nasty, noisy boys would spoil everything."

"Some of the sorority sisters could do with a boy friend or two," Ginger assured her mother. "Fern's crazy to get married, in spite of all her talk about carrying the torch for the solitary."

Sarah sighed. "I don't think she'll ever marry."

"You don't think you'll have a grandson, either, but you may be surprised," Ginger warned. "Hoke's going to send it back, if I present him with a girl."

After she has a child we'll be closer than ever, Sarah thought. *No man can come between us then.* Aloud she said, "Let's hurry and get out of the way before anyone comes. I promised Fern the family would keep out of sight."

Once or twice during the news reel when Sarah felt conversation disturbed no one, she whispered that Fern would never forgive her if Miss Porter barged in on the games. Miss Porter was one of the two school teachers who rented the second floor front room. Ginger in reply hissed that it was a wonder Fern didn't set pails of water on the front stairs and so force the roomers to go up and down the back way. The concentrated hate stored up in Fern against these people who happened to rent rooms in her home, would undoubtedly consume Fern some bright day, Ginger predicted.

"Not that I'm mad about renting rooms myself—I never did go for it," she confided to her mother when they walked slowly toward the confectionary store, after the feature picture. "It's just that I have sense enough to know you're darn glad to get the money. Fern feels it degrades her."

Sarah was rummaging in her purse for the slip of paper on which Fern had written her order for ice cream. "Fern's all mind," she murmured. "She ought to meet lawyers and doctors and college presidents—people like that. I wish we could send her to college."

The candy and ice cream shop proprietor had no one to make deliveries, resented the movies which made it expedient for him to keep open past ten o'clock, and offered only two flavors of ice cream with the stipulation that sherbert must be taken with each order.

"You're lucky I have any to go out." He spoke with the peculiar ministerial air assumed by so many of the small shopmen since rationing had given them the whip hand. Mr. Tucker, short and stocky, peered over his marble soda fountain as if it had been a pulpit. "This summer I couldn't have let you have this much," he said.

"I hope your cream's better than it was this summer," Sarah, rather nettled, told him. "The last we had tasted as if it was made out of skimmed milk and I paid just as much for it as before the war."

Mr. Tucker leveled off a carton, closed the top firmly. The government controlled the amount of butter fat, he reproved, the armed forces needed ice cream more than the civilians did. Some of the places run by Jews didn't seem to know there was a war on, but he was an American, he added, handing over the last package.

"Some men make me sick!" Sarah extended a trembling hand for her change. "Charging ice cream price for sherbet, which is only water, and has nothing to do with winning the war. It's skinning the public, that's what it is."

The last word was Mr. Tucker's, called after her before she could slam the door. "You don't have to buy it, if you don't want it."

That was the bewildering truth Sarah conceded, feeling the creeping chill of the cardboard containers against her arm and side. Daily she battled with grocers and butchers who need make no effort to please her, who could afford to be indifferent to her criticism or complaints. The steady demand exceeded their variable supply, and they could watch irritated customers flounce out empty-handed, secure in the knowledge that by night their shelves and counters would be bare.

"I never did like that Al Tucker," Sarah stated, feeling the cool night air smooth her flushed face. "He's just plain dumb."

Ginger, tranquil throughout, agreed. "Mama, I just thought—the baby'll have a ration book as soon as he's born. Won't that be cute? Look at our house from here—Fern's left the porch light on."

They quickened their steps. Sarah, intent on reaching the

kitchen through the narrow strip of side yard, strode ahead. Ginger suddenly pulled her sleeve.

"Mama! What do you know—Papa's there. Fern will be fit to be tied!"

Sarah whirled sharply, but she had already passed the one side wall window and to return might attract attention. She heard the faint murmur of voices—it would be like Lion to take the floor and monopolize the conversation! Anxiety as to how he might be dressed, whether he had taken more to drink—she searched the house every morning, but sometimes he succeeded in hiding a bottle—a quick fear that he might defy her before Fern's guests, assailed Sarah with the force of blows.

"Hurry!" she whispered to Ginger. "I'll handle him. You mustn't get excited."

The kitchen was lighted and Mabel, a flowered smock over her light dress, stood at the gas range, stirring chocolate in the double boiler. The familiar, rich fragrance permeated the room and mixed with the odor of percolating coffee. Beyond the swinging door the sound of the radio, playing dance music, mingled with an undertone of laughter and talk.

"I'm glad you're here, Mama. Fern's all set to have hysterics." Mabel's red mouth was nervous and tense. "Papa came down—I tried to coax him out with cake and coffee, but he won't budge."

Sarah tumbled the ice cream packages on the table. Her eyes blinked against the strong light, but she forced them open. "How long's your father been in there?" She seemed to have grown taller and Ginger and Mabel looked at her as they had when they were children.

Papa had been wandering around the living room for an hour, according to Fern, Mabel said. He hadn't been too bad; about all he had done was to make a nuisance of himself. "He kibitzes and says silly things to the girls. Fern came out and cried, when she was dummy. I got home about twenty minutes ago, but she wanted me to stay up until you came."

"You stay out here, both of you," Sarah commanded. "Ginger, sit down and rest. I'm not going to have any trouble in front of Fern's company. Don't let the ice cream melt, Mabel, and pull out the percolator cord—that coffee's done."

She did not know what she intended to say or do, when she pushed back the swinging door and let herself into the tiny pantry. The light was on—every light in the house was probably on—and someone had left a bright red compact on the shelf under the dish closet. A faint haze of tobacco smoke hung in the air—Sarah disliked the idea of high school girls smoking, but comforted herself with the assurance that Fern had not begun.

The radio was louder in the hall and in the brief instant she hesitated, Sarah saw the four bridge tables arranged strategically to utilize the two table lights as well as the two bridge lamps. She saw with photographic clarity the light and dark heads of the girls and their hands, accented by their tinted nails, and because each chair was filled she knew that everyone had come. Her eyes automatically sought out Fern and in one swift, appraising glance the mother measured the anger and humiliation and youthful despair that fed the color burning under Fern's cherished "Tawny Dawn" rouge. An answering rage, fierce, protective, shot through Sarah, standing gaunt and dark behind the rep portiéres. Her hands clenched and in her loosely-fitted shoes her toes curled in a tight grip, too. *I could kill him,* she thought, her mouth as dry as if it had been blotted.

Her husband stood between two of the card tables, obviously confident of his role as a welcome guest. He wore his good suit, Sarah noted, but had forgotten his necktie. His hair looked the same, combed or not, so presumably he had tidied it. He had provided himself with a clean handkerchief, for as she watched he pulled a white square from his pocket and blew a tremendous blast.

The girls jumped and Fern cried out. It was difficult to credit so small a man with producing such a volume of sound. Sarah gulped, held herself rigid for a moment. She had resolved not to create a scene. As she fought for self-control, she saw Lionel reach over the shoulder of Fern and help himself to candy from the dish.

"Lion!" In spite of her intentions, Sarah's tone was commanding. The faces of the girls turned toward her, increased her embarrassment. "Lion, I need you to help me in the kitchen."

A confused remembrance of the etiquette books she borrowed from the library and studied in preparation for school parties and dances, assailed Fern. Introductions bristled with complications as she recalled the instructions, but she would not shirk when something was expected of her.

"Ma—" her voice was a mere whisper and she tried again. "Mama, these are the girls. I guess you all know my mother." That was over, thank heaven! Even if she had been short on savoir-faire, the girls had not listened. They were wondering about her father and mother.

"You need me?" Lionel Eustice looked alarmed. He had been having a delightful time for the past hour, but he could read his wife's displeasure in her grim face. A man was never looked up to in his own family; he need expect no appreciation, unless strangers gave him a few crumbs.

In the doorway Sarah waited until he shuffled past her, headed for the kitchen. Then she spoke across the room to Fern's angry, hurt young eyes. "You'd better clear the tables, darling," she suggested. "Mabel and I will bring the chocolate in right away."

Lionel was standing at bay before his two daughters when

Sarah reached the kitchen. She heard him protest that he had interfered with no one, that he had merely been sociable; in his day the father of a daughter always met her friends when they came to the house.

"And a fine father you are!" Sarah's emotion turned her face a dark, painful-looking red. "All you've ever done for your daughters is to disgrace them. But this is the last straw—positively the last. If I can't go out of the house without you sneaking down stairs to humiliate your children, I'll lock you up every time I put foot outdoors."

Ginger and Mabel exchanged a frightened glance. It was one thing to have Mama take their side against Papa, but quite another to have her go blind with fury. There was something terrifying in the undercurrent of her voice, keyed low so that the guests should not overhear. Above its gritty, creeping quality, the radio blared insanely and the rhumba's beat added a weird touch to the kitchen scene.

"I guess I can walk around my own house," Lionel protested, squaring his narrow shoulders. His timid eyes met the anxious gaze of Ginger and Mabel. "You two tend to your cooking," he directed with a wave of his arm, meant to be an impressive gesture.

Sarah sprang across the room. She snatched a long, shining cake-knife from the table and whirled, like a fencer, to point it at her astonished husband.

"Don't you give your daughters orders!" Her flushed face deepened to purple, but mindful of the sorority she still kept her voice low. "And don't you ever, as long as you live, presume to parade yourself, when the girls have company." She carved an aimless circle in mid-air with the knife and Lionel flattened himself against the sink.

"Do you promise to let 'em alone?" Sarah lurched forward and her husband dodged. "The idea of you, half drunk, making a spectacle of yourself at Fern's expense!" Sarah gritted.

He had meant no harm, Lionel placated. If he had known she would be so upset, he would have stayed in his room. "Anyway, I'm not drunk. I'm as sober as you are. I'll go in and ask those girls, to prove it."

Sarah raised the knife again and took a long step that brought her within striking distance of the terrified little man backed against the sink. "You go near those girls again tonight—or any other time—and I'll kill you!" She swung the knife blade to the left. "See that door to the cellar? You open it and march yourself down there and stay. Do you hear me?"

He bleated, "All night?", but began to sidle toward the door, keeping his face turned toward his wife.

All night or forever, it was none of his business, Sarah retorted, following him with the knife blade pointed at his ribs. "Fern's party is going to wind up in peace if I have to drag you out of the way by the hair of your head."

Still facing her, Lionel pulled back the door of the cellar. He opened his mouth to speak, but Sarah pushed him in, closed the door and bolted it as if she locked a vault. A scratching sound indicated that her prisoner was feeling for the light switch at the head of the stairs. Another second and the listeners heard his footsteps clopping down the wooden steps.

"I'll dish out the ice cream." Sarah recovered her normal, loud tone. "You'd better go in and ask who wants chocolate and who wants coffee, Mabel. If you're worn out, Ginger, you go right up to bed. I'll bring you a tray as soon as I've finished helping Fern."

"You can choose between him and us," Fern said, when the last sorority sister had departed and she had turned off the lights in the living room. Her mother would "clean up" the next day.

The kitchen was in disorder, too, and the dirty dishes piled on the drainboard haunted Sarah whose fingers itched to get at them, if only her daughters would ever go to bed. Ginger had undressed, but had trailed down again in pajamas and negligée, curious to learn if her father had remained in the cellar. She sat on the lowest step of the front stairs, her mother beside her. Fern and Mabel occupied the top of the carved box-seat in the hall. They were safe from intrusion for, as Sarah said, one of the comforts in taking only women lodgers was that they came in at respectable hours, went to bed and stayed there.

"I don't think your father will bother you any more," Sarah comforted Fern. "I gave him a good talking to. He knows when I mean business."

"You have to choose," Fern said again. "Mabel feels the same way I do. It isn't only Papa—it's the whole mess we live in. There was Miss Porter tonight—she came down three times to hunt for her eyeglasses. When she got through Papa prances in and undertakes to be amusing. I won't live like this any longer. That's flat."

Mabel began more temperately. She and Fern had talked it over and they had decided to leave home, if something drastic wasn't done. "I can go in with three or four other girls and have a nice apartment. Fern could stay with us—she'll get a job when she graduates."

They would prefer, Fern resumed, to have their mother take an apartment and all live together—without roomers. "Papa can have a furnished room somewhere by himself. He won't care as long as he can get drunk every night."

Ginger murmured that an apartment would be convenient before the baby came, because if they rented in a building with a self-service elevator there would be no stairs to climb. But later she would miss a porch and yard. "Besides, the tenants will be apt to fuss if the baby as much as moans in his sleep."

"Just what am I expected to run the apartment on?" questioned Sarah. She put out her hand to draw Ginger's negligée snugly around her ankles. "You mustn't take cold, darling," she murmured.

Mabel lifted her chin. "I pay board."

Five dollars a week wouldn't go far, Sarah commented without malice. She had to have money coming in, renting rooms gave her an income. "Your father always brings me his pay envelope, too. Unopened. What he spends on whiskey he earns extra. All his life he's given me his money."

"You can't get hotel service for five dollars a week with a bunch of girls, Mabel," Ginger observed.

They mustn't be edgy, Sarah interposed, they were tired out and in no condition to see matters clearly. In reality she knew that Mabel fiercely resented the fact that she paid five dollars a week board and that Ginger gave her mother nothing. Ginger had fifty dollars a month from Hoke Steel, Mabel complained, it wouldn't hurt her to contribute to the family finances.

"Well, I'm not going to stand for it, that's all," Fern muttered. "The rest of you have your own money and you can go out and get away from Papa. I have to have my friends here and I'm ashamed to have them see my father."

Sarah sighed. "Was the cake good? They didn't leave any."

The cake was all right and so was the ice cream, but the sherbet was terrible, Fern reported. "You tell Papa I'm going to leave home as soon as I get a job, will you, Mama?"

Their emotions talked out, a weariness seemed to grip them all. Ginger complained that the hall was cold, Sarah urged her to go to bed. "All of you go. I'll put out the light—it's past one," she yawned.

"Are you going to leave Papa down cellar all night?" Ginger's expression of curiosity was reflected in the faces of her sisters.

The cellar wasn't cold, it wouldn't hurt their father to spend the night there, Sarah decided. "Maybe after this he'll appreciate his nice room and his clean bed. If he'd stayed upstairs where he belonged, he wouldn't be in the cellar now."

Once in bed herself, she lay awake listening to the intermittent street noises, tracing the familiar outlines of the furniture in the shadows of the room. Once or twice she fancied she made out a mound in Lion's empty bed on the other side of the night table and she raised up, only to have the mound dissolve into the shadows.

She didn't blame the girls, she reflected, lying down again; it was a shame that Lion had to be such a failure as a father. She could have forgiven him his shortcomings as a husband, had he been a better parent. The clock in the living room down stairs struck three, then after a long interval, one. Sarah hoped that Lion wasn't asleep in a drunken stupor on the cold cellar floor. It might be better to let him up—they could do the dishes, which the girls had persuaded her to leave—and then she could bring him upstairs and let him sleep until it was time to get him off to work.

Chapter Four

AFTER Mabel had left for the office in the morning, Sarah discovered a box on the hall table. It contained a pair of shoes. A note in pencil explained that the shoes were to be exchanged. The clerk could not put up a fuss about the stamp, Mabel had written, because she had warned him that she expected to return them.

Sarah ascribed her headache and depressed state of mind to the calendar. It was the first of the month, the rent was due, and she thought she shared, with the late Sarah Bernhardt, an inexplicable distrust of October. The mail had brought in the usual bills; her charge account at Houseman's was staggering to contemplate. Ginger and Mabel had bought several items they had not thought to mention and possibly Fern had also been having articles charged. In time, Sarah supposed, the girls would repay her, but with the new rulings the account could not be allowed to run. When her daughters urged her to leave Lion and take an apartment, they conveniently overlooked the bills they ran up for her to settle.

It would do her good to go downtown, attend to Mabel's shoes, and have a respite from the house, Sarah decided. It irritated her to be heavy-headed in the morning, she who had resolved never to slow up. The loss of one night's sleep ought not to make such a tremendous difference in her energy, she reasoned.

Why, in her girlhood she had often danced all night and put in a full eight hours' work the next day.

She dressed and, alarmed at the sight of her pale face in her mirror, applied lipstick and rouge, borrowed from Mabel's supply, for Ginger still slept. Sarah used artifice badly, but comforted herself with the assurance that no one could call her vain. The same reasoning enabled her to clothe herself in the misfits casually donated her.

Once out of the house, however, she insensibly relaxed, finding the bright sunshine and crisp air delightfully buoyant in spite of their October associations. The other passengers in the bus saw only a tall, angular woman in a dark blue skirt too tight across the stomach and too short in the rear, revealing stockings with half a dozen darned runs. Sarah's green coat had faded to an indefinite tone, her hat was one Mabel had discarded two seasons before. Her lack of chic meant nothing to Sarah, whose contentment increased as she savored the possibilities before her. Her conscientious scruples seldom permitted her to get downtown in the morning, unless on an errand for one of the girls, but she adored the shops and was devoted to the five-and-tens. Today she might even lunch at a soda fountain, she mused; she hadn't eaten a tomato and bacon sandwich for weeks.

To her disappointment, the exchange of shoes required only a few moments. The clerk made no demur—indeed his matter-of-factness as he concluded the transaction rather nettled Sarah. She had been prepared for debate and argument, and for her the absence of friction resulted in a lack of color. When she left the shop it was with a vague distrust of the quiet clerk. "You want to watch the deep ones," she frequently warned her family.

Then, turning into the stream of pedestrians flowing north, Sarah found herself beside a tall, slender girl whose stone marten scarf, tiny, forward-tilted hat, and beautifully tailored black suit looked, Sarah later reported at home, like the photographs in the fashion magazines.

"Cecilia! Cecilia Warren!" Sarah's voice rose sharply and several passers-by turned to look over their shoulders.

On the other side of the girl a man in uniform, tall, handsome, smiling, gently manœuvred her and Sarah out of the crowd, piloted them to an open space before a bank's plate-glass window.

"Aunt Sarah!" Cecilia's charming face lighted affectionately. She kissed Sarah as simply as when a child, patted her cheek with one gloved hand. "Auntie, may I present Sergeant Silverstein? Tag, this is my aunt, Mrs. Eustice. How are the girls, Auntie?"

They were well, Sarah murmured, but for once the images of her daughters retreated in her mind. She stared at Hyman Silverstein whose twinkling eyes and up-curling lips urged her to smile at him in return. Sarah clutched haphazardly at her convictions, reminded herself that men were all alike. "I've been hearing about you," she said, and watched the dancing eyes sober, the smiling lips alter to form a straight, firm line.

"I suppose Grandfather—?" Cecilia faltered, looked across Sarah to meet Tag's glance of reassurance. "Nothing is decided, of course," Cecilia asserted, but she might have been in a trance.

She looked happy, Sarah admitted to herself. They made a good-looking pair. Both of them young and pliant and with the undefeated look in their eyes that Sarah could recognize and envy, without being able to analyze it. A mounting nervousness within her, rooted in the fear that she would say the wrong thing —specifically some reference to the Jewish race—fixed Sarah's gaze in a prolonged blankness disconcerting to Cecilia, but apparently rather amusing to Tag. His bright, dark eyes resumed their twinkle, the firmness of his lips yielded to an upward curve.

"We're window-shopping, Mrs. Eustice." His voice was warm and deep with a vital power to which Sarah unconsciously responded.

He hasn't any of the traits, she told herself, floundering in a panicky endeavor to recall what some of the traits were. *You'd never think*—and then she perceived in the smiling dark eyes that Tag mysteriously fathomed her line of reasoning and she blushed. The slow, painful blood forcing its way upward to the roots of her gray hair added to her confusion and she spoke thickly. "I'd love to have you both come to dinner tonight, but I just remembered we're having ham."

Her horror and regret were instantly so apparent that Cecilia's impulse was to steady her as she would an empty box bobbing on a rocking sea. "Dear Aunt Sarah, we have no time." Cecilia's lovely compassion was as ageless as the engaging awkwardness of her slim body was young. "Tag goes back to camp tonight. This is our last day together. We're going to a matinée this afternoon."

The girls would be so disappointed, Sarah babbled, Ginger was expecting a baby, they all would love to see Cecilia. "It's a shame, the way you've been allowed to grow up, hardly knowing the relatives on your mother's side of the house. It's none of my doings as I hope you've explained to Mr. er—Mr.—your friend. When I like somebody it doesn't make a bit of difference to me what their religion is. But I guess your grandmother was always a little afraid we might turn you into a Protestant."

She had not been at home with her grandmother, Cecilia said. "Remember I spent sixteen years in the convent." Could she and Tag give Sarah a lift, she added; they had a car parked two blocks away.

Sarah shook her head. She had errands to do for the girls. She kissed Cecilia, held out her hand to Tag. "I'm real glad to have met you, Mr. er—" she stammered, but although she avoided pronouncing his name, her harassed, good-natured face told him that she genuinely liked him.

At luncheon Cecilia and Tag laughed a little over the episode as they ordered a hearty meal in the crowded grill. Aunt Sarah had had a hard life, Cecilia recalled, she had always been obliged to work to keep her family housed and fed. "She hasn't an atom of tact, but she's honest." Cecilia, glancing up from the menu looked into Tag's eyes and forgot Aunt Sarah from that moment on.

But Tag remembered her and the uneasiness that he hesitated to quiet, lest it be a warning, fed on his recollections of her inexpert pretenses. "There will be lots of people like your aunt," he worried when they had fixed on fried oysters as their choice. "I'm afraid it may affect you, after a while."

Cecilia surveyed the bright blue walls, the yellow painted tables and scarlet leather chairs and for her the color scheme might as well have been black and white. What were people? A shrug of her shoulders disposed of the critical and bungling and left her only Tag upon whom she turned the radiance of her smile.

"All right, but how do you think you'll feel when you're called Mrs. Silverstein?" Tag privately wished that she were older, although maturity could guarantee no solution of their problems. He saw now that the intended significance of his question had passed her by and that she sat opposite him lost in a dream of what it would mean to be his wife.

"Ceil, you're simply lovely!" He supposed he stifled his conscience, but what did it matter if only they were strong enough to need no one or nothing outside themselves?

Her face, with its unchanging stamp of sincerity that never

altered even in the varying expression of its emotions, deepened in color as she sighed. "But we decided to wait."

They *must* wait, he reminded her; his leave was up. Would she come away with him now, if he asked her, he wondered? He said suddenly, "Darling, do you remember your mother?"

"A little." Cecilia smoothed the soft fur in her lap. "I was three when she died. But I remember once she lifted me over a mud puddle that looked as wide as the sea. And I remember going to church and sitting between her and my father."

"I wonder how she looked." Tag was a little puzzled by his own persistence.

The waitress served them—the salad plates looked, Tag thought, like designs for a particularly cheerful wallpaper.

"Why, I look exactly like my mother!" Cecilia seemed surprised in turn. "Grandmother says so and my Grandfather Ferris stared and stared the first time he saw me when I came home from school."

They would remember Cecilia's mother as always young and fair, Tag thought. Like the picture of his own mother his father had carried in the back of his watch. No, he had no recollection of his mother, he answered Cecilia's question; she had died when he was two.

"I've thought more about her, since I've known you, than ever before," Tag said. "She was a Gentile, but I think she was very happy with my father."

She had died, he added, in her sleep following an attack of pneumonia from which she was believed to be convalescent.

"My mother was expecting another baby and she died with the flu." Cecilia's dark eyes were unshadowed and clear. "But you had your father, Tag. Until you were twenty, you said. What would he have thought—about us?"

Tag considered. "He would be glad, I think. While he lived

he made me feel that whatever I did would be all right with him. He was that kind of father."

"Well, Grandmother likes you—she said so." Cecilia began to pour the neglected tea. "We'll be all right." The act of passing Tag his tea cup conferred on her an irresistibly matronly air that made him long to lean across the basket of rolls and kiss her.

"It's easy enough to say we'll be all right," he conceded, "but we have to be sure—more sure than most, my darling." He read acquiescence in his judgment in her lovely smile, but perversely he questioned whether it might not also mean that she cared too little. He had no wish to make her unhappy or to have her tormented with doubts and fears until his next leave; yet if she could wait indefinitely and be content what else was he to think if not that her love was that of an unawakened child's? Then as he placed a bill with the check on the waitress' tray, he saw Cecilia's lashes sweep down but not in time to hide the tears brimming her eyes.

Tag had been apologetic about the cocktail date with the Goldbergs. The sister and brother-in-law of one of his friends in camp, he had been committed to look them up before he left on his furlough.

"I don't know them—never saw them—but I've a feeling they're not your kind of people," he said to Cecilia. "But when I called them and tried to break the date, they cornered me and made me promise to bring you."

He had made it clear that dinner was out, he continued, but it looked as if they'd have to drop into the Prince Albert for a few moments after the matinée. "We won't stay long," Tag promised. "It's only that Sidney will be hurt if I go back and tell him I didn't see them."

The ornate, littered lobby of the Prince Albert was filled at five-thirty with a raucous crowd, most of whom appeared to be slightly tipsy. The air was heavy with smoke and the odor of strong perfume. Women with smartly-styled hair and silver fox jackets sliding from their shoulders leaned against the green and gold columns, lolled in the pink-striped love seats, or bent at right angles to dial the phones at the desk. As Tag spoke to the clerk, Cecilia noted how markedly the fat, bald-middle-aged men outnumbered the young escorts who were, like all young men now, in uniform.

"We're to go up." Tag, turning, looked at her anxiously.

Even in the elevator people shouted, thinking perhaps that by screaming they convinced each other that they were gay. Cecilia, cornered at the back of the car by two women, one in black velvet slacks and a rhinestone-studded silver lamé blouse, the other in gray riding clothes, had to be hauled out at the fifteenth floor by Tag. Both were unprepared for the peach-colored carpet that, Tag asserted, was as lush as pasture grass.

"It tickles my ankles," he insisted.

A door at the far end of the corridor opened, before Cecilia could reply. A short, heavy-set man beckoned to them hospitably. He wore a sports shirt and matching blue slacks, an informal costume that accentuated his curly blond hair and the freckles and thick blond down that covered his fat arms. "Greetings!" he boomed.

Mrs. Goldberg promptly displaced her husband by stepping in front of him. "You're late. I thought maybe you were in the lobby, the service is so terrible we don't always know when people get here," she said without punctuation.

Cecilia shook hands with her hostess and stepped into a small, hot room that to her confused senses swarmed with people. Actually, as she discovered presently, there were not more than twenty or twenty-five guests, but the mirror-lined walls, mirror-topped tables, screen, waste-baskets, and various ornaments, multiplied the count.

The reflections showed Mrs. Goldberg to be a stout matron, perhaps forty years old, strongly corseted and zippered into a silk jersey robe elaborately shirred to insure a smooth fit over bust and hips. The flamboyant print of purple morning glories on a white ground, set the color key for matching lace stockings and elaborately cut-out high-heeled purple suède shoes with glittering rhinestone ankle straps. Mrs. Goldberg displayed bracelets, clips, and earrings of amethysts and diamonds and she wore her jet-black hair in a towering pompadour. Her coarse, good-humored face was thickly masked with dead-white make-up, gashed by her wide mouth lipsticked into a square and filled with large, strong white teeth.

"You're my little brother Sidney's friend," she said in her appallingly loud voice to Tag. "Nadine! Oh, there you are—Nadine, give Hyman Silverstein a drink."

Cecilia found herself, a glass in her hand, watching a short, plump girl with magnificent black eyes and a great cloud of blonde hair, hand Tag a cocktail. The girl's fingernails looked to be two inches long, painted dark green and highly lacquered. *I never saw such long ones,* Cecilia thought, *but her hands are lovely, with that row of dimples.*

"They make a nice couple, don't they?" Mrs. Goldberg, carrying a tray of canapés, smiled up at Cecilia. "Take a lot—they're so small. Miriam—my daughter, Mrs. Singer, Miss Warren—Miriam, you look after Miss Warren. But get her a napkin, first."

Miriam Singer reminded Cecilia of a seal. The girl was so slim, so sleeky tailored, so brown of skin, and her small, bright eyes stared coldly and unwinkingly at her mother's guests as if she found them alike in their capacity to bore her. She dutifully fetched Cecilia a heavily-embroidered square of linen, then drifted away to stand beside her father who put his arm across her shoulders.

A table built of octagon mirrors and set in the angle of a mirror-paneled screen, afforded Cecilia a place to put the Manhattan she did not drink and the cigarette she did not smoke. A half-dozen reflections of herself met her eyes wherever she looked and it was distracting to attempt to sort out the flashing images of the others who, when she turned her head, were never where she expected them to be. The impact of talk and laughter was as brittle as glass, too, and when someone turned on a radio, Cecilia fancied that she was whirling dizzily in a mirror-lined nightmare.

There was too much light, too much noise, too much food and drink—two old waiters were converging upon her with fresh trays—and all the women were overdressed, overjeweled and calcimined with make-up. *It isn't prejudice, I just don't like them,* Cecilia thought.

"Ceil!" Tag had come up behind her. "Mr. and Mrs. Litcher are anxious to meet you."

Mrs. Litcher was plump and gray-haired and her twin silver fox scarfs came to within three inches of the floor. She found it less work to wear them than to carry them, she assured Tag, who had evidently suggested the room was too warm. "Saul, we need another chair," she said to her husband.

Like his wife Mr. Litcher was plump, but he had no hair, except half a dozen spears above the fat roll of flesh at the back of his neck. He fetched the chair, saw that they were all supplied with drinks—he had kidney trouble and couldn't touch a drop, he said—and filled a plate with fish canapés which he carefully selected from the trays, for his own refreshment. "Now we're comfortable," he beamed, patting Cecilia's cheek, for she sat next to him.

For the next half-hour Mrs. Litcher conducted a monologue with the skill of a veteran conversationalist ably equipped to anticipate and fend off all interruptions. She talked about her nine-room apartment with three baths and a terrace where she served Sunday night suppers for twenty people, week after week. They spent the summer in the city and entertained so much it took her all winter to recover her strength, she assured Cecilia and Tag.

"We always winter in the South," Mrs. Litcher explained.

She had two married daughters and she described their households at length, dwelling on their furniture, their silver, their illnesses, and their operations. Her references to "My Selma" and "My Baby" quite ignored the parental claims of Mr. Litcher, but he said nothing, only continued to munch and smoke. When addressed directly by his wife he said, "Yes, Judith," or "No, Judith," grinding out his cigarette each time he spoke.

Cecilia wondered what Tag was thinking as he sipped his glass and listened in a grave silence that she suspected was something less than complete attention. Mrs. Litcher had fingernails as long as Nadine Goldberg's, but blood-red and when they touched her glass or the mirror table-top, they made a sharp, scratching sound. Once Tag leaned forward, apparently intent on studying her huge cocktail ring, a square-cut sapphire; once he lighted her cigarette when her husband did not hear her request for a match.

Cecilia welcomed the little flurry that signaled the departure of two or three of the younger guests. She read relief in Tag's glance, too, and at the first opportunity murmured to Mrs. Litcher that they must go.

"We'll look up Mr. Silverstein in camp on our way to Miami," promised Mrs. Litcher, and finished her Manhattan in a gulp.

"The girls will be with us and maybe a couple of their cousins and you young people can have a good time."

Mrs. Goldberg, most of whose lipstick had become transferred to the handkerchief tucked conspicuously in her bosom, asked Tag to take her love to her brother. Her daughter Nadine drew his head down so that she might whisper a confidential message —Cecilia saw the small, plump hands and long green fingernails grasp possessively at Tag's sleeve, but in another moment Mr. Goldberg had pulled her to him and kissed her.

"I kiss all the girls good-bye," he informed her, his wet, red lips grinning at her confusion.

Four other couples were taking their leave, too, and those remaining streamed into the hall to congregate at the elevator where they rattled the gates, rang bells, and screamed derisive messages through the gratings, until the elevator, already nearly filled, stopped at that floor.

Cecilia, clinging to Tag's hand, would have held back, but they were pushed forward by those behind them. Despite the remonstrance of the operator, all ten managed to squeeze themselves in, to the discomfort of the other passengers. Cecilia, crushed against an elderly couple, saw the white-haired woman's lips speak soundlessly to her old, courtly husband beside her. One word encompassed the wife's silent communication—"Jews." Cecilia, glancing at Tag, perceived that he had read the message, too. Her back to the gate, Cecilia's eyes met the contemptuous gaze of another woman in the far corner of the car—hostile, coldly insulting eyes that labeled her by their expressed loathing for her and her kind.

In the lobby Tag abruptly, almost rudely, separated himself and Cecilia from the party group and hurried her through a narrow door, evidently a side entrance. They found themselves in a bricked alleyway lighted only from the windows of the hotel and a stone building opposite that might have been a club.

Tag drew a deep breath, as if glad to be in the open air. "You see how it would be, don't you?" he said roughly.

"How what would be?" countered Cecilia.

"If you were married to me." Tag, standing still, his back against the brick wall, sounded very tired.

Anger, humiliation, and a bitter self-disgust lashed Cecilia's spirit like a hot, searing wind. The remembered touch of Irving Goldberg's loose, wet mouth on hers infuriated her—she hated herself for having accepted his hospitality. "It was ghastly—all of it!" she cried, her face flushing in shame. "I can't endure people like that—noisy, commonplace exhibitionists! I thought I'd lose my mind."

"You see how it would be," Tag repeated.

"And in the elevator . . . women looking at me as if I were a—a—"

"—a Jew." Tag's eyes searched her face. "When we talk of marriage, this is what worries me."

It was quiet in the alleyway and they had it to themselves, except for a dingy white cat sitting on a window ledge in a compact huddle, his tail wound neatly about his feet. Far up in the hotel—perhaps on the fifteenth floor—a radio blared and at the far end of the narrow passageway street traffic, flowing past, was muted to a rhythmless hum. Some of the tension and all of the senseless anger went out of Cecilia, leaving her body weary, but her mind strangely relieved and clear.

"If we were married, our friends wouldn't be like them," she said, slipping her ungloved hand into Tag's.

His fingers curled about hers. "They're Jewish—that's the whole trouble."

"Oh, Tag, it is not!" She spoke to the hurt in his stricken eyes. "I know plenty of people—Christians, Gentiles, whatever you choose to call them—who are just as cheap show-offs. You've met them, too."

Tag lifted her hand to his lips. "These were the first Jews you've met as a group. Could you be happy, living among them?"

"Well, not the Goldbergs," Cecilia admitted. "But neither could you, so that doesn't frighten me. They're no more your kind than they are mine."

He persisted. "I'm Jewish, Ceil. Didn't everything they said and did grate more on your nerves because they were Jews? Didn't that make it worse?"

Cecilia pulled her hand free and in the privacy of the shabby, dim alley, put her arms about his neck. "I didn't lose my perspective, I merely mislaid it, darling," she assured him, sincerity warm in her voice. "It only *seemed* worse because they were Jews."

The following morning Cecilia arrived at the bank practically on time. She and the three other girls who worked in the North branch of the Security Trust Company represented the president's reluctant and belated concession to the labor situation. The branch, in the residential section of the city, was mainly patronized by housewives and neighborhood tradesmen whose relations with the bank employees had always been on a more informal basis than that fostered in the large main edifice located downtown.

In the third year of the war it was conceded that the supply of serious young men to be trained at the branch for gradual absorption into the main organization, had finally trickled to a stop. This left the president with no alternative except to employ more or less serious young women, an innovation that did not altogether displease the two elderly tellers and the vice-president who was a comparatively frisky sixty-eight. Cecilia's grandmother had kept a handsome balance with the Security Trust for years, so that when the girl had announced her intention to earn her living, old Mrs. Warren suggested the bank as the logical place to apply.

The pay for untrained workers was twenty dollars a week, but the hours were not too rigid and the atmosphere pleasant, even kind. Cecilia's fellow clerks, like herself, had been trained for no definite employment and perhaps none of them appreciated the patience and courtesy with which their mistakes and blunders were parried. They took the friendship of their depositors for granted, and when they learned the grizzled janitor's fifty-seventh birthday date, they bought him a layer cake at the bakery where they went for their lunches. Their tendency to make a casual and cozy affair of the banking business might have worried the president had he not convinced himself that the war would be over before women in banking could become a menace. He would be the last to encourage any girl to take the work too earnestly. The problem of what women would do after the war did not alarm him, since he planned to do without them.

Norma Cleves had the desk next to Cecilia's and had just uncovered her machine when Cecilia strolled in, not rushing awkwardly but moving slowly, like a girl in a dream. She murmured, "Good morning," seated herself at her desk.

"In a trance?" Norma, blonde, incisive, had a sharp voice to match her sharp, clear features.

The two other girls, Grace White and Kitty Carroll, turned from the files. They saw that Cecilia still wore her calot and coat and that she continued to smile as if at some pleasant secret.

"In love—I knew it." Grace White, who was married to a man overseas, closed a steel drawer with a bang. She crossed the rug and held out her hands for Cecilia's jacket. "I'll hang up your things—you tell Mama all about him," she urged.

Kitty came to sit on Norma's desk and the three gazed expectantly at Cecilia who laughed and blushed, protesting there was nothing to tell.

She had had the previous day off, so the man must be in the service, the amateur detectives, relentless, shameless, reminded her. The bank gave women employees time off when their husbands or men friends came home on furlough.

"Don't be mean—is he handsome?" prodded Kitty.

"Stunning." Cecilia sat up straighter. "Absolutely immaculate—the cleanest soldier I ever saw."

They pounced. Then he was in the Army? Commissioned? No? Not even a second lieutenant?

"If you put in your time at the Officers' Club on Kincaid Street you'd meet plenty of commissioned men." Norma was a member of the Junior League and Kitty and Grace privately considered her rather a snob.

"Where did you meet him? Is he going to be a candidate for a commission?" Grace had married her husband on the day he had finished at Officers Candidate School.

Cecilia lifted her dark head. She spoke distinctly. "I met Tag in the USO. He's a top sergeant—he was helping a soldier get a message through to his family."

"Can't he get a commission—is he a college man?" Kitty had given her heart to the Navy—providing "he" was made an ensign soon, she stipulated.

She didn't think Tag would try for a commission Cecelia said. "We haven't talked about it. He was working in the day and going to college at night—he hasn't graduated."

"I'll bet he knows more right now than plenty of college men," Grace White snapped. "Now you take my cousin in the Navy—

he's been in two years and wouldn't know a ship if he saw one." Paul, Grace went to say, was book-perfect, but relied on enlisted men to back him up when he got into deep waters. "He says give him experienced men from the ranks any day before what the personnel calls ninety-day wonders—the college kids who take a three months course and pull down a commission."

Norma Cleves with a swift movement lifted Cecilia's left hand and inspected the fingers. "No ring," she reported.

If she married Tag, she would probably not have an engagement ring, Cecilia explained composedly. "But nothing is decided yet. We are to wait until he has his next furlough."

"What do you call him—Tag?" Norma puzzled. "Is that his nickname? What's his right name, anyway?"

The level gaze of Cecilia's dark eyes did not falter. "Hyman Silverstein."

"Hyman Silver—but where does the 'Tag' come in?" Norma stammered, exchanged a bewildered glance with the other girls.

"His father was Jewish. His mother was a Gentile. Taget was his mother's name and it's his middle name. He's always been called Tag." Cecilia felt as if she was reciting something she had learned by rote.

Kitty Carroll began to talk too rapidly. "You must bring his picture down and let us see him. I'll bet he's good-looking and has brains. It's not so easy for an enlisted man to work up to be staff sergeant."

"Doesn't his race hamper him—promotion and things like that—in the Army?" Norma asked. "I should think it would hold him back. Even if he didn't look Jewish, his name would give him away."

Grace put her hand to her head in mock dismay. "Such tact, Miss Cleves! Haven't you heard that we live in a democracy? In fact are said to be fighting a war for equality and justice and things like that?"

To which Norma replied with considerable heat that she was no hypocrite. "I've heard every one of you girls make cracks about the Jews. I can't see why we should change simply because Ceil Warren has fallen in love with one. When you come down to plain facts, I've heard her say plenty about the Jews who deposit their money in this noble bank."

It's true, thought Cecilia. *Oh, Tag, how could I?*

Chapter Five

IT had been a shock to Mrs. Hubert Warren when her only grandchild, upon leaving the convent, had insisted on—abominable phrase—getting a job. She had trusted the nuns to educate Cecilia in the hope that the girl would escape the taint of modern ideas which did nothing, the old lady was convinced, to further a woman's happiness.

When Cecilia had insisted that she must earn money, her distracted grandmother had suggested the bank as offering a dignified environment and one where good manners might still be an appreciated asset. She had scarcely adjusted herself to the possession of a granddaughter who left the house at eight-thirty in the morning and seldom returned before five, when Cecilia had subjected her to another and greater shock—the introduction of Hyman Silverstein, who completed the grandmother's confusion by his ability to charm.

It was this clash between her mind and heart that alarmed the old lady, for never before had her fixed prejudices and pet intolerances been dissolved by any such simple alchemy as a young man's smile. Cecelia must not think of marrying him, of course, but as long as she continued to see him she remained in danger of being swept off her feet. Her own grandmother's footing was none to secure, old Mrs. Warren dryly admitted to herself, when Tag chose to devote himself to her. She had no wish to prolong the vast and horrible war, she muttered piously, but if a power beyond her control should transport Hyman Silverstein overseas and keep him there long enough for Cecilia to forget him, the problem would be solved.

The day after Tag's leave expired it occurred to Mrs. Warren that it might be the part of wisdom to take counsel with others. She had little or no communication with the relatives of her daughter-in-law after the deaths of Lucy Ferris and Post Warren. But they *were* Cecilia's kin, she reminded herself now, and if she didn't talk to someone about this Hyman person, she would certainly have a nervous breakdown.

The name of Tobias Ferris in the phone book promised her little relief. She preferred to talk to his sister, Annabel—what was her name—Annabel Pinn. A widow like herself, Annabel would be more sympathetic than Tobias, whom Mrs. Warren remembered as the possessor of a quick tongue.

Discreet inquiry established that Annabel lived anonymously—for telephone purposes—with a married daughter and it was Molly Cotter who answered the call. She had a Red Cross meeting that afternoon, but her mother would be at home and would love to see Mrs. Warren. "It's been ages since you've been to our house," Molly said cordially. "I don't believe we've seen you since—" her voice trailed off.

Since Lucy's death, old Mrs. Warren reflected, as the bus jerked its way along the boulevard. None of the Ferris connections had attended the funeral, although a number had come to the house before the church service. She had been surprised then at their curious distrust of her religion, betrayed in their awkward and voluble excuses to avoid entering St. Bernard's. Afterward she had scarcely remembered their existence. Her son had died and she had hoped that she might die, too, but now she was beginning to think that God had spared her to safeguard the happiness of Cecilia.

"For the child is very young and the young can not know that values alter after marriage," old Mrs. Warren confided to old Mrs. Pinn, as they faced each other in Molly Cotter's living room.

The Cotters lived in the suburbs and ordered their lives on a conventional pattern. Their house probably duplicated the interiors of twenty others on the same tree-shaded street, old Mrs. Warren reflected a trifle disdainfully, for she prided herself on her old mahogany and silver. There was nothing the matter with the room, really, except that it lacked imagination. Perhaps that had always been the trouble with the Ferris family—a lack of vision. Annabel Pinn had been a Ferris and at seventy-four or five she looked older than her visitor who was nearly eighty.

"You can't explain marriage," old Mrs. Pinn said, knitting on a navy helmet. "How can you explain an experience that is never twice the same? Your marriage, or mine, would mean nothing to Cecilia." Old Mrs. Pinn let her knitting drop into her aproned lap. "Even Cecilia's mother, if she had lived, couldn't do much explaining. Young people refuse to believe love can ever change. They're afraid of the word."

What older people could do, said Annabel Pinn thoughtfully, was to influence and control, without putting their plan into words. "My daughter Molly was terribly worried a few years ago about the love affairs of her children—she has two, you know. A daughter and a son."

Molly, old Mrs. Pinn revealed, had been distressed to learn that both young people were prepared to insist on making marriages that could only be expected to turn out disastrously. Their mother had refused to be dismayed. "My son-in-law, Mr. Cotter, was afraid to act, but Molly went right ahead and saw to it that the children met plenty of eligible young men and women. In no time at all they were both engaged—suitably in every way."

They were both married now, the boy in the service, the girl expecting, old Mrs. Pinn concluded cheerfully, taking up her knitting as if her energy had been renewed.

She was a tiny woman with soft, cream-colored white hair and quick, flashing movements of her small hands and feet. When she spoke she seemed to bite off her words neatly, almost as though she put a period between each one. Because she was dependent upon her daughters (she had two) she retained a fierce independence that extended not only to her speech but impelled her to refuse physical assistance, although her arthritis at times made it difficult for her to lift her arms.

In contrast old Mrs. Warren appeared the younger, for she was a tall and stately woman who still found pleasure in clothes and jewels and furs. The details of living had never wearied her and, since she had always had money, she had never been in bondage to her child, although since the death of her son she had been isolated and alone. She paid well for service, accepted it graciously, and believed that certain types of human beings were designated from birth to be servants.

Out of touch with reality to an extent possible only to a well-protected old age, nevertheless her concern for Cecilia had opened her eyes to the dearth of eligible young men. It wasn't practical, she pointed out now to her hostess, to arrange parties for a young girl.

"All the young men are in the service and any war marriage presents an appalling array of risks," old Mrs. Warren, a handsome picture in black crêpe and a lace ruffle and pearls, observed.

Mrs. Pinn glanced up from her knitting and the light made her glasses opaque. "Just where did Cecilia ever meet a Hebrew?" she inquired.

"At the USO." She had misunderstood the arrangement from the first, Mrs. Warren sighed. As it had been explained to her, the girls served on shifts, simply as a patriotic gesture. "One of my friends was chairman of a committee to get young, pretty girls to hand out chocolate and cigarettes, serve coffee and tea and things like that, down at the lounge in the Terminal station."

She had been so careful, old Mrs. Warren reiterated, she had stipulated that Cecilia was not to work at night, since her bank position made it necessary for her to keep regular hours. It was understood that the girls were not to have "dates" with the men who came into the lounge between trains. Cecilia, her grandmother said, had given her Saturday afternoons at first and later had gone down Sundays, after mass.

That was the trouble, both women agreed—you couldn't be with a young girl every moment and no matter how carefully supervised, she would, given the smallest opening, break away and head for trouble.

"Boys are easier to raise," old Mrs. Pinn said, her wrinkled face very earnest. "I always wanted a boy."

Sometimes, at the end of life, it was all the same, Mrs. Warren returned. "You're fortunate to have your two girls. There's no one to take care of me and after I'm gone Cecilia will be all alone."

"She has her mother's people—quite a number of them." The white knitting needles raced. "But she's grown up without knowing us."

Old Mrs. Warren murmured. She had seen little of Cecilia herself. "I wanted her to grow up in a safe and happy environment, with girls her own age. What the Sisters are going to say about her infatuation for—for—this person, I dread to think. They feel as if Cecilia is their charge still."

Mrs. Pinn, whose knowledge of the Catholic sisterhoods was extremely sketchy, even fantastic, sidestepped the subject by offering to fetch her visitor a cup of tea. She was relieved when her offer was declined and secretly pleased when Mrs. Warren decided that she must make the four-thirty bus. She hoped that she had not seemed unsympathetic or cold, old Mrs. Pinn reflected as she closed the front door, but she could not help feeling that this affair of Cecilia's was in effect a judgment of the Lord's upon her Grandmother Warren: they had not been satisfied to let Lucy remain a Protestant, but had worked upon her until she had turned. It would be interesting to see if Hyman Silverstein insisted that Cecilia adopt the Hebrew faith, after she married him. That would give St. Catherine's Convent something to think about.

At dinner that night old Mrs. Pinn enjoyed the role, unusual for her, of bearer of news. Her son-in-law, a restrained and silent man, seldom spoke at the table. When he did, it was always to address his wife, a practice he followed to the point of embarrassing her when outsiders were present. He was punctillious about the physical comfort of his wife's mother, and he saw to it that she was supplied with what she needed; but his resentment against her, kindled on his wedding day, had mounted steadily throughout the years.

"Mother had a visitor this afternoon, dear," Molly Cotter announced when she had finished serving the vegetables at her end of the table. "While I was at Red Cross. Mrs. Warren—Mrs. Hubert Warren."

Charlie Cotter frowned, not in irritation, but because the name held no association for him. He said politely, "A new neighbor?"

"No, Mrs. Warren, dear. Cecilia Warren's grandmother. You know—my cousin Lucy's daughter. Mother is her great-aunt."

Charlie said, "Oh!"

Mrs. Pinn murmured that she thought it was very strange her brother Tobias had not taken the trouble to let her know. It must have looked odd to Mrs. Warren that Cecilia's own great-aunt didn't know of her engagement. "For it amounts to an engagement. I suppose Cecilia went to her grandfather first because she felt she wouldn't upset any household arrangements."

Molly's thin, nervous face tightened, she brushed back an imaginary strand of hair, for her almost white head was beautifully waved. "Why, Mother, what a strange thing to say! What do you mean?"

"Eat your dinner, Molly," her husband urged.

She meant, Mrs. Pinn said, that Tobias was the head of his own house and people felt free to go to see him at any time. "He's the main one. Dora and Quilty are under his direction." *There are times,* the old woman thought, *when I would give my soul to have my own home. One room, perhaps, but absolutely mine.*

"Well, anyway, wait until you hear what's happened, Charlie." Molly, not knowing what to say to her mother, chose to ignore the reference to Tobias' independence. "What do you think—Cecilia Warren wants to marry a Jewish boy."

Charlie glanced at his wife's and mother-in-law's plates, helped himself to a second chop. "Thought the Warrens were Roman Catholics," he shrugged, rising to fill his water glass from the pitcher on the buffet.

His wife nodded. Of course the Warrens were Catholics, she confirmed. She would never forget what the family had gone through when Lucy married Post Warren.

"Now it seems that Ceil's grandmother is terribly upset about this," she declared. "Mother says she looks to be in a kind of daze. Apparently she doesn't know how to stop it."

"It's terrible, a young girl barely twenty," Mrs. Pinn sighed. "After all the money that's been spent on her education."

Charlie addressed his wife. "Christ was a Jew."

It always embarrassed Molly to have him use what she vaguely called "religious terms" although, since he was a Presbyterian elder, she considered him to be a religious man. As a matter of fact, any discussion of or reference to religion outside the regular church services, which she attended faithfully and in which she sincerely believed, made her uneasy. She said now, "Oh, that was different."

"How was it different?"

Molly saw that her mother, seated on her right hand, was ready for more food. "Give Mother another chop, Charlie," she instructed her husband. "Why, so far back when—when Christ lived, the Jews were different. They were the way we are now." She meant the dominating race, but although she stopped short, Charlie, familiar with her reasoning, understood.

"What is Mrs. Warren upset about?" he persisted. "If Cecilia marries this Jew, is a difference in creed bound to wreck their marriage? Don't you believe—doesn't Mrs. Warren believe—that there is only one God?"

It wasn't a question of religion, Molly objected, well, at least it wasn't religion alone. Jews were a separate race. Or weren't they? "Are Jews a race, Charlie?"

"Suppose they are? We happen to live in a country that allows no discrimination in race, color, or creed," he reminded her, obviously enjoying the sound of his voice. "What's dessert?"

His troubled wife murmured that she had made a chocolate icebox-cake. "I've finally learned how to whip evaporated milk."

Mrs. Pinn choked on a bit of bread, gulped a swallow of water. "Nobody seemed to think there was only one God when your Ellen wanted to marry a Catholic boy," she suggested.

"Charlie didn't object to the difference in religion, did you, Charlie?" Molly appealed. "It was only—only—"

He had thought it wiser not to subject his daughter to the inevitable strain of the adjustments such a marriage would have imposed, Charlie explained. "Ellen is very happily married now and I think my judgment was vindicated."

His wife, because she had never been sure that God would forgive her the part she had played in breaking off her daughter's romance, must assure herself of the worth of her son-in-law. "Albert is a very fine young man in every way," she testified.

Afterward in the kitchen, when she and Charlie washed the dishes together as they had done since their first married year, Molly confided that she couldn't bear to think of Lucy's child marrying a Jew. "The poor girl hasn't met enough nice boys, that's the whole trouble. Mother says his name is Silverstein—Hyman Silverstein. Are you listening to me, Charlie?"

"There's a convention next week, in Chicago. I want you to go with me." Charlie dried a plate with a snowy towel, placed it carefully on the immaculate porcelain table-top.

Molly at the sink looked distressed. "Mother—"

"Let your sister Ida take her. Call her up tomorrow. We'll only be away for two weeks and it won't kill her." Charlie realized that his grip on a china cup threatened to crack it and he loosened his long, firm fingers.

Her sister Ida would be furious; she always resented a request to have her mother visit her, Molly worried. But the last visit had been more than a year ago, and Ida ought to be willing to let them close the house for two weeks. Ida, a registered nurse, worked in a defense plant; she had crazy hours and most of the responsibility would devolve on Frank, her husband—well, heavens, thought Molly spiritedly, didn't she have that responsibility day and night?

"I'll call Ida tonight, after Mother's in bed," she promised. "I don't believe she's heard about Cecilia."

Charlie suggested that it might be better not to mention Cecilia, lest Ida seize upon that and ignore the real issue. "You stick to pinning her down to take your mother for two weeks. Tell her she's got to."

It did not greatly surprise Molly the next day to meet Cecilia Warren in Frank Ferris' office and to learn that he had invited the girl to lunch with them. Frank had created something like a family scandal by his marriage to Molly's younger sister ten years ago when he was forty and Ida thirty years old. They were first cousins and its was confidently predicted, both by Frank's father, Tobias, and Ida's mother, Annabel Pinn, that no good could come of such an alliance. Frank had not allowed criticism to deflect him from his course, but he had never been quite at ease with his relatives since his marriage. Whenever forced into social communication with them he automatically sought to protect himself against private or personal disclosures.

Molly understood perfectly that he had invited Cecilia to make it difficult or impossible to bring up the subject of a visit from his mother-in-law. Ida, he had said, was working on the night shift, which meant that she could not be asked to answer the telephone during the day. Molly discounted the night shift excuse—she suspected that Ida took refuge in that evasion to escape the necessity for making unpleasant or difficult decisions.

"The two of them are as slippery as eels," the exasperated Molly had complained to her mother, "but Frank has got to take me to lunch and say yes or no; he made the appointment with me as if I were his dentist."

Cecilia, delighted to be asked out to lunch in her noon hour, charmed Frank who had not seen her since a child. Not only was she a new personality and not likely to harass him, but her touching confidence in his interest and sympathy, her acceptance of him and of Molly as her kin and therefore to be cherished, would have impressed a much less sensitive man.

Molly forgot her own irritation, when she saw how eagerly Cecilia turned to him and how wholeheartedly he listened to her extravagant praise of her "Angel," as she designated Tag.

"I wish you could have met him," Cecilia reiterated for the twentieth time. "Aunt Dory and Grandfather both like him."

They were waiting in Frank's office—he was manager of a fire insurance agency—for a delayed phone call. His good-natured, incompetent secretary, the third in a month, he grumbled, could handle only the simplest routine, and the slightest deviation from her memorized business school course plunged her into despair.

"What does your grandmother—Mrs. Warren—really think of"—Molly gulped—"Mr. Silverstein?"

The clear, dark eyes, their candid gaze so like a child's and yet with a steadfast quality in their depths that no child eyes mirrored, turned to Molly. Her grandmother, Cecilia said, liked Tag when he was with her. "She admits he has great charm. But when she hasn't seen him for a week or so she says it is just infatuation and that there are plenty of boys as nice and good Catholics."

Frank was too short to have a good figure, but he kept his weight normal and his blond hair was still thick. "Well?" standing beside his desk he smiled down at Cecilia, who sat beside Molly on a straight-backed settle.

Cecilia lifted her chin. "There is no one like Tag, no one so—so genuine." She twisted her hands in a young gesture, oddly appealing. "His principles are exactly right!" she assured her listeners in a tone of triumph.

The phone rang sharply and Frank seized the receiver. He began to speak in a low, rapid voice.

The two women left their seat and crossed the rug to the window which opened upon a vista of tidy chimneys and well-kept roofs.

"What are his principles?" Molly, who seldom lost the thread of a conversation, whispered.

Cecilia, unable to command a list upon short notice, answered in some confusion. "Oh—why—well, Cousin Molly, we think alike. About the important things, I mean."

Molly's stare betrayed her utter lack of comprehension.

"Well, for instance, Cousin Molly, take Tag's sense of honor." Cecilia put a beautifully gloved hand on Molly's arm. "Plenty of men I've met lack a sense of personal integrity. They think it's smart to be dishonest, if you're not found out. No one could persuade Tag to be dishonest in the tiniest detail," Cecilia insisted, pride shining in her eyes. "Not even me."

Frank took them to lunch in the restaurant at the top of his building and afterward Cecilia went back to the bank and Molly off to a lecture she vaguely identified as "something for the French." She had not succeeded in pinning him down to consideration of her problem, but frustration only increased her determination.

That evening she patiently and systematically called her sister's number until Ida finally answered the phone. If Molly was about to have a nervous breakdown, Ida observed, by all means let Mother come to them. "But she'll have to get along with Frank. I'm home so seldom and my hours change." She had a woman come in to get her daughter's lunch, Ida added, and to start dinner, but Frank managed the rest. "Mother will probably think we let Leidy run wild, but I can't pay any attention to her criticism."

Molly's voice dropped. "Frank tell you about Cecilia?"

"Yes. Isn't it queer about her? Frank says he heard about it through his father." She thought Cecilia was making a great mistake, Ida asserted; it was one thing to be head over heels in love with a man and another to face criticism of him as his wife.

A wife found enough flaws in her husband, Ida added, without having other people constantly on the alert to detect them. "Anyway, a woman at the plant told me that Jews are terrible gamblers and will bet their last dollar—that's a fine prospect for Ceil," Ida said.

"How much do you suppose Ida makes at that defense plant, Charlie?" Molly asked when the sisters had said good-bye.

"Not so much. She has plenty taken out of her envelope before she even sees it." Charlie went on to explain that the only people who really made money in the large plants were those families with half a dozen or more members employed. "You take these Italians, with a man and his wife and maybe eight or nine children, all working—they bring home enough to buy a house in the city or a farm outside. Ida and Frank, both working, don't get far ahead—with Leidy their only kid and living expenses what they are."

Old Mrs. Pinn looked arch. "You should have married an Italian, Molly."

But Molly answered in all seriousness. "My goodness, I never would! All Italians beat their wives. Everyone says so."

Chapter Six

TOBIAS FERRIS, in moments of depression, complained that he had been cheated in the matter of grandchildren. To be sure he had five—Cecilia Warren, the child of his dead daughter Lucy, the three girls of his daughter Sarah, and Leidy, the daughter of his son Frank. Tobias liked to suggest to Dora, "the unmarried one," as the family designated her, that if she had taken a husband she might have produced a son. It was extremely disappointing to a man to have reached the stage in life where he could not reasonably expect more grandchildren, Tobias said, only to realize that the line lacked a male.

To Dora's suggestion that his grandchild, Ginger Steel, might present him with a great-grandson, or that her sisters were likely to marry and have boys, Tobias remained indifferent. Not only did he think it unlikely that he would live long enough to take a great-grandson to a ball game, but he deemed it still more unlikely that his daughter Sarah would permit a grandson to be introduced to this world.

"I wouldn't put it past her, if Nutmeg should have a boy, to dress the kid up like a girl and give out that he *is* a girl," Tobias informed Dora in the course of the argument. "How do we know that Nutmeg and Mabel and Fern are girls, when it comes to that? Maybe they're boys and Sarah has hoodwinked us all these years."

Dora said significantly, "Well, they happen to be girls. I know."

There were women, Tobias insisted, who thought they could control sex, or at least refuse to admit it defeated them. "I read the other day in a magazine down to the library, about a woman wanted a girl so bad she dressed up her boy baby with ribbons and curls and kept him like that until he was twenty or so."

Dora sniffed. Such a fantastic situation might exist, but only in an isolated community without school or social contact, she pointed out. "Are you going out to Frank's tomorrow, Father? I hope you don't suspect Leidy of being a boy."

No one could mistake that tyke for a boy, Tobias retorted. Besides, Ida had been crazy for a son. "If she had had a boy, she wouldn't have stopped talking about it yet."

He had never admitted it, perhaps not even to himself, but Tobias stood somewhat in awe of the niece who had become his daughter-in-law. Ida, he reflected when he set out for Frank's house the next afternoon, was so damn efficient. He always suspected that she measured exactly what could be expected of her in any given situation and did that much, cheerfully and accurately, but no more. Tobias groped in his mind for the word he wanted and found it just as the bus reached his stop. Mechanical—that was what Ida was.

"Watch your step, Pop!" the bus driver advised, eyeing Tobias' descent to the curb with an intentness embarrassing to his elderly fare.

The suburban town of Melon was a link in a chain of standardized, well-planned communities peopled, as is the American custom, by families who had effected a compromise for the sake of their children. They paid for an expensive school system, they were reasonably certain that their neighbors were "nice" and that the youngsters who overran the lawns and swung from the trees were normal in body and mind. For themselves, they had city conveniences, good train and bus service—in peacetime—and the wives could get into town to the theatres and shops. The servant problem, serious for years before the war, had resulted in an increasing number of women, like Ida Ferris, putting their reliance on elaborate electrical equipment.

Mrs. Holdfast, the middle-aged widow who came five days a week to prepare a hot noon lunch for little Leidy, answered Tobias' ring. She had a good memory for faces and recognized him smilingly. His sister, she told him, was in the sun parlor. The house was rather chilly, Mrs. Holdfast confided, but Mr. Ferris wanted to put off starting the oil burner as long as he could—what with no one home all day, oil rationing, and all.

"Well, Annabel—don't get up." Tobias kissed his sister awkwardly. "You look first rate."

The October sunshine poured over Annabel's small, neat figure in its dull blue dress. She tossed her head as one accustomed to compliments, for she had been beautiful when a girl. Yes, she was enjoying her visit, she answered Tobias' question, delighted to have someone with whom to talk. Leidy was the only person she saw to say a word to, from morning till night. "Oh, that Mrs. Holdfast, of course—I don't count her. We don't need her—I can get Leidy's lunch. But Ida tells me she has to have her the year round or not at all."

Mrs. Holdfast, Annabel revealed, was in great demand throughout the neighborhood. She "minded" children at night, when their parents went out; she did marketing and mending and cooked dinners, all tasks for which she charged by the hour. She could not do heavy work, like laundry and cleaning, but she was excellent to leave in charge.

"I give her her due," Annabel assured Tobias. "She isn't a

good cook and her prices are outrageous; but she's the widow of a clergyman and very conscientious."

The sun parlor, furnished in maple with orange and green for the decorative scheme, was the warmest room in the house, Annabel chattered. Frank built up a fine fire in the fireplace at night and then the living room was comfortable. "But I get so stiff during the day I can hardly move out of my chair. I don't know what the fuel rationing board expects old people to do—we can't all live in Florida."

Tobias listened, hitching his chair at intervals to keep it in the pool of sunshine that shifted, he complained, "at the edges." Annabel Pinn knitted steadily on a sweater for the Red Cross, the reliable Mrs. Holdfast went home, and at quarter-past three a small, freckle-faced girl tapped on the glass pane and grinned to see Tobias jump.

"Hello, Grandpa!" She let him kiss her when he opened the door and she stood docilely beside her grandmother to be kissed again, but she appeared to be relieved when the performance was over.

"You were sound asleep—in the daytime!" Leidy accused her two elders.

Her grandmother indignantly denied the charge, but Tobias explained that he had not slept well the night before. "My bed," he explained, "was restless."

"Tell me more rhymes," the child commanded, her clear green eyes bright with mischief.

She was tiny, even for her eight years and extremely plain, with a thin, sharp-featured face and straight, fine hair screwed into tight pigtails that looked as if they might come out, roots and all, at any moment. Tobias thought now, as he had at each encounter with her since her babyhood, that she was the neatest creature he had ever seen. She looked thoroughly scrubbed: her tight, bright yellow wash dress was spotless, her white socks immaculate, her shoes polished. Tobias regarded her with awe, knowing that her mind was like her mother's, relentless, quick.

"What kind of rhyme you want?" he parried cautiously. Leidy had a retentive memory and it behooved him to instruct her only in such verse as would be socially approved, her mother had once warned him.

Leidy considered. "Oh, like—

"Smarty, smarty had a party—
Nobody came but big fat Artie."

Annabel interposed. "Why do you want to waste your time learning trash like that?"

"When I was a boy, I knew hundreds of 'em." Tobias' thoughts traveled backward seventy years and resurrected one of his favorites with an ease that never failed to surprise him. And he couldn't remember where he had left yesterday's paper, when he wanted to work the crossword puzzle!

"Dan, Dan, was a very nice man,
He washed his face in the frying pan,
Combed his hair with a wagon wheel,
And died with a toothache in his heel."

Tobias beamed upon Leidy. "How's that?"

The child recited it word for word. "Tell me another."

"Your teacher might not like this." Tobias hesitated, "We used it a lot, when I went to school." He began to recite slowly, while Leidy stared at him as if hypnotized.

"Liar! Liar!
Your pants are on fire!
Your nose is as long
As a telegraph wire."

"That," announced Annabel with finality, "will be enough."

Leidy, on her way to the kitchen, glanced over her shoulder. "Well, anyway I know the old ones—like

"Marguerite
Go wash your feet:
The Board of Health's
Across the street."

She let the swinging door close behind her with the force of a rushing wind.

Before Annabel could deliver the lecture trembling on her tongue, the child returned. The note on the bulletin board in the kitchen said that Frank would be home early, Leidy announced.

"I want to ask him if he'd sell our house to Jews." Leidy gathered up her plaid lumber-jacket from the chair on which she had flung it.

Tobias asked, "What are you talking about?" This was practically an automatic question in any conversation he held with this grandchild.

One of the children on the block had told her it was a dreadful thing to sell one's house to Jews, Leidy confided. "They ruin a neighborhood. I don't see exactly why, because look at Cecilia. If she marries a Jew, I don't think she'd ruin a neighborhood."

"Stop that nonsense." Tobias wondered why such talk sounded abominable in the mouth of a child. Glancing at Annabel, he saw that she, too, was aghast. "You don't know anything about it," he scolded Leidy. "Nice children don't say things like that."

But Annabel was curious to know how Leidy had learned of Cecilia's attachment. "Who told you your cousin Cecilia may be married, dearie? It's something of a secret, or is supposed to be."

Frank had told her, Leidy said, he told her everything. Years ago, when she had been younger, she had planned to marry Frank when she grew up. Now she wasn't sure that she wanted to marry anyone. "If he had to go to war, I wouldn't like that. Cecilia's boy friend is in the war and I don't think she likes it, either."

She thought too much, that was what kept her looking like a razor blade, Tobias informed her gruffly. But when Frank came in at half-past four and found the two old people solemnly discussing his daughter, he said their anxiety dated them.

"Ida knows all about child psychology—she reads all the magazines and books," he assured his agitated relatives. "We believe in encouraging Leidy to use her mind."

"My good godfrey, I should think you could do that without treating her as if she was a woman of thirty," Tobias objected.

Annabel, who practiced tact as a younger women practiced to perfect a tennis stroke, suggested that she had been waiting to hear Leidy play her new piece. Yes, they would wait while she went to the bathroom.

"I had a heck of a time at her music teacher's recital last week," Frank lit a cigarette, walked nervously about as the older people re-established themselves in the living room which did not looked lived in at all.

Leidy, he went on, had taken part in the recital and he had represented the family, since Ida could not get off. "No one had ever told Leidy what 'Intermission' meant, so when the first part of the program was completed, she saw her name was next, after the intermission. She dashed right out, her teacher after her, and both of them landed on the piano keys with a crash. The audience was all steamed up."

Frank listened with rapt attention while Leidy rattled off a noisy march, then murmured something about potatoes. No, he'd have to attend to them, he assured his mother-in-law; he was used to getting dinner.

"Ida said we should have mashed potatoes, not boiled the way you like them," Leidy instructed him from the piano bench.

She followed her father into the kitchen and her shrill, eager voice, evidently pitched high to hold his attention, made her every word audible in the living room.

"Frank, what religion do you like best?"

A moment's hesitation, then, "Why Congregational, I guess. I'm a Congregationalist."

"Oh! What's Ida?"

A rattle of dishes punctuated Frank's reply. "Your mother's a member of the Methodist Church, or was."

"Then I like the Methodist religion best. But Frank—say, Frank?"

Tobias grinned as Frank's tone sharpened. "What?"

"You know what religion I like best, next to the Methodists? The Catholics. Because Gertie Kendall is my best friend and she's a Catholic."

In the living room Annabel asked Tobias to turn on the floor lamp beside his chair. "I can knit in the twilight, but you can't see to work your crossword puzzle."

He was on his way, he was waiting only to speak to Ida, Tobias answered as the lamp shade glowed like a yellow pumpkin shell. "Annabel, have you seen Cecilia lately? To talk to?"

His sister shook her white head. "I saw Mrs. Warren. She called while Molly was at Red Cross. I was so afraid I'd say something against the Catholics." Cecilia was only a child, Annabel added, too young to know her own mind. "You ought to use your influence, Tobias. You're her grandfather."

"She's in love." Tobias spoke with a simplicity that surprised himself. "You know something, Annabel? I think Ceil's got a better chance of making a successful marriage than anyone in her family—on either side of the house."

That was queer talk, Annabel reproved him; happy marriages had been the rule, not the exception, among the Ferrises and the Pinns. "We've never had a divorce—very few families can say that, Tobias."

His children had stayed married and so had hers, Tobias admitted, but that in itself proved nothing. "One or the other getting the upper hand isn't my idea of married life. Sarah holds the reins in her marriage, Lucy was so dominated that she stayed away from us. Of your two children, Molly is afraid of her husband and Ida has hers under her thumb. No one's divorced, I grant you, but that's only because the household Facists win."

Annabel sniffed as the odor of something burning came from the kitchen. She did not dare go into her daughter's kitchen, except to help in clearing away a meal. Irritation at her imposed helplessness tinged her response with asperity. "I'm sure I don't see why you're so sure that Cecilia will be happy," she frowned above her clicking needles. "If she marries that man she'll be handicapped from the start. She's never been up against public opinion. How can she, a protected young girl, guess how cruel people will be, what kind of things they will say?"

"I imagine she's had a taste of it already." Tobias shifted in his chair to get more light. "But you see, Annabel, the thing is she and Tag won't be saying mean things to each other and that's what really counts. In this family we have a kind of gift for meanness. I notice it more as I get older. We've infected each other. Ceil and this lad haven't the taint. If you once saw them together, you'd know what I mean."

Annabel twitched her yarn. "But he's Jewish." She amplified. "There's his name and all."

Her face looked pinched and she was probably chilly, Tobias

thought. He was sorry for Annabel, living in the homes of her children, Tobias mused. For that matter, he was sorry for all women—for Sarah and her Nutmeg, for Dora who had nothing of her own. Ida, too, was a pathetic creature although, or perhaps because, her husband and child regarded her with awe. And Molly, Annabel's daughter, for years had been pulled two ways, between her husband's demands and her mother's love.

But Cecilia—ah, Cecilia, about whom all these women fretted, had no need for pity. It pleased Tobias to fancy that he could look beyond the circle of lamplight and see her standing, young and tall and dark and so sweetly awkward, with Tag, the smiling, steady glow in his eyes, straight and proud beside her. It was the way they looked at each other that Tobias found he remembered—the gentle kindness that was like a golden core in the flame of their love. The outside world could not harm them when their concern was all to save each other from a wound.

It was lucky Annabel couldn't read his thoughts, Tobias decided, getting stiffly to his feet. Up to this moment he had reached no conclusion regarding Hyman Silverstein, but he perceived now that he had liked him from the first.

"Don't go!" Annabel looked up at him. He was of her generation, she was lonely, her expressive face pleaded. Hastily she cast about in her mind for some questions, something to delay him, like the touch of her hand on his sleeve. She let the words tumble from her mouth, scarely aware of what she said. "Tobias! Then you've seen him—this—this Silverstein?"

"Had him to dinner—at least Ceil came and he called for her." Tobias dropped his pipe in his pocket. "You never saw anything handsomer on two legs. If I was a girl, I'd do just as Ceil has and fall head over heels in love with him."

Annabel reiterated that she was thinking of their lives together after marriage. The brunt would fall on Cecilia. Men didn't mind or didn't notice the jabs and side glances and whispers, but Cecilia wouldn't miss one of them. "Her grandmother's afraid and I am, too, that she's heading for a lifetime of heartaches."

Two old women would figure it out that way, Tobias snapped. His own buried doubts sharpened his irritation. "Has it occurred to you that she won't have a monopoly on heartache, even if her marriage is a washout?" he growled. "Look at Sarah, with a husband who's been drinking steadily for years. Not that I altogether blame him. Look at Frank." Tobias discreetly lowered his voice. Ida, he conceded, was a wonderful woman, as perfect as the mechanical washer that was the pride of her heart. "And while we're at it, take a look at your other daughter, Annabel. Her husband is a good man, but not good enough to lay off nagging Molly about—about—"

"Me," said Annabel's tired old voice. "I know."

Before Tobias could recover from his embarrassment, Frank burst into the room, Leidy like a small terrier, panting at his heels. "Mother, will you come out and look at the ham?" he implored. "It's perfectly dry."

Annabel began to roll up her knitting. "You're cooking veal," she instructed. "Not ham. Don't you know the difference?"

It all looked alike to him, Frank confessed, but Leidy suddenly pointed an accusing finger at him.

"The whole trouble, Frank, is that you were trying to keep the pan so it would be easy to wash," the child said. "You thought gravy would be greasy. Now you haven't even got any juice."

Annabel sometimes felt that she had not much more than a speaking acquaintance with her daughter Ida since her marriage ten years before. Ida was twelve years younger than Molly, which was offered as an excuse for the lack of communication between the sisters; but the truth was that Frank and Charlie were hopelessly antagonistic. Even if she had not furnished a focus point for argument, Annabel acknowledged, the two men would have opposed each other with a vehemence that amounted almost to hatred. Ida might have been able to ignore, or pretend to ignore, the tension between them, but Molly suffered agonies whenever her husband and brother-in-law were in the same room. Molly, more sensitive to spiritual currents than Ida, dreaded the silent clashes almost as much as the verbal.

It was for Molly's sake that Annabel submitted herself to the strange and tortuous adjustments demanded of her now in Ida's house. Charlie would be so glad to be alone with Molly, he would be sweet to her, they would be as happy as though newly married, Annabel reminded herself, when her difficulties as guest threatened to overwhelm her. Charlie was deeply in love with Molly; after twenty-five years of marriage, he still liked to be alone with his wife. He had welcomed the marriages of his children, since he then felt free to make more demands on Molly's time. Only his wife's mother now disputed his claims on his wife.

Well, thought Annabel, waiting as it were on the sidelines for Ida to summon her to dinner, *Molly and I could be very happy together, too, by ourselves. Without Charlie.* But the import of such an arrangement, even in fancy, was too shocking to contemplate. Annabel turned away from it in quick relief as Leidy dashed in to announce that "Ida's here."

The room's chill had further stiffened Annabel's knees and for a moment after rising from her chair, she stood perfectly still. Then she moved at top speed for her, toward the dining room.

Ida, already seated, ready to carve the veal, looked thirty instead of forty, even after a full eight-hour day at the plant. "I have a meeting at seven, Mother," she said in explanation of her poised knife. She began to slice the roast with firm, competent strokes of the shining blade.

She was a slender woman, immaculately neat in a tailored gray wool suit, for she changed her uniforms at the plant. Her gleaming blonde hair, built into a high pompadour, made a rather hard line above her face, the flesh of which was hard and firm, too. Everything about Ida was healthy and vital, but with that same hint of steeliness like a metal finish. She had a habit of holding her head motionless and glancing rapidly, from left to right, so that her small, round, agate-colored eyes seemed to click. All her movements were quick but precise and her voice, crisp and distinct, pleased her mother who could always hear every word.

"And what happened to you today, Leidy?" Ida asked her daughter, when the meat, potatoes, two vegetables, one green and one yellow as the nutrition chart directed, had been served.

Ida cared nothing about food as such, but she conscientiously followed the recommendations of the government nutritionists, grateful, she said, to be relieved of that much planning.

Leidy beamed. "I'm head of my group in spelling," she announced.

"That's fine." Ida glanced significantly at the glass of milk before Leidy's plate. She wondered whether Mrs. Holdfast had been firm about the soup for luncheon. Leidy was apt to make an issue of soup and her grandmother was not much moral support to Mrs. Holdfast.

Annabel, who had been champion at many a spelling bee in her childhood, forgot the rule she had set herself, which was not to speak before she was spoken to. "Does that make you the highest in the class for spelling, darling?" she asked.

"Oh, no." Leidy, across the table, regarded a carrot thoughtfully. "No, I'm head of the lowest group."

This puzzled even Ida, who sought an explanation.

The class was divided into three spelling groups, Leidy revealed. The Air Corps was first, the Signal Corps second, and the Coast Guard third. "I'm head of the Coast Guards."

Her father laughed. "Does that mean you can spell at all?"

But Ida, pressed for time as always, was instructing Leidy that she must dry the dishes. "Your father will wash them and you are to dry them. Grandmother isn't to go into the kitchen. Light the fire in the living room, Frank, so Mother will be comfortable."

She would like to help with the dinner work, Annabel protested. She was far happier if allowed to be useful.

"Heck, you're useful," Frank assured her. "What about all that Red Cross knitting you do? And all that thread I got you downtown today—what's that for?"

"I thought"—Annabel glanced at Ida—"that I'd make a bedspread. For Cecilia."

A lace bedspread, she specified, in answer to Ida's question. Or a tablecloth. She might not get it finished in time for Cecilia's wedding, but that wasn't important. "Molly tells me so many of the girls don't plan to keep house right away. They store their presents for the duration."

Ida said nothing—perhaps she didn't even hear, Annabel thought charitably—but when she hurried off to her meeting, Leidy came to stand beside Annabel's chair in the living room. She was not a demonstrative child and she saw her grandmother so seldom that a feeling of mutual confidence had never been established between them. Now Leidy appeared to watch her father, kneeling on the hearth to light the fire, but she spoke to Annabel.

"Will you make me a lace bedspread, Grandma? I mean when I get married?"

"If you don't put it off too long." The old lady in the big arm chair nodded confidentially to the small, serious-faced girl.

"Would you like to have the star pattern? That's the old one I'm going to make for Cecilia."

Frank, fanning his blaze with a folded newspaper, protested. "I thought you were never going to be married, Leidy. You said you would always live at home with me."

The child gazed past him, into an ecstatic future. "No." She rejected any past commitments. "I'm going to get married when I grow up and have a nuptial mass in St. Columba's."

She couldn't be married in a Catholic church, her grandmother interposed. "You're not a Catholic, dearie."

Gertie Kendall was going to have a church wedding, when she grew up, Leidy said; they wanted their weddings to be just alike. "Gertie's going to wear her mother's wedding dress. Can I wear my mother's wedding dress, Grandma?"

What had Ida worn to be married in? She and Frank had had a City Hall ceremony; their families had not been told until the next day. Ida was not the type of bride to be interested in white satin and orange blossoms, nor did one offer to crochet her a lace bedspread.

A tongue of flame curled up around the kindling and pierced the spiral of white smoke mounting lazily between the sticks. Frank sat back on his heels and wiped his face on a plaid-bordered handkerchief. "Doggone those dishes!" He frowned, then laughed as he noted Annabel's solicitous expression.

She coaxed. "Why don't you let me do the dishes, Frank? I can get them done while you read the paper."

That would be all wrong, he said firmly. Ida intended to train a certain young person to do her share. "Come on, Toots, you and I have a job in the kitchen."

Leidy demurred. She lay on her stomach, a book open before and thrust partly under her. "I got to do my research," she declared.

Her father and grandmother regarded her with open distrust. Research in the third grade was a little *too* much, Frank complained. Besides, the last time Leidy had upset the house with her research, she had discovered the next morning that she had been looking up the wrong thing.

"I remember you had me flying to the library for all kinds of books," Frank reminded his complacent and prostrate child. "We did research on the elephant—or was it the giraffe? Anyway, when you went to school the next day you found out you were supposed to have studied the cow."

She was doing history now, Leidy murmured. "About war."

"There'll be war, if you don't come out and dry the dishes for me," Frank warned her. "Come on—you've stalled long enough. You can do your homework afterward."

A gust of anger shook Leidy, who recognized her defeat. "You're a bully!" she stormed, rising like a camel, rear first. "A great big bully—that's what you are. If I was your size, you wouldn't dare talk to me like that."

"You'll be doing dishes all by yourself when you're big," he consoled her and ran for the kitchen, the child in pursuit.

But a few moments later Annabel heard them laughing as they clattered dishes and silver with cheerful industry.

For a moment she wondered if Ida intentionally planned to make her feel unnecessary; then she tried dutifully to dismiss the idea as morbid and the type of reasoning to be avoided by the aged. Tobias was always exhorting her to respect herself; he assured her that others would accept her at her own valuation. But Tobias, Annabel reflected, had his own home, and he could order Dora and Quilty around. They might not do as he told them, but at least he was the nominal head of his household. The fact that Tobias had his pension from his firm contributed heavily to his position of independence, Annabel perceived.

However, an evening or two later her innocent reliance on a cash income as the solution to the problems of the aged, sustained a severe shock. She even wondered whether old Mrs. Warren might not have her moments of despair when she tried to foresee the years left to her.

Ida had suggested the dinner at the Doyle. Mrs. Holdfast consented to be a "sitter" for the evening and Ida arranged that Frank should take her and her mother to the hotel to dine in the softly-lighted shadowy pit that was the sunken dining room.

To Annabel it was like eating in the dark and the blast of music from the small orchestra on the platform directly behind their table drowned out the conversational efforts of Frank and Ida. Presently they went to dance in the tiny, cleared floor space, Ida neat and assured and somehow determined in her blue rayon crêpe, Frank looking as foolish as he felt.

Annabel, peering past the flickering candle's fan of light, thought all the middle-aged husbands seemed ill at ease, the expressions of their wives to be a little grim. Only the lithe service men with beautifully small waists and broad shoulders, danced as if they heard the music, and the girls with them all had masses of shining, shimmering hair.

They reminded Annabel of Cecilia as she must be now. Twenty years old, her grandmother had said, and wanting to marry a man named Hyman Silverstein. If her daughters had chosen to marry Jews she never could have endured it, Annabel admitted, leaning over the table to inspect the celery and olives, neither one of which her teeth could manage.

It was all very well for Tobias to praise this Silverstein and to take Cecilia's part, but when his daughter Lucy had been determined to marry Post Warren, he had made a terrible fuss. Jennie, Tobias' wife, had grieved principally because she had set her heart on a home wedding, but Tobias had been openly bitter against the Catholic faith. There must be a perverse streak in the family, somewhere, Annabel decided, delighted to have discovered a stuffed olive tucked under a celery curl. At home Molly always mixed a few stuffed olives with the hard green ones, when she served appetizers.

A row of small tables, seating one or two, lined the long, blank wall to Annabel's right. Reserve cards had marked each of these when the waiter had first seated her and gradually the little tables had filled. Annabel, when she looked away from the dance floor saw that now each chair held an old lady.

"My heavens, what a collection!" Ida looked amused as she and Frank returned to their cooling soup.

Annabel asked rather timidly if the old ladies lived in the hotel, but Ida did not hear and it was the waiter who answered.

"They have rooms or suites in the hotel, madam. Some of them have been here for years."

He was old himself and he moved as though his feet hurt him. But watching him, Annabel perceived how kindly and how patiently he waited on the old ladies, changing their orders, returning dishes that displeased them, laughing at their little jokes. They all seemed to like him and to prefer him to the pretty young waitress who supplemented his efforts. It was she, however, who stooped to retrieve the handkerchiefs and napkins and black silk handbags and eyeglasses their trembling fingers dropped. They were so thin, so shrunken, in their decent black dresses; their gray and white heads shook with palsy, their beads and chains rattled against their own bones, so scantily covered with flesh. Fascinated, yet dismayed, Annabel scarcely noticed when Ida and Frank left the table again to rhumba.

"Haven't they children? What do they do with themselves?" she said to the old waiter who hovered at her elbow.

The old ladies visited in each other's rooms, he assured her, they had little card parties and were quite gay. "The short one, far over, she's eighty-six and she signed a ten-year lease on her room yesterday," he confided.

In the taxi on the way home, Ida condemned exhibitionism in the elderly. "It's disgusting to see those old women drinking cocktails and smoking. And carrying on with the waiter, too! At their age!"

"They're well off, I guess." Annabel sighed. "Some of them wore beautiful diamonds."

"Jews." Ida yawned. "They always have diamonds. And furs."

Frank grumbled that the price charged for drinks had been highway robbery. "And that kyke orchestra leader murdered the music."

An uneasy wriggle from Ida, seated between Annabel and Frank, attracted attention to her whisper.

"What? What you saying?" Frank grunted. "I can't hear you."

Ida coughed. "I say I think the taxi man's Jewish."

"So what? You started the talk." Frank smelled of gin and tobacco.

She just wanted him not to be so free with his remarks about kykes, Ida whispered. After all, people had feelings.

"My father always said that the Jewish people are very good to their aged," Annabel observed, wondering why she didn't feel more festive after dining at a large hotel. Her only sensation was one of overpowering fatigue.

Frank stretched his legs full length and gravely contemplated his shoes. "I wonder how Ceil will like being called Mrs. Silverstein," he mused. "That is, if she really does marry the guy."

The day after Annabel returned to Molly's house, the trustworthy Mrs. Holdfast requested a week off to enable her to care for her daughter, just out of the hospital with a new baby. A friendly neighbor took Leidy in for lunch with her own children and Ida planned the after-school period dexterously to keep the child occupied, either with errands or with companions, until Frank should reach home.

"But tomorrow we're up against it," Ida phoned Tobias one night. "My firm is to receive the Navy 'E' in the afternoon and we're having a dinner at the plant. That means I can't get home before ten or eleven. Frank is all tied up, too. He has a regular monthly meeting all afternoon and a dinner at night. That leaves Leidy completely alone, you see."

Tobias said he saw. "Bring her into town," he suggested. "I'll make her up a bed on the sofa."

"Then she wouldn't go to school tomorrow morning," Ida objected. "It's awfully important to keep her to routine. I thought maybe you'd come out."

Leidy wouldn't be a juvenile delinquent if she spent an evening with her neighbors next door, Tobias suggested. For himself, he had a movie all picked out.

That was what ailed the children of this generation, his daughter-in-law informed him. Nothing was more valuable than a child's life, yet adults put their own amusements, comfort, and leisure, first.

"No wonder the papers are full of horrible things that happen," Ida scolded. "How can you expect children to grow up right, if no one is interested in supervising them?"

"My good godfrey, I've brought my children up!" Tobias sputtered. In the living room, opening on the hall, he saw Dora flash him a delighted grin. "Leidy's your young one, not mine. Why don't you stay home with her and keep her out of—of delinquency?"

It was her duty to work at the plant, Ida rebuked him. Woman power was needed to help win the war. "Well, suppose I do like the job I'm trained for ten times better than housework!" she snapped in answer to a gibe from Tobias. "Does that alter the fact that women are needed outside the home?"

It made her a little less the martyr, Tobias thought, but why question her patriotism which was probably no more mixed than the general run-of-the-mill human motives. He hinted, with deceptive meekness that she might get one of the neighbors to take Leidy in for lunch and he would come out and get dinner for the child.

"I can't impose on Mrs. Taylor too much," Ida countered. "Leidy has been there for lunch half a dozen times. Besides, she's quarreled with one of the Taylor children."

And was Mrs. Taylor the only neighbor? questioned Tobias, who died hard.

"Well, there's Mrs. Levy. Two doors down. But naturally I can't ask her."

"Why not?"

Ida repeated, "Why not?" on a rising note of exasperation. Surely Tobias recalled what a fuss she and Frank had made when the Levys bought the Marshall house. "The whole neighborhood was furious. They've turned out to be nice, quiet people, but I certainly can't ask favors of them. Anyway, I don't want Leidy running in and out of their house. Why? Good heavens, you'll drive me out of my mind. Because they're Jewish, of course. You know that. They don't live the way we do."

How did she know? Well, she just knew. No, she'd never been inside the Levy home and she had no intention of going. "I meet her at the Red Cross and we speak on the bus and at the grocery —that's enough." Ida added, evidently to clinch her argument, "They don't eat the same things we do."

In the end Tobias capitulated, as he always did. Yes, he would come out in the morning, in time to give Leidy her lunch. And he would stay and make dinner for her and see that she went to bed on time.

"Don't ever retire on a pension," he warned Dora, when he had replaced the receiver. "The sight of anyone with a little leisure on his hands drives the folks who are still hard at it right out of their so-called minds."

It might not be a bad idea for him to get himself a job, he grumbled, turning the radio dial in search of a program without a news commentator. He could push little carts around a department store. "Saw an old codger who looked to be a hundred, pushing one of those bins on wheels through the aisles the other day. Down at Houseman's. Lots of pretty girls tossing him smiles along with the bundles they threw in."

That was probably the reason old men took such jobs, Dora observed. "Man power doesn't run by gasoline alone."

Tobias conceded that man's motives were as mixed as woman's. "That is to say, Ida's. She's making more money than she ever did in her life and they'll have the house paid for, if the war lasts long enough."

His granddaughter's motives were also mixed he discovered the next noon when she dashed in from school and flung herself upon him assuring him in one breath that she was glad to see him and that she had to have a quarter.

"I've got to buy a defense stamp, Grandpa."

He corrected her mechanically. "War stamp." The early drilling must have been intensive, but it did seem to him that after so many months of war the school children might have been conditioned—that was Ida's word—to the use of another phrase.

Leidy seated herself at the table in the breakfast nook and waited to be served. In addition to a defense stamp, she must also have some tin cans. "Flattened out, Grandpa. Fridays we have a patriotic program in the afternoon."

Ida had left elaborate directions for Leidy's lunch and for her later dinner. Tobias had reheated vegetable soup, baked the macaroni and cheese already prepared, and set out the chilled stewed pears. While Leidy ate he found the empty cans where she told him her mother kept them—on the platform of the stairs leading to the cellar.

He laboriously cut the lids from four cans and jumped upon them, under his grandchild's watchful and critical gaze. She needed a quarter, she reminded him, as he finished the fourth can.

"What for?" he liked to tease her because she kept her neat, unruffled appearance no matter how greatly irritated.

"I have to buy a defense stamp."

"What for?"

She was ready for him there. "To help end this destructive war," she recited, her mouth filled with macaroni and cheese.

"My good godfrey, what other kind is there?" demanded Tobias, but the child sensed that the question was rhetorical.

She accepted her tin cans and her quarter as her due and rushed away to the afternoon session. This compulsion to hurry remained a characteristic of the school child still, in spite of modern educational methods, Tobias reflected as he ate his own lunch. He remembered the school days of his children and that it had seemed to him then as if he and his wife played a perpetual game of battledore and shuttlecock. They propelled the youngsters toward school and the school shot them back, and always the children were in transit, nervous, excited, out of breath.

He was prepared to have Leidy fling open the kitchen door at half-past three, with the effect of ripping it from its hinges, but he had not expected her to be carrying a burlap bag, like a pack, over her shoulder.

"My good godfrey, what's that?" Tobias asked.

"Cans." Leidy let the bag drop to the floor, pushed it toward him.

"Cans?" It occurred to Tobias that he and Leidy needed less

than the eight hundred words of basic English to conduct their dialogues.

Leidy consented to explain. "Some of the kids brought cans to school without having them flattened. The teacher said maybe you'd do it."

"My good—" Tobias exploded. "Is there any good reason why your teacher shouldn't do it herself?"

Leidy didn't know. She wanted to take her bicycle and play out till five o'clock. "What'll I tell the teacher?"

Tobias grinned. "Tell her I have only two hands—and one head. Did you get your war stamp?" He kicked the bag as an outlet for his feelings and the cans rattled with a hollow sound.

She had bought her stamp, Leidy assured him. Now she had more stamps in her book than any child in the class, except a colored boy. "He buys the most every week, because he has a paper route. I don't care as long as I have more than Anna Hagen."

She didn't like Anna, Leidy confided, and she had needed the extra quarter to put Anna in her place. "She always buys two stamps and today I bought four. Ida gave me a quarter, Frank gave me fifty cents and you gave me twenty-five, so I bought twice as many stamps as Anna."

All the kids tried to keep ahead of each other, Leidy said, especially when they disliked some other child. "Now Gertie Kendall, my best friend, had a fight with Diana Morielli. So Gertie got an extra stamp today. She didn't know Diana wasn't coming back this afternoon, or she could have spent the quarter."

"War *and* peace," her grandfather muttered piously. "Where you going now?"

She wanted to ride her bicycle till five o'clock, Leidy repeated. Ida liked her to stay outdoors till five o'clock. Well, at least till half-past four, she improvised, when Tobias suggested that it was dark by five o'clock, in November. Her bicycle was in the back hall and she had trundled it down the steps before he could offer to help her. He saw that a group of children waited on the pavement for her—a bicycle was a valuable possession in these war days.

Half an hour later, sounds of commotion drew him to the front windows. Leidy appeared to be surrounded by a milling group of children who screamed raucously and pushed each other about, apparently in an effort to gain the center of the ring. Three or four women shuttled back and forth on the edges of the circle, their agitation betrayed by a general tendency to flap their arms.

Tobias opened the front door, then stepped back for his hat, as the rush of cold air crisped his thinning hair. He cut across the dead, frozen lawn and felt the earth ridges crush under his shoes. The children were partly on the lawn, partly on the adjoining strip of pavement. At his approach they stopped screaming with a suddenness as abrupt as the slamming of a door. Wide-eyed, silent, they turned to stare at him. Leidy, straddling her prostrate bicycle, stared, too. So did the women, who were presumably neighbors.

"What's the trouble?" Tobias noted that most of the children looked older than Leidy, but of course she was small for her age.

His granddaughter squared her shoulders, courage restored. "I won't let La Verne Tolley ride my bicycle."

"She ought to be ashamed of herself," one of the women said hotly. "She let every other girl have a ride."

"Why aren't you willing to lend your bicycle to La Verne?" Tobias asked. If these fatheaded women had had sense enough to keep away, the kids would have settled the quarrel themselves, he thought.

Leidy scowled. "I don't like her. That's why."

Tobias guessed La Verne to be the only colored girl in the

group. A girl with dark hair standing beside the colored child, spoke jerkily. "She doesn't like La Verne because she's colored. She said so."

"Well, this is a free country, ain't it?" Another of the women, short and stout, with a bundle of groceries in her arms, stirred impatiently. "We can have likes and dislikes, I hope."

The firm, neat face of Leidy tilted so that her direct, troubled gaze met her grandfather's eyes. "La Verne grabbed my bike," she testified. "She tried to take it away from me. And Edith was helping her."

"Once they get up here from the South, they'll do anything," the woman with the groceries declared. "I've had to wait hours at the butcher's, while they bought their meat first. Down South it's altogether different."

The woman who had spoken first laughed. "A fine place, the South!" she gibed.

"Now wait a moment." Tobias settled his bifocals more firmly on his nose, a familiar gesture when confused.

The cold dusk of early winter had already begun to blur individual features, but he could still make out the faces of the little girls—he counted eight of them, including Leidy. La Verne was the only colored child, but a mixture of races was apparent in the noses and cheekbones, the chins and brows, of the others. Only their eyes, wide with the uncomprehending, steady gaze of innocence and ignorance, were alike. They regarded him as Authority and relied on him to tell them what to do. *A kid's quarrel,* Tobias thought, and if only those old hens would move on about their business—

"You've got a first-class chance to nip prejudice right in the bud," a tall, lean woman informed Tobias. "It's disgusting to see children taking on the faults of narrow-minded, racially influenced parents."

The fat woman with the bag of groceries snorted. "Is that so? I notice you send *your* kids to private school, so you won't have any racial problems to bother you," she said.

So this was a racial problem, was it? Tobias up to this moment had considered it to be only an ordinary row—a kid's quarrel, he repeated to himself. But La Verne was set apart, or felt herself to be, by her black skin and Leidy and the other white girls were unconsciously being forced to consider the Negro problem.

If I knew where I stood myself, Tobias ruminated uneasily. But the children were waiting and he had left his dinner cooking on the range.

"You're all wrong, all of you." His sweeping gesture encompassed the circle. "If Leidy let everyone ride her bike, except La Verne, she didn't play fair. And if La Verne tried to grab the bike, why she had no business to do that. It's Leidy's bike, whether she's mean or nice about it. Two wrongs don't make a right," he added, confident that the children wouldn't grasp the connection since he himself didn't.

He waited while La Verne rode twice around the block on the bicycle. The women went on, the children disappeared, and he helped Leidy bring her wheel into the house. Later, when they were playing checkers after dinner in the living room, he asked her why she had refused to allow La Verne Tolley to ride her bicycle.

Leidy knew exactly why. She spoke with cold precision. "It's her brother who has the most defense stamps of anybody in the class. I want to have the most stamps."

Her grandfather protested. It was La Verne, not her brother, who had asked to ride the wheel.

"She gives herself airs," Leidy assured him. "On account of her brother having the most defense stamps of anyone in the class."

Chapter Seven

WHEN, one snowy day in December, Frank Ferris found himself passing the Security Trust Company's building, he remembered that Cecilia Warren was employed there. He had not seen her since the day he had taken her and his sister Molly to lunch. Ida asked him almost daily whether Cecilia planned to be married soon and he always answered that he didn't know. His father mentioned the girl at infrequent intervals, but apparently he saw her seldom and if he knew of her approaching marriage, he had carefully refrained from discussing the subject.

Frank looked at his watch. A little early, perhaps, to ask a young lady to lunch with one, but he was suddenly curious to survey Cecilia in her work-day setting. Besides, he told himself, he really ought to become better acquainted with his sister's child. Molly had talked so much the last time, that he and Cecilia had hardly exchanged a personal word.

Funny, Frank mused, turning in at the bank's pink marble entrance, how rapidly the members of a family lost touch with each other, once they were on their own. Not estranged—except in the case of Lucy who had married that Catholic chap—but no longer interested in each other's lives, or dependent on each other for sympathy and love. Perhaps if his mother had lived, more solidarity might have been preserved, Frank thought. Still, his mother had accepted Lucy as lost to them when she had married Post Warren.

Frank found himself remembering Lucy vividly again as he spoke to one of the white-haired guards who summoned Cecilia from a row of high book-keeping desks visible in the rear. She came toward Frank awkwardly, yet with a young, rushing movement that was eager and endearing. Her mother had been like that, he recalled, and a pang of regret that Lucy could not see this tall, sweet daughter stabbed him.

"Uncle Frank! How nice!" Cecilia put a firm, slim hand into his.

She asked after Ida and Leidy, was frankly pleased to be invited to lunch. It lacked twenty minutes of her lunch hour, but she was sure one of the other girls would "trade" with her. They often did—it was no hardship, when one didn't have a date.

In a few moments she came back to him, a fur coat thrown over the shoulders of her brown tweed suit. A tiny hat, flat as a pieplate, balanced precariously atop the long, straight bob that curled softly just before it touched the fur. She had nice legs, he noted as she preceded him in the revolving door, and wore good-looking shoes. Ida always selected shoes that were too fancy and looked cheap, even when they were expensive.

"New coat?" Frank inquired, when they were out on the street. "What kind of fur do you call it?"

The coat was sheared beaver, Cecilia told him, a birthday gift from her grandmother. "I'm glad I happened to wear it today. The girls wanted to see it. It's too warm for every day and besides it looks kind of silly when everyone knows I get twenty dollars a week."

He took her to a place much patronized by business men for its good food and where women seldom went unless escorted. The day's special chanced to be corned-beef and cabbage and Cecilia confided that she adored the dish and had not tasted it for many years. She asked if it were difficult to cook and admitted, when he teased her, that she knew next to nothing about cooking.

"And you planning to be married?" he probed with the freedom of an uncle.

She nodded, coloring, and he asked whether it was "Still Silverstein, or somebody else?"

There could never be anyone else, she flashed. "We're more in love than ever, Uncle Frank. I'm hoping we can be married before Christmas."

"You're probably heading for a lot of trouble." He sliced his boiled potato thoughtfully. There wasn't much use in trying to talk to a girl in love, he admitted, but she ought to know that marriage was difficult enough in itself, without racial or religious complications.

Cecilia twisted the stem of her water goblet with her left hand. She wore no ring. "Religion doesn't worry me," she said in a low tone. "My mother had—complications. But she married my father and they were very happy."

Her mother had "turned," Frank reminded her. Lucy had adopted her husband's faith as her own. "She practically gave up her family for him, too. We saw very little of her, after that."

"But you could have." Something like accusation flickered in Cecilia's dark eyes. "She was alive, she was in the same city. If I marry Tag, it won't cut me off from my own people."

Marriage did such strange things to people, how could one foretell which relationships would remain, which be destroyed? Not an especially sensitive man, Frank yet hesitated to be too explicit.

"Listen, Ceil, it's a little different in your case." He waited while she helped herself to rolls from the basket the waiter offered. "You can't turn Jewish, you know."

She laughed, conscientiously sat up a little straighter, as she glimpsed her poor posture in a wall mirror. Tag was always admonishing her to throw her shoulders back, she murmured "We won't have any trouble about religion," she said.

On the other side of the room Frank saw an acquaintance and, catching his eye, nodded to him. His companion, a handsome woman, wearing a high-crowned fur hat, glanced up sharply, for a moment stared.

"His secretary." Frank saw that Cecilia's interest had been flagged. "The poor chap married a woman out of his class and he soon gave up trying to keep up with her."

Cecilia lifted her chin. "That sounds like an English novel to me. They probably never were in love."

There were classes in America, Frank argued, always had been, always would be. Equality was just dandy, up to a certain point. "But to live with a man or woman, you've got to share a level. I'm anxious to have you consider these things, my dear, before it is too late."

She leaned forward at that and her earnestness so impressed him that the slight absurdity which tinged her words carried no weight. "Uncle Frank, Tag is an angel!" she said clearly. "He is so far above me in every way that I expect to spend the rest of my life trying to scramble up to where he is. The wonder is that he leans down to love me."

After that dessert would be an anti-climax, Frank suggested lightly and he guided the conversation into a discussion of her work at the bank, her grandmother's health, and like safe topics that carried them through their coffee and apple pie. Cecilia mentioned innocently enough that she wished she had known her mother's people as a little girl and Frank again reminded himself that the family had always lacked clannish traits. As a matter of fact, although Cecilia might never know it, the news of her pending engagement had welded them in a solidarity as impermanent as it was rare. Their curiosity about her, coupled with their eagerness to be the first to confirm or deny rumors, had driven the Ferrises, the Eustices, and the Cotters into keeping tabs on each other to a degree hitherto unknown among themselves—and not without its drawbacks, Frank had lately admitted.

Cecilia did not smoke, but she urged him to have his cigar when he revealed that he was rationed to three a day. The slight constraint still visible in her manner urged him to abandon the serious and in his eagerness to put her at ease, he committed a fresh blunder. "Don't take my warnings too much to heart, my dear," he counseled, blowing out his match. "If you and Tag find you can't hit it off, you can always be divorced."

She shook her head. "You forget I am a Catholic."

Irritated, feeling balked, he became perverse. "What about children, then? I suppose you won't practice birth control?"

"No, of course not. Why should I?" She looked less the child when she challenged him like that.

He thought it only fair, he said, in all marriages to wait and see how things turned out, before taking the responsibility of bringing children into the world. If a man and woman were unable to live together happily, surely it was only common sense to spare children the spectacle of their cat and dog life.

"In your case, with the odds so much against you," Frank set forth, "the kindest thing you can do, for Tag as well as yourself, is to postpone having a family." Funny, he told himself, no youngster flinched from a discussion of birth these days, not even convent-bred girls like Cecilia. Well, he could also remember when no pregnant woman went out of the house until after dark. And look at them now!

"Wait a few years, Ceil," he counseled. "If you're happy, fine. If you and Tag find you've made a mistake, there won't be so much harm done."

Cecilia suddenly smiled. "Don't be silly," she said. "We both want children."

He wondered if she thought of them as Jewish children, but let that go. She was his guest, he ought to have given her a better time. From her surreptitious glances at her wrist watch, he judged that she was worried about getting back to the bank on time.

"I'll put you in a taxi," he promised, picking up the check. "Well—I suppose you two kids will work out your destiny somehow. Luckily you haven't many close relatives to hamper you and Tag's an orphan, isn't he?"

His parents were dead, Cecilia returned, but he had "swarms" of cousins. "I'm going to see one of them this Sunday. She's visiting her husband's cousin in town. Her name's Mrs. O'Neill. Mrs. Patrick O'Neill." Most of Tag's cousins seemed to have married men with Irish names, Cecilia concluded wistfully.

"My God!" Frank said.

The cousin whom Mrs. Patrick O'Neill was visiting lived uptown in a block of brick and frame one-family houses that looked not precisely dilapidated but unquestionably in need of immediate minor repairs. Cecilia, a bright color in her face, for she had walked five blocks from the bus, rang the bell of Number Eight. She noticed as she waited that every shutter hung by one hinge and that several sections of the clapboards were missing, revealing gaps through to the masonwork.

A woman who, like the house, could have done with a little extra attention to appearances, answered the doorbell. Yes, Mrs. O'Neill was in, she would call her. "You can wait in there." She pointed to a doorway, curtained with heavy, old-fashioned, dark red portieres, that evidently opened into a room.

Cecilia slipped between the curtains and found herself in the "front room." A gallery of family portraits, photographs and crayons, massively framed, stared down from the walls. The floor was carpeted to the dark baseboards and on top of the faded weave half a dozen smaller rugs made a helter-skelter pattern like small islands.

Bundles of books, loosely tied together, filled two or three of the chairs, but Cecilia discovered an empty tufted stool and seated herself gingerly on the edge. No one came and the longer she stared at the contents of the room, the more she marveled. Three knee-hole desks had the spaces beneath them filled with bundles wrapped in newspaper and tied with string. The wooden mantel above the empty fireplace was a parade ground for a collection of empty medicine bottles; table-tops were cluttered with curtains folded as if to be put away, dusty china cups and plates, ornaments without purpose, and lamps without shades. Almost, the puzzled visitor reflected, like an antique shop, except that nothing was very old, only very shabby and probably of no intrinsic value, even when new. Two tall, narrow windows, fitted with folding blinds, let in a dim light through grimy panes and the air was musty and chill. Mrs. O'Neill's cousin, Cecilia decided, probably had trouble getting coal.

"So you're Cecilia Warren!" A short, dark woman thrust her compact body through the portieres, advanced smiling, one hand outstretched in greeting. "I'm so sorry you had to wait but I was hunting for my picture of Tag's mother."

The small photograph showed a young woman with a gentle face and masses of soft, straight hair piled high on her small head. Everything about her, the quiet composure in her steadfast eyes, the serenity of her expression, marked her as tranquil and sweet.

"I never saw her." Mrs. O'Neill answered Cecilia's mute question. "My mother said she was just lovely. You can keep the picture—Tag would want you to have it."

This cousin had warm, dark eyes like Tag's and something of

his charm of manner. Cecilia thought she must be in her thirties. Her mother, she volunteered, was keeping her three children and she had come to the city to find herself a job.

"My husband's had the luck of the Irish so far," she grinned, patting her curly dark bangs into place with one hand, and pulling the short skirt of her red wool frock over her knees with the other. "He's in the Navy, but after the war I want him to get into something steady." She planned to build up a nest-egg for him, she said; "Pat" had no more sense of money than a child. If there was any saving done, she had to do it.

"My Jewish blood comes in handy, I can tell you." She laughed, glanced sharply at Cecilia. "How do you think you're going to like it, marrying yourself a Jewish boy, dear?"

Cecilia felt her face flush. "Does that matter?" She spread her handkerchief on her knee, began to pleat the hem. "Tag is such an angel—that is, I think he's so fine that any girl would be proud to be his wife."

Mrs. O'Neill, who had seated herself on a kitchen chair, first tumbling a pile of magazines to the floor, hooked her enormously high heels over the round and rocked sturdily back and forth. "There's more to it than that," she warned.

"Well, you look happy," Cecilia flung at her. "And you're Jewish and married to a Gentile."

"My mother was a Gentile," the other explained. "So was Tag's mother. It seems to be a habit in our family for the men to make mixed marriages." Her gaze swept the chaotic room and she laughed. "This interior decoration is pure, undiluted Irish," she chuckled. "My husband's cousin Mona is Irish on both sides, for as far back as history goes. Would that be to the Garden of Eden?"

Cecilia stared at the row of medicine bottles without seeing them. "Your husband's Irish, isn't he? Then he must be Catholic."

Her Pat was a devout Catholic, Mrs. O'Neill attested. And she had another sister, married to a Scotchman. "They ought to be millionaires, if you believe the funny papers." For an instant her lips twisted in bitterness, but relaxed quickly into their natural smiling curve. "Esther Goldberg MacTavish—there's a combination for you," she said.

Somewhere in the house a radio blared wildly, blurring the stations, then a door slammed with force sufficient to shake the walls.

"But if you and your sister are happy, why shouldn't I be?" Cecilia pulled her handkerchief straight again, began to crimp finer pleats.

Mrs. O'Neill hesitated. "Well, for one reason your children will be Silversteins."

"You mean they'll be discrim—discriminated against, because they have a Jewish name?"

"And how!"

Cecilia shook her head. "It may have been like that once. Not now," she protested.

"It's exactly like that now," Mrs. O'Neill retorted. "Wait until you've seen your friends' queer looks when your husband's name is mentioned. Tag is a wonderful boy, as you say, and he can charm birds off trees. But nine out of ten Gentiles will stiffen when they first hear his name. Your children's name, too, remember."

Of course it is outrageous, she admitted when Cecilia rebelled in anger, but that was the kind of world they were living in and it was just as well to know what to expect. The war? Perhaps for purposes of war racial differences had been buried, but certainly in no deep grave.

"Sometimes I think nothing's been buried, only covered up, the way poor housekeepers sweep dirt under a rug," Mrs. O'Neill said. "Or if some folks have buried their racial prejudices, the chances are that they've got the graves marked and will have no trouble disinterring their pet hates."

"Then you think Jewish girls who marry men with Christian names are luckier than the Jewish boys who have to keep their family names?" Cecilia suggested. "You make me wish that Tag's name was O'Neill. Then there wouldn't be any trouble."

The Irish had had their troubles, Mrs. O'Neill sighed. Her husband's grandmother remembered well when the Irish were looked down upon in many cities and towns. Had Cecilia never heard the slur aimed at the "Shanty Irish"? And God knew there was always the difference in religion. "Pat's grandmother was forever making cracks about the black Protestants, he says, and the Protestant neighbors practically spit upon the Papists. Oh, I tell you, the Irish haven't always had clear sailing."

But they had outlived prejudice, Cecilia insisted; it would be like that with the Jewish race, too. "Tag holds no resentments, no bitterness. He knows people like him. How can they help it, when they see his smile?"

"It's of you I'm thinking." Mrs. O'Neill's grim look softened. "It will fall the hardest on you. But you're right about the Jews outliving prejudice. In another five hundred years they'll be accepted everywhere, as Christians are accepted today." She laughed and again her mouth twisted in bitterness or disdain. "And in another thousand years you can bank on the colored people getting a fair deal, too," she pronounced. "By that time everyone will have been killed off in a series of co-operative wars to make all men brothers."

On New Year's Day, 1944, Cecilia and Tag were married in the Army chapel at Fort Jackson. Cecilia had gone down to "talk things over" with Tag and their decision to be married seemed to them logical if not leisurely. The Warren and Ferris relatives, conditioned to war weddings, expressed regret that Cecilia had had none of her own family with her and that she should be a bride in tweeds instead of white satin and a veil. Old Mrs. Warren telephoned Tobias, agreed with him that Tag was a splendid boy and that announcements should be mailed to relatives and friends on both sides. "In spite of—" old Mrs. Warren concluded vaguely.

Naomi O'Neill sent Cecilia another photograph of Tag's mother, taken in her wedding gown and framed in faded rose-colored velvet. Tag had never seen it and he studied the lovely, tranquil features with as much absorption as Cecilia. To the young bride there was tragedy in the thought that this happy woman's life had been so brief. She had died when Tag was barely two years old and she must have dreamed so many dreams for him.

"But your own mother died when you were a child," Tag remonstrated. "Your father, too. My father lived until I was almost twenty. It doesn't really matter when we die—it comes early to some, late to others. But it's all the same in the end."

Cecilia put down the velvet frame and hurled herself into his arms. She burrowed against his heart, as if seeking to shut herself away from some secret fear.

"That isn't so!" Her muffled voice choked. "You know it does matter, Tag. That's the horrible, untruthful bromide everyone mutters when a plane crashes. 'It doesn't matter when we die—we all have to go sometime,' they say. The chumps!"

She laid her face against his shoulder, tightening her arms about his neck. "Darling, let's neither one of us die until we are very old, and then together. It's terrible to die when you are young. Why, so many are dying before they ever marry, or have babies, or build themselves homes. We want to taste life, don't we?" She added, less vehemently. "Your mother would rather have lived. I know she would. She would love to see you now, she would have liked to have seen us married. If ever I have a little baby, I just can't die and let him grow up without me."

Tag kissed the tip of her ear. "Why do you always specify a 'little' baby? Aren't they always little at first?"

She laughed and that pleased him for he suspected her mind was running on the bad plane crash of the previous day. One of the pilots had been married less than a week and the same Catholic chaplain who had married Cecilia and Tag had officiated at the wedding and would have the funeral mass, too.

Cecilia lifted wet eyes to his and their lips met. Strange that, although they were so happy, the impulse to comfort one another stirred in each heart. *It is better this way,* Tag thought, his wife in his arms; *we take nothing for granted. Life least of all.*

"Tag?" Cecilia turned slightly so that she might watch his face. "Tag, do you feel as if time whirls faster and faster? Grandmother always said that was a sign of old age, but I don't know. It seems to me as if we were being hurled forward, blown down a road as if by a powerful wind."

Tag agreed. "Time does go fast. Too fast. I wish I could hold back the years. I don't want our life together to be over too soon."

"There!" cried Cecilia in triumph. "You feel it. Why are we talking so much about the end of life when ours is just beginning?"

Tag said it must be because they were influenced by the ghastly wall paper in the only furnished room they had been able to find. It was enough to make anyone think of the hereafter, he grumbled, when forced to live with a design of caterpillars crawling over rhubarb pies. "If we don't find an apartment soon, we'll be some psychiatrist's pets."

"You just imagine they're caterpillars," Cecilia argued. She expected to hear of an apartment any day, she added hopefully. "In fact we almost moved this afternoon. Mrs. Meadow caught me washing my stockings in the bathroom again."

The landlady's most stringent rule forebade light laundry work in the bathroom, but most of the young wives installed in the house stealthily rinsed out their stockings and underwear in the bathroom washbowl. Any kind of outside service was high-priced and unsatisfactory, due to overcrowding and scarcity of labor.

"Don't do any more washing until we know we have an apartment nailed down," Tag begged. "This is the best place we've had so far and if we spend all of our money moving, we won't have anything for food."

Cecilia had started to dress to go out for dinner with him. Now she turned back to the shadowy mirror hung above the dresser and resumed making up her mouth.

"Not too much!" Tag, sitting on the side of the bed, warned. There was only one chair in the room and they used that as a table, because there was no other.

The thing that burned her up, Cecilia murmured, trying to talk without moving her lips, was that all the landladies possessed such patriotic motives.

"Every last one of them will tell you that she is putting herself out to take in service people. Her family is sleeping on the grass, to hear her tell it, so that service men and their wives can have rooms. And yet look at the prices they charge—they're making more money than they ever made in their lives. They *like* the war."

Tag said, "Don't be a snob, darling."

"Well, I'm not." Cecilia ran the comb through her soft, dark hair, and over it put a tiny, black felt piece with wings like a Dutch cap. "I don't mind them making money, not really. If only they wouldn't insist that they're doing it simply to help their country!"

She was eager to find an apartment, two rooms, any place where she and Tag could keep house. He didn't have too much time off the Post, but there were nights when he came home and then they both disliked to wait for their dinners in the cheap and noisy eating places in Columbia. It wasted time they might otherwise spend together and the food cost far too much. Her grandmother didn't see why they didn't simply put up at a good hotel; the South to old Mrs. Warren was Pinehurst or Asheville and she cherished a vague, pleasant conviction that all service men had access to the lavishly appointed type of USO photographed in the newsreels. She had hinted that she might run down and see "the love birds," a caption which made them both laugh, in spite of the consternation the suggestion invoked.

"Tag and I think the same things are funny," Cecilia had explained to Jorry Read, a top sergeant's wife she had met at the soda fountain in a drugstore.

Jorry seemed always expecting Cecilia to explain her marriage, ever since the afternoon when, comparing nostalgic notes about their home backgrounds, Cecilia had said, her frank eyes on the pretty, rather childish face of the blonde Mrs. Bracer Read, "My husband's a top sergeant, too—Hyman Silverstein."

It was, perhaps, something like pressing on a sore tooth, she confessed secretly to herself. She would never tell Tag but in the four weeks since their marriage she had learned to watch for that sudden stiffening of the facial muscles in both women and men hearing the first mention of Tag's name. It was involuntary, and they carefully erased it as if they drew a sponge across a slate, their eyes veiled. Then they would glance up brightly and speak, almost as spontaneously as if there had been no block. Almost as spontaneously, but not quite. "Sergeant—is that so?

What outfit?" And after that, always, "How you making out for a place to live?"

Anger, fierce, blazing anger such as she had never guessed could flame in her heart, an emotion so primitive, so devastating that the gentle nuns would have gasped in terror at the spectacle of a favorite pupil abandoned to the Devil's grip, shook Cecilia, whenever she met this instinctive recoil. She never fully forgave it in anyone, even in those who later became her friends and Tag's. His attitude, she perceived, was healthier than hers, less bitter, more understanding.

"No, Tag doesn't resent people's stupid prejudices as I do," she admitted to Jorry, who accused her of carrying a chip on her shoulder. "But look at the years he's been training himself not to care! When he was a little fellow the boys in his home town wouldn't have him on their baseball team because he was Jewish. He had to learn not to care when he was a *child*."

Jorry pointed out that Tag was a good ball player now. "Brace says he could be a professional, if he wanted to. Or if he wasn't in the Army."

Tag had gone on by himself and played football and baseball with the Jewish and colored boys on the sandlots, Cecilia recounted proudly. "He made himself so good that in high school they begged him to join the baseball nine. There's no resentment in Tag—he says people are more thoughtless than unkind."

Brace Read, in the same outfit but another company, had made his adjustments, if any, before Cecilia met him. He apparently accepted Tag wholeheartedly and suggested from time to time that it would be swell if the two couples pooled their resources in a housekeeping apartment. The girls, he said, could share the work, and would be company for each other when the men went on manœuvres.

Tonight the restaurant where Tag and Cecilia dined would

have made any kind of an arrangement which permitted any kind of housekeeping attractive in contrast. The tables were too close together, the room was blue with smoke and heavy with stale air. The overworked, irritable waitresses frankly informed impatient customers that the damyanks would be waited on after others more deserving had been served.

"Brotherly love does certainly get a kick in the pants when you go to war to preserve it," grinned Tag. "Who you staring at, honey—or is it whom?"

Cecilia laughed. "Isn't that the nice boy you introduced to me last week at the movies? Over there at the table by the door? The one you said was headed for Officers' School? And, oh, Tag, that isn't his wife? It can't be!"

"Uh-huh." Tag glanced swiftly toward the couple, away again. "She's probably his ideal. Mustn't be too fussy, darling, you see all kinds of people in the Army, you know."

Cecilia nodded, knowing that he could not endure to think that she judged anyone harshly. It wasn't judging, she protested silently, giving up the struggle with her chop. She peered through the smoke that blurred the figures of girls, most of them young wives like herself, with their men glad to be off Post for a few hours in which they might do as they pleased, even if there wasn't much to do.

She wasn't critical of these girls, Cecilia reflected, they were lonely, worried, in love, making the best of situations which confronted them in wartime. But she couldn't help seeing—and feeling—Cecilia acknowledged, that many of these marriages were doomed to fail. Tag would think it snobbery if she told him; she meant never to tell him. The fact that the girls had married the men they loved in haste and under the excitement of imminent separation, lent their unions a synthetic glamour; but when the glamour faded the majority of the men would go on, either with wives able and willing to keep up with them, or without the girls who could not keep in step. A few of the weaker men would be held back by their wives—men like the nice boy sitting over there by the door.

Cecilia looked again at his wife—at the straw-colored, frizzed hair, the too-plump, badly made-up face, and the tight black satin dress wrapped around the sausage-like form. *He wants to be an officer and she's his wife,* Cecilia sighed. He looked to be about twenty; he had married for love, as she and Tag had done. But Tag, she reminded herself, had grown up first, he controlled his life. She thought with a thrill of pride that not even Tag's wife could ruin his life. She could hurt him, she could cause him deep and lasting unhappiness, if she destroyed his trust in her; but she could not "wreck" him, he would never go to pieces, lose his grip permanently, as she had often heard Jorry Read boast her power could accomplish. Jorry declared that Brace would go to pieces if she ever left him.

"We might take ice cream back with us and eat it on the bed," Tag proposed, having disposed of the final strands of his canned spaghetti. "Or doesn't Toots allow such liberties?"

He referred to their landlady as Toots in private conversation, principally because she was in her early sixties and blessed with grandchildren and not likely, Tag decided, to be known as Toots.

Cecilia thought that ice cream in their room was permitted and she preferred it to the deep dish apple pie which was tonight's table d'hôte dessert. She and Tag had almost reached the drugstore when Jorry and Brace Read, turning a corner, collided with them.

"Ceil!" Jorry, chubby, short, and smiling, squealed in unaffected delight. "We went up to your place, but the landlady's husband insisted you were out."

Brace had gone up and rapped on their room door, Jorry went

on, for they had no faith in the veracity of the landlady's husband. He was so soaked in gin, Jorry complained, that the wonder was he could speak at all.

"Guess what!" Brace Read, who had hair the color of red brick and whose face was burned the color of brick, too, grinned happily at them. His teeth were widely spaced so that when he laughed he looked even younger than his twenty-two years.

Jorry tugged at his sleeve. "Let me tell!" she begged. "I found it, Brace."

Then both chorused, "We've got an apartment!"

"Five rooms!" Jorry exulted.

"We want you two to come in with us." In his excitement Brace stepped over the curb, into the gutter. "Jorry says she'd rather have you than any other people we know."

Cecilia, tall and dark, drew closer to Tag, as she unconsciously did when anything happened. Could they really leave that ghastly one room for which Toots charged them fifty dollars a month and openly repented of her agreement to furnish them with four towels a week?

"Tag!" breathed Cecilia. "I can make that cake I saw in the magazine advertisement!"

They finally persuaded the Reads to return to coherence and a consideration of details. Jorry had overheard ("And suppose I hadn't been there!") a girl in the seat next but one to her at the movies, tell a girl friend that she must rent her apartment. Her husband had been rejected by the Army doctors, but she had been so confident of his acceptance that she herself had joined the WAC. "She said her husband intended to live with his mother, so I leaned right across the friend and asked her to rent it to me," Jorry testified, rocking joyously on her rickety stool at the soda fountain.

The WAC recruit had taken her home to look the apartment

over and Jorry had agreed to take the place that same night. It was too wonderful an apartment to let slip, she sighed, it had everything. She couldn't reach Brace to consult with him, so she had left her engagement ring as a deposit and early the next morning had hastened to cement the deal with cash. The six months' lease had been signed, possession would be hers the first of the week, and would Cecilia come and look *now?*

It was an opportunity, Tag agreed, when he and Cecilia could talk alone—it was then past midnight and he must leave at six in the morning. The apartment was comfortably furnished, it was clean and reasonably modern. Stores were within walking distance, so that the girls could market without having to depend on a bus. If Cecilia could be happy, doubling up with the Reads, he was all for it, Tag said, but the girls would have the most difficult portion of the arrangement: if they got in each other's hair, neither one would be contented.

They could manage, Cecilia assured him. Jorry wanted the same thing she did—to make a home for her sergeant when he could get a pass. There would be a bedroom for each couple, they would share the kitchen and the living and dining rooms. She and Jorry had talked it over, each would do the cooking one week, the housework next. They were to keep an exact account of expenses, share equally.

"If anyone wants extras, he has to pay for them," Cecilia said. "Brace can't enjoy his dinner without beer and you never touch it. So Jorry is going to buy that, but it doesn't go on the joint account. And she has to buy her own cigarettes."

Chapter Eight

JORRY had had a little experience in cooking, Cecilia none at all. But to their mutual surprise, Cecilia proved to be the more successful in the kitchen, probably because she followed the cookbook directions with mechanical exactness. She never questioned a recipe, never experimented, deviated, or deleted.

"You ought to see her measure out a quarter of a teaspoon of salt," Jorry reported. "You'd think she was back in school, struggling with fractions."

Both Tag and Brace astonished the girls by confessing to a nostalgic longing for homemade bread; Tag because, he said, he had heard so much about it and never tasted it, Brace because he remembered his mother baking twice a week when he had been a boy. Not, they assured their wives, that marble cakes and devil's food and elaborate icebox structures, were not delicious and appreciated, but there was something about a crusty loaf of homemade bread.

"I can make baking-powder biscuits," Cecilia offered.

Biscuits were fine, but you take homemade bread, Tag insisted, there was something about homemade bread.

"You both said you liked my date muffins," Jorry reproached them.

The date muffins were swell, Brace agreed, but there was something about homemade bread.

"There's a recipe in the book," Cecilia capitulated. "I'll try it and see what happens."

Brace, glancing doubtfully at her slender wrists, suggested that she might not be strong enough to knead bread dough. His mother had been forced to give up making bread because of the strain on her wrists and hands.

Jorry submitted that some people had mixers. You turned a crank and it mixed the dough.

"We haven't any mixer," Cecilia, intent on the cookbook, murmured. "It says here that you set a sponge."

"Where?" demanded Tag. "In the bread dough? Let me see that fool book."

There were too many recipes, he complained, as he turned the pages. Four different ways to make bread was enough to distract any cook. Just one sensible formula would fill the bill.

"Well, pick out your one sensible formula," Jorry directed, rising to begin clearing the dinner table, "because we'll make homemade bread tonight. If Cecil and I can't knead it, you boys can show off your muscles."

Brace took the butter plate and cream pitcher his wife handed to him, but stood still. "Look, Jorry, you can't make bread the way you do cake. It takes more time. Mom used to set hers at night, cover it up, and bake it the next morning. She used to get up at five o'clock to take care of it."

"If anyone gets up at five o'clock to take care of bread dough, it will be you," Jorry declared.

"It says here the sponge must be put in a warm place," Tag contributed. "How can we keep it warm all night?"

Cecilia laughed and Jorry looked grim. She had no intention of rising in the night to take the temperature of a pan of bread dough, Jorry proclaimed. "You and your homemade bread!"

Cecilia, reading over Tag's shoulder, gave an exultant crow.

"Oh, Jorry, this is just right for us. It says the whole process takes from five and one-half to six hours. Baking and everything."

"It's after seven now," Brace demurred. "Do you mean to say we have to cook until one or two in the morning?"

That was the price of homemade bread, Jorry grinned, but there was nothing compulsory about the matter. "Ceil and I are just as willing to be taken to the movies, or we'll take you on for bridge."

Cecilia thought it would be fun to try the recipe. "You and Brace will have to get us a cake of yeast, Tag. Everything else we have. You can get that while Jorry and I do the dinner dishes. And I remember I saw some bread pans way back in the pot closet—I'll get those out and wash them."

The dishes finished and the yeast at hand, they all gathered about the nervous Cecilia to watch her set the sponge. Tag read the directions—making them sound like the burial service, Brace criticised—Jorry sifted the flour, and Brace decided when the water was lukewarm. Both he and Tag insisted on carrying out the admonition to "beat well."

"Beat well, like hell," sang Tag joyously as he delivered his strong, even strokes with the sturdy wooden spoon. "Now what do we do?" he demanded when Cecilia decided that the mixing was accomplished.

"'Cover, set aside to rise about one and a half hours in a warm place,'" she recited, her cheeks pink with excitement, a smudge of flour on the pocket of her rose-colored apron.

They might play a few hands of bridge while they waited for the stuff to rise, Brace suggested. He approved the clean white towel Cecilia spread over the mixing bowl, but he doubted whether the kitchen was warm enough to encourage the bread to rise. His mother had put her bread pan in a rocking chair and left it beside the coal stove all night, he testified.

Tag began to laugh. "We can take it in the living room with us, where it won't be lonely," he suggested. "Perhaps the heat from the bridge lamp will keep it cosy."

Cecilia giggled, but to his amazement, approved the plan. The electric stove did not warm the kitchen and if the sponge didn't rise, they might have to sit up with it all night, she warned. She placed the mixing bowl on one of the chairs, lowered the light to bring the rays within two feet of the protecting towel, and said she was ready for the card game.

"Maybe we could hatch eggs with that lamp," Jorry pondered as she cut for the deal. "You boys may laugh, but lots of important inventions have been made by people who saw the possibilities in simple things."

Brace, who was an expert player, was quite unprepared some time later, to have Cecilia put down her hand a moment after his opening bid and rise precipitately to her feet. He could only stare at her.

"What's the matter?" Tag asked in quick alarm.

"It's time to knead the bread!" Cecilia pointed dramatically to the covered bowl. "It said to let it rise one and a half hours."

Jorry protested. "It hasn't risen a half-hour yet."

"It's one and a half hours by Tag's watch," Cecilia affirmed. "Come on, we have to knead it now."

"I told you she was a methodical cook," Jorry groaned. "You can't have a grand slam and homemade bread, too, Brace—not when Cecil is your partner."

Cecilia, a stickler for the twenty minutes' kneading recommended by the cookbook, watched the kitchen clock relentlessly while Tag and Brace took turns in working the dough. "It must be smooth and elastic to the touch," she quoted each time they asked her if they had kneaded long enough. The dough was too soft, they complained, if she would add more flour it would stiffen up.

"I put in just what the directions said," Cecilia insisted. "You knead it for seven more minutes and it will be smooth and elastic to the touch."

Unbelievably it was. Tag and Brace, puffed with pride, watched while Cecilia turned the smooth ivory-colored mass into the bowl Jorry had ready and greased.

"Now what do we do?" Tag inquired interestedly.

Cecilia gazed upon him placidly. "We cover it and let it rise from one and a half to two hours," she said.

He collapsed against the ironing board and Brace fell upon him. Jorry revived them with water sprayed from the bulb sprinkler she used for dampening clothes, and they went back to the living room and the abandoned game. Each time she was dummy Cecilia disappeared into the kitchen to peek at the bread and when Tag's wrist watch showed twelve o'clock, she all but leaped across the table, Brace said, scattering tricks in her wake.

"I have to mold it into loaves," she explained, when the others followed her, more sedately.

They watched respectfully while she divided the sponge into two parts and put a portion into each of the two bread pans.

Jorry admitted that it began to look like bread. "What's next?" she yawned.

"It has to rise for one hour," Cecilia said.

They groaned, but by the time they had made coffee and some generous-sized sandwiches and disposed of them, the bread could be put into the oven. It must bake fifty minutes, Cecilia read from the cookbook; it should be done by two o'clock.

Tag and Brace offered to sit up and take it from the oven—it wasn't necessary for the girls to lose their sleep, they gallantly insisted. Yes, sure, they knew when bread was done.

"Just instinct," Tag grinned when Jorry hooted. "Native intelligence."

But Cecilia, anxious to see the results of her labors, sat sleepily in the kitchen, her eyes on the clock, and the others waited with her. At the end of fifty minutes two beautiful, fragrant, delicately brown loaves rewarded them.

"Do they look right?" Cecilia hovered anxiously over the pans, placed on a wire rack on the kitchen table.

His mother's bread had looked like that and smelled like that, Brace enthusiastically responded. "I used to love the crust end, hot from the oven, and heaped with fresh-churned butter."

"We will *not* make butter," Jorry declared hurriedly. "And Cecil's in a trance, so we'd all better go to bed. Wake up, you champion baker, what are you dreaming about?"

Cecilia's dark, sleepy eyes smiled up at Tag, then she let her head rest on his shoulder. "I was just thinking," she murmured drowsily, "there is something about homemade bread."

Jorry, good-natured, amiable, could not conceal her curiosity about Tag's racial traits. Quite innocently she revealed that she had thought it better for her to make all arrangements for renting the apartment when she had signed the lease. This, she assured Cecilia, was proof of her friendship.

"You're not Jewish, of course, and people who know Tag don't mind that he is," she said lightly. "But I could tell from the things that girl and her mother said that they wouldn't be very favorably inclined toward anyone with that kind of name. I don't believe in stirring up controversy, life's too short to be always jawing. Besides, apartments are scarce."

She was frankly astonished when Tag accompanied Cecilia to Mass on the Sundays he could get off. Didn't it make him feel funny? she probed. Well, perhaps not funny, but certainly a little queer? The Jewish religion and the Catholic religion couldn't have much in common, could they?

"They have one God," Cecilia said.

She kept to herself the dear and sweet things that Tag said to her on those Sundays. He always insisted that she put a dollar in the box, whether he was with her or not. "I guess we can afford to give a dollar a week to God," he rebuked her when she had demurred, murmuring something about the budget.

At first she had worried lest the service tire him. The little church had no kneelers and her own knees ached from long contact with the unprotected hard wood. He didn't have to kneel throughout, she whispered to Tag; no one would criticise him if he sat back comfortably in the pew before the congregation rose.

"I guess I can stay on my knees one hour a week," Tag returned, his young face suddenly as reproving as a young priest's she remembered from her convent days.

There were other times when he looked at her with a lovely reverence she felt confusedly should have been given to the High Altar, but which she found infinitely precious. After all, she told herself, all love eventually found its way to God.

Jorry and Brace did not attend church, being of that vast multitude mentioned in statistics and surveys as "unchurched." They believed in being broad-minded they said—one religion was as good as another. Except that, Jorry amended, she had been relieved when one sister had had her baby baptized in the Congregational Church. Two other sisters had married Catholic fellows, Jory said, and their children were being brought up as Catholics, which naturally distressed her mother.

Grace had married a Catholic fellow, too, Jorry confided; all her sisters for some strange reason had been attracted to Catholic men. "Of course where we live there are lots of Catholics and I think the men like Protestant girls because they'll practice birth control. Well, anyway, Grace isn't going to have her child separated from her by religion. The baby's going to be a Protestant."

Cecilia, peeling potatoes at the kitchen table sighed. Religion had divided her family, too, she said. "My mother's people were Protestant. They seemed to stop loving her when she took my father's faith."

The older generation were like that, Jorry asserted cheerfully. Her voice sounded muffled, for she was half-way under the sink, collecting empty beer bottles to be returned. Grace's in-laws were fit to be tied because she had had the baby baptized, but they might as well get used to it, for there was nothing they could do. "My God, look at the refund I'll collect!" Jorry emerged triumphant. "Sixteen of 'em!"

"But don't you ever think," questioned Cecilia, ignoring the beer bottles, "of what queer ideas that baby will have of religion? I mean when she's old enough to know her people have quarreled over their creeds?"

To that Jorry responded that when Cecilia had a baby she might feel differently and to Brace that night Jorry said that she hoped she hadn't made a mistake in inviting Grace to visit them. Grace was dead set against Catholics, Jews, and colored people and here she was heading for a house where she'd have to live with a Catholic *and* a Jew and in a town filled with coons.

"She can keep her mouth shut about Ceil and Tag," Brace directed tersely, "but the way niggers are treated down here ought to suit her fine."

Grace proved to be the kind of guest who relaxed and let her cares and responsibilities devolve upon her hosts. Her active, fifteen-months-old baby roamed the apartment unsupervised, unless Cecilia or Jorry looked after her. Grace declared herself exhausted from the trip down. There had been two thousand babies on the train she moaned, none of them trained.

"In all the thousands of years that babies have been born, wouldn't you think something would have been invented to do away with diapers?" she demanded at the dinner table the first night both men were free.

Brace, who was clever with his pencil, obligingly sketched a device which he offered to have patented. Something like the old opera hat, he explained. "You attach it to the infant by a shoulder strap harness. It collapses when the kid sits down, or lies flat. Rest of the time it's er—inflated for service."

Cecilia had watched Grace's acceptance of Tag with interest. It still irritated her when strangers stiffened at the mention of his name, but she was beginning now to be amused at their quick capitulation to his charm. He had only to smile at them, that slow, warm smile which began far back in his eyes; he had only to speak a few words, listening for their reply with his dark head bent as if he counted on the assurance of their friendship, to have them eating out of his hand, as Quilty would say. What the pert, pretty, red-headed Grace had expected she had failed to state, but obviously she had not been prepared for Tag. With her own husband overseas she might suddenly have decided that it would be pleasant to be escorted to movies and perhaps to a dance—if they had dances in this one-horse town—by anything so good-looking in the khaki uniform.

"The boys will stay home, do the dishes, and take care of the baby, while we three girls go to the movies." Jorry shattered her sister's half-formed dreams with magnificent assurance born of previous experience. The men, she added, had to go to bed early, anyway, for they turned out at an ungodly hour in the morning.

But Grace wanted to talk to Tag and another night she offered to help Cecilia clear away dinner while Brace took Jorry to the early movie show. The baby, who had never been introduced to any routine, refused to go to sleep and Grace said she would have to be allowed to stay up until she put herself to sleep on the rug. "My nerves can't stand it to hear her yell," Grace explained.

So the child continued to patter about, getting in Cecilia's way as she cleared the table, until Tag diverted her attention with the old device of making shadow pictures on the wall.

"Where on earth did you ever learn that?" Grace put down a pile of plates and stared.

He remembered his father making pictures for him as a kid, Tag smiled, twisting his thumbs to provide a rabbit with convincing ears.

"Why my father used to do that for us at home!" Grace almost gasped. "I think that's the strangest thing!" She stared at the wall, as if transfixed.

Cecilia, from the kitchen doorway, smiled at the baby's evident fascination. She could recall watching the nuns' shadows on the walls at school, she murmured; all children were probably awed by the mysterious movement and exaggerated size.

"I thought it was . . . . " Grace's voice trailed off. "Only Americans . . . an old American pastime," she faltered. "I read about it once in a book at the library."

Tag glanced at his wife's face, buried his own face in the baby's tangled hair. His shoulders shook with laughter. "Pioneer stuff!" he gurgled. "Could be."

But Cecilia's sense of humor refused to function. The dish towel twisted in her hands. "Don't you think Tag is an American, Grace? What do you suppose he is doing in the United States Army?"

Grace giggled. She was not vicious, merely stupid. "I didn't mean Tag isn't an American. I was thinking of his folks, I guess. What I really meant was that making shadow pictures goes 'way back to *early* American families."

"Colonial," suggested Tag, who still seemed to have difficulty with his speech.

"Yes," agreed Grace, grateful for co-operation, "colonial."

Cecilia, her lovely face troubled, untwisted her dish towel and resumed her task of putting away the food. No, she wasn't ready for Grace yet—she would call her when she had the kitchen in better order. She heard the baby laugh in the dining room and then Grace's voice with a confidential note in it because she was practically alone in a room with a man. Even if his wife could overhear.

"My, you certainly are fond of children," Grace said. "You'd make a good father."

Tag took that seriously. "I hope so."

"I hope you don't mind if I say it, but if I were you I wouldn't be in too big a hurry to have any." Grace, mysterious, was pretty awful to listen to.

If she tells him my build indicates I'm sure to have a miscarriage—Jorry had repeated that remark to Cecilia, adding that she didn't know where Grace collected her medical theories.

But to Cecilia's relief, Tag strode out into the kitchen and kissed the nape of her neck as she bent over the dishpan. He would wash the dishes, he proclaimed, gently pushing her aside. Let her dry them and save her manicure, for a change. Grace? Oh, he had turned the damp baby back to her. She was busy in the bedroom, changing the kid, "I'm too old-fashioned to enjoy discussing my future family with a strange female," Tag observed, rolling up his sleeves. "Where do we keep the soap?"

It was wonderful to have Tag to herself in the kitchen. They had not been alone together since Grace's arrival, for the sleeping arrangements had been completely upset to allow the visitor a bedroom to herself. One week wouldn't kill anyone, Jorry had assured them all, but afterward she admitted that she had not known that seven days could seem so much like seven years.

"What do you suppose Grace meant by saying that if she were you she wouldn't be in a hurry to have babies?" Cecilia asked hurriedly, half whispering to avoid being overheard.

"She meant I ought to realize what is before them." Tag whispered, too, liking to tease.

"What is before them?" Cecilia demanded.

"Well, if we have a girl and she grows up and marries a man named Lincoln or Grant, that won't be so bad; but if we have a boy, he'll be Silverstein to the end of his days." Tag's eyes twinkled as he blew a collar of soap bubbles from a tumbler he had fished out of the suds.

If the silly and cruel things that people said had no power to hurt him, surely she need not dwell upon them, Cecilia told herself, counting the days until Grace should return North. Tag didn't look for slights, and he could laugh at Grace's confusion when, as she often did, she tried to be subtle and succeeded only in being vulgar and cheap. She was no worse than many of her friends back home, Cecilia honestly acknowledged, remembering how many jokes about Jews she had listened to. But that was before she had met Tag and since her marriage it hurt her to recall that many of these stories had been told by Jewish people themselves; she knew now that ridicule could be a two-edged sword.

She and Jorry put Grace and the baby on the train at the end of the week's visit, with relief they hoped they decently concealed. To their startled eyes the coaches appeared to bulge with babies and Jorry swore that she saw diapers hanging from the ventilators to dry. Her nerves demanded refreshment, she confided as they left the station; she intended to go to the movies and eat downtown.

"Better let the baby smell air out before you try to cook dinner again," she counseled. "Even if Grace is my own sister, I think her conception of sanitation is subnormal. Come on, let's relax."

Cecilia walked as far as the theatre, but she would not go in. She had a couple of errands to do, she explained—she had put off everything, but now she could make up for lost time. One of the postponed errands she did not specify was to see the doctor at the hospital. There was no reason to worry, she had hardly thought of it at all, but there was a little lump . . . Not so little now; in fact it seemed to grow so rapidly that for a week, ever since Grace had kept them all so stirred up, Cecilia had not dared to touch it. This was because she didn't want to be nervous, with company in the house. Not that there was any reason to be nervous about a lump. The doctor would probably laugh at her for even mentioning it.

On the contrary, he was quite fierce about it. He barked at her and pounded his desk, when she became confused under his questioning. Overworked, brusque, long enough removed from civilian practice to have forgotten his bedside manner, if he had ever had one, Major Delbert felt no obligation upon him to conceal his impatience with the frailty of female constitutions. His examination of Cecilia was skilled, but he chose to ignore the psychological implications of her terror-stricken eyes and shaking hands.

"Cancer? Certainly not. But you'll have to have it out. As soon as possible. Get your husband and make arrangements for say next Monday morning. Private room? What in hell do you want a private room for? We'll be doing well to get you into one of the wards. Give me a ring as soon as you've made up your mind."

She could go home, Cecilia thought, on her way back to the apartment. Grandma would see that she had a private room at All Souls, and even with the present scarcity of nurses she would be assured the best care that money could buy. But she was Tag's wife, a sergeant's wife—Tag supported her on his pay. He had a profound admiration for the medical attention the Army offered service men and their families. Tag was proud of that; to him it was tangible proof that he was part of the best cared-for fighting force in the world. He thought of Democracy as an operating dynamo that "ran things," not perfectly perhaps, but hopefully and bravely.

Cecilia had learned that he fancied he had an individual agreement between himself and his country—he was to perform certain duties, like fighting a war, in return for services performed in exchange for him. He had his own code of how much he ought to accept and his reasoning often surprised Cecilia, but only endeared him the more to her. For instance, he would not frank his mail, arguing that the government paid him enough to allow him to afford postage. "That's only my feeling," he explained carefully to his wife. "Don't say that to the fellows."

Yes, Tag would have faith in the Post hospital, in the Army surgeons' skill. She would persuade him to let no one at home know; it would be easier to be lonely than to undertake to cope with the affectionate, worried letters from her relatives in the North. Her grandmother might even come down and she would unquestionably lean heavily on numerous long-distance calls. Grandmother would drive Jorry, who hated the telephone, right out of her mind.

It was worse than she had expected. Cecilia in the dragging horror of the long night following the morning operation, thought she must drown in the pit of her despair. She had not been prepared for the use of a local anesthetic, or for the pain which set in as the operation approached the finish. The rows of ward beds and the short tempers of the weary nurses intimidated her, too. A terrible feeling of helplessness overwhelmed her, the more devastating in that the memory of a previous hospital experience returned to her, mercilessly clear in the smallest detail. The removal of her appendix then had meant a private room and nurses, flowers, a kindly, attentive doctor, but above all assurance and security that gave her confidence to endure the pain.

Did all these women in the narrow beds in this ghastly place feel as she did, Cecilia wondered, too weak to turn her head on the pillow soaked in her tears? Did they fear lest they suffocate in the queer, gray darkness, a murky darkness that she fancied must be smoke from the great, consuming fires of pain, racking their feeble bodies. It seemed to Cecilia in other moments that the anguish of these suffering women formed a heavy, compact weight that pressed down upon her and slowed the beating of her heart.

Perhaps you're going to die, she told herself and realized that for the first time in her life the idea of death ceased to be remote. She and Tag had talked about death and dying, but they had not really believed it could touch them. Now this horrible, grinding pain had become a thing to be escaped at all costs, even if it cost one's life.

Are you afraid to die? Not if the pain stops. She asked herself the question and supplied the answer, as, when a child, she had played games with an imaginary partner. *I would just as lief,* she decided, and was amazed to find how much simpler the process of dying was than she had been taught to expect. Without a thought for priest, or Tag, or God, without fear or anxiety or regret, one had only to close one's eyes....

She did not, however, wake in Heaven, but in the same ward, with the eyes of a girl in the next bed fixed on her in staring curiosity.

"Hello, feel better?" chirped the watcher. "You sure handed

that Wop nurse a turn last night. I was glad to see her doing a little work for a change. I guessed you pretty near went through the pearly gates."

At first bewildered, in a moment Cecilia understood. She asked what day it was, heard that it was Thursday afternoon. She had been operated on Wednesday morning. A glucose transfusion had been given her, Cecilia was informed; the nurse had been kept hopping under the doctor's orders.

"They talked about sending for your husband, but I guess they saw you'd pull through." The girl in the next bed laughed. "I'd better pause for station identification, as my husband says. I'm Mrs. Ned Fuller. My husband's a Corporal in the 374th."

Cecilia gathered breath for the effort to speak, pushed the sheet away from her mouth. "I'm Cecilia Silverstein. Sergeant Hyman Silverstein's wife. He's in the 397th."

She saw the girl in the other bed hesitate for the fraction of a second. *I wonder, did I used to do that, too?*

"Some people think I look Jewish," Mrs. Fuller said. She reached under pillow for a handglass, studied her brown, square face gravely. "You don't show it at all!" she assured Cecilia in a burst of generosity.

Cecilia's head ached, her sheets felt hot and wrinkled, but probably the shortage of nurses was duplicated in the laundry force. It worried her to think that Tag must see her with her hair uncombed and not even a fresh nightgown, but at least she would have strength to talk to him. She was getting well!

Mrs. Ned Fuller said that she couldn't "get over" Tag's good looks. "You'd never know," she chattered, putting up her copper-brown hair on curlers for the night. She could see now, she went on, why Tag had married a Christian girl. "That type wouldn't go for Jewish women."

Cecilia could still see Tag's face as he had stood at the foot of her bed, when the last visitors were being ushered out. A lot Mrs. Fuller knew about his preferences.

Jewish women were too aggressive and bossy, Mrs. Fuller was explaining confidently; a man like Tag wanted his girl to be soft-spoken and willing to let him lead. A curler fell to the floor and Mrs. Fuller said "Damn!" It was funny, she owned, but years ago when she had finished high school and was hunting a job, she had thought the word "Christian" in the advertisements specified a church member. She had let a couple of good chances go by, because she was sure the firms would demand proof that she had joined a church.

"Wasn't I the dope! It never dawned on me they didn't want Jews to apply. An employment agency tipped me off and we had a good laugh." Mrs. Fuller suggested kindly that if Cecilia thought of getting a job—say when her husband was shipped out —she could use her maiden name.

Cecilia said, "I'm not ashamed of my married name."

No, perhaps not, Mrs. Fuller agreed, but why not look facts in the face? "Plenty of Jewish employers don't want too many of their own race on the pay roll. They don't think it looks too good. I believe in equality and all that myself, but what I say is there's no harm in looking out for yourself. Between the Jews and the Catholics—"

"I'm a Catholic." Cecilia had just time to get that in before the tall figure of the nurse stepped between the two beds and Miss Ricci inquired whether they knew that there were other patients in the ward who would like to get a little sleep?

At that Mrs. Fuller had the final word. Wops, she whispered when Miss Ricci had returned to her desk, loved to display their authority. A few grains went to their heads every time—look at Mussolini.

Chapter Nine

CECILIA had been home from the hospital for a week when the telegram came. Jorry answered the bell, signed for the message, and carried the envelope to Cecilia, ironing in the kitchen. If she sat at work, she had almost as much strength as before the operation, Cecilia insisted.

"My grandmother is very ill." She glanced up from the single line of typed words. "Oh, Jorry, I think I'll have to go home. She is so old, she might die."

Jorry was practical. She said that Tag must get the train reservations, because the ticket agent turned down civilians. "May Evans told me that when she went to get tickets for Milt and herself, they wouldn't sell her a thing. She had to produce Milt."

Cecilia scarcely heard. The task of getting herself home presented a formidable challenge in view of the physical exertion required and her limited strength. She dreaded the separation from Tag, harbored a superstitious fear lest the vague forces labeled collectively the government, take advantage of her absence to "ship out" Tag to another post, or overseas. She was his good luck piece, he constantly assured her, his talisman and charm.

Yet, with the first flurry over and the wheels of preparation set in motion, there was something oddly calming in the knowledge that she was returning to familiar scenes to be among her kith and kin. The old phrase swam up to the surface of her mind from the shadowy depths of memories stored in her school days.

She had thought so often of the convent in the long, lonely hours when pain had kept her awake at the hospital, had gravely considered whether such reflections indicated that she was growing old. It was only, she had decided, because she had been so happy there, so free from the necessity for being patient, or brave, or able to endure pain. The lovely serenity of those happy years flowed like a bright river in the stream of her unconsciousness, but she could recall them without fear of drugging herself with nostalgic dreams. No wish to return to sanctuary ever plagued her. She thought of the placid Sisters without envy, nor yearned again for the shelter of their loving care. Married to Tag, nothing that had happened to her or could happen, had power to harm her. It was very simple, she told him the night before she went North; they had only to remain in love to be invulnerable to all the forces of destruction.

"People can't hurt us," she assured him, her arms about him tightening their clasp. "Or Time."

Tag, they had planned, would stay in camp and already another couple had agreed to move in with Jorry and Brace. Cecilia did not know how long she was to be gone, but the newcomers professed themselves willing to be received on a temporary basis. In fact, Jorry observed, they would have been grateful if allowed to stay overnight. She hoped Cecilia didn't mind frankness, but the arrangement would be a relief to her in one way, Jorry said. "I get so tired of hushing up Brace, when he's dying to tell a new joke."

Brace could tell all the jokes he knew in his Jewish dialect, of which he was inordinately proud, Cecilia reflected, trying to sleep in the noisy, crowded train the next day. The traveling public seemed to her to be more notable than ever for the capacity of its appetite. Men, women, and children, up and down the length of the car, and probably the train, ate continuously, consuming vast quantities of food, most of which they carried with them. They ate in the diner, if they could be served, but if not there were always boxes and bags on which to draw. Sandwiches, fruit, and cake, washed down by milk, coffee, and soft drinks, made the coach in which Cecilia sat one composite buffet. The rustle of waxed paper and the smell of oranges became obsessions to torment her.

Yet good-temper prevailed and everyone in the main made allowance for shortages, rolling up coats when the porter announced there were no more pillows, helping each other to swing luggage up and down from the wall racks. Service men yielded their seats to young mothers with babies and when an older child lost his soft rubber ball under the seats, a dozen passengers patiently heaved themselves out into the aisle to permit him to scramble about on all fours in search of it.

It seemed to Cecilia that the car would never settle down for the night. She had given the lunch box Jorry had packed for her to a young corporal who had had the seat next to her until mid-afternoon; but although she had had nothing since boarding the train except a container of milk, she was not hungry. Passengers spoke in hissing whispers when the lights were dimmed, they crawled over each other, grunting, as they grimly tramped east and west to the wash rooms. Tired children and tired mothers bickered over the problem of knotted shoestrings, hitherto cherubic babies spasmodically wailed.

Cecilia lay back in her tilted seat, sternly reminded herself not to be a snob. It was just as hard on all these weary people to be traveling in this confused fashion, as for her. She would close her eyes, say a prayer for dear Grandmother, and then perhaps she could sleep and dream of Tag.

Hers was an aisle seat and next to the window a middle-aged

woman snored, not loudly but in an undercurrent of plaintive squeaks and gasps. She had confided to Cecilia earlier that there was no use trying to get into the dressing room—"Gentiles haven't a chance"—and she had proceeded to tie her face up in a gauze mask and tape a black disc over each eye. The mask, she volunteered, would bleach her skin while she slept, the discs screened her eyes from the lights. Once arrayed, she promptly went to sleep and began to whistle through the slits she had cut for her nose and mouth.

Cecilia, her prayers said, found it impossible to sleep. Her eyes and ears remained persistently alert, the motion of the swaying train failed to lull her into drowsiness. She heard the whispered dialogue of the two girls across the aisle as to which one should take the sleeping baby into the dressing room and change him *again,* and she caught the impatient comment of the man in the seat behind them.

"My God, if they can dehydrate beans, why not babies?" he growled to his seatmate.

After the girl returned with the baby, someone opened a candy box, releasing the odor of chocolate, rustling waxed paper in a frantic search for the favorite variety.

Cecilia, wide-eyed, motionless, heard the door at the end of the car open, felt a current of air. The porter tiptoed into view. He swayed down the aisle, glancing automatically from left to right, as she had noticed every trainman did. His sober, brown face, something in the intentness of his peering look, impressed Cecilia. She turned slightly and the movement caught his attention.

"You awake, Miss?" He stopped at her seat. "I got to get someone."

She pulled herself up to a sitting position, shivering as her coat slid to her knees. A chill frosted the air. She whispered, "Can I help? What's the matter?"

"For Christ's sake, can the chatter." A man further down the aisle, his legs wrapped in newspapers for warmth, raised himself on one elbow.

Silently Cecilia stepped into the aisle. She signed to the porter to go back and that she would follow. In the dim light the hazards presented by the portions of the passengers' anatomy projecting from their seats were further complicated by their suitcases and bags and, in some instances, their shoes. Cecilia stumbled twice, but managed to retain her balance, although she grasped thankfully at the arm of the porter who waited for her in the vestibule.

A man waited, too, disheveled, coatless, his collar opened at the throat. "My little girl!" he gasped when he saw Cecilia. "She's awfully sick, maybe dying. In there!" He pointed to the door lettered "Ladies." Could she go in and do something to help, the father implored.

In the dressing room Cecilia found a girl in her early teens, doubled up on the couch and crying hysterically. It was all her father's fault the child sobbed; he had not brought any whiskey with him.

"Nothing cures me of cramps except whiskey." She rolled over and buried her face in the towel she had spread over the red plush. "You tell him he's got to get me some."

Cecilia found that Sunny's hands and feet were cold—the patient apparently saw nothing incongruous in the contrast afforded by her name and her copious flow of tears—and decided that a cup of hot tea and an aspirin might bring relief. In spite of Sunny's indignant insistence that nothing except whiskey was good for cramps, she was persuaded to drink the tea the porter fetched and to swallow an aspirin. Yes, she would stay with her, Cecilia promised; no, she needn't go back to her seat in the car —it would soon be morning, anyway.

The father, who had no seat for himself, but who could now sleep for an hour or so in that vacated by his daughter, was voluble in his expressions of gratitude. He didn't know how to handle a girl; Sunny was the hysterical type and always frightened him whenever she was laid up.

"I'm sure I don't know how to thank you enough for what you've done, Miss—Mrs.—"

"Mrs. Silverstein," Cecilia said. "And I am more than glad to have been able to help you."

He gulped audibly, then put a hand on her arm as she turned to go back to the girl, now asleep. "Well, I sure appreciate what you've done, just the same. I've always told my wife there were some white Jews and now she'll believe it when I tell her about you."

"Now we've got you, we'll have to see if Quilty can't fatten you up a little," Tobias said.

They were all shocked to see Cecilia so much thinner, her natural awkwardness intensified by the self-conscious knowledge that they thought she looked "peaked." Her grandmother, out of danger but weak and exhausted, occupied the room which she had endowed in All Souls. She was pleased that Cecilia had come to her, but brief visits satisfied her and the Sisters reported that she slept most of the time, so that they had to waken her, like a baby, when she was to be fed. Her mind wandered at times and she had forgotten Tag. Had she ever met him? she mumbled, when Cecilia mentioned his name. Tobias insisted that Cecilia stay with him and Dora, since the grandmother's apartment was closed. He would not hear to Cecilia's suggestion that she get the keys from the superintendent and open the rooms.

"A fine, cheerful arrangement that would be," he scolded. "No one to get you a cup of tea when you come back from the hospital—your grandmother's help went into defense factories, even before she was down sick."

He knew how it took the tucking out of a person, he added, to make regular visits to the hospital. It was a new-fangled notion, this being carted out of your own home and laid out on a hospital bed, the instant you developed a touch of indigestion or what not. Tobias regarded the modern passion for hospitalization with suspicion.

"They tell me you had a taste of it yourself, down to Fort Jackson," he said, watching the light from his hearth fire warm Cecilia's pale face into tints of rose. "Makes you eligible for the 'My-Operation' club, I guess."

Cecilia had no desire to talk of her hospital experiences, but later, one afternoon when she returned cramped and cold from the long trip to All Souls, she could not refuse to answer Quilty's soft-voiced questions. The colored woman had made tea and cinnamon toast and had laid a place in the breakfast nook. The coal range heated the kitchen more evenly than the oil burner, converted to coal, served the dining room.

"You ought to take the bus home, Miss Cecilia," Quilty admonished, noticing that the girl rubbed her thin hands to warm them.

She had to get the hospital air out of her lungs, Cecilia returned; it always seemed to her that even her clothes smelled of drugs when she had visited her grandmother. "I thought of being a hospital aide before I married Tag, but now I don't believe I'd be much good at it."

Quilty poured boiling water into a pink china teapot, carried a small tray, arranged with cup and saucer, the tea, and a plate of toast covered by a pink napkin, to the waxed pine table.

"A dish of tea will set you right—won't spoil your dinner a bit. What kind of a hospital did they have down South, Miss Cecilia?"

Cecilia, seated on the high-backed settle, let her tea steep. The hospital had been all right, she answered cautiously; everyone said the surgeons were wonderful. They performed the most delicate and expensive operations at a fraction of what they would have charged in civilian practice.

"They're short of nurses, of course. All hospitals are." Cecilia revealed that the doctor had been unable to get a private night nurse for her grandmother. "I managed," she went on. "My husband rubbed my back for me one night and Mrs. Read—we have the apartment together—used to do things for me in the daytime."

The fragrance of the hot tea as she filled her cup, the perfection of the thin strips of toast, and the delicate smoothness of the pink linen napkin in her fingers, suddenly brought back to her the contrast presented by her hospital trays. No one had had time or inclination to make them attractive, or even to see that the food was eaten, once served.

"Oh, Quilty!" Cecilia hesitated. There had been that night when, too weak to feed herself, she had cried to see the dishes within reach and not be able to lift the fork or spoon. Mrs. Fuller had called the nurse who had cranked the head of the bed to a sharper angle, scolded Cecilia for making a fuss, and flounced away without waiting to see whether she had bettered the situation.

Cecilia said slowly. "They didn't have to *yell*. The doctors shouted at me. If I didn't understand their questions, they acted as if I must be feeble-minded. And the nurses had no patience—I supposed they were dead from fatigue. Yet if people are well, they don't come to doctors or nurses for help. It's dreadful to be sick and so helpless, Quilty, and to be treated as if you had committed a crime."

"You eat your toast." Quilty, solid and comfortable, opened the oven door to put in her potatoes to bake.

"There was one doctor," Cecilia's tense young voice went on. "He said to me, 'How do you feel?' and when I answered, 'Doctor, I think I have a cold,' he pounded his desk and shouted, 'I didn't ask you what you think—you leave the thinking to me. All I want to know is how do you feel.' "

Cecilia looked at Quilty. "I cried."

The oven door clicked shut, Quilty rose from her knees. "Why, Miss Cecilia, that's only what we been used to all our lives."

To the girl at the table the pathos in the simple statement seemed a rebuke. The hospital clinics on which Quilty and her friends must depend when long or expensive illness forced them to ask for free treatment, were manned by competent, skilled physicians, Cecilia knew. She had heard professional nurses say that if ever they were ill, they would ask to go into the wards, because the nurses there were in constant attendance and the poorer patients were not dependent on "floor nursing."

But now Cecilia had learned, through her own bitter experience, that knowledge and skill and experience were not enough. She had not been a charity patient, strictly speaking, but she supposed that the modest fees Tag had paid had been far below the actual costs, certainly not to be compared to the surgeon's charges in civilian practice. Women who consulted doctors in their private offices and women who submitted to examination at the clinics, were alike in their capacity for anxiety and pain. *Money buys even compassion,* Cecilia thought and knew that Tag would say the doctors did not mean to be unkind. They were overworked and tired, they carried far too heavy a load, he would excuse them. Tag excused everyone.

He would have laughed, Cecilia reminded herself the next day, when the night nurse the hospital Sisters had finally succeeded in getting for her grandmother, mentioned her previous case. She had taken three days off to rest, Miss Lake confided—this twelve-hour duty was hard, after a nurse had become accustomed to an eight-hour shift.

"Even if, as they tell us, it's your patriotic duty to work like a dray horse, it means a girl never has time to get her hair done." Miss Lake, seeing Cecilia's glance at her smartly-waved blonde head, admitted that she had just returned from the beauty parlor. She had gone there to "blow in" the money gift presented to her by her last case.

"My last case," volunteered Miss Lake, patting her front curls into a graceful bang, "was a Jewish lady. But nice."

He wouldn't be surprised if his daughter Sarah landed in the hospital before her first grandchild arrived, Tobias informed Cecilia, when she questioned him about the expected baby. "Nutmeg kind of overdoes the dramatics, if you ask me."

She must go to see her cousin Ginger, Cecilia said; she had intended to send the baby something weeks ago. "Now I'll get two knitted blankets, I think. I can use one for Hildegarde Williams' stork shower next week."

That involved her in a rather detailed explanation of what a stork shower was and why Hildegarde, who wasn't married, was giving a shower for Etta Carver who was the mother-to-be. They were girls with whom she had been at school, Cecilia said.

The invitation had been mailed to her Grandmother Warren's address. Cecilia had found it in the mailbox in the apartment house lobby. She did not tell Tobias that the superintendent of the building, a curt, dour-faced man with cropped black hair that appeared to be inserted in his scalp like tufts in a hairbrush, had declined to be responsible for any mail that might come for her.

"I'm not sure that anyone will write to me at this address, Mr. Veal," Cecilia had told him, "but letters or packages may come in my married name—Mrs. Hyman Silverstein. You'd know if there had been anything for me up to now, wouldn't you?"

The superintendent had scowled at her, a compressed version of his lowering face faithfully reflected in the polished brass mailboxes lining the immaculate white marble vestibule walls.

"Miss Warren, this isn't that kind of a house," he informed her. "Your grandmother never has mail with that sort of name on it and neither do any of the other families. White people live here. This is a restricted neighborhood."

The scene was to recur to Cecilia again and again, as fixed in detail as a photograph imprinted on her brain. The white walls of the vestibule, the bright brass mail slots, even the great yellow cat sprawled in the entrance where the early March sun heated the stone sill. And in the center of the freshly-mopped tiled floor, the stocky, dark figure of the shirt-sleeved Mr. Veal, always so anxious to please on the few previous occasions she had transmitted her grandmother's orders to him. But she had been Cecilia Warren then, living with Mrs. Hubert Warren, and her name in the mailbox had presumably been approved.

She had not known how to meet the situation—that was always the trouble, she admitted, when she looked back at such encounters. It might be a confession of cowardice on her part, but she had no talent for combatting insolence. She lacked both the power of the great lady who, in fiction at least, could put a forward person in his place simply and effectively with one piercing glance, and the belligerence of Jorry who relished "run-ins" with customers and clerks at the cash grocery stores.

To Cecilia it seemed that the superintendent's rudeness was directed not at her, but at Tag; if she lashed out at the man in anger, or worse, took advantage of the authority invested in her as her grandmother's agent, she lowered herself to his level and so harmed Tag's cause. Nothing could hurt her, she assured herself, if it did not touch Tag. The superintendent wanted her to know that he despised her for marrying a Jew, but the verdict of such a man carried no weight. She would continue to ask for her mail, and he would not dare destroy anything actually addressed to her, but it was a relief to know that Tag would write to her in care of her Grandfather Ferris and that when she shopped her packages would be sent to the Ferris house.

The day before the stork shower she suggested to Tobias that she go with him to see her Aunt Sarah Eustice and the girls, if they should be at home. Nutmeg would be home all right, Tobias assented, but one could never count on Mabel or Fern. Mabel had one day off a week, but she kept it a secret so that, she said, her friends should not parcel it out for her.

"Sarah tells me she has her room done over every time they change the model rooms down in the department stores," Tobias gossiped as he and Cecilia walked with heads bent against the wind. Sarah would kill herself some day, the old man added, in her efforts to make up to her children for giving them such an unsatisfactory father.

"Course, he's no shakes as a husband, either, but I guess a woman figures out that at least she had the fun of gambling with her marriage. Children don't have even that much chance."

Beside him Cecilia lifted her beaver coat sleeve to screen her face as the wind gained in fury. "But Grandfather, Aunt Sarah's children don't *blame* her, do they? She can't help it, if Uncle Lion drinks to excess."

It was surprising, what children could blame their mothers for, Tobias retorted. In Sarah's case she had taught her children to regard her marriage as a mistake, in the process thoroughly destroying her own self-respect. "She all but tells them she's been a fool. And the queer part of it is that sometimes I think she really cares for Lion."

"I think she cares," Cecilia said.

Sarah, gaunt, tired-looking, but beaming with honest good-will, kissed Cecilia with great warmth and ushered her and Tobias into the dining room where Ginger was enjoying a malted milk. With an egg in it, Sarah explained—the doctor was hipped on the value of fresh eggs in pregnancy.

"Don't you need one of these yourself?" Ginger hinted, unfolding the pretty knitted baby blanket Cecilia dropped into her lap.

If Cecilia wasn't pregnant, she was about the only war bride who wasn't, Ginger remarked instructively; the baby crop was breaking all records. "But something tells me there'll be an awful lot of families with an only child." If she had a boy, she confided, once would be enough for her.

Tobias, following Sarah to the kitchen, called through the doorway. "Your mother says you can't have a boy. It's got to be a girl."

Ginger ignored the interruption. "You'd better have a boy the first time, Ceil. If a Jewish woman has a son, that lets her out. Lots of Jewish girls have told me they can stop right there."

She intended to have more than one baby, Cecilia asserted, determined not to be irritated by the inevitable reference to Jewish customs. Tag had once said, with his heavenly grin, that he had learned more about his race since his marriage to a Gentile, than in all the years he had gone his way a lonely Hebrew.

If she had known how her figure would look, she would have sidestepped the experience, Ginger mourned. No one knew what it was like to be uncomfortable for nine long months, except the women who lived through them. "Hoke isn't very sympathetic, either. I wrote to him that I was simply petrified, worrying that our baby might smother himself in his carriage or crib. You read of accidents like that almost every day."

Her husband, Ginger scolded, had written to assure her that smothering was a peculiar accident and seldom happened. He had asked some doctor, Hoke related, who had been anything but soothing to a woman's shattered nerves. "The doctor said that one baby in one hundred thousand might smother and that there was nothing you could do about it."

"Well, is there?" inquired Tobias from the doorway.

Sarah pushed him aside. "The men ought to take turns having babies!" she stormed. "There wouldn't be so many, then. Imagine having a husband who was going to have a baby around the house for nine months!"

Tobias said he couldn't imagine it, and should he bring in the cocoa?

When he had carried in the tray of steaming cups, Sarah followed with a plate of brownies. These, she proudly announced, had been made by Fern. Her girls could do anything they put their minds to, Sarah said; it was a shame they couldn't meet the right kind of people.

Above the rim of her milk glass Ginger winked at her grandfather. "Mama means Fern. The girl has a boy friend."

Cecilia wondered at Sarah's evident distress. Her face reddened, she crumbled a cake on her plate without seeming to know what she was doing. Fern didn't have a beau—a boy friend, Sarah protested; if only the family would keep still about it, things would work out all right.

"Not that I'm not glad she is a success with boys," Sarah said rather illogically. "At least I don't have to worry that she will be an old maid on my hands."

How can they be so brutal to each other, Cecilia thought, as Sarah and Ginger in a sort of animated duet—the one indignant, the other amused—dragged Fern's poor little young romance out, exposed it to the public gaze. The fellow's name was enough for her, Sarah grumbled; she wasn't going to have a child of hers getting mixed up with anyone named Kotoski.

"He claims he isn't a foreigner," Sarah said. Her large hands, the knuckles distorted from hard work, began to roll the cake crumbs into brown pellets. She had told Jim Kotoski that, if he was an American, he had no business with such an outlandish name. "I told him outright that I thought it showed a lack of ambition to go around sounding like a Polak, when he was born in this country. People judge you by your name, I says to him."

Cecilia's dark lashes swept down to hide her eyes. "I don't think all people do." *But she's right, I used to do it, too, God forgive me.*

Tobias coughed, prophesied he'd hear from the nut that had gone down his bronchial tubes. "Where did Fern meet this fellow, anyway?"

"In school." Ginger answered for her mother. "He was two classes ahead of her. Captain of the basketball team—I guess the coal heavers make the huskiest players, boys named Dumbrowski and Olansky and the like."

There was no use beating around the bush, Sarah said, she had never known any people like the Kotoski family—they could have nothing in common with a girl like Fern. Jim's father worked sodding lawns, cleaning furnaces, in spite of the fact that he owned his own house and had sent one daughter to college. "A fine snob she is, too. More cocoa, Ceil? At least you don't have the problem of Tag's family to contend with."

Tag had relatives, Cecilia said firmly. She liked Naomi O'Neill, the cousin she had met. It was a pity Tag's mother had died so long ago that his wife could know her only through her lovely photographs.

"No one in the Kotoski family *ever* died," Ginger interposed, helping herself to a third brownie.

"I thought you were so afraid of gaining weight, Nutmeg," Tobias suggested and instantly regretted his remark.

She was entitled to gain twenty-five pounds, his granddaughter instructed him; that included the child "and everything," she announced modestly. "The doctor took me off B-1 because that increases appetite and heaven knows I have all the appetite I need. I look like a Fifth Avenue bus from the rear, but I go right on craving sweets. What was I saying?"

Sarah murmured, "The Kotoskis never die," as one giving a cue.

"Oh, yes." Ginger adjusted the gathers of her maternity dress across her swelling breasts. "Your mother-in-law wouldn't have been Jewish anyway, Ceil. But if Fern has any sense, she'll think twice before she marries into the Kotoski tribe. Jim's mother was raised in an orphanage and is very much alive. She has nine other children, all alive, too."

They had taken Fern to Fort Monmouth where two of the brothers were stationed, Ginger went on. It was funny to see Fern surrounded by that husky, noisy troup—they were the kind of family who always talked at the top of their lungs. "And such clothes! The brighter the better. There must be a strain of Zulu in them, I told Mama."

Tobias gazed fixedly at the green and red plaid of Ginger's own dress. The neck and waistline, gathered on red ribbons, tied in large, flat bows. "Nutmeg, I've seen quieter taste in clothes than you've got yourself," he decided.

It did make the girl's figure look awful, Cecilia had privately concluded, or was it only that she looked as all pregnant women must look, as Cecilia herself would be some day? *Only I'm tall,* Cecilia reflected. *I'll probably resemble those vases they have in the drugstores, fat in the middle, with long, thin necks and round glass stoppers.*

Modern maternity clothes were a great improvement on those worn by women of Tobias' generation, Ginger was kind enough to explain. Even her mother had gone in for long, dark coats and ugly, chocolate-colored garments on the theory that she must conceal her shame. "Just because a girl's pregnant, Grandfather, doesn't mean she has to take her exercise after dark. Not any more. Bright clothes cheer us up, so we wear them. Sure we look a sight, but it's harder on us than on the men who are responsible, so we trot right along beside them in broad daylight. I'll bet Mama never went out once with Papa when she was pregnant, except on the nights when there was no moon."

The house suddenly shook as the front door slammed. The dishes in the Dutch cupboard rattled alarmingly. The cupboard, painted black and decorated with quaint sprays of pink roses didn't harmonize with Sarah's golden-oak suite, but Mabel had given it to her at Christmas, with the announcement that she planned gradually to replace the oak set.

"Hello!" Fern, looking ten years old in a red coat, a babushka tied over her flowing bob, stood in the doorway. "Why, if it isn't Ceil!" She dodged behind Ginger and leaned over Cecilia's chair to kiss her.

"Baby come yet?" Fern grinned at her sister, circled the table to kiss her mother and grandfather in turn. She saw the solitary brownie left on the plate and her small, fair face changed.

"You didn't *eat* them?" she almost wailed. "Oh, Mama, my brownies that I made especially for Dave!"

For a moment no one answered. Fern had jerked off her babushka and her foaming hair seemed to pull her small head back. Her face was as white as though the blood from it had all drained into her red coat. In contrast her lipsticked mouth was vivid scarlet.

She had the others at a disadvantage, because they were seated.

Ginger, her arm linked in her mother's—they invariably kept close enough to each other for their hands to touch—kept turning Sarah's wedding ring round and round. Tobias, elbows on the table, propped his chin in his palms. The sound of his foot tapping the floor added to the nervous tension. Sarah stared at Fern and Cecilia, blushing uncomfortably, looked overwhelmed with guilt.

"Darling, I didn't think you'd mind." Sarah, recovering voice, was apologetic, pleading. "They were perfectly wonderful and there's one left for you."

Fern, her hands clenched, said, "They were for Dave, I promised."

Her grandfather, whose passion for asking leading questions had not been dulled by age, muttered hopefully, "Dave the boy friend? Thought his name was Jim?"

"His brother." Ginger supplied the information in a low tone. "David Kotoski—that's an American name for you."

It *was* an American name, Fern reiterated with fierce emphasis. All the Kotoski boys had been born in the United States. Four of them were in the service. "And you have a God damn nerve to eat up the brownies I made to send Dave at Fort Sam Houston."

"You let me hear any more such language out of you, young lady, and I'll turn you up and blister your bottom!" Tobias, outraged, sputtered. "Don't think I can't do it, either."

She hadn't thought the war depended on Dave Kotoski getting his brownies, Sarah argued; Fern could make another batch as soon as there was sugar to spare. "You might show a little more hospitality toward your cousin Ceil, don't you think? How do you suppose she feels with you making such a scene?"

"I'm sorry—I didn't know." Cecilia looked distressed. There was a French bakery on Duane Street, she suggested, perhaps if they shipped a box of brownies to Dave—"Of course, they won't be homemade, but they used to be very good. You could walk over there with me, Fern. I'll get a box for Tag, too."

Fern blinked wet eyes, unbuttoned her coat. "It wasn't your fault, Ceil. I promised Jim I'd make them for his brother and Mama knew it. She doesn't want me to have anything to do with Jim."

"You have absolutely nothing in common with his family or him." Sarah's response was so automatic that Cecilia perceived she had used the same words many times before.

Fern laughed. "I wouldn't say that, Mama. Not when Mr. Kotoski and Mr. Eustice get drunk in the same tavern."

Tobias agreed to walk home alone and leave Cecilia and Fern to go their own way to the French bakery and from there to the post office. Cecilia promised to bring him a napoleon as a reward for returning without her and to Fern she confided that old people apparently never lost their sweet tooth.

"They do if they drink," Fern maintained gloomily. She took long strides as she walked and her moccasin shoes slapped the pavement at each step. Her father never touched candy or dessert, Fern testified; liquor satisfied his craving for sugar. Jim had told her that his father wanted nothing sweet, either.

Jim, Fern said, had made a study of the way liquor affected the different nationalities. "He's decided that Germans sing and dance, the Italians want to fight, Poles argue first, then start a fist fight, and the English go quiet when they're drunk. He doesn't know much about the French, and Americans are all different," Fern concluded.

Cecilia smiled down at the small figure loping beside her. "Tell me about Jim."

"Mama's so silly!" Fern complained. "She calls him a foreigner. Jim is as American as I am. He's in the Navy. He's never been to Poland. He can't even speak Polish. None of the boys can. If it wasn't for his name, no one would ever think Jim was anything except a nice American guy."

If it wasn't for his name, Cecilia repeated silently. *If it wasn't for his name.*

She had made up her mind, "When I was younger," Fern went on, never to marry. Now she wasn't sure. Mama was always beefing about how little women got out of marriage and yet in the next breath she said she despised old maids. "Every time Mabel or I do something she doesn't like, Mama will say, 'Do you want to be an old maid, like your Aunt Dora?' Or else she'll predict that some day we'll have to live alone like Aunt Dora, because no man will have us."

But Aunt Dora, Cecilia objected, didn't live alone. She had her father.

"Well, when he dies she'll be alone," Fern amended. "I wonder why she never married? Do you suppose Grandma was too fussy? I mean about her picking out a man?"

Cecilia didn't know. Her only memories of her Grandmother Ferris were dim pictures gained, she now suspected, in brief, uncomfortably formal calls. Ahead of her she saw the bakery's blue and white sign on the next block as the traffic light turned red.

"Mama ought to stop picking on Jim," Fern said, as they waited on the curb. "At least he isn't a Catholic or a Jew. She's always been worried for fear one of us would marry someone—" she gasped. "Gee, Ceil, I never thought! I'm sorry—I didn't mean—"

"I'm used to it," Cecilia assured her. She moved with the traffic as the lights changed. "Why doesn't Aunt Sarah like Catholics?" she probed.

Fern answered that she didn't know, but she thought it was because of Aunt Lucy. "Your mother. Mixing religions makes trouble in a family. You ought to know that."

"Did you ever stop to think it might be the families, not the religions?" Cecilia asked, but she thought, *Aunt Sarah is such an unhappy woman, how could she teach her children to be kind?*

Fern set her lips in a prim line. It was better for a couple to think the same about religion. "Mama says she doesn't see how you and Tag can get along, believing almost exactly opposite parts of the Bible."

Cecilia laughed, wondering how much Sarah knew about the Bible. "What is Jim's religion?" she questioned.

"He's an atheist."

"An atheist?"

She sounded like Mama, Fern pouted, stopping before the bakery window to survey the tiers of cakes. "There's nothing wrong with being an atheist. Plenty of pleople don't believe in God. It's got nothing to do with the question of whether a man will make a good husband or not. But try to convince Mama!" Fern sighed. "Let's go in."

Cecilia bought and paid for the brownies, but while Fern importantly wrote out the card, delighted to learn that the bakery attended to the mailing, Cecilia pondered the subject of marriage to an atheist. If a man denied the love of God, could he believe in love at all? She thought of Tag who never "talked religion," and yet believed that God was his friend. A woman married to an atheist might find him a "good" husband, but surely she must find his world a dreary place. *I have never known anyone who didn't believe in God,* Cecilia reflected. *I have never known anyone who tried to live without hope.*

Fern was spelling out the name to the clerk. "K-o-t-o-s-k-i—that's the way I wrote it. Yes, that's right." She turned to Cecilia, her small features earnest, tense. "If Mama is so set against the Catholics and the Jews, what's she got against the atheists?" Fern demanded.

Chapter Ten

HILDEGARDE WILLIAMS lived in Melon, the suburb where Frank Ferris and his family lived, but in a more pretentious section. Mrs. Williams had been determined to give her two pretty daughters "social advantages" and had bullied her husband into buying a too-expensive house in the right neighborhood. When the girls married, providing they made what she called good marriages, Mrs. Williams would be able to relax.

To Cecilia, caught up in the flurry of talk and laughter as the guests for the stork shower assembled in the Williams' living room, the half-forgotten atmosphere of careless happiness emphasized how long she had been away. Not long, perhaps, counted in weeks or months, but long enough to have separated her from the life these girls led; long enough, she discovered with wonder, to have the sound of their laughter fall strangely on her ears. *I haven't been with a bunch of girls who do nothing but play . . . or heard them laugh . . .* she thought, and when she recalled their school days together, the past seemed unreal and dim.

Bridge was to precede the shower and Hildegarde, called to the phone, returned to announce that her mother would have to fill in. "Althea Woody says she has to meet her fiancé—he has only three hours at the station. The telegram caught her just as she was leaving the house."

Mrs. Williams played bridge badly and her curious attitude toward her daughter's guests handicapped her still further. She had created in her imagination an alarming monster labeled

"Society" and had endowed it with a capacity to devour the ignorant or poor. She had been poor, she suspected she remained ignorant, and etiquette, as she conceived it, terrified her. In her pitiful efforts to conceal her panic at being forced to mingle with her children's friends, she became overbearing, condescending, vain.

"Your grandmother's better, Cecilia?" she asked, when it had been settled that she should play opposite Cecilia. "How long do you expect to stay?"

It depended partly on her grandmother's recovery, partly on her husband's plans, Cecilia returned. If Tag should be shifted to another camp—

"I guess you find it quite different being married, don't you?" Mrs. Williams, who never under any circumstances dared make a bid, murmured that she passed. "I mean, it must be quite a step down from being Cecelia Warren to—to—I never can remember your married name."

It annoyed Cecilia to feel the hot color warm her face. The others at the table, pretty, blonde Etta Carver, the guest of honor, and Pauline, Hildegarde's sister, were watching her, curiosity in their eyes. "It hasn't been a step down, Mrs. Williams," Cecilia said.

There was nothing like a fine old American name, Mrs. Williams insisted; she always told her girls that they owed it to their heritage to hand their traditions down to their children. Her tormented glance rested on Cecilia, turned away. When Mary Ann Finnegan had married Henderson Williams she had made sure that her children would not have to live down the label, "Shanty Irish," and from that moment the Finnegans, as far as she was concerned, had ceased to be. Hildegarde and Pauline had descended from the Williams and had inherited, so their mother passionately proclaimed, only Williams traits.

When she was dummy, Etta Carver, turning her diamond circlet on her plump finger, confided that her husband was bored to death with his Army work. "Of course he's glad he isn't overseas and they probably won't send him, but an office job does get so tiresome, day in and day out."

"But it's lovely to have him a captain," Mrs. Williams approved. "He looks grand in his uniform, Etta."

Uniforms cost enough, they ought to look grand, Etta sighed. "Paul says he spends every day from nine till twelve at his desk, figuring out how he can become a major. In the afternoon he works on the same question from two till five. He owes it to his child, he says, to be a major. That is, if we have a boy."

Cecilia, whose game had suffered for lack of practice, tried to keep her mind on the cards, but the chatter distracted her and the score wasn't important, after all. The room was blue with smoke; the neat maid kept replenishing the dishes with miniature chocolates and salted nuts. Most of the girls did so much dancing, Etta confided to Cecilia, that they didn't have to worry about their diets.

"The Officers' Club Lounge was furnished by Melon girls." Etta selected a fresh cigarette. "Is there a club where you're stationed?"

Cecilia smiled. "Tag is a non-com."

"Why, I certainly thought you'd married an officer!" Mrs. Williams' explosive astonishment was genuine. There were so many officers, she added vaguely, all the girls in Melon married officers and had grand times. "Plenty of boys go into town every morning and come out every night, just as they used to, only they're in uniform." She always said, Mrs. Williams babbled, that all war work was of equal importance. "The main thing is to do the best you can."

Finally the games ended, the prize was awarded Etta, and a hamper, filled with ribbon-tied parcels, was set before her. Tiny saques, fairy bootees, flower-embroidered pillow slips, all the fascinating, inconsequential furbelows that women always associate with gifts to a baby, tumbled from the packages. Etta, fingering them, murmuring "Adorable," "Precious," "Sweet," seemed half bemused, and the dreamy expression in her eyes was repeated in the absorbed circle of faces surrounding her.

This would be the "class baby," someone said, the first child born to a graduate of June, 1943. Sister Mary Agnes would be radiant over the news; she was worse than a doting grandmother when it came to the babies of her girls.

"Sister is a snob, too, at heart and don't you forget it," laughed Yolande Banks, helping Etta to fold up the tissue paper.

Mrs. Williams had overheard. "Sister Mary Agnes comes from a very fine family. Her people were one of the bigwigs in Pennsylvania."

And from the hearth, where she knelt to put a fresh log on the fire, Hildegarde grunted: "Someone ought to tell her that a Catholic can't get into the Junior League. Not here."

That was Hildegarde's chief resentment, Cecilia recalled her previous complaints. She had no means of knowing whether it might be true. She remembered, too, with sudden clarity, certain talks Sister Mary Agnes had held with her pupils, confidential, earnest chats in which she had sought to impress them with a realization of what she called their place in life.

"You girls are to remember that you are different." Cecilia heard again the cool, clear voice of the blue-eyed nun, a beautiful woman past her sixtieth birthday. "You will not have to earn your living ... or to compete. ... It is important that you cultivate your minds and spirits, that you may be able to order your homes graciously for the comfort and welfare of your husbands and children."

Sister Mary Agnes had taught every girl here for Etta's

shower, Cecilia reflected. The sunny, peaceful years at St. Catherine's had been happy, but now she wondered could they have been wasted time? *I wasn't fitted for living,* Cecilia thought, *none of us were.* The Sisters had assumed that the children placed in their care would be perpetually sheltered, that security was a birthright of the fortunate few.

"I think some of the things they taught us at the Convent were terrible," said Cecilia slowly, as if thinking aloud.

Mrs. Williams, helping the maid to set the tables, looked horrified. She had not been sure that it was "correct" for her to supplement Helen, but it behooved every housewife to lend a helping hand to the maid in these days of precarious service.

"Your grandmother will have a stroke, if she ever hears you say a thing like that," Mrs. Williams reproved Cecilia. "There isn't a better, or a higher-priced, school for girls in the East than St. Catherine's."

Hildegarde lost her bored, resentful expression for a moment. "Why do you say that, Ceil?"

"I was thinking about how little preparation for actual living they gave us," Cecilia looked troubled.

Etta, her arms heaped with packages to be replaced in the gift hamper, stood up. "The majority of us won't need to be prepared to live with Jewish husbands, I hope." She let the parcels cascade into the hamper's padded depths.

Something in Cecilia tightened like an elastic band about her heart. A bright sheet of flame flashed once before her eyes, vanished. She had never believed that anyone saw red, it was merely a figure of speech. Her limbs felt heavy as she struggled up from the cushions of the fat, blue velvet chair and for a moment she thought that her knees would refuse to stiffen. Then she was on her feet, facing the blur of faces in which she could distinguish only staring holes that must be eyes.

"I'm tired of listening to your silly, cheap cracks about Tag!" Her voice, repressed, fiercely rapid, startled them more than if she had screamed. "None of you has ever met him. You don't know him. You don't know anyone like him. Men like him don't go around with our crowd."

Cecilia's tall figure, in a silver-green crêpe frock, stood out against the dusty rose of the wall. Her face had gone white, her eyes looked blacker than her hair. She lifted one arm, perhaps to steady herself, and her hand touched the crystal prisms on the table lamp. The glass tinkled, a faint, artificial sound.

"You think it's terrible, that I've married a Jew!" Cecilia fixed her gaze on the bulging corsage of gardenias pinned to Etta Carver's shoulder. "What you can't understand is that I've married a man. I know the boys you go out with, have married, or are going to marry." She had danced with them, flirted with them, let them kiss her after cocktail parties, Cecilia recalled, but she would let that go.

"They haven't brains, or energy, or courage," she said, in her disciplined voice. "Perhaps they're not dissipated, but they're limp and weak. They haven't any convictions, because they can't think. My husband is strong in mind and body, good to look at, and heavenly to live with. What can the boys you know give you? Nothing except what they've inherited from someone else—money and a good American name."

The fire sent out a shower of sparks and in the hall the telephone bell rang. Cecilia drew a deep breath. In the doorway that led to the dining room, she saw Mrs. Williams and the maid, each transfixed with a tray in her hand.

"I beg your pardon, Mrs. Williams." The realization that she had complicated Mrs. Williams' rôle as hostess distressed Cecila, who had not intended to make a speech. "I'm sorry I lost my temper so completely."

Chapter Eleven

WHEN it became apparent that old Mrs. Warren's convalescence might be a matter of months, Cecilia said that of course she must return to Tag.

"We may have so little time together," she urged, dismayed at the opposition her decision encountered.

Her grandmother presumably had little time left to be with her only grandchild, Sarah Eustice pointed out and even Tobias hinted that it would "look a little better" if Cecilia stayed until the old lady could travel.

"She ought to go off somewhere for a rest," Tobias suggested. "Young people got their lives before them, they ought not to begrudge a little attention to the people almost finished with this world."

Cecilia, drying dishes for Quilty, said gently, "Tag's in the Army. How can he tell how much life he has before him?"

But Frank Ferris's wife, when Cecilia went there to dinner, took the stand that Cecilia's grandmother had been a mother to her and that a girl owed her mother everything. "Some women have five or six husbands," Ida stated significantly, "but you can't replace a mother."

Leidy, who was a veritable little pitcher—indeed the entire lemonade set her exasperated father had once said—when it came to listening, argued that a girl could have more than one grandmother. "Gertie Kendall has three."

"That has nothing to do with what we're talking about," Ida admonished her. "Your grandmother brought you up, Ceil. I think you owe her a great deal. Your husband will understand, if he is the right kind of man. There are some debts we're in honor bound to pay."

Frank, cutting Leidy's ham steak for her, stared at his wife in astonishment. "You put up an awful fuss when your mother wants to visit you," he observed with the faculty of saying the wrong thing, a tendency which, his wife frequently complained, never failed him.

"She has Molly," Ida snapped. "Besides, she isn't sick, is she?" Her mother's visits were usually timed to fit in with Charlie Cotter's plans, Ida added, and she didn't intend to have her brother-in-law dictate to her.

The truth was that she was continually torn between a natural antagonism to her mother, and her respect for convention which made it imperative that she preserve a fictitious bond of affection. She was far more like her mother than Molly and the element of domination, strongest characteristic in mother and daughter, inevitably produced a clash whenever the two came together. Away from her mother, Ida thought of her lovingly, believed that she adored her, and remembered her personal anniversaries with meticulous care. Only when her mother insisted that Ida relied on telephone calls rather than on visits, or suggested that a woman ought to divide her time between her two daughters, was Ida conscious of a fierce reaction, so dark and oppressive that she refused to examine it.

No claim should be allowed to come before a mother's, or one who stood in place of a mother, Ida emphasized when, after dinner, a neighbor dropped in to seek advice about her service flag. Cecilia, Leidy, and Frank were playing parchesi in one corner of the living room, but Ida and the visitor, a Mrs. Lind, sat on the other side of the bridge lamp to get light for their knitting.

"It's my daughter-in-law." Little beads of perspiration dotted Mrs. Lind's forehead, under her gray pompadour, although Cecilia and Leidy wore sweaters, for the room was cool. Her daughter-in-law, Mrs. Lind panted, said that she had no right to display a service flag.

"I told her I had two sons in service, that they were my boys and always will be." Mrs. Lind choked indignantly. "She says they don't live with me and I got no right to put me a service flag with two stars on it in my front window!"

Ida twitched her khaki wool into position, inspected her small, neat stitches. She had to guard against pulling her work too tight. "Any mother with a boy in service can hang up a flag for him and wear a service pin," she said. "He'll never have but one mother."

That was what she had told her daughter-in-law, Mrs. Lind confirmed; but young wives, if they had their way, would pretend that men came into the world as orphans. "My boys worship the ground I walk on, if I do say it myself, but they're afraid to let their wives see it. If they come to see me, they got to make sneak visits."

The rattle of the dice caught her ear and she turned to inspect Cecilia. "You're married, aren't you? I didn't catch your name."

"Mrs. Silverstein."

"Silverstein? Oh." Mrs. Lind dropped a knitting needle and Cecilia restored it, before Leidy could scramble down from her chair.

"Thank you—thank you very much." Red-faced, confused, the visitor could not refrain from staring at Cecilia. "I'm sure you treat your mother-in-law right," she mumbled.

Her husband's mother had died years ago, Cecilia answered

She knew what Mrs. Lind was going to say next—it would be something about the way Jews treated their old people. Apparently everyone admired the devotion to kin which tradition ascribed to the Jewish race. Cecilia wondered whether any Jewish girl ever had mother-in-law trouble, concluded that human nature was probably stronger than tradition or creed.

"I certainly admire the Jews for the way they take care of their old people," Mrs. Lind said.

Cecilia wanted to laugh. If Tag had been with her his grin would have been too much for her resistance. They had joked about the cliches to which people clung when they discussed racial differences and Cecilia voted her favorite the statement that Catholics could do anything wrong they pleased, and "fix it up" in confession; but Tag insisted that his pet bromide was that the Jews always took care of their old people.

"If you were a Jew, Mrs. Lind, would your sons take care of you?" asked Leidy with the disconcerting logic of the very young.

Mrs. Lind retorted sharply that she needed no help from her sons. As a matter of fact, she confided in a lower tone to Ida, part of the trouble with this daughter-in-law was because she had refused to have the girl live with her. "She thought while my son was in the service she could move right in and have me look after her baby and no expense whatever."

Her daughter-in-law had eighty a month, as regular as the sun rose and set, Mrs. Lind declared, and of course that meant that she herself lost her government check. Frank couldn't pay his wife and his mother, too, and many a mother was actually suffering because hussies were marrying men right and left for what they could get out of them.

"I should think you'd like to have your son's wife live with you," Leidy suggested, quite as if she had a place in the discussion. "If she lived with you, you'd need only one service flag and you wouldn't have to quarrel about whose it was."

But Ida said that Leidy ought to be in bed and Mrs. Lind remembered that she had put some clothes to soak and if Ida and Mrs. Goldberg—Oh, Mrs. Silverstein, of course—would excuse her, she'd run right home.

"I know exactly how you feel," Molly Cotter assured Cecilia a day or two later when they met unexpectedly on the hospital steps.

Cecilia had spent the afternoon with her grandmother. Molly, a Nurses' Aide, had been assigned to four hours' duty in the blood bank. Last week, she confided, she had washed dishes at City Hospital for three hours straight.

A broad stone coping encircled All Souls and afforded a natural seat for hospital visitors. Molly drew Cecilia to a sunny spot flanked by two iron urns from which trailed the dead tendrils of ivy plants. She had been planning to call on Dora Ferris for months, Molly apologized. "But even though I don't go to business as she does, I never have a minute to spare."

Like her sister Ida, Molly Cotter loved to talk, but her interests were those of the born housewife. She had never earned a cent in her life, but she prided herself on being a far better manager than married women who worked and had no more to show for the two salaries than she and her Charlie, with his one envelope. Ida had kept them informed about Cecilia's grandmother, Molly said; she wanted Cecilia to know that anyone who thought there was but one answer to the problem was crazy.

"It isn't simply a question of whether your place is with your grandmother or your husband." Molly had a high, nervous voice with very little breath control and she sounded perpetually rushed. She could understand that Cecilia's grandmother took the place of her mother, and any woman pulled two ways, between her mother and her husband, had her sympathy, Molly said.

"Why, I've been torn to pieces for years and no one can see it." The words tumbled from Molly's mouth, her heels drummed against the stone wall. "There have been times when I thought I'd go out of my mind, trying to plan how to placate Mother and Charlie, both."

Cecilia regarded her with astonishment. Molly was middle-aged, she had grown children, and she expected, so Ida inferred, to be a grandmother in the fall. If, in all the years that she had been married, Molly had not succeeded in reconciling her duty to her mother and her husband, did that mean there was no solution, at least none that satisfied one's conscience?

Cecilia's troubled eyes looked out across the hospital lawn faintly green with the first tints of spring. "But your mother and husband are both here," she reminded Molly. "I can't decide whether to stay North with Grandmother, or go South to Tag. In my heart I know Tag comes first."

"I suppose the trouble is we're not willing to run the risk of suffering later remorse." Molly's fingers snapped and unsnapped the catch of her purse. "We're trying to save ourselves pain. Men say to hell with duty and they get through life with a lot less wear and tear than we do."

If it were her children, Cecilia probed, hesitated. "Suppose your children and your mother made conflicting demands upon you, Cousin Molly?"

"You would think of that." Molly grimaced. "Let's walk. I'm atrophying, sitting on this stone."

Cecilia carried the question in her mind home to Tobias, whom she found sunk in his favorite chair, intent on a crossword puzzle.

"Grandfather, why do you suppose Cousin Charlie and Aunt Annabel don't get along well together? It's so hard on Cousin

Molly to have to be the buffer between her mother and her husband." Cecilia gazed hopefully at the long, thin old gentleman who had lived so long he ought to have solved life's puzzles, too.

Tobias grunted. "Uh-huh."

"I suppose a psychologist could explain it."

He was no psychologist, Tobias pointed out. Personally, he thought a lot of people who ran to a psychologist were just plain dotty and could save themselves time if they ran up to the State Hospital instead. "It doesn't take a psychologist to recognize jealousy, I hope. It's a run of the mill failing."

"You mean Cousin Charlie is jealous?"

Tobias nodded. A seven-letter word meaning green-eyed, he amplified. "Charlie Cotter and my sister Annabel are jealous of each other. Always have been. Each wants to be first with Molly."

"Why, that's a triangle!" Cecilia's naïve astonishment suggested a puzzle solver unprepared for the solution. She had read of triangles in love stories, she faltered, but this was different.

Her grandfather snorted. There were love stories and love stories, he said. "That reminds me of a story I heard this morning. The drugstore clerk told me. Seems there was one of his customers, a Jew, tangled with the OPA." Tobias checked himself, glanced up furtively from his puzzle. "I forgot," he apologized.

"It's all right," Cecilia assured him. "Go on."

"Well, the clerk's a Jew himself and he told it," Tobias offered in extenuation. "This Jew customer had to go before the board for some kind of a hearing and he stopped in the drugstore to tell his friend, the clerk, about it.

" 'Sam, you know what they got down to the OPA?' he says, mad enough to bite nails. 'Jews, all Jews. Nothing but Jews.'

"Seems another customer overheard and he horns in to say,

'Why, Mr. Levy, you're Jewish yourself, aren't you?' And the first man says, 'That may be, but there are Jews *and* Jews.' "

Cecilia laughed, moving behind her grandfather's chair to look over his shoulder. "Tag says there are plenty of Jews he dislikes intensely. But not because they're Jews. He says we're not supposed to like everyone, but when he makes an enemy his reasons aren't based on race."

"How's Tag get along with folks?" Tobias rubbed out a word.

He was an angel, Cecilia maintained, he made friends wherever he went. All Tag had to do was to smile and people felt that they had known him all their lives. "Jorry Read—we shared the apartment with the Reads, you know—said she wouldn't want her husband to be as good-looking as Tag. Girls do make a play for him, of course, but I'm not jealous. Well, hardly ever."

She watched in silence for a few moments, while Tobias succumbed to temptation and looked up a word in his puzzle dictionary. The definitions, he muttered, drove any sane person crazy. The screwy idiots who designed the puzzles needed to have their heads examined.

Crossword puzzles were easy, compared to her puzzle, Cecilia reflected, resting her chin on the high, tufted back of the wing chair. Should she stay with her grandmother, or go back to Tag? No one seemed willing to make the decision for her; she supposed a mature adult would not ask anyone to. *Well, I'm not a mature adult,* Cecilia admitted, *and I'd love to be told what to do.*

Tobias put his left hand up to his shoulder and she slipped her smooth, narrow hand with its wedding band, into his.

"What's the doctor say about your grandmother now?"

Old Mrs. Warren's heart was bad, the doctor's verdict read; she might linger for a year, or die in her sleep any night. Cecilia had learned in the hours spent with her that old age did not guarantee peace. Her grandmother wanted to live with an intensity that surprised the nurses. They declared her limited strength continually frustrated her and that she exhausted herself in rages directed at the feebleness of her failing body.

"Grandmother wants me to stay and go with her to Atlantic City next week," Cecilia sighed. "Doctor Ambrose believes she'll be well enough to make the trip and that the change will be good for her. I'd planned to go back to South Carolina as soon as she could leave the hospital."

Yes, she had written to Tag, but he had told her to do as she thought best. "Grandfather, Tag says I owe more to Grandmother than if she were my own mother. Tag says parents have a responsibility toward their children that grandparents do not share." Tag had told her, Cecilia said, that whatever her grandmother had done for her had been a double sacrifice, a free-will offering that imposed a heavy obligation on the recipient.

"Tag feels that ingratitude is the unpardonable sin," Cecilia finished.

Tag's steadfast, dark face rose before her, his dear grave eyes untroubled by doubt. Love in any guise was so precious to Tag! He forgave the cruelties, the stupidities, the mistakes committed in its name and believed with passionate sincerity that its gold always outweighed the dross.

"Never stop telling Tag that you love him," Naomi O'Neill, his cousin, had written Cecilia in one of her infrequent letters. "He needs to hear it every day. He has such a hunger for love, and no one has ever given him enough since his mother died."

It was settled that Cecilia would accompany her grandmother to Atlantic City. Frank Ferris's wife, Ida, agreed to go in the capacity of nurse. She had hesitated to take a week off, she said, although entitled to a vacation with pay—she couldn't afford a trip. By the time her group insurance, social security taxes, bond payments, hospitalization, and Christmas club was taken out, her "take-home-money" as Ida called the residue, left her next to nothing to spend. Her household expenses mounted steadily, she complained, in spite of her efforts to do the marketing herself.

"It will be a rest for me to go down to the shore and get a few sun baths," she assured Cecilia. Mrs. Warren wasn't a difficult case, Ida said competently, the care of her would be like play, compared to the work at the plant. She disposed of Frank and Leidy with the statement that they would probably kill themselves with frankfurters and ice cream, but that she did not intend to worry about them. The only way a wife and mother could get a vacation was to forget her family cares.

The train trip sorely tried the invalid's nerves, for old Mrs. Warren had not been prepared for the discomforts of wartime travel. She had relied on her luxurious car and chauffeur through the years for journeys of this sort; if for any reason the automobile had not been available, there had been the "parlor car" with its trained, polite porters, its privacy and comparative freedom from dirt.

Cecilia and Ida did what they could for her, supplied her with pillows, fed her at intervals from the lunch box Quilty had thoughtfully provided, forebore to whisper when she slept. It was difficult to settle her long enough for her to enjoy a doze, since when they had her in the seat next to the window, the baggage racks above her head made her nervous; but when she found herself in an aisle seat, children dashed against her knees, apologetic service men dripped water on her from their paper cups, and each influx of new passengers barricaded her with their suitcases and grips.

"She gets herself so worked up over things like that girl trying to smoke a cigarette before the conductor catches her, that a *year* in Atlantic City won't put her on her feet," Ida observed in a rare interval when her patient scanned the headlines of an afternoon paper. "I guess she's the type that always takes everything hard."

Tag would say that it was hardening of the arteries that made old people fretful, that no matter how unreasonable they might be, they deserved patience and consideration. Once at the movies in South Carolina, Cecilia remembered, an old lady in the row with them had changed her seat four or five times, always forcing the entire row to rise to let her pass. Some of the other patrons had finally remonstrated, but when the usher interfered, Tag had upheld the fidgety old soul. She was only trying to find a seat from which she could see, Tag had said; her dimming eyesight entitled her to the sympathy of the lucky ones with good vision.

When the bustle that signified the journey's end began to sweep the car, Ida glanced a little anxiously at Cecilia. Better let the crowd and their luggage get out of the way before they attempted to leave the train, Ida suggested. "Your grandmother wants you to register for all of us at the hotel," she added.

Old Mrs. Warren's hands were busy with her hair and veil. The diamonds flashed as she fastened wisps of gray hair with tiny, invisible silvered pins. "Our reservations are in the name of Warren," she said.

Cecilia bent above her to help adjust the black and white dotted veil—Grandmother still was anxious to look her best.

"You always do take rooms in your name." Cecilia wondered a little at the mention of an established custom.

"I mean you must register yourself under the name of Warren—your old name." It was dreadful, the way people crowded into the aisle as if they could all get off first, old Mrs. Warren scolded.

She didn't understand, Cecilia protested. What did her grandmother mean? How could she sign herself "Cecilia Warren" now?

Ida jerked Cecilia's sleeve and hissed into her ear. "For heaven's sake, don't upset her! She's dead tired and likely to collapse and be carted off to the hospital, instead of the hotel. Humor her, just until I can get her into bed."

"I should think you might be a little more perceptive, Cecilia." The fretful, tired voice dropped at the end of each sentence as if the effort to speak demanded too much of old Mrs. Warren's breath. "You know the King's Arms is restricted. It always has been. That's why we've gone there for years."

Restricted. The word hit Cecilia like a blow in the face. *Why, I'm not Jewish!* She felt the blood rush to her temples and hot tears burned her eyes. She was Cecilia Warren, the same Cecilia Warren who had been a guest at the King's Arms since a child, with her parents, later in her grandmother's care. "They know me," she argued stupidly. "They've had the same clerk for years."

Old Mrs. Warren took a fresh handkerchief from her purse, dabbed at her lips. "It's your name," she whispered as one guarding a shameful secret. "It would be embarrassing if anyone saw Silverstein on the register."

Ida, lifting down a suitcase, said over her shoulder, "Once they let one in, they can't keep the rest out. You can't blame the management."

As Cecilia Warren Silverstein she couldn't stay at the King's Arms. If her beautiful, tall, strong Tag had been with her, they would both be turned away. So this was what the hateful word "Restricted" meant. And she heard it all her life, taken it for granted and, God forgive her, had never questioned its implications.

The crowd still jostled in the aisle, though the train had

stopped. Baggage piled in the vestibules momentarily dammed the human stream. Cecilia, hopeful that the woman's room had not yet been locked, muttered that she must wash her hands. Fortunately the door yielded to her touch and she found herself alone in the stuffy little room littered with crumpled, soiled towels, empty pasteboard lunch boxes, and battered paper cups.

"I'll take the next train back!" Cecilia stormed to the crimson-cheeked, hot-eyed girl who stared miserably at her from the mirror over the wash-basin. "I won't go any place where Tag couldn't go. Or where I have to pretend I'm not married."

The door opened and Ida slipped in. The porter was squawking, she warned, he wanted to lock up. "I told your grandmother I'd ask you to hurry."

"I'm taking the next train back. Then I'll pack up my clothes and go home to Tag." Cecilia began to powder over the tear streaks. "I ought to have gone home long ago."

Ida sat down on the green velvet sofa. "Good Lord, this feels as though they'd given the padding to the scrap drive and kept the metal," she groaned. "Don't be a mule, Ceil. You can't leave me alone with your grandmother. She's likely to die on my hands."

The faucet shuddered as Cecilia let water run into the basin. "I don't believe she's sick at all. She just wants to keep me and Tag apart." She had read about old people who used illness as a club over their families, in order to have their own way, Cecilia related childishly.

"Well, if you mean your grandmother is faking, she isn't." Ida was blunt. "She has a heart that may give out any moment. Her blood pressure's high and she has two or three degenerative diseases in an advance stage. That's enough for any one woman to worry about. You bring on a quarrel with her and she'll pass out—the least excitement can carry her off. Do you want that on your conscience?"

Cecilia dried her hands slowly. In the full-length mirror set in the door frame she saw her tall, young figure, her favorite black suit topped by the handsome stone marten skins her grandmother had given her because, old Mrs. Warren had said, tall women could wear neck furs.

"It isn't legal." Cecilia's lips trembled. "I mean it's against the law to restrict hotels open to the public."

Ida shrugged. "As far as I'm concerned laws only confuse the issue. What you have to cope with are the facts. Suppose you made a fuss, evoked the law and the hotel took you in: would you be comfortable when you got the cold shoulder from the other guests? Having the law on your side isn't worth two damns, unless you have public opinion rooting for you, too."

Someone knocked, rattled the door handle. "Ladies, we're in the station. Everybody got to get off here," the porter called.

"Come on—your grandmother will be having a stroke." Ida linked her arm in Cecilia's, drew her out into the car, nearly empty now.

Old Mrs. Warren was standing, clutching the back of her seat for support, her anxious eyes peering up and down the aisle. When she saw Cecilia, her face broke into a smile, relieved and sweet.

"You'll have to register." Cecilia spoke to Ida in a fierce undertone. "I won't sign any name except my own. It'll be bad enough to be living a lie."

Ida agreed to register. Then she proceeded to give her entire attention to getting her patient out of the car and into a taxi, where old Mrs. Warren dozed exhaustedly until they reached the hotel. A wheel chair was brought to the curb and in this the weary invalid rode to the lobby where Cecilia waited with her while Ida registered for all three. That accomplished, they were free to enter the elevator which carried them to the eleventh floor and their two comfortable rooms.

When she had old Mrs. Warren luxuriously arranged in bed—from which she could have heard the breakers pounding on the beach, had she not gone to sleep almost before her white head touched the pillow—Ida confessed that she had been worried.

"She was in a bad way on the train—her pulse was terribly slow for a time. I think now she must have been fretting all the way down about how you were going to take this hotel business."

Cecilia was registered as Mrs. C. C. Warren, Ida revealed, to avoid any possible comment about her wedding ring. It would be asking a little too much to expect Cecilia to remove her ring and become Miss Warren again, Ida said. There was no reason why Cecilia should feel at all uneasy, or make any fuss. "We haven't done anything dishonest. You're not going under false pretenses, either—you're not Jewish, if your married name is. And Warren is your own name, you're entitled to use it. In fact it's more yours than your married name, for you inherited it."

Her husband, Cecilia suggested mildly, when she could insert a word, would be apt to write to her, even at Atlantic City, and to use her married name.

"Good Lord, I never thought of that!" Ida wailed. "Well—we'll have to take the chance. Most likely he'll send his letters in care of your grandmother and that will be a help."

Early April in Atlantic City pleased old Mrs. Warren. The sunshine was not sufficiently powerful to burn her fine skin, yet permitted her to spend hours baking in its beneficial rays. Another advantage, she pointed out, was that it was still too chilly for bathing, so that spring visitors were spared the exhibits furnished later in the season by practically naked young women posed on the beach.

She could walk only short distances and usually Cecilia or Ida wheeled her in a roller chair. The boardwalk, so crowded with uniformed men, interested the invalid and she liked to knit and watch them as they passed. Already there were large numbers of convalescents, men recovering from wounds or illness, who walked slowly and whose tanned faces turned toward the sea when they passed civilians who nudged one another and stared.

Cecilia and her grandmother had settled themselves on the sunny, protected side of one of the piers on a bright but windy morning, when three sailors took possession of the bench next to theirs. They looked seventeen or eighteen, but Cecilia noted their foreign service bars. How they kept their caps glued to the back of their heads in such a strong wind mystified her, but she had never seen a sailor lose his white headpiece.

Old Mrs. Warren, who felt that her seventy-nine years entitled her to comment on whatever interested her, asked Cecilia if it was a mandolin that the short, blond boy carried.

"Music annoy you?" The lad, the center of the trio, included both women in his impartial smile.

They shook their heads, urged him to play. The pier swayed as a heavy breaker crashed against the pilings. Between the floor boards' cracks Cecilia glimpsed the green, foaming water racing toward the sand.

The mandolin player alternated "jive" with "classical," obedient to the requests of his friends whose musical tastes seemed to have as little chance as the East and West of meeting on common ground. But when the musician interpolated numbers to please himself, he fingered Russian sea songs as if their haunting theme, melodious and sad, expressed the hidden emotions in his heart. He stayed after his two companions strolled on in search of hot dogs and he seemed scarcely to know that they had gone. Over and over he picked out the Russian songs, head bent, eyes closed, absorbed in self-communion.

"What is that he keeps playing?" old Mrs. Warren demanded in a loud whisper.

Cecilia replied that it was something Russian, probably a folk song. "He must have learned it from real Russians. I wonder where."

The sailor overheard, half turned, smiling. "Like it?"

"Very much." Cecilia decided when he smiled that he couldn't be seventeen. Perhaps twelve.

Old Mrs. Warren surveyed him through her gold-rimmed glasses. "Where did you learn Russian songs? My granddaughter says they're Russian."

"They are. Sorry I can't sing them."

He had, alas, no voice at all. With the other two he had hummed the words of some of the song hits they had called for, but he had been dolefully and systematically squeaky.

"Have you been in Russia?" Old Mrs. Warren looked at the sailor as she might have looked at a geographical globe.

He evaded her scrutiny, glanced at Cecilia.

"Grandmother, they're not supposed to talk about where they've been. But one can't disguise music, can he?" Cecilia thought, *I hope a beautiful Russian girl taught him the songs on a moonlit river.*

"Russia is a terrible country," said old Mrs. Warren, beginning to knit again. "Ida and I were talking about it the other day. You can't trust a word those people say."

Cecilia, startled and distressed, blushed, but the sailor showed his handsome teeth in a wide grin.

"You and my grandmother ought to get together, ma'am," he suggested. "I take it you've never been to Russia, just don't like it on general principles. Same way with my grandmother and the Catholic Church. She's never been inside one, but she says it's simply scandalous, the goings on that take place. My girl's a Catholic and I tell her one religion is as queer as another," the boy finished happily. "I'm broad-minded."

Cecilia began to laugh. The contrast between her grandmother's horrified face and the kindly, tolerant expression of the sailor, evidently vastly pleased with himself as a liberal thinker, was too much for her self-control. She laughed until she caught her breath in deep, painful gasps and her grandmother, alarmed, begged her to keep still.

Ida, coming to tell them it was lunchtime, said sharply that when folks got hysterical it was time to stop.

"I could hear you from the boardwalk," Ida said in disapproval. "At first I thought it sounded as if you were crying."

Chapter Twelve

"IN the movies," Ida Ferris said with some bitterness. "your father would have an old friend turn up with a fortune and marry my mother and everyone would be happy."

"Speak for yourself, Priscilla," advised Frank.

Well it was necessary that she did, Ida retorted. As it was now she was going completely out of her mind. No one knew what she was enduring. "Eat your dinner and stop mooning," she admonished Leidy and was immediately vexed with herself. All the psychology books favored ignoring a child indifferent to food.

"I'm not mooning," her daughter informed her with dignity. "I'm deciding which dessert I'd have, if this was a restaurant."

Frank reminded her that it wasn't a restaurant, but something like a cafeteria. "Home style," he added. "That means you are to help with the dishes."

Ida surveyed them with disfavor. Here she had returned from Atlantic City rested in some ways, in others more tired than when she had gone away. But her family, not only Frank and Leidy, but her mother and her sister Molly and above all Molly's husband, Charlie, chirped insistently that her lovely vacation must have done her a world of good.

"I told Cecil while we were at the shore that it was probably a mistake for me to take any time off from the plant." Ida salted her potato for the third time. She took little interest in her food and ate almost mechanically. "I had a premonition that if I went away, I'd be expected to do more when I came back."

Frank sighed. "The one week your mother is to be here won't kill us."

It was all very well for him to say "us," Ida scolded; a husband used the plural when he knew the responsibility would devolve upon the wife. "I'd like to know what you or Leidy do when Mother's here. You tinker down cellar and Leidy stays up in the attic and reads."

That was so she and her mother might visit together, Frank explained; presumably they had confidences to exchange, secrets meant only for each other's ears. Ida sniffed at this bit of rationalization and turned to take the salad from the buffet within arm's reach. It was, she told the two spectators, a combination salad and dessert.

"Ceil told me how to make it. That girl she shared the apartment with in Columbia taught her. I wonder if anyone's heard from Ceil."

"She won't like it in Texas," Frank predicted. "Hot and dry around Fort Sam Houston. Too bad they transferred Tag."

Ceil was so thin the heat wouldn't bother her, Ida declared, placing a quivering mound of gelatine and lettuce in front of Frank. Old Mrs. Warren was the one who dreaded the coming summer. The doctor had advised her to go to a quiet country place, far from the confusion of the city and preferably some distance from a town.

"She doesn't want to go because with gas so scarce, she may not be able to persuade the sanitarium people to drive her to church. It's really a rest home—no radios, no visitors, no contacts with the outside world." Old Mrs. Warren, Ida said, had been positive that she could get as good care and as complete seclusion in one of the Catholic retreats.

"That's the trouble with the Catholics," Ida observed. "They won't mingle. But at least they follow a religion and that's more than you can say for Fern Eustice's boy friend. Sarah would rather have a Catholic than an atheist in the family—that is, I think she would."

Leidy chewed a lettuce leaf to shreds, remembering the talk on good teeth in the hygiene period that afternoon. "Ida, I think I ought to do something about my immortal soul," she said, still chewing.

"Your what?" Her startled father dropped his fork.

But Ida's lips folded in a thin line. "I suppose your friend Gertie has been worrying about your immortal soul?"

The bewilderment of Leidy answered the question. Gertie Kendall had never mentioned her soul. "Why would she worry about my immortal soul, Ida?"

"I'm sure I don't know," Ida admitted, "except that I'm always expecting her to try to convert you. I don't know why you can't pick out a child of your own faith to have as your best friend."

Leidy pondered. "What is my own faith?"

"How did you happen to hear about your immortal soul?" her father interposed with real curiosity.

She had just heard of it, Leidy answered vaguely.

Ida said that there was nothing to laugh at and that things had come to a pretty pass if a child didn't know she was a Protestant. "Your Grandmother Pinn would be horrified to hear you talk. She's a very religious woman."

"I'd rather be a Catholic or a Jew or an Episcopalian," Leidy announced. "They get excused from school for religious instruction. I never get any."

She didn't need any, Ida returned, pouring Frank's coffee. "I don't believe in any one creed, nor does your father. Plenty of very good people never see the inside of a church. They worship God in the great outdoors."

"Especially the golf links," Frank amplified.

Then would it be all right if she went to church with Gertie

Kendall? Leidy asked. And when her mother rebuked her with a sharp negative, the child protested that she didn't want to worship God in the great outdoors. "I like an organ and people singing," she said.

Ida put down the cream pitcher with a thud. The cream got thinner every day, she complained; it would be more honest in the government to label everything grade B milk and let it go at that. "As if I didn't have enough trouble, with your grandmother coming to spend a week, you have to worry me about this church business," she accused Leidy.

Frank pushed his plate aside, felt in his pocket for cigarettes. Ida asked for one and he lighted it for her. She couldn't smoke when her mother was around, not without a fuss, Ida murmured, so she might as well enjoy the time left before the visit.

"There's the church on the corner of the next block," Frank suggested. "What—er—make is that? Why couldn't Leidy go there to Sunday school or something?"

The church was Baptist, Ida thought. "But I don't want her going to any of the neighborhood churches, Frank. You know exactly what it will mean. The minister will call and the church leaders will call and they'll expect us to come to church. Then there'll be all kinds of meetings and discussions for parents and I simply haven't the time. If you want to get into that sort of thing, all right."

"Well, where do want her to go?" Frank reflected uneasily that they ought to settle the issue when Leidy wasn't around.

Any church that wasn't Jewish or Catholic, or too near home, would be all right, Ida assured him. Leidy didn't walk nearly enough, it would do her good to get out on Sunday and walk to Sunday school or church. Later Ida confided to Frank that she didn't expect Leidy's interest in her soul to last very long. Most children, especially girls, were apt to be strongly religious for brief periods, but usually they outgrew piousness, although of course one could never tell.

"A woman worker at the plant told me the only thing you can count on in your children is their perversity," Ida mourned. "Her children grew up in church and Sunday school, she said, and as soon as they were on their own they never put foot in a church again. But her brother didn't even have his kids baptized, they never saw inside a church until they married—and now they are all devout church members."

According to that reasoning, Jim Kotoski must have had an overdose of religion in his childhood, Frank commented. "Funny, but when you hear a fellow's an atheist, you don't feel that you'd hanker to have him for a friend." Not, Frank amended hastily, that he was one to choose his friends among the saintly and devout.

Tobias Ferris assumed that he fulfilled his duty to his immortal soul by attending church twice a year, at Christmas and at Easter. He had behaved well, he reported to his sister, Annabel Pinn, when he went to call upon her in Melon, the day after Easter. She was to spend the week with Ida while the Cotters paid a brief visit to their married daughter in Pittsburgh.

Tobias shrewdly surmised that Annabel might be lonely since, breakfast over, there would be no one left in the house to bear her company. Ordinarily Leidy would have no school the week following Easter, but the suburban schools had closed for a week in the winter to conserve fuel; that had canceled the customary spring vacation. Tobias maintained the Easter spirit by taking as gifts a dozen eggs dyed by Quilty and a ginger cake with the boiled icing that "Ol' Miz' Pinn doted upon," Quilty said.

The house depressed her, Annabel confided when she had seated Tobias in Frank's chair in the living room. It was like a ghost-house, with the rooms in order and no one to speak to. Ida had finally consented to give Mrs. Holdfast the week off, so that Annabel remained quite alone during the day, except for the noon period when Leidy rushed in to eat and rushed out again in haste to return to school.

Tobias thought that the house would depress him, too, if he spent much time there. If Leidy had been a boy she might have upset the appalling neatness of the rooms, but perhaps Ida would have been too much, even for a son. Long ago Tobias had decided that her furnishings meant nothing to Ida, that they represented not her taste, but the hybrid decorative theories of magazines and department stores. She was so damn efficient that ready-made effects contented her.

"I'm used to having people coming in," Annabel was saying. "Not that so many come at Molly's, but there is usually someone. When I had my own home, I always had company. You know, Tobias, I think people were kinder then, than they are now."

He repeated, "Kinder?" and began to fill his pipe from the tobacco pouch he carried.

"Everyone had more time." Annabel's voice was wistful. "Maybe it only seemed that way, but I feel we were all kinder. And I'm sure women were happier."

That was only because she had her home, her husband and children, she was young and strong, Tobias reminded her. "Leastways, I suppose you're thinking of your early married years. And don't forget, Annabel, when life tastes bitter to you now, that you were young in peacetime. So was I. We got that to be thankful for."

Annabel put up a hand to her white hair, tucked in a fringe of net. "My husband didn't have to go to war, like Cecil's husband, and Ginger's, but I lost three children between Molly and

Ida, Tobias. It's a good thing a girl can't see ahead when she marries."

"We all pay a high price to be young," Tobias said. "At that the kids are paying more than we did. Yet when they're seventy-eight, like me, I suppose they'll decide it was worth it."

She didn't consider it worth while living to be seventy-five, Annabel stated. The lace edging she was crocheting to edge a baby dress for her expected great-grandchild, fell to her lap. "Tobias, what ails my girls? We took care of our parents—we never had much money, but we didn't make a hardship of it. Now I'm a burden on my two children and what can I do?"

The set-up was wrong, Tobias diagnosed, she ought to have her own home. "Even one room, Annabel. Independence is sweet."

Annabel said, "You don't live alone."

"Well, then, maybe you ought to get yourself an old-maid daughter," Tobias conceded reasonably. He and Dora didn't always hit it off together, he owned, but in the main they got along. "She'll be living alone some day, I suppose. I can't imagine her moving in with Sarah—or Frank."

Old maids used to be a worry to their folks, he went on; they had no future except to do the chores in their married brothers' and sisters' home. "You think that people aren't as kind as they used to be, Annabel, but you'll have to admit the old maid finds it a better world."

Dora would have been much happier, had she married, Annabel corrected him. "I think Sarah is better off than Dora, even if Lion is such a cross to her. She has her children." Annabel picked up her crochet work. "She'll have grandchildren, too. When does Ginger expect her baby?"

Tobias believed sometime "within the year." He had always thought nine months was the customary waiting period, he grumbled, but Ginger had been discussing her pregnancy for two years. Maybe more. There was something to be said for the Victorian conventions which kept a woman's mouth shut almost to the day of the baby's birth. "Ginger's always telling me birth is a perfectly natural function, but there are plenty of natural functions she'd shriek at if I sat down to discuss 'em with her."

"That will do," said Annabel uneasily. "It's the fashion just now to tell about a baby months in advance. The movie stars announce it practically the day after—" She checked herself, refused to notice Tobias' grin.

"My great-grandchild will have a good American name and that's something to be thankful for." She changed the subject more swiftly than coherently. It was terrible, she declared, to see names like Silverstein and Kotoski replacing substantial names like Warren and Eustice. "Your granddaughters don't care for family tradition, do they, Tobias?"

Fern, Sarah's daughter, wasn't married to her Kotoski beau yet, Tobias objected. As for Cecil, she had a fine husband and one who loved her devotedly. "What in time does Tag's name matter, when he is the salt of the earth?"

"Well, but people who don't know he is the salt of the earth assume she's married to an ordinary Jew. You know yourself that some of them are pretty dreadful." Annabel glanced at the clock, for she was to put the lamb stew on over a low flame at three o'clock. You'd think she had never cooked a meal in her life, she sniffed, the directions Ida left for her.

"I suppose if Tag's name had been Lee, people who heard it for the first time would assume she had married into the F.F.V.," Tobias contended stubbornly. "Yet there's a Chinese laundryman two blocks from us, named Lee."

People couldn't help their reactions, Annabel argued; there were established associations with certain names. "For instance, Kotoski doesn't suggest a sound American background, does it? Neither does Silverstein."

"The lousy part of all this is that there's some truth in your ramblings." Tobias stretched his long legs. "We go by labels. But you'd think we'd forget them when the kids step out in uniforms. Only we don't. Lots of damn fools think of Tag as a Jew first and a soldier second."

The clock hands pointed to three. She hated silly electric clocks, Annabel said. There wasn't a clock in Ida's house that struck the hours. Years ago, when one couldn't sleep at night, one could listen to the clocks striking slowly and clearly, as the hours wore away. Clocks were like old friends, Annabel continued, getting to her feet stiffly; you learned to recognize their different tones.

"I expect the lamb will be tough." She pulled her mind back to the present. "Ida buys in a chain shop, and the butcher doesn't know anything about good meat." There was nothing like the old neighborhood butcher store, where the butcher knew each family and married daughters traded where their mothers had bought, Annabel said. "The Jews just ruined the butcher business. Mr. Morey, our old butcher, told me so. They don't care anything about the best meat; all they want is to make money. They forced the independent butchers out of business. There's hardly a Gentile butcher left, Mr. Morey says, and lots of men behind the cutting blocks don't know a decent piece of beef when they see it."

The telephone on Ida's desk rang, startling both old people. Annabel always fluttered through the simplest phone conversations, knocking books to the floor, interrupting the person at the other end, worrying lest she not hear or not be heard. Tobias, watching her, rapidly calculated that the telephone had been in use for some forty years of her life: it did seem that in forty years time one should become accustomed to a gadget like the phone.

"It was Ginger Eustice." Annabel hung up with obvious relief. "She's here in Melon—came out to see a girl friend who has a new baby. And she's going to drop in and see me for a few minutes."

Either Ginger had concluded her visit before she had expected to, or Fern, who was to pick her up in the car, had sent word she would be late, Annabel elaborated. "I never get things very straight on the phone. There's a fine lying-in hospital on Main Street and I take it Ginger's friend had her baby there."

A few moments later Ginger, very smart in a black and white checked dress and matching long coat, rang the doorbell. Surprised to see her grandfather, she kissed him dutifully, appeared pleased. She had taken a chance, when she called, on finding anyone at home. "I thought Mrs. Holdfast might let me wait in the hall—no one told me you were visiting Ida, Aunt Annabel."

The size she was, pattered Ginger, she couldn't just sit out on the curb and wait for Fern. "They turned me out at the hospital because the doctor came to examine Hortense. Something's wrong—she didn't have a normal birth."

"Nutmeg, I'm an old man and I can't endure any more lectures on obstetrics," Tobias warned. "Besides, I should think you'd better fix your mind on more cheerful matters."

There were no cheerful matters, Ginger retorted, gazing in obvious astonishment at the glass of milk Annabel presented to her. On the same plate was a cupcake. Sponge cake, Annabel said, and not rich enough to hurt her.

"Well, I'd rather have a cocktail, but I suppose the milk is for Junior," Ginger grinned. "I hope you're both admiring my new outfit. Each part, dress and coat, cost thirty-nine, ninety-five and the advertisement promised no one would ever know I was expecting a baby. Bunk!" Ginger bit into the cake. "When you get toward the eighth month there isn't a maternity dress made that can help you. I look like a hillside and Hoke agrees with me."

Tobias and Annabel chorused together, "When did he have a furlough?"

"He didn't. But Fern took snaps of me, side view, and I sent them to him."

Annabel glanced at Tobias.

"What do you hear from Cecil?" Ginger asked. "I'll bet she's pregnant." She looked hopefully at her grandfather.

Cecilia was in Texas with Tag, Tobias reported, he had heard from her a day or two ago. She was worried now, lest Tag be shipped across.

"Well, plenty of women's husbands have gone over," Ginger commented. "I should think he'd be anxious to go. On account of being Jewish."

She looked ill, Tobias decided, she was probably worried about her own man. "You're a little tuckered out, Nutmeg?" he suggested. "Why don't you lie down on the couch to wait for Fern?"

"The baby kicks just as much when I'm lying down as when I'm up," Ginger said. "I wonder if Ceil *will* have a baby! I'd be afraid it would look and act Jewish. Even if Tag's mother was a Gentile."

"How do you suppose she came to marry his father?" Annabel speculated.

It was just barely possible that she fell in love with the man, Tobias pointed out. "I can't imagine a mixed marriage entered into for any other reason, can you? God knows staying married is difficult enough when a couple has everything in their favor. Toss in differences in race or religion and you got a ticklish proposition calling for patience and love."

Ginger squealed, "Why, Grandpa!" but a horn sounded outside and through the front window they saw Fern seated in a small car at the curb.

"It's Mabel's car. She won't let Fern drive her Kotoski around in it, but she let's us use it now and then and we pay her in different ways." Ginger frantically powdered her nose. "I hope there's gas in the tank when I have to go to the hospital," she said. "Papa will undoubtedly be drunk and we may not be able to get a taxi. I'll be all right, Grandfather—you don't have to take me to the car."

But when he insisted on accompanying her to the curb, she confessed that she was grateful for his hand under her arm. "I can't see my feet and I'm in mortal horror of missing a step or something," she told him. "Boy, this is the last baby I'm going to have for a long time."

By four o'clock the fragrance of simmering lamb filled the house, and Leidy had not returned from school. She was supposed to come directly home and report before she went out to play, Annabel admitted. But the temptation to go home with some classmate often proved too strong, especially if the hostess lived on the other side of town.

"Ida ought to stay home and take care of the child." Annabel shaded her eyes with her hand for she had followed Tobias to the door and the sun in the west was still high.

If he ran into Leidy on his way to the bus he'd send her home, Tobias promised, remembering that his own children had furnished a similar problem in their school days. Why should kids be expected to voluntarily dash from one form of discipline back to another, as if attached to overhead wires in a neat groove?

"... juvenile delinquency," Annabel said. "You read about it in the papers every day."

Tobias guessed she had made some reference to the stories prevalent about unsupervised children and he tried to set her fears at rest by confiding Leidy's expressed interest in her immortal soul. "She'll go to church with you, Annabel. The only person in this heathen household who will, if I am not mistaken."

"Episcopal." Apparently Annabel referred to the church attended by her grandchild. "I can't get up and down on my lame knees, and anyway they're altogether too much like the Catholics."

She had nothing against the Catholics, she assured her brother when he reminded her that Cecilia was a devout communicant, it was only that she preferred her own church. "Besides, Tobias Ferris, land knows you made enough fuss when Lucy wanted to marry Post Warren. All you had against him, that I ever heard, was his religion."

Tobias let her have the last word and started his walk to the bus, indifferent to schedules and determined to enjoy the April sunshine. It seemed strange to him now that he and Jennie, his wife, could have been so shocked at the idea of their daughter marrying a Catholic. When he tried to reconstruct their objections they persistently eluded him, remaining shadows without form in the recesses of his tired old brain.

Dora had had a Catholic beau, too—funny, he hadn't thought of that for years. He couldn't even recall the fellow's name, but he didn't doubt that Dora remembered it. The boy—he had been young and shy—had called at the house a few times and Dora had gone once to church with him. With Lucy's love affair upsetting the entire family connection, Tobias had been in no mood to be sympathetic toward the prospect of a second Catholic son-in-law. He had delivered an ultimatum—either Dora dismissed this suitor or he, her father, would send him packing.

She had broken with the lad and Tobias had, he recollected now, been illogically disappointed in her submission and the apparently limp acquiescence of the young man. A girl was well rid of such a weakling, Tobias had assured himself.

He sat on the steps of the Melon National Bank to wait for the bus. Drat Annabel, her chatter had started him meditating about his children and he liked to feel that they were outside his mind as well as outside his life. They were settled, even Dora who presumably would never marry now. It annoyed Tobias to discover that he wished these adult children were happier. Sarah had led a miserable life, really—Lionel had humiliated her pride for years. Frank's marriage—well, he adored his daughter, but it would have been more natural if he could have adored his wife. And Dora—Tobias decided that he knew little about Dora, but he wondered if a single woman felt herself cheated, whether or not she had succeeded in disciplining her heart. Happiness was a childish word, Tobias conceded, his framework creaking as he rose, for the bus was now in sight. He thought of his fourth child, the dead Lucy, and with her memory, as always now, came the lovely face of Cecilia.

He had said something like that to her, taking her to the train when she left to join her husband in Texas, and she had looked up at him with grave and beautiful eyes.

"But you let me grow up—I am twenty now—without knowing you," she had said.

He had muttered something about her being shut away in a convent school and she had laughed and asked him if he feared to face the nuns. He had laughed, too, but her teasing was uncomfortably close to the truth. The only time he had ever spoken to a nun in his life had been at the hospital the night Lucy died.

Although he had missed one bus, he expected to reach home by six, the dinner hour from which Quilty permitted no deviation. None of the passengers was prepared to endure a half-hour's delay with fortitude or calm when on the main boulevard, the vehicle broke down. The harassed driver explained as usual that it was the war. It was all very well to pass around the banana oil, a chorus muttered, but everyone knew the buses had been ready for the junk heap two years before the war.

"So what?" barked the driver in the democratic habit of give and take. "Can I get out and weld the rear axle, if it breaks? Maybe the bus was ready for the junk yard, so were some of you. But I notice you keep right on working."

They laughed, but as a crowded bus rushed past, the grumbling was renewed. Tobias, reluctant to lose his seat, became increasingly aware of the rank half-smoked cigar his seatmate held in a fat, soiled hand. The man's soft, heavy body took up more than half the space and overflowed into the aisle. He caught Tobias' glance and grunted.

"Rotten service," he said.

"Uh-huh."

Politics controlled the transportation system, the fat man stated. The head of the line was in cahoots with the city commission. "The whole town's run by Italians. That's what ails it."

"We got three Irishmen on the commission," Tobias objected.

They were figureheads, the fat one growled. You could spot the influence of the Italians in the city government, he said, by the gradual rot and decay of the various departments under their control. "Italians aren't constructive. They let things fall apart. Look at this neighborhood, for instance—why I remember when it used to be a fine residential section."

Seen from the bus the streets were dirty, the houses shabby, and the apathetic citizens who stared listlessly from the curb, appeared to lack ambition. "Maybe if they collected the garbage through here now and then it might help morale," Tobias submitted.

Well, the contract was let to an Italian, the fat man retorted. The guy collected his money regularly, but let the refuse go until the Board of Health prodded him.

"Nearly every house has a service flag," said Tobias, peering through the grimy window which he had not been able to open. "I can see two and three stars on some flags, just from here."

"Italians are lousy fighters," declared the fat man. "No guts."

Tobias yawned. "I would have said you're Italian yourself," he remarked. "But likely I'm a poor guesser."

His father was Greek, his mother Armenian, the other disclosed. "I'm a one hundred per cent American myself."

"Tell that to the bus driver," Tobias suggested, for he had intercepted a glance from the man slumped over the steering wheel. The driver stared straight ahead, but the flustered passenger belatedly read the name in the metal plate above the dashboard—A. Petrillo.

"Christ! Why didn't you tell me to pipe down?" he demanded, glowering at Tobias.

It was quarter of seven when Tobias finally let himself in at his front door. He moved cautiously and paused in the hall. From the kitchen came the sound of pots and pans striking against hard surfaces and a quick glance into the dining room showed him the table set with only one place.

Paris hurtled down the stairs on velvet feet and went to work to weave himself gracefully in and out between his idol's ankles. Tobias stooped and patted the cat absently. "Sounds like Quilty went early and Dora's expressing herself on the pots and pans," he whispered.

The swinging door flew back and Quilty fixed him with a stern eye. "You home, Mr. Ferris?"

Tobias admitted the indictment. "The bus broke down," he said. "Where's Miss Dora?"

Miss Dora had phoned she wouldn't be home for dinner, Quilty rejoined. That had been before Leidy came.

"Leidy!" Tobias gasped. "Why, she couldn't—that little kid?

She lives in Melon, you know. Besides, she's in school until three o'clock." He remembered that Annabel had been waiting for Leidy to return from school and hurriedly he asked where the child was now.

"She went home." Apparently Quilty saw nothing unusual in eight-year-old Leidy's bus travels. The children Quilty knew looked out for themselves at an early age and often took care of two or three younger by the time they had reached the ripe old age of seven.

Tobias let his dinner wait while he called Annabel. Yes, Leidy had reached home, she was all right and her father had refused to spank her. It was no wonder juvenile delinquency was such a problem, Annabel's thin old voice crackled on the wire. Parents let their children run wild.

"I must have passed the child on the bus," Tobias mused as Quilty brought him a cup of thin, clear soup. "It's a shame to have her come all this distance and then miss me. Why didn't you try to keep her for dinner, Quilty?"

Leidy had been fidgety to get back, Quilty said. "She didn't want to see you, Mr. Ferris. She come to see me."

"You?" In his astonishment Tobias spilled a spoonful of soup. "Something special?" he ventured.

He might call it special, Quilty frowned. She stood, large and quiet, her back against the swinging door. But the brooding anger in her face, so different from her customary benign calm, impressed even Tobias, ordinarily not sensitive to emotion unless expressed in action or words. Something had upset Quilty, that was plain. He'd know it, if by no other sign than the soup which was goshalmighty salty.

"She ought to have let her Grandmother Pinn know she was coming here," Tobias remonstrated.

"Leidy? She didn't want to have to go around explaining to

folks." Quilty squared her shoulders. "I'd like to get my hands on the kids she plays with. I'd shake every last one of them until their teeth fell out. All of their teeth," emphasized Quilty, as if to be less explicit might lay her open to a charge of coddling the enemy.

Tobias blinked, then choked, for the last spoonful had tasted like solid salt. "What's it all about?"

"You know what that poor child come to tell me?" Quilty took a step forward, a menacing gesture when coupled with her glare. "She ain't going to have no birthday cake this year! She come over to tell me on no 'count to make her a cake. Her mama wants her to have a party, but Leidy says she'll spit in the kids' faces, if they come."

Tobias grunted. "Nice, hospitable gesture. Not to mention hints on how to get along with the neighbors. You going to string along, Quilty?"

She had disappeared into the kitchen to take up his main course. Tobias, still puzzled as to the reason for Leidy's surprise visit, recalled that Quilty had made the little girl an imposing birthday cake for the last three years. Leidy's name and age always decorated the icing and the dimensions were such that party guests were invariably stunned at their first glimpse. Something far out of the ordinary must have befallen Leidy, if she had determined to forego her birthday cake.

Quilty brought in a plate she had kept hot in the oven, filled Tobias' water glass, arranged the salt and pepper shakers in an even line and stepped back to her favorite station by the swinging door. "Leidy's papa ought go out and shoot those kids," she said.

"Now look here—" Tobias paused, momentarily diverted by his first taste of the meat on his plate. Pork chops again! How in tunket, if Wallace had plowed under so many little pigs, could the markets be continually flooded with pork? Tobias began to estimate how many pork chops he had eaten since the start of the war, recollected that Leidy and her birthday cake were current problems and abandoned his statistics. "Just what is all the fuss about, Quilty?" he asked.

Quilty muttered that those nasty little hoodlums... "Leidy say she won't have no birthday party this year, 'count of her birthday's the same as that ole Hitler's."

"My good godfrey! Is it?" Tobias clutched wildly at his meager knowledge of family dates. "When is Leidy's birthday—what day, I mean?"

The twentieth of April, Quilty informed him. "That old Hitler has the same birthday. And the kids Leidy plays with have been tormenting her ever since they found it out. They say she's a Nazi, with a birthday the same day as that ole son of a bitch."

"Now, now," Tobias reproved absently. "I suppose children pick up their meanness from the people around them," he speculated. "They copy our cruelties."

Quilty shook her head in violent negation. "Don't you believe that, Mr. Ferris. Children is born mean and cruel and nasty-like. You got to beat it out of 'em. The sweetest looking little angels ever was will tear the legs right off a kitten, if you don't interfere. They'll laugh at a boy with only one arm and if there's a deformed child on their block they won't play with him. Savages—that's what kids is born like."

"Well—" Tobias hesitated. "But I don't relish this business about Leidy's birthday. We'll have to do something about that."

There was nothing for anyone to do, Ida announced crisply when, following Dora's advice, he telephoned her. Certainly Leidy would have a birthday party—she had had a birthday party every year of her life and a few wretched little brats were not going to make any difference in the customary observance. Ida was convinced, she said, that the Jewish children in Leidy's class had started all the trouble and she didn't intend to give them the satisfaction of boasting that they had the say-so about her child's social life.

"But how you going to give a party, if the children won't come?" Tobias persisted.

They'd come for ice cream and cake, Ida predicted grimly. She had never met any children who would turn down sweet stuff—they might strafe Leidy before and after the serving of refreshments, but you couldn't keep them away from the dining room table.

"It sounds kinda gloomy to me," Tobias reported to Dora. "You don't suppose any of the little guests will come armed with sawed-off shotguns, do you?"

Dora thought that was within the range of possibility, but suggested that the adults use their heads. It didn't take a psychologist to know that children—the abominable little prigs—would trample on anyone who was down, but would as quickly fall over themselves to bask in the smiles of the successful. Let it be demonstrated, Dora said, that the twentieth of April was the most highly desirable birth date in the year and Leidy's youthful friends would swamp her with avowals of their admiration and love.

"You don't sound any too sweet on human nature," Tobias objected. "And just how do we go about making April twentieth a date to conjure with? Thirty years from now Leidy may be president of the United States, but that's a long wait."

Ida and Frank could "think up" something, Dora said. "Why should a child be burdened with parents if they throw up their hands in every emergency?"

Frank, considerably more worried than Ida, welcomed his father's visit to the office one damp, misty morning a few days before the eventful twentieth. He couldn't be sure the children invited would come, Frank confided, but he and Ida were going ahead with their plans.

"I gather that a number of the mothers are quite upset over the whole affair," Frank said. "Ida blames a couple of Jewish kids, but as nearly as I can make out, it's just the hunting pack instinct. Leidy let them see she was vulnerable and they set upon her like hounds after a fox. Nice little beasts, children."

He had been building an outdoor fireplace, he revealed, the party was to center about that, with hamburgers and buns to be toasted and Quilty's tower of a cake and ice cream, for dessert. Frank took out the blueprints of his fireplace and showed them to his father with a builder's pride.

"Say, I've got a glimmer of an idea," Tobias remarked as he examined the tracings. "What do you think—"

For half an hour he and Frank conferred earnestly. When Tobias finally left, Frank was whistling "Among My Souvenirs," to the astonishment of a waiting client and the relief of the typist who recognized the signal that all was well.

The day of the party—a Thursday—obligingly provided sunshine and a warm breeze. The hour set, four o'clock, allowed Leidy time to reach home from school and exchange her dress for blue denim overalls and a white blouse. The girls had been asked to wear overalls, since it was conceded that skirts handicapped the feminine wearers around an outdoor fire.

"Everyone's trying to guess why we asked them to bring examples of their best work, Frank." Leidy, her tight, shining braids smoothly coiled, her small features immaculate from soap and water polishing, slipped a small hand into her father's as they sat on the front steps to await their guests.

The children were coming then, Frank thought, relieved. Leidy would have known had they planned otherwise, for there existed some mysterious underground system of communication between the youngsters.

"Ida said she'd try to get here in time for the ice cream," Leidy revealed, "but we don't really need her. Not with Quilty."

Frank found the picture of Quilty established in the kitchen, prepared to hand out the stacks of hamburgers and buns, a comforting one, but he felt vaguely that his daughter might display a little more affection for her mother. Before he could remonstrate, Leidy rose to her feet and swung her arm.

"Hi!" She called as the vanguard of guests turned the corner and marched noisily toward the house.

Fifteen minutes later they had all arrived—twenty-nine of them, the roster of Leidy's class in school. No one had stayed away. Each had brought a present. Seemingly etiquette demanded that if one attended a birthday party, one took a gift, regardless of what one might have said about the hostess behind her back or to her face. The little heap of packages thrust upon her quite overwhelmed Leidy who whispered to her father that she "ran out of thank-you words" before she had untied them all.

In addition to a present, each child had brought, as requested by Frank, a specimen of his or her best work. In some instances this proved to be a pencil or crayon drawing. Others brought neatly copied poems, or examples of their "social studies"—the curriculum fell down somewhere there, Frank suggested to Tobias later—or bits of art work achieved by grimy periods of toil. They were to bring these out to the stone fireplace in the back yard, Frank instructed them.

The fireplace, built at the end of the deep lot, was in a clearing but slim, young maple trees, brave in new foliage, shaded the clipped lawn. Their branches swayed gently above the children, grouped in a natural semicircle, with Frank in the center, his back to the fireplace.

He had something to say to them, before they started to toast hamburgers, he said, something about the twentieth of April as a birthday. The children stirred uneasily at that, he fancied, but no one spoke. Leidy, on the edge of the circle, sitting on the ground cross-legged, chewed a blade of grass. A movement of the curtains at the kitchen window suggested that Quilty was numbered among the audience.

"I don't know whether you know about people who have been born on April twentieth," Frank began, dodging a shaft of sunlight that pierced the maple shade.

April twentieth was a pretty special day, he went on, in fact as a birthday it was tops. He envied persons born on that date, since they were almost sure to grow up to be important people, much more important than people born say in March, or June.

"Perhaps a hundred years from now, people will be celebrating April twentieth as the birthday of—well, say of Leidy." He looked toward his placid daughter and the children's eyes followed his glance. "I can see them!" Frank announced dramatically. "They will be opening a cornerstone and in it they'll find the early drawings of a world-famous artist—Leidy Ferris. Do you know what the date on that cornerstone will be? April twentieth, nineteen forty-four."

A freckle-faced, solid boy sitting on his heels struggled desperately with mental calculations. "That's today!" he cried.

"Sure." Frank dodged behind the fireplace, returned with a small bucket and trowel. "We're going to lay that cornerstone today. The cornerstone to this fireplace. You kids can help."

He explained, as they surged forward, that a cornerstone was usually laid at the beginning of a building project, but that he had had to work on the fireplace in his spare time and had been unable to wait for a ceremony. However, the hollow space behind one of the stones was ready, they would put a tin box in it, then seal up the opening—to be opened years and years from that day.

The boys and girls were to put the samples of their work in the box, Frank said, signed with their names and the date. Then each one might handle the trowel and help seal the stone in place.

"Leidy may put the first paper in, because she is the birthday girl," Frank announced, carefully despositing the bucket of mortar on the fireplace coping where no child could step into it.

The youngsters, formed in an orderly line, moved past him, faces serious, fingers gripping their contributions tightly. Overhead an airplane droned, green shrubbery rustled in the light breeze. *One hundred years from now,* Frank thought. *I wonder what kind of a world it will be then.* Presumably not one of these sturdy, grave-eyed children filing past him would be here to see it, but conceivably a silly metal box filled with childish scrawls might outwit death and rust. It suddenly seemed monstrous to the dreaming man that human beings should live so briefly and inanimate objects be handed down through the centuries. *I'm a heck of a lot more interested in this world than I am in the next,* Frank told himself. *I'd like to know what will be going on two hundred years from now.*

"Everything's in, Frank!" Leidy jerked his shirt-sleeve. "Let me use the trowel now, Frank? Let me put the box in the stone hole, because this is my birthday."

Frank, kneeling on the grass, showed her how to slip the box into the hollow tile he had ingeniously fitted into a space between two of the stones. The other youngsters crowded around, pushing each other aside in their efforts to see. Each one insisted on an actual, unobstructed view of the box and most of them poked exploring fingers into the cavity to satisfy themselves that it was really there.

"You can't dig this out tomorrow and look at it, you know." Frank thought it prudent to warn them. "Nobody's going to see this box again until the fireplace falls down from old age. Then strangers, people we have never seen, will come and pry the stones apart and discover the cornerstone. They'll chip off the mortar, pull out the tin box, and find your stuff."

"Will they be commandos?" the solid boy asked hopefully.

"Naw," another lad interposed. "They'll be supermen. From another planet. With secret weapons and beams of light."

Frank handed the trowel to Leidy. "We'll seal it up," he said. "Before the supermen get started."

Leidy put the stone in place, as he showed her, and the guests were obvious impressed by the date line—April-20-1944—done in dashing black paint. Each guest in turn smeared mortar in the crevices and each had to be forcibly torn away to make room for the next in line. He could give a successful children's party with no equipment other than a mix of soft cement and a couple of trowels, Frank decided.

Once he had the fire started he dared not leave the children alone with it, so he dispatched Leidy to the kitchen to tell Quilty to bring out the hamburgers and rolls. He had sharpened sticks, in lieu of the scarcity of metal toasting forks, and soon the fragrance of roasting meat perfumed the twilight air. Ida, letting herself in at the front door, reached the kitchen before Quilty heard her.

"If noise is a sign, they're having a wonderful time," Ida commented. "Was anyone mean to Leidy? Did they heckle her, Quilty?"

Leidy was queen bee, she had those children begging for her favor, Quilty said. "Near as I can make out, those kids got the idea now that only people born on April twentieth rate a cornerstone!"

Chapter Thirteen

"THE trouble with your paper," said Mrs. Henry William Prexton, "is that you're afraid to give any space to Protestant news."

Dora Ferris shook her head.

"Why I can show you, day after day, week after week, nothing in your society columns but articles about the Catholics and their doings." Mrs. Prexton patted her large, moist face with a small, black-bordered handkerchief. "Even all your pictures are of Catholic activities," she continued. "Yesterday you had the inside of St. Michael's and the day before that a group picture of the Ladies' Sodality of St. Anne's."

Dora thought, *if she gets it out of her system, perhaps she'll amble off. I wonder why my proofs don't come down.*

"And everybody's commenting on your big society stories—all the weddings are those of Catholic girls." Mrs. Prexton fanned herself with a copy of the *Bulletin* she had brought with her as evidence. "Everyone wonders when you'll run the picture of a Protestant girl, just for a change."

The cuts in the society pages were not selected on the basis of religion, Dora said, more solemnly than she felt. If she glanced across her desk it would be to see Trudy Spinelli opposite, dark eyes dancing, lips curling in a sardonic grin. "We can't use the story of your church meeting for the simple reason that it is a week old, Mrs. Prexton." Dora stood up. Sometimes these complaining women accepted that as a hint. More often, like Mrs. Prexton, they remained firmly planted in their chairs.

"But the women who couldn't attend will want to see it,

and the secretary will keep the clipping for her scrapbook," urged the vistor. "Of course, I know we're a little church, without much influence, or any wealthy people in our congregation—but we do have some rights. This isn't a Catholic country yet."

The story was stale, she couldn't use it, no amount of argument could give a week-old story value, Dora insisted, marveling that her phone never rang when she had a pest on her hands.

Mrs. Prexton struggled to her feet, clutching her crumpled newspaper, her sagging cheeks mottled with tiny, red veins. "Are you a Catholic?" she demanded.

"I am not." Dora resisted the temptation to add that twenty years on the society desk had knocked all the religion out of her.

She nodded and grimaced mechanically as Mrs. Prexton made her stately farewells, then waited until the elevator gates had clashed behind the bulky figure. "This," prophesied Dora, "is going to be one of those days."

The white-haired Mrs. Potter who did women's clubs in winter and helped out at the society desk in late spring and summer, paused in her typing. Her desk, a few feet from Dora's but ruled off from it by a column of low steel files, enabled her to be attached to or detached from the department as convenience dictated.

"You know I've heard other peope say we carry too much Catholic news," Mrs. Potter commented. "I suppose it's the Wops. They have so many children. One of them is always getting married, or having someone made a priest or something."

A faint flush stained Trudy Spinelli's smooth, olive skin. She wasn't as impervious as she liked to think herself, Dora noted. She had spoken to Mrs. Potter before about her tactlessness, but without effect. Mrs. Potter was the kindest woman in the world and would be the last person to hurt another deliberately. She was an incessant talker, however, and appallingly frank. Trudy harbored no resentment against her, admitting freely that Mrs. Potter would give you the shirt off her back, if you needed it. Not needing a shirt, it was expecting too much of Mrs. Potter to ask her to exhibit those qualities with which the Lord had neglected to endow her.

Dora, gathering up a litter of photographs, spoke over her shoulder. "I'm going to the art department. Does it ever occur to you that so far no one has come in to squawk about the number of Italian names we run on the military service page? Or the number of Catholic obits for the boys who have military funerals?"

The men in the art department said that it was a wonder she wouldn't bring in a good-looking bride once a fortnight or so and the layout artist, who was supposed to have communistic leanings, grunted that a good-looking girl couldn't get her picture in the society section because she wouldn't be a blue-blood.

Any time the art department wanted to take over and interview the girls and their mothers, Dora suggested—

"The trouble with you is you're afraid to tell 'em to go to hell," the layout artist said.

When Dora returned to her desk she found a small, slight figure waiting her in the customer's chair, as Trudy called it. Trudy was busy at the phone and Mrs. Potter appeared to be absorbed in addressing wedding blanks.

"Society editor?" The small, dark woman's bright eyes smiled as she fumbled in her knitting bag to produce a tissue-paper-wrapped parcel.

Dora thought, *More photographs. And May used to be considered an unlucky month for brides.*

"My daughter—" The visitor placed a photograph on Dora's desk blotter.

A fuzzy print of a girl perhaps twelve years old, in an artificial pose against a lattice, the child's features indistinguishable in the black shadow cast by poor lighting.

"My son—" the woman dropped another photograph on the blotter. The boy, wooden, unsmiling, was backed against the same lattice pattern.

"They're graduating," the woman said. "From grammar school. I'm having a party for them Saturday."

Dora sighed. "I'm sorry. We can't use the pictures."

"Why not?"

The *Bulletin* didn't publish photographs of high school graduates, let alone grammar school, had not for years, Dora explained. "With the present paper shortage, we haven't space for half the material submitted to us, anyway. We'll use the story—that's the best we can do."

The woman made no movement to take the pictures. Instead she said, her eyes no longer smiling, "I guess you don't want pictures of Jewish children in your paper."

"That has no connection with the ruling—we cannot use graduation photographs, no matter whether the children are Jewish or Gentile." Dora leaned forward and dropped the pictures into the capacious knitting bag. "You haven't seen commencement pictures in the *Bulletin,* have you?" she challenged.

Mrs. Cohen admitted that she had not, but then she seldom saw the *Bulletin*. She bought the *Globe* because her children liked the funnies. "Would you mind copying what I gave you about the party?" she asked. "I want to take it around to the *Globe,* too."

"Go on and laugh," said Dora coldly, when she could turn her attention to Trudy, doubled up in silent mirth across her typewriter. "I'm glad if you see anything cheerful in this damn job. What are you mumbling, Trudy?'

"She said, 'Why don't the Catholics come in and crusade?' " Mrs. Potter repeated, evidently a little mystified. "It's queer how all the complaints seem to come on the same day, isn't it?"

Perhaps if she went out to lunch early the spell would break.

Dora suggested. Anyway, she meant to go half an hour ahead of schedule and stop in at Houseman's, before she ate. "My niece in Texas can't find a double boiler. Brides are out of luck, if they want to keep house this year."

"Is that the girl who married the Jew—what's-his-name?" Mrs. Potter inquired with sincere interest. "Are they still making a go of it?"

Cecilia was still married to Tag Silverstein and they were very happy, Dora returned. She admonished herself that no one ever minded Mrs. Potter—the poor soul didn't know how the things she said sounded to sensitive ears.

Trudy, having wiped her eyes, began to sort her notes. "Before you go, Miss Ferris—what's candlelight satin?"

Dora had no idea.

Mrs. Potter said she thought brides invented fabric names for their wedding gowns. "They want to be so romantic and they just make up a name as they go along and then we spend hours trying to track down the silly, highfalutin stuff."

Tension slacked in the afternoon—the *Bulletin* was an evening paper—and with their pages planned for the next day, Dora and Trudy could check the date books, work on the card files, and search for photographs which Elaine was supposed to have returned by mail the week before. Trudy said that her dream-paper was one in which no photographs of any living person ever appeared and Dora agreed with her that existence would be simplified if no brides, at least, were allowed to be exhibited to an apathetic world. It was undoubtedly as great a sin to encourage vanity as to be personally vain, Dora pointed out, and Trudy suggested that they discuss the issue with the mothers of the brides.

"Well, it's begun to rain, so maybe we won't have any squawks this afternoon," Trudy observed hopefully, when she had returned from her lunch hour. "Did you find a double boiler, Miss Ferris?"

Before Dora could answer, an angry, hoarse voice spread through the city room.

"Where's your society editor?"

A large, stocky woman stood at the entrance gate. She wore a vividly-patterned green and white dress and her red hair, built up into a high pompadour, supported an enormous, flaring, black hat. Her voice suggested that she had a throat of brass and she glowered threateningly at the faces turned in her direction.

Elaine, the office girl, towed her reluctantly toward the society desk. She preferred to see someone in authority, she wanted to talk to a *man*—words rumbled from her in a steady stream.

"Yes?" Dora wondered in some alarm how much she remembered of her first-aid course. The woman looked as if she might have a stroke.

"I'm Mrs. McCarthy. You sent back my daughter's picture." Mrs. McCarthy pounded the desk. "What do you mean by sending it back?"

Neither Dora nor Trudy recalled the name, but the photograph, triumphantly produced, supplied the clues. It has been published in three other papers, Dora recounted; she could use only exclusive photographs. "We used as much of the story as we could. That was in all the other papers, too."

Well, she wanted the picture in the *Bulletin,* Mrs. McCarthy insisted, and she intended to see that it got there. "We've been readers for twenty-five years and this is the first favor I ever asked. You put it in tomorrow, or the next day, and I'll make it all right with you."

"Mrs. McCarthy, we can't use it."

She had another photograph, one of the couple coming out of St. Anne's Church, Mrs. McCarthy said. "How about putting that in? I'll pay you."

The wedding was past, it had been in all the city papers, there was nothing she could do, Dora reiterated. The city room might be enjoying the row, but she was sick of these eternal dialogues.

"You discriminate between the Catholics and Protestants, don't you?" Mrs. McCarthy turned the color of a red plum. "I said to my sister it's nothing but discrimination. None of the girls married in St. Anne's ever get their pictures in the paper."

Trudy rebelled. It was against all ethics to "horn in" on arguments in which she was not involved, but she pushed back her chair and walked around the mountain of flesh that was Mrs. McCarthy, so that she faced the irate woman.

"Look!" Trudy smote her chest dramatically. "I'm a Catholic. I know plenty of girls who were married in St. Anne's and St. Michael's and all the other saints and they've had their pictures in the *Bulletin*. But they gave us exclusive photographs."

Mrs. McCarthy whirled. She grabbed at her slipping hat and opened her wide mouth to shout. "I don't give a damn about your filthy paper! You can take it to hell, for all I care. I'll never read another line of it again as long as I live and no one in my family will."

She tramped across the room toward the elevator and Benny, the operator who had been listening, fascinated, to her tirade, scuttled into the cage and shrank back as she crashed in beside him. Her voice could be heard as the car descended, screaming expletives against the *Bulletin* and all whom it employed.

"Boy!" Across the room the bald-headed man on the sports desk passed a shaking hand across his eyes. "Don't cheer, fellows, she's somebody's mother-in-law!"

Trudy turned to the pile of exchanges on her desk, ready to attack them with her clipping shears. "I just happened to think today is my saint's day," she murmured.

"Don't mention it," Dora begged.

"I've always said the Catholic religion is mostly form," said Mrs. Potter reflectively.

Trudy made a face. "Miss Ferris, I didn't have the heart to tell you, but while you were out to lunch, a patriotic soul came in with a Great Plan. To promote unity and show the boys in the fighting forces that the home front will keep the flag waving free —you know it all by heart." The chairman of the committee, Trudy related, had fumbled with a sheaf of notes and fragments of names.

"I pulled a few first names and initials out of her by main force," Trudy said. "Exercising sweetness and tact, I persuaded her that it did matter how we spelled them. But when I came to a Father Barrow from some out-of-town church I was lost and so was she. It never occurred to her that priests *had* names, she said. I explained that we couldn't use a last name like that and that I was awfully sorry, but unless she could get me Father Barrow's Christian name, we'd have to leave him out.

"Miss Ferris, that woman looked at me and smiled. 'That doesn't bother me in the slightest—I'm a Presbyterian,' she said. Honestly, I almost asked her why she was a church member and when."

Dora put out a hand automatically as the desk phone rang. "This would be a perfectly beautiful world," she hissed between clenched teeth, "if it wasn't for the Protestants, the Catholics, and the Jews!"

In the eyes of her sister Sarah's children, Dora Ferris ranked as a second Emily Post. It was one of the penalties exacted by her job and she was fairly resigned to the rôle. Nor did she marvel at the slavish, if intermittent, devotion of her nieces to formal etiquette, since the majority of *Bulletin* readers leaned heavily upon the same staff. "Is it proper?" they always asked and in their anxiety to be correct they confused ethics with good manners, made themselves unhappy, spent money they could ill afford, and "perished in the formal flames," Trudy Spinelli liked to chant.

But when Mabel Eustice, whom Dora suspected of sleeping with a volume of Emily Post under her pillow, drove her smart car around to the Ferris house one evening, it developed that she sought support on a formal ruling.

No one ever called Mabel pretty, but she had a flair for style and she was passionately concerned with good grooming. She was always heavily in debt, although the shops no longer permitted her charge accounts to run indefinitely. The several hundred dollars she owed her mother was never mentioned between them, but Mabel often assured her sisters that when she married she would do "something nice for Mama." Meanwhile her mother gratefully accepted her cast-off clothes and wore them with a dignity that went far to alleviate their unsuitability in color and style.

Tonight Mabel intimated that she wished to speak confidentially to her Aunt Dora. It seemed to Mabel that her grandfather tended to monopolize the living room, a situation of which she did not approve.

"You'd think he owned the house," she had once said to her mother.

Sarah had mildly offered the excuse that it was his house and that he lived there.

"Does he live with Aunt Dora, or does she live with him?" Mabel had probed.

And when she had learned that her grandfather owned the house, but that her aunt shared the upkeep and the living expenses, Mabel had decided that Aunt Dora didn't sufficiently assert herself.

"Look at Papa! He doesn't hang around the living room in our house." The home, Mabel added, was the woman's domain, it represented her labor, her taste. Perhaps, she concluded charitably, no one had told her grandfather that.

No question of his right to smoke in the living room assailed Tobias. Unaware of his grandchild's disapproval, he continued to lie relaxed in his lounge chair, feet comfortably elevated, Paris camped on his stomach, puffing in blissful ease.

"How's your mother?" He beamed upon Mabel, his sharp old eyes studying her more intently than his screen of smoke disclosed.

The family were well, Mabel sighed. She told herself that she might as well go through the list, before her grandfather asked. Ginger was as big as a house, Mabel recounted, Fern was as pigheaded as ever over her boy friend, and Papa was doing his bit as usual to disgrace them all. "The house is just running over with happiness," Mabel summed up resentfully.

Tobias lay still, the cat's silky body moving gently with each breath. "What about your mother?"

"Mama's trying as usual to decide whether it would have been better if she had divorced Papa the time she left him, just before Fern was born. We all tell her the big mistake was in not divorcing him before any of us had the bad luck to land in this world." The flippant note in the young voice could not conceal the real bitterness behind the careless words.

From the dining room where she had been putting away the silver for Quilty, Dora observed that she had seen Mabel walking with a handsome young officer on a downtown street. "Last Thursday. You were so wrapped up in each other you passed me by."

"You never told me," Tobias objected.

She wasn't one to relay gossip, Dora rebuked, she only mentioned the incident now to remind Mabel that she was not unblessed.

There was no pleasure in having Lieutenant Bentley at the house, Mabel complained. She never knew in what condition her father would be. That was probably the reason Fern had decided to be satisfied with Jim Kotoski. "He doesn't expect much in the way of background."

Lieutenant Bentley, she confided more animatedly, came from a fine family. They not only had money, but social position. "You ought to know his mother, Aunt Dory. She was Elvira Cameron."

"Now, wait a minute." Tobias leaned across the protesting Paris to empty his pipe ashes into the metal stand beside his chair. "I knew her father. Old man Schwartzhauer. Ran a fine type of saloon down in the South End."

Mabel stared. "Lieutenant Bentley isn't German."

His granddaddy was, Tobias affirmed. "His mother was old man Schwartzhauer's youngest girl, no matter what she's done to her name since."

Old Gus had made every cent of his money over the bar, Tobias said. He gazed ecstatically at the two women. "What a place he kept! None of your taverns, but a respectable saloon that didn't need a juke box and women sitting on high stools to pull in the crowds. My good godfrey, the free lunch old Gus used to set out! I wonder if this grandson of his ever eats pigs' knuckles and sauerkraut. Washed down by draught beer."

She hated saloons, Mabel cried fiercely, and if she thought Lieutenant Bentley ever touched a drop, she'd be through with him then and there. "I've seen enough of drinking in our family to last me all my life."

Her grandfather remonstrated that beer wasn't intoxicating and that anyway she couldn't judge all men by her father, but Dora terminated the argument by taking Mabel upstairs to the large, pleasant room used as a sitting room. It was time for Tobias to hear his favorite commentator, Dora said, and besides she and Mabel wanted to talk female talk, not discuss pigs' knuckles.

"Aunt Dory, I really came to ask you something special, but now I want to ask you something else first." Mabel looked about for a mirror. "Mind if I powder my nose in your room?"

Dora turned on the lights in the adjoining bedroom, stood in the doorway while Mabel seated herself at the vanity table. Her compact was one of the huge pancake designs brought out that spring. Mabel considered accessories important and prided herself on keeping in step with the advertisements. Before she could talk easily with her aunt she must reassure herself as to her make-up and her shining hair-do.

She applied fresh lipstick and said, "Did you ever hear that the Bentleys changed their name?" Her eyes met Dora's in the mirror, turned away.

"Of course." Dora was matter of fact. "It's no secret. Fred Bentley was originally Franz Hausmann. He changed the family name in the first World War."

"Why?"

"Oh, heavens, because it was German. He was second or third generation himself, but I imagine he was sensitive and his wife more so. You don't know anything about the violent reactions against anything German, back in those days; sauerkraut changed over night into liberty cabbage."

Mabel did not smile. "Were the Hausmanns Jewish? Or the Schwartzhauers?"

"Jewish? Not that I ever heard of. They were just plain German stock, I've always understood, and apparently they couldn't take the sniping of the neighbors. Father thought then it was the wrong thing to do, but I suppose they had children who were being plagued in school."

After a moment Mabel said, "Rolfe Bentley went to Princeton." She dampened her finger on her tongue, ran it over her eyebrows to remove the powder. "After the war he'll practice law, at least I think so."

"Do you like him?" Dora spoke awkwardly. Young people resented prying, yet they criticized indifference, too.

Mabel wasn't sure. "The main thing is that he's an officer. I can't get interested in a service man unless he's commissioned. It's lots more fun in every way to go out with an officer. But," she blotted her lips on a tissue, "if he drinks, I'm through. I wouldn't marry the—the President, if he liked booze."

She thought Rolfe Bentley's father had been "bright" to change his name, Mabel asserted, blowing powder from the vanity top to the floor, which was one way of achieving neatness. If more people with the wrong kind of names changed them, fixed them up like American names, a lot of trouble would be saved.

"Look at Ceil. If her husband would do something about the Silverstein, don't you suppose she'd be happier? And if Jim Kotoski turned himself into Jim Cotter, maybe Fern could marry him with the family blessing." Mabel rose, smiling at her image in the glass. "I guess I'll do," she said.

It was as if she shut the door on her personal affairs, when she followed Dora back into the sitting room. What she had really come for, Mabel disclosed, was to ask her aunt about the propriety of giving a stork shower for Ginger.

"Mama thinks it's awful that Fern and I haven't done it months ago. But we keep telling her that relatives don't give stork showers for mothers-to-be, as she calls Ginger." Mabel dropped into the chintz-covered rocking chair. "Just the name, 'stork shower,' gives me the horrors," she groaned. "It's so coy."

She didn't suppose it would make any difference to Sarah, but it was not considered in the best of taste for a close relative to sponsor any kind of shower, Dora admitted. "You know, of course, it's nothing but a bid for gifts."

There ought to be a law against showers, Mabel shrugged. She had attended a thousand, more or less, mostly for the office brides. The scheme was a flagrant hold-up, any way you looked at it, and had grown to such proportions that she dreaded to be introduced to a new girl. "The next day she invites you to a shower she's giving for a friend of hers. Someone you never *did* meet."

Dora pointed out, with middle-aged calm, that one did not have to accept.

"You have to keep your end up," Mabel instructed, rocking gently.

They had wandered from the main issue, Dora perceived. Why, she asked, had Sarah set her heart on a stork shower for Ginger?

"She wants her to have presents!" Mabel straightened, ceased to rock. "Mama says she knows a shower is for gifts and that Ginger's friends will just love to bring things for the little stranger."

What irritated her and Fern, Mabel disclosed, was their conviction that they would be labeled ignorant if they yielded to their mother's insistence and arranged the party for Ginger. "We know what is correct and what isn't, Aunt Dory, and it's maddening to have Mama trying to force us to act like yokels. She wouldn't mind making us a laughing stock, if only the baby duds came in."

Ginger didn't care one way or the other, Mabel said; all she wanted for the baby was diapers, she told everyone that. She couldn't be sure of getting the service—

"For heaven's sake," Dora interrupted at this point, "don't go into that. Your generation has gone mad on the subject of diapers. Maybe you'd better please your mother by giving a shower and letting etiquette go hang."

Half an hour later Mabel left, still undecided. There were so many angles, she lamented. Her mother would be sure to want mention made of the party in the *Bulletin* and Lieutenant Bentley's mother might see that and leap to the conclusion that the Eustice family were a bunch of hicks.

"Look on the bright side of life as I do," Dora admonished. "At least we've never been asked to run a photograph of the expectant mother for whom a stork shower is given. That's a break, if you ask me."

Her father called to her from the living room as she closed the door behind Mabel and Dora marveled anew at his faculty for putting her on the defensive. Most old people had the gift, she decided; they resented being excluded from the lives of their children and mysteriously they retained the power to foster a feeling of guilt.

"We were talking about a stork shower for Ginger, Father—you wouldn't have been interested." Dora took the chair opposite him.

Evenings were lonely for him, she thought. He managed fairly well through the day and so did she, but they were both lonely at night. He had been playing solitaire as he listened to the war news and his crossword puzzle lay on the card table, too. But what he wanted was to hear the sound of his own voice.

"Where's Paris?" Dora asked.

The cat had asked to go out, Tobias said. "He's very agile, socially, in the spring."

Dora laughed. "Mabel looked well, didn't you think, Father? She has good style."

Mabel thought she had "Ow," Tobias grumbled. "Well, then oomph. Quit your giggling. Sarah told me it takes the girl two hours to get fixed up to go to work every morning. That makes me wonder if she is good-looking to start with."

No one looked very beautiful in the morning, Dora argued, scanning the advertisements in a magazine.

"I'm just as good-looking in the morning as I am any time of day," Tobias insisted, and when Dora intimated that was his misfortune, he grinned, no longer aggrieved.

It would be funny, he mused aloud, if Mabel should marry into the Bentley family. She was a smart girl and knew what she wanted, but she was in danger of turning into a prig. This trying to set up rules about drinking for her young man—

"That's Lion's fault," Dora spoke quickly. "Mabel thinks every man who takes a cocktail will be like her father."

Tobias struck a match for his pipe which had gone out. He had never been sure how much Lion drank, he said, and he doubted whether Sarah did. "The women hustle him out of sight the minute he sets foot within the door. Sometimes I think if they'd let him alone he might sit in a corner and never attract attention."

"Well, he's made it almost impossible for his daughters to contract normal marriages," Dora charged, apparently intent on a fashion drawing. "Ginger will never be happy away from her mother and Mabel will sue for divorce if Lion takes a whiskey and soda. And Fern is willing to marry an atheist, not for love, but simply to prove everything her mother says is wrong."

Tobias twisted in his chair, conscious of a back twinge. Lion was no great shakes, he admitted, but his son-in-law wasn't to blame for more than fifty per cent. "Your sister Sarah's had something to do with those girls."

It was their whole ghastly married life, Sarah's and Lion's, that had warped the girls, Dora said. "Sarah hates all men. But she preaches that old maids are social outcasts, so her daughters feel obliged to chose between living with brutes in the form of husbands or a life of humiliation, like mine."

"I've often wondered." Tobias cleared his throat. "Do you?"

Dora's black and silver head lifted sharply. The tired lines beneath her eyes faded in the lamplight, the shadows were kind to her neck and chin. "Do I what?" She challenged the twinkle in her father's aquamarine eyes.

"Worry about not being married. Or let what women say, or you think they say, hurt you." *Parcel of cats, women,* Tobias thought. *Always ready to claw.*

Her friends had accepted her single state, no one expected her to marry now, the worst was over for her, Dora assured him cheerfully. The greatest cross the single woman had to bear, she confessed, was the efforts made by her friends in her behalf.

"Their attempts to marry you off are heartbreaking. They trot out actual derelicts, the inference being that you'll be thankful to take anything. Lord be thanked, I don't have to go through that, any more."

She turned a page of her magazine. " 'Old maids are the happiest, once they quit a-struggling,' " she quoted. "I've quit."

Tobias reflected that she was almost a stranger to him. He knew nothing of her conflicts, her sorrows, her regrets. How much would she have told her mother had Jennie lived? Dora didn't look resigned to him, he mused, studying his daughter's half-averted face. There was a restlessness about her, a stirring like a ceaseless movement, not as if she had found peace. *I'm so old I have no more authority,* Tobias thought. It seemed to him that if the gulf between parent and child had collapsed, that perhaps Dora and he could talk as friends.

"What's on your mind?" he said, because he wanted to leave the way open for her to escape.

Dora lifted her head again. She did not look at her father but past him into the pool of shadows beyond the rim of the lamp. Her hand fingered a silver clip at the neck of her black and gray frock. "There is always one more trap." She might have been speaking to herself.

The old man waited and in the silence between them the ticking of the clock dropped slow, measured pellets of sound.

"When I realize now that I shall never have a child..." For an instant Dora's glance met her father's. Her face was bleak with tragedy, but bitter rebellion flared in her dark eyes. "It's a shock to *know* that you will never have a child."

Tobias thought, *Nature hands them the little end of the deal.* Aloud he said, "I been wondering lately—about that Catholic fellow. The one you went out with, once or twice."

"Dick Huber?" Dora laughed, almost naturally. "What about him, Father? And why should you think of him?"

"Well, was there anything serious between you? Maybe you ought to have married him."

Even a heartache may wear itself out in twenty-five years, Dora reflected, *but I cared more than I realized.*

It was a little late, she pointed out briskly, to be talking about what ought to have been. "You might try out your advice on Fern, Father. She feels that if she doesn't marry Jim Kotoski, no one else will ever ask her."

"Maybe they won't. She ought to think about it."

"Father! Fern's only seventeen. As Sarah says, she can afford to wait ten years."

Where her children were concerned, Sarah was a plain damn fool, Tobias announced, feeling himself back upon safe ground. He discovered that his pipe was out, decided against refilling it. All mothers were alike, he grumbled, never got an honest look at their young ones.

"If Fern doesn't marry this Kotoski boy, it will be a good long time before she finds anyone else," Tobias predicted. "Maybe she'll never find anyone else."

Dora stammered, "Wh-y-y?"

"You don't see any boys cluttering up her doorstep now, do you?"

But Fern was young, all the boys were in service, no girl had as many beaus as she would have in normal times, Dora protested.

"A fine list of alibis." Mind, Tobias interposed, he didn't say that Fern should marry her one beau regardless of whether she loved him, but it wasn't fair to let her expect more than the world was going to give her.

"If you're intimating that her sex appeal is limited, that may be," Dora admitted, "but you'd be the first to criticise her if she was anything like Jim Kotoski's sister."

Lena Kotoski? Oh, she was a big, coarse-looking girl, supposed to have a handsome figure.

"Her bust is large, but she does have nice legs," Dora conceded. "Oh, stop grinning, Father. She's had one illegitimate child and her mother takes care of it. Foreigners don't seem to think marriage is so important, do they?"

"They don't seem to lay such stress on divorce, either," Tobias acknowledged. "Say, you trying to tell me that Fern's fixing to be an unwed mother? I never thought it of her."

He was not to start thinking of it, Dora rebuked him. "We don't have unwed mothers in our family. Jim's mother has already asked Fern to have a boy. Foreigners talk everything out, Sarah says. She thinks they haven't a shred of modesty."

"My good godfrey!" Tobias choked. "Sarah can say a thing like that, after hearing Nutmeg! Why, if there's anything in connection with having a baby that girl hasn't mentioned I'd like to know what it is. I'll bet she could make the Kotoski girl blush. Did you ever hear Nutmeg get confidential about diapers?"

Ginger talked about diapers because she wanted to avoid having the house festooned with them, Dora said coldly. People like the Kotoskis had diapers hanging from every nail, their rooms smelled of babies from morning till night. "It's no worse to discuss disposable diapers, as Ginger does, than never to dispose of them, the way foreigners do."

Tobias caught at her repetition of the word. "How come you're so set against foreigners, all of a sudden? Not so long ago you were standing up for Jim Kotoski. According to you he was fighting the war for me as a seaman, first-class."

She didn't know what was the matter with her, Dora apologized. She was probably tired. What she needed was a good night's sleep. "I'll read myself drowsy with a lovely little article in this magazine I'm taking up with me—'The Woman Approaching Fifty.'"

At the door of the living room she turned. "Maybe you don't mind having Jim Kotoski fighting the war for you," she said, "but I mind like hell his sister having the babies for me."

Cecilia wrote that she was worried about her Grandmother Warren, Dora revealed a few mornings later. She had read the letter standing as she drank her coffee, a practice her father hopelessly deplored.

Tobias, who in contrast to his daughter seldom left the breakfast table until he had solved the crossword puzzled and emptied the coffee pot, dropped more bread in the toaster. Old Mrs. Warren, he observed, must be getting on.

"I'll drop around there late this afternoon," Dora decided. "Before I come home. Ceil says her grandmother's letters aren't coherent and she doesn't answer questions about her health. Just tells how lonely she is and begs to know when Ceil is coming North to stay."

The Portsmouth Apartments, where old Mrs. Warren lived, had exacted high rentals and offered good service for a decade previous to the war. The rents were still high, Dora had been told, but the service had been much curtailed. At half-past five in the afternoon the main floor appeared deserted, with no one at the switchboard and one of the two elevators marked "Not Running." When the other car came down, the operator assured Dora that it was "all right" to go up without being announced. Mrs. Warren didn't answer the switchboard calls half the time, anyway, he said.

"Why, it's Dora Ferris!" Old Mrs. Warren came to the door of her apartment herself and she had the half-startled, half-suspicious expression of a woman who has few callers. "Do come in," she fluttered, putting her hands up to the white knot of her hair. "I'm so glad to see you."

She led the way across a square hall into a large living room with a dropped end, furnished as a dining room. The windows were closed and the air had a faint, musty odor, as if they had been like that for a long time.

"Sit here." Old Mrs. Warren indicated the divan before the fireplace where a great sheaf of waxy, green leaves filled a copper jug. "This is the first time you've been to see me, isn't it?" She sat down beside Dora. "Do you smoke? There are cigarettes in the china box."

Dora thanked her absently. She was thinking, *this is the first time I have ever called on Ceil's grandmother. And she has never been in our house.* Aloud she said, "I have been intending to drop in, ever since Ceil went to Texas. But you know I'm a business woman and the days go by so quickly."

She found that she was staring at the wrinkled hands of her hostess. An old lady's hands would not be plump and smooth, perhaps, but why should they be red and rough, marred with scratches, with broken fingernails and bits of tape wound around the knuckles?

Old Mrs. Warren stared, too, as if she might be seeing them for the first time. "My hands—they look awful. I've been doing all my own work and there's no use having a manicure, if you have to oil your own floors and sweep and dust."

She looked around the room, her glance lingering on the heavy, striped, silk rep curtains at the three large windows. Her winter draperies were still up and it was nearly June, she sighed. "But what can I do? The dry cleaners won't take them down this year and I can't get a woman to clean. If I had had someone to hold the ladder, I could have done it myself long ago.

The old lady had serious heart trouble, Dora recalled. No wonder Cecilia worried. "You must have someone to help you, Mrs. Warren," Dora urged. "Can't you get a maid? I don't see how you manage in this large place with no servants at all."

Some distance away, probably in a bedroom, the telephone began to ring. Old Mrs. Warren murmured apologies, limped off to answer it. When she walked she put out one hand stiffly, as if none too sure of her balance. Her black dress showed wrinkles in the skirt and the belt hung down, unfastened.

Left alone, Dora perceived the room to be crowded with beautiful things that avoided a cluttered effect because of clever grouping and a nice color sense. The chairs and sofas and ottomans were slip-covered, but the heavy winter rug, an old-rose broadloom, looked out of place. *My Lord, it must take a week to dust the place,* Dora calculated. *Quilty would have a fit.*

The shelf above the fireplace, the two and three-tiered tables, the hanging cabinets on the walls, and the book shelves, all were filled with exquisite ornaments. China, glass, figurines, bits of brass and copper—the treasures of a lifetime had been assembled here with loving care. *Who takes care of it?* Dora marveled, hearing the fumbling step returning.

"The agency called to tell me they haven't found a reliable maid for me yet." Old Mrs. Warren resumed her seat on the divan with a heavy sigh. "It's stuffy in here, isn't it? But if I open a window, so much dust comes in." She had spent two days that week cleaning the living room, she said. "I work so slowly. And there is so much to be done."

Well, how were people to manage, she demanded, when Dora remonstrated. The defense factories had drawn off all the maids. She had always kept two maids, sometimes three, and treated them well. But the girls today wanted exorbitant wages, outrageous privileges, and then they stayed only long enough to earn their first week's pay. "My dear, one has to pay them by the week, now. That's so they can leave before their month is up."

No, she had written nothing of this to Cecilia, she didn't want to worry the child. Besides she had no time to write. Old Mrs. Warren flexed her poor, scarred hands as if they might ache. They were small and well-shaped; she had probably kept them in beautiful condition and been proud of them, before the war.

"This is a seven-room apartment and I haven't had a good maid for months—even before I went to the hospital I had a dreadful time. The house porter came in once or twice to help me, but they get a new one nearly every week and they drink up my liquor." Would Dora like a cocktail, old Mrs. Warren asked belatedly. Or a cup of tea?

Dora declined absently, for she was trying to remember if Cecilia had ever mentioned any relatives of her grandmother who might be influential in remedying the situation. Probably the old lady was the last of her line, Dora reflected, hastily deflecting her glance from the dust curls under a carved antique table.

"You haven't the strength to do all this work," she expostulated helplessly. "I'll get Quilty to find someone for you. Quilty's the woman we've had for years, you know," she added as old Mrs. Warren looked blank. "She's wonderful."

"Isn't she colored?"

Dora looked blank in turn. "Colored? Why certainly she's colored."

Well, she had never employed colored help, old Mrs. Warren said. "I wouldn't want to begin now. I don't think I'd feel quite comfortable with a colored woman handling my things and I know I wouldn't be able to eat anything she cooked."

Quilty was a fine cook and a fanatic about cleanliness, Dora testified. She told herself it was foolish to argue, she had the feeling that she had run full tilt into a stone wall, but she couldn't stand by and watch Cecilia's grandmother committing suicide, could she?

"Oh, I realize plenty of people feel as you do; I'm not saying it isn't a foolish reaction on my part." Old Mrs. Warren spoke indulgently, making allowances for the common attitude. It was only that she had never had a colored cook or laundress, not even a woman by the day.

"One reason of course is that you can't mix them with your white help," she explained patiently. "The house here has had the same trouble. The superintendent had to run the elevator himself for a week a short time ago. The only operators sent him were colored men and of course he couldn't use them."

Give me patience, prayed Dora, *I have been brought up to be respectful to the aged. The issue isn't one of race, merely one of the common, garden-variety of sense. Is it quite bright for an old lady to invite a heart attack by scrubbing a seven-room apartment rather than to hire a colored woman to clean?* Not that she was at all sure such a woman could be found, Dora admitted to herself.

Aloud she said gently, "Wouldn't you rather have colored help, than none at all, Mrs. Warren? Don't you want me to ask Quilty to find you someone, say to tide you over for a time and save your strength?"

That was very kind, she appreciated the offer, especially as Dora was so busy, old Mrs. Warren returned. She didn't want to seem peculiar, she disliked to appear obstinate, but the truth was she didn't trust the colored. "I've always heard that they're light-fingered and I have so many small valuables they could pick up and carry away in their pockets. Besides, if they're from the South they're lazy and if they're bred in the North they are overbearing and cocky. I'll go on as I have been doing, I think." Old Mrs. Warren smiled, "If you don't mind."

Chapter Fourteen

"MAMA wanted me to tell you," said Mabel's carefully modulated voice over the telephone, "that Ginger went to the hospital at five o'clock this morning."

Tobias felt behind him for a chair, sat down, finding the support grateful to his knees. He asked the inevitable, inadequate question. "She all right?"

The doctor said everything was fine, Mabel reported. She had driven her mother and Ginger to the hospital, both of them in a state of jitters. Her mother had stayed, Mabel said, and no one expected to see her again until the baby arrived.

"Where's your father?" Tobias thought, *If no one asked, you wouldn't hear Lion's name from one year's end to another.*

Mabel believed that her father had left home "for the duration." He had disappeared while she was at the hospital and Fern had discovered that his clean collars were gone from his bureau drawer. That was his usual concession to personal luggage, when he planned to absent himself for an indefinite period.

"Fern and I have to do everything—he didn't even carry out the garbage," Mabel said. "He's a lot of help in a crisis."

If her mother wasn't back from the hospital that night, he'd lend a hand the next day, Tobias promised. Meanwhile, if a lodger went without a clean towel, Mabel was not to worry. A baby wasn't born every day—

"That's what you think," Mabel interposed. "They had eight deliveries at Rinnell Memorial yesterday. One of the nurses told me."

When Dora telephoned the Eustice house that evening, Fern answered. Her mother, she said, was still at the hospital, no one knew where her father might be, and Mabel was dating Lieutenant Bentley. "She doesn't feel secure enough to break a date with him," Fern disclosed. "Anyway, there isn't anything we can do. They think Ginger may have to have a Caesarian."

The next morning Tobias set out for Sarah's house, the brilliant June sunshine tempting him to walk part of the way. It was rather appalling, he reflected, checking his impulse to swing the neat fabric bag into which Quilty had packed a meat loaf and a fresh sponge cake, to perceive how little interested his children were in each other. Poor, distracted Sarah could count on no practical assistance from Dora or Frank at a time like this and presumably she would pay as little attention to them when their personal affairs became involved. Tobias pondered whether his family were less united than others and, if that was the case, whether he might in a measure be to blame; or whether the absorption in their own households, the preoccupation, the apparently selfish narrowing of interests stemmed principally from the pressure of modern life that made it imperative for each human being to put his welfare first as the relentless wheel of competition turned.

The key, Fern had telephoned, would be tucked behind the mailbox and Tobias found it there—all ready for the burglar, he grumbled—when he reached the house. He let himself in and the insistent stillness of an empty house met him in the hall. It was funny, he mused, how spooky a house could be, even in broad daylight, if no human beings were about. Sarah might have been downstairs, washing, and the atmosphere of the house would be different, although she could be neither seen nor heard by anyone standing in the front hall.

This unbroken silence, as suffocating, thought Tobias, as a down comforter wrapped about him, choked every room into which he went. He put the meat loaf into the refrigerator, the cake in the tin box. There were dirty dishes on the drainboard and the garbage pail was full. Damn fool girls, he grumbled, they'd rather have typhoid than run the risk of breaking a fingernail.

He tramped upstairs, deliberately noisy, and again silence enveloped him. The bedrooms were disordered, the bathroom a jungle of wet towels and scattered toilet articles. No one had washed out the tub, the shower curtain was a damp wad, and the door of the medicine cabinet stood open ready to catch a luckless skull.

Tobias in his capacity of helper had self-imposed limitations. He would make the beds, collect the wet towels and hang them on the line to dry, in preparation for the laundry; he would wash dirty dishes, carry out garbage, empty ash trays, and dust the high spots in the living room. Scrubbing and mopping he declined to do and it was manifestly not his duty to put the rooms of the lodgers in order. The bathroom was a mess, he conceded, but he had no intention of cleaning the tub; when he came upon two combs, one pink, one red, both filled with combings, he gingerly disposed of them by tossing them in the basket of trash he later set out upon the curb.

Neither Mabel nor Fern came home at noon, but at one o'clock Fern called him. It was a study period, she explained, she had been talking to her mother at the hospital. "Mama is terribly upset. Ginger just suffers and suffers and they don't give her anything. Have you seen Papa?"

Tobias answered in the negative, somewhat startled to realize that he had not once thought of Lion, since entering the house.

"You don't think Ginger will die, do you, Grandpa?"

Millions of women had babies every year and most of them lived, Tobias assured her. Nutmeg—Ginger, was in good care, everything would be done for her. "What about Hoke Steel? Anyone sent him word of what's going on?"

Fern was vague on the subject of Ginger's husband. No, she didn't think her mother had sent him word. She went on to say that the birth announcements were addressed and ready, except for filling in the spaces. "Ginger has three hundred and forty names on her list, Grandpa. Mabel and I helped her do the envelopes."

"My good godfrey! Three hundred and forty names—what they for?" Tobias was bewildered.

"Oh, her friends and Hoke's friends. Lots of them are girls she met while she was in camp. They've all had babies and have been sending Ginger announcements, so of course she wants to send them hers. She made us promise to fill them out and mail them as soon as we hear."

She wasn't coming home right after school, Fern warned. If nothing had happened at the hospital by that time, she intended to look for white shoes to wear at her graduation. Her father had given her his shoe coupon and Mabel had been furious. "Mama," Fern babbled into the telephone, "gave all her shoe coupons to Ginger, of course. Mabel thought Papa ought to give her his. But he said my graduation was more important than for Mabel to try to catch herself a man."

Tobias, when allowed to talk, said that he was leaving food in the icebox and that the house needed a thorough going-over, in spite of his contributed labor. It seemed to him, he hinted, that two girls as old as Fern and Mabel, could manage to run things in a little more ship-shape fashion during their mother's brief absence. "How do you expect to run your own homes, when you get married, if you can't pick up after yourselves now?"

"Mabel won't get married if she can't have servants, and Jim and I will most likely live in a trailer," Fern comforted him.

Sarah came home from the hospital at the end of the second day. She looked, Mabel informed her, as if she had had the baby herself.

"Is Ginger glad it's a boy? What will she name it?" Mabel, who had made her mother a cup of tea and carried it up to the bedroom, stood at the foot of the bed. She felt uncomfortable for, as she said, none of them knew what to do when Mama was flat on her back.

If not precisely flat, Sarah at least reclined, her big, old-fashioned pillow bunched between her shoulder blades. She was fully dressed, but had consented to having her shoes removed. Her face was haggard, deeply lined, and her eyes looked sunken behind the heavy lids. She gave no indication of having heard Mabel, but lay inert, a handkerchief clutched in one work-roughened hand.

"Shall we send out the announcements, Mama?" Mabel spoke as a little girl might, asking to be directed. "Ginger didn't settle on any name for a boy. Do you think she'll want him to be Junior?"

Sarah stirred. "Don't send out the cards. Wait." Her eyelids fluttered, but she seemingly lacked the strength to raise them.

The tea was hot, Mabel urged, she could make toast. "Mama, you ought to eat something. You'll be sick, just when you want to go back and stay with Ginger. Won't you drink your tea, Mama?"

"Where's your father?" Sarah sat up. She put out her hand for the cup and as the light from the headboard lamp fell across her face Mabel was shocked to see that she had aged.

No one knew where Papa was, Mabel said. "He just stayed away."

"Where's Fern?"

Fern was having her new permament at the Empress Beauty Shop. "We didn't know whether anything was going to happen . . . or when . . ." Mabel took the empty cup from her mother. "Fern graduates tomorrow night, Mama She broke the appointment twice and she couldn't put it off any longer."

Sarah rested her head on her knees. She had lost all track of time, she murmured; it seemed to her that she had been at the hospital for weeks, not days. "It was so awful—my poor little girl!"

"But Mama, everybody says the first baby—and Ginger's all right now, isn't she?" Her grandfather had telephoned the hospital at six o'clock, Mabel said, and they had told him Mrs. Steel had been delivered of an eight-pound son. Mabel decided not to mention that her grandfather had wanted to bet her a quarter that Sarah would send the baby back.

"We ought to send the announcements soon, don't you think, Mama?" Mabel recollected that the baby had a father presumably interested in the news. "Mama, did you telegraph Hoke Steel?"

Sarah groaned. "Not yet. Mabel, the doctor doesn't think the baby will live."

"Won't live?" Mabel unconsciously shrieked. "Mama, you mean that after all Ginger went through—why, what will she *do?* Can't they make the baby all right? What's the matter with it, Mama?"

She didn't know, Sarah returned dully. Several doctors had said the baby didn't have a chance. Ginger herself would be all right. She was exhausted, of course, and no one could see her until she had a twelve hours' sleep.

"Doctor Ryneer sent me home. He's going to tell her himself —that is, if the baby dies. After that he'll let me know when I can see her. And he says we must put all the baby things out of sight, if—"

Mabel stared, eyes frightened, for she had had no experience with either birth or death. Did Mama mean they were to carry all the new furniture up to the attic? The bassinet and the little chest of wicker drawers? And the clothes the girls had sent? "But Mama, what can we do with the announcements? Three hundred and forty of them. It's lucky I didn't put the stamps on them."

Doctor Ryneer had told her to remove everything that might have painful associations for Ginger, Sarah repeated.

"But Mama, doctors don't know it all. Maybe the baby won't die. Lots of times people who are given up to die go right on, living to be eighty. Ginger's a healthy kid, I'll bet her baby has a good chance." Mabel found herself struggling against the impression that this was a dream. Presently she must wake up and some day she would tell Ginger, "What do you know, I dreamed your baby died."

Sarah began to retrieve the hairpins scattered on the counterpane and to thrust them at random into her untidy hair. "I think the baby died at birth," she said in a low, monotonous tone. "Doctor Ryneer thinks I'm the hysterical type so he wouldn't tell me, just hustled me off home, to get some rest, he said. Yes, I'm sure the child is dead and Ginger will never see him. He almost killed her, but I don't suppose that was his fault."

Later that evening Sarah telephoned the hospital and was told that all inquiries about Mrs. Steel were to be referred to Doctor Ryneer. Sarah, looking shockingly decrepit in a faded housecoat of Ginger's, dialed the doctor's office. The child had died, he admitted; he planned to break the news to the mother the next morning, if he found her in good condition. He didn't want her to have visitors for at least five days; one member of her family and one only might be allowed to see her during the regular visiting hours, through that probationary period.

"If her husband can get leave, it might be well for him to spend a little time with her," the doctor advised. "She'll need all the comfort and reassurance she can get."

The doctor should have given Mama something, Mabel confided to Fern, when the younger girl reached home a little after midnight. Mama was on a rampage, she wouldn't go to bed, she wouldn't sit down and let Mabel wait on her, in fact she seemed to be determined to wear herself out.

"She cleaned up the kitchen and baked a cake and two pies," Mabel whispered. "She burned the announcements in the cellar furnace. The bassinet is all done up in paper, waiting for Papa to carry it to the attic." You would think from the way Mama acted, that Ginger was expected home the next day, Mabel grumbled. "She'll be in the hospital for two weeks at least. Mama'll land there herself and all the rest of us with her, if she doesn't calm down pretty soon."

Fern's solution of difficulties was to go around them. She managed to reach her room without meeting her mother and once there she put on a bathrobe and proceeded to examine her hair. She had been profoundly shocked to hear from Mabel of the baby's death, but like Mabel she thought of the tragedy in terms likely to affect her mother rather than her sister Ginger. If Mama should be too much "upset," she might not attend the graduation exercises and her ticket would be wasted. The class was large, the auditorium small, and tickets had been limited. Besides her mother, Fern had been able to ask her grandfather and Aunt

Dora. The fourth ticket, assigned to her father by the committee, she had offered to Mabel whose regrets, couched in unflattering language, were directed at commencements in general and not specifically at her sister's alma mater. Fern had given the extra ticket to Rita Kotoski. Her folks, Rita said, adored any kind of a school affair, for there was always a Kotoski child somewhere in the curriculum.

"Do you think Mama will go tomorrow night?" Fern asked, when Mabel came up to examine the permanent, which had been her gift. "Is it too tight? Do you like the way she set it?"

Mabel thought the wave would "loosen" a little the next day and look more natural. Chemicals were hard to get, a girl couldn't be sure of a good wave since the war. "But I think you'll do—tie it up in a net cap and don't touch it until tomorrow night."

"Did Mama say anything about going?" Fern persisted.

Their mother talked of nothing but Ginger, Mabel said. "She'll be camped at the hospital, if she can talk the doctor into letting her help take care of Ginger. Nurses are so scarce, home talent isn't sneered at any more."

The next day Fern worked industriously and silently, intent on her own concerns. She washed and ironed, because Sarah who normally laundered the underthings of all three girls, had apparently overlooked the little heaps of silk things left for her in the two bedrooms. Sarah haunted the phone stand and at intervals she dialed the doctor or the hospital. She did the routine housework mechanically and Fern could not persuade her to take food. Even hot tea, she complained, made her sick. Late in the afternoon she succeeded in gaining permission from the doctor to see Ginger for a few moments during the evening visiting hours. It would be better if she waited till morning, he pleaded, but if she would promise to stay no longer than fifteen minutes and if she thought she could in some measure soothe her daughter—

"He means don't cry all over her," Fern advised.

She had no intention of crying, Sarah retorted, her eyes filling as she spoke. Fern was too young and hard to know the meaning of grief, but Ginger, Sarah exulted, was closer than ever to her now. "If Mabel isn't using her car, do you think she'll be willing for you to drive me over to the hospital tonight, Fern?"

"Sorry, Mama, I have a date."

"A date? Oh, your commencement. Well, dear, you'll have your grandfather so it won't be as if you had no family there." Sarah, obviously bringing her attention to bear upon her youngest child, rubbed her eyes fretfully. "Darling, I've been so worried about Ginger that I didn't buy you a present. Would you like the money, to get something yourself?"

Fern stood the electric iron upright on its plate and walked around the ironing board to hug her mother. She would love to have the money, Fern said, there was something she wanted very much. Her plain little face, framed in the dark net which protected the precious permanent, was suddenly so radiant that Sarah hesitated. She found words for her anxiety. "Will that Kotoski boy be there tonight?"

Jim had liberty and his cousin was graduating, Fern said. Afterward—she checked herself as the phone rang and her mother rushed to answer it. The Kotoski party would only worry Mama, it would be better not to mention it, Fern reasoned.

"I feel more cheerful about the world," Tobias stated as he trudged homeward from the high school commencement. "There isn't anything so bad the kids can't mend it."

He and Dora had elected to walk, finding the soft darkness of the early June night restful and cool. The stars, Tobias had already observed, were almost as far apart as the street lights and a grateful breeze stirred at intervals.

"Isn't that a man sitting on our step?" Dora halted as they came in sight of the house.

She could dimly trace the outline of a human figure crouched in the shadows.

Tobias, unable to see anything at that distance, said if it was a man, the fellow was undoubtedly drunk. Dora, he instructed, should wait for him and he would go on and send the loiterer packing. "Let go my arm, Dory. How in tunket do you expect me to do anything with you hanging on me like a—a albatross?" he whispered angrily.

"I intend to hang," Dora informed him. "If you think you're going to get yourself murdered, you're mistaken. I'll get the pol—why, Father, it's Lion!"

Lionel Eustice stood up as they reached him. He looked very tidy and composed in the flickering light of the street lamp. He had come, he announced matter-of-factly, to ask them to take him in for the night. "Sarah's locked me out of our house," he said.

He added, politely, that he wasn't drunk and that he disliked to trouble his wife's relatives, but the embarrassing truth was that he hadn't a cent of cash.

On her way to the hospital, the smell of frying hamburgers from a dinner wagon reminded Sarah that she had cooked nothing for her family that night. For a moment the unbelievable lapse from routine staggered her. Then, as she mentally checked the whereabouts of the individual members, she decided that no great harm had been done. Fern had no time for food, she was absorbed in her commencement plans. Sarah hoped the child's grandfather would send flowers to the school—it was likely that Dora would remind him. Fern's father had gone too far this time—Sarah pictured him lying drunk in a gutter. As far as she knew Lion had never been drunk in a gutter, but neither had he ever stayed away from his home over night.

Had Mabel said anything about dinner? Sarah moved to make room for a fat woman to sit beside her in the bus. No, Mabel, had stayed down town for dinner. She kept her own counsel. It was difficult to guess whether she and the lieutenant were serious, but she had dinner with him three or four times a week. If Mabel should marry an officer, that would be something to write Cecil, Sarah reflected. It was a shame that Ceil, with her looks and her education and old Mrs. Warren for a grandmother, had not married an officer. Mabel made no secret of her ambition —she intended that marriage should better her, not pull her down.

The fat woman next to Sarah wriggled uneasily. It was a wonder they wouldn't do something about the ventilation in these buses, she fretted. "It's worse on this line because people go back and forth from Rinnell Memorial and they carry germs. You're going to the hospital, aren't you?"

Sarah assented. "My daughter, my oldest girl, is a maternity patient. She lost her baby. A little boy. It was her first. Her husband's in the service. At some post in Alabama. I forget the name."

"My!" The fat woman had listened avidly, her face bright with attention. She herself was on her way to the hospital to visit her sister, a patient in the surgical ward. "We never thought, when she was married, that Helen would ever have to go in a ward. But I must say she gets good care. Her doctor's a Jew, but he's real nice, if you know what I mean. And smart! He put himself through medical school, the nurse told Helen."

"They can live on next to nothing," Sarah murmured, and then wondered if she had confused the Jewish race with the Chinese who lived on rice.

The fat woman wiped a powder puff over her moist, pink face, her skin showing a faint golden down, like the fuzz on a peach. "Did you ever notice how the Jews want their sons to be doctors and a Catholic family feels set up if they have a son who turns out to be a priest?" She looked about her hastily, to see if she had been overheard.

She thanked God every day of her life that she had never had a son, Sarah said. Nasty, dirty, noisy brats, who grew up into men and made the lives of women miserable. "If it wasn't for my children, I would a thousand times rather have been an old maid."

Her vehemence surprised the fat woman, who clucked like a comfortable hen. Men weren't so bad, she soothed, and as for children, give her boys every time. Girls always got into trouble and with the war on nine out of ten mothers didn't know what went on behind their backs.

"I got two boys in high school and it's the girls who put ideas into their heads. Mostly foreigners at that. I tell you, when I went to school things were different. We didn't have any but good American names in our class and not more than one or two coons."

Sarah fancied that a passenger across the aisle eyed them malevolently, so she attempted to lower her naturally strident voice. "Don't talk to me about foreigners! My youngest daughter is all taken up with a boy—well, of course, he was born in this country, but that doesn't make any difference. His folks are Polish." And, as if that wasn't enough, he was an atheist, Sarah added in a fierce undertone.

The fat woman said, "How perfectly dreadful!" She hesitated. "What is an atheist?" she fumbled.

She wasn't quite sure herself, Sarah admitted; she had been told, but it was difficult to keep straight. "I always get atheists and communists mixed," she confided. It had something to do with religion, she continued more firmly, just what she couldn't say. But it wasn't likely that a girl brought up in a normal American family could find much happiness with a fellow brought up to eat differently and to think differently.

"I always say marriage is hard enough, when you have the same ideas; why make it any harder? At least my husband was an American and he was willing to be married by the minister I picked out," Sarah concluded.

The bus jolted to a stop beside the hospital sign. Half a dozen passengers filed out, the pay-as-you-leave rule forcing them to stand in line while the driver made change.

"Did you notice his name over the wheel?" The fat woman straightened her hat as she started up the walk beside Sarah. "He's a foreigner, all right. I hope he didn't hear what we were saying."

She didn't care, she wasn't ashamed of anything she had said, Sarah retorted. She believed in always letting people know where she stood. And no one had ever accused her of being two-faced.

Her new acquaintance left her at the entrance to the maternity building. Sarah was early, the nurse's aide at the desk regretted, she would have to wait fifteen minutes or so. Two other visitors, a man and a woman but evidently not together, were already waiting, seated in slippery leather chairs.

Sarah sat down on the edge of the couch and tapped an impatient foot. Another visitor, an elderly woman, approached the desk, demurred at the enforced delay. The clock in the corridor, she insisted, read seven o'clock.

The minutes dragged interminably. No one spoke. The lone man, obviously a new father rattled the paper tied around his bunch of flowers, shuffled his feet, and occasionally sighed. Sarah thought, *"Why, they're all going to see new babies. All except me.* She had been so glad, so thankful that Ginger's life had been spared that she had given comparatively little attention to the fact of the baby's death. *Well,* she reflected now, *she never held him in her arms, she had no chance to become attached to him. And she was so ill, she probably doesn't realize what happened.*

"All right!" The aide smiled and everyone looked startled, then hurried for the self-service elevator.

On the third floor Sarah began to tiptoe down the corridor, convinced that absolute quiet was a hospital rule. The doors of the private rooms were open and as she passed she glimpsed the mothers, most of them absurdly young, propped up on the high beds and surrounded by neglected-looking bouquets of expensive flowers crammed into inadequate containers.

I wonder if Ginger has flowers, Sarah thought. Mabel had declared the nurses to be dead-set against flowers since the war, for they could not give precious time to hunting up vases and changing the water. But now, seeing all these rooms, each decked with flowers, maybe—Sarah realized that she was passing the numbers 306 on a door and that 306 was the number of Ginger's room.

She entered cautiously and Ginger, lying inert, faced her unsmilingly from the bed. Her hand, the left hand with its wedding ring, lay on the coverlet, and Sarah was shocked to see that it looked almost bloodless.

"My darling!" She bent down to kiss the girl. "You'll be all right now, dear, after *such* a time. You haven't anything to do now, but rest and get well."

The chair beside the bed was the only place to sit. It was too low, Sarah fretted inwardly, it made her feel remote from Ginger and surely the bed was cranked unnecessarily high. She had satisfied herself that there was no fever, for Ginger's forehead had been cool and moist to her hand. But she didn't look natural—perhaps it was too soon to expect her to be on the mend.

"I haven't anything to do, have I, Mama?" Ginger pleated the sheet hem into fine tucks.

Sarah agreed. "Except to get well."

Ginger said levelly, "Well, I suppose it turned out the way you wanted it to."

"The way I wanted? What do you mean, darling?"

"My baby—he was a boy and you never could endure boys. So now you won't have to have him around. Did you see him, Mama?"

Sarah shook her head. Her lips felt stiff.

"I never saw him, either. Not once. Hoke's son." Ginger, from the height of the bed and her pillows, looked down at Sarah with inscrutable eyes. "Did you tell Papa?"

Astonishment galvanized Sarah into speech. "Your father? Me tell him? Why, he hasn't been home since we took you to the hospital. I haven't had a chance to tell him."

He had been to see her, Ginger said. Before visiting hours. The doctor had been there and had talked to him when the nurse telephoned from the reception desk. "Papa told me that all his life he had wanted a son. He cried, when I told him."

Sarah sat as if paralyzed. She turned her head, when Ginger pointed to the bureau, and her movements were stiff and slow, her features expressionless. The red gladioli had come from Papa, Ginger said. The flowers were arranged woodenly in a can of water, leaving space for Ginger to see herself in the mirror. "I don't suppose he knew what to get, so he bought red to look cheerful." Ginger put the back of her hand across her eyes, as if to shut out the sight.

"You wouldn't have liked a grandson, would you, Mama?"

The pain amounted almost to terror in Sarah's heart. Ginger, to whom she had always been so close! The doctor had said she must not be upset, it would be dreadful if she ran a temperature

—Sarah, confused and frightened, ached to take the girl in her arms and soothe her against her breast.

"Ginger, darling, don't talk that way. I can't begin to tell you how sorry I am about the little baby. Boy or girl—I would have loved your baby—you know that."

Ginger reiterated. "Not a boy." She shifted her position slightly, so that by raising one shoulder she could not see her mother. "I wish you'd go now, Mama," she said.

"You want me to go home? To leave you?" Poor Sarah fumbled helplessly with her worn purse, her gloves, "We haven't talked at all. I don't know what you'd like me to bring you."

A bell rang in the corridor.

"Oh, Mama, please go!" Ginger's voice rose to a shriek. "Leave me alone. I don't want you to bring me anything. Only go away. Go quick."

Sarah stumbled blindly to the door. People hurried past her, down the corridor, all going in the same direction, all intent on a common goal. Unable to think, Sarah hastened with them, turned when they did, stood grouped with them outside a door. The top of the door was glass and behind it a white-capped nurse gazed out placidly at the cluster of strangers.

A little, gray-haired woman stepped to the door, opened it a crack, and said, "Buckley."

While Sarah watched dully, the nurse stepped back, revealing a room lined with orderly rows of cribs. She selected a blanketed bundle, held it aloft. A tiny baby stared from the wrapping, his mittened fists flailing the air.

"Isn't he sweet? Isn't he grand?" the little, gray-haired woman demanded proudly. "He's three days old—my first grandchild."

She stepped back, allowing another woman to take her place. Sarah touched her sleeve. "What is it?" she questioned. "What are they all doing?"

Hadn't she heard the bell? the new grandmother asked, surprised. "That's the signal to visitors that they can see the baby. I stay and see them all, they're so sweeet. I've been here twice a day for three days now. We're all so crazy over having a boy."

It was that way in wartime, she confided; the hospital had been swamped with boy babies. "Which is yours? Why, aren't you going to wait to see your baby?" She stared after Sarah who had murmured something incoherent and was feeling her way to the elevator, blinded by the tears running down her face.

It took Mabel fifteen minutes to get her hair to look natural and careless and after that she had to put on fresh make-up and change her accents. She and the other girls in the office stocked their lockers as completely as their dressing tables at home. They knew all the secrets of working till five, or five-thirty, and then transforming a plain crêpe into a date dress, a businesslike hair-do into something glamorous. Most of the girls preferred to go from the office on a date, rather than from home. It saved explanation, wear and tear, and embarrassment to the boy friend, they thought.

"Big night?" A stenographer carefully applying mascara to her eyelashes questioned Mabel as they shared the wide mirror.

Just dinner, Mabel said, with an officer. They might dance afterward.

"You've been out a lot with him." The other girl winked rapidly to dry her lashes. "If he isn't sent overseas, it might not be so bad. Have you seen those pictures where they have crossed swords and everything?"

Mabel had seen them—the rotogravure sections were dotted with pictures of smiling brides and their officer bridegrooms, leaving the church.

Tobias had argued with Mabel that to be effective, the sword-bearers would have to be evenly matched. "Now you take the Knights of Pythias," Tobias illustrated. "I saw them cross their swords for one of their commanders to walk through. And some short fellers was opposite some tall fellers and the commander was fat, so he damn near got stuck under his honor arch. He had to tell the little fellers to stand tippy-toe, so as to leave him head room."

The Knights of Pythias were not members of the United States Army, Mabel had retorted. Anyway, if she had a military wedding, the ushers would be properly paired. "All my life I've dreamed of a formal wedding—maybe I'll have you give me away, Grandfather. I don't suppose Papa will be in any condition to face the limelight."

Lion would be all right, Tobias predicted, if no one told him where to find the champagne. "I'd like to drink a toast myself, in some good champagne."

"There'll be no liquor at my wedding—not a drop." Mabel stiffened. "I'm surprised that you'd mention it, Grandfather, knowing what my home has been, all because of Papa's unfortunate habits."

The only reason he'd mentioned champagne was because it went with a formal wedding, Tobias, who had a child's persistence, said. "You don't have to drink it—your guests will attend to that." Mabel, he reflected, was a contradictory creature, with her devotion to fashion and beauty parlors superimposed upon her rock-ribbed mind. Here she was dead-set against liquor, even in the abstract, and yet planning to marry a man whose money came from beer. She'd better mention it to young Bentley that she was pledged never to fill a drunkard's grave, Tobias brooded.

Tonight Mabel, seated opposite Rolfe Bentley in the small, quiet restaurant famous for its German specialties, perceived that she was the only patron in the place not drinking beer. She preferred cigarettes, she said, beer made women fat. No, light or dark, it made no difference—she didn't know one brand from another, she wouldn't have anything but coffee and that later.

Rolfe had ordered sauerbrauten for them both, and the potato dumplings were the waiter's pride. His grandmother, Rolfe said, had made dumplings, too. She had been a wonderful cook and his grandfather's saloon had owed its success to her free lunch.

"Did you know my grandfather kept a saloon?" he challenged Mabel. She looked uncomfortable.

"I—I heard. But Rolfe, you're a lawyer, aren't you?"

His firm jaw hardened almost imperceptibly. "Yes, I passed my bar exams before I went in. I am also an American citizen. But I am the third generation of a German family in this country. My grandfather kept a saloon. Like you, my mother is ashamed of facts. The brewery operates under the original name."

Mabel patted her small hat still further over one eye. In the mirror behind Rolfe she glimpsed a reflection of herself, slim, well groomed, not the type of woman who ate potato dumplings and let her figure go. She thought the green beans had a queer taste, too, but at least they couldn't be fattening.

"I don't see that you have any connection with the brewery, or with your grandfather's saloon, Rolfe." She smiled, meeting his serious, blue eyes. "You're a lawyer, you have your own life."

Rolfe was silent.

"After the war you'll have your law practice," Mabel urged. "And your father had the good sense to change your name."

The waiter brought the salad and Rolfe spoke to him in German. "I told him my grandmother didn't serve salad on the free lunch," he translated. "Look, Mabel, are you against beer, or saloons, or Germans? I can't make you out."

She loathed liquor in any form, Mabel said. "My mother's whole life has been ruined by my father's drinking. I hate the smell and sight and name of the stuff. So does Mama."

"Well, why do you feel my father displayed good sense when he altered the family name? Because it was German?"

She hadn't thought of that, Mabel admitted. Her aunt had said that in the last war people were down on anyone with a German name, but no one seemed to pay much attention now. "I never think of you as German, Rolfe. What I meant was that as long as you are a lawyer, it's nice for you to have a name that won't be connected with—with beer."

He saw that she was very honest and had forgotten to be coquettish. How much she cared for him, he could not be sure. "Beer put me through college, Mabel," he said.

The waiter suggested dessert and when Mabel had taken ice cream and Rolfe apple-cake, Mabel spoke less vehemently.

"Rolfe, I can't see what the brewery business has to do with you. You're a lawyer."

He had never practiced, he had gone into the Army the day after he passed the bar, Rolfe said. After the war it would take him several years to become established. "You must realize that what money I have now comes from beer. I own a good many shares in the brewery. If I broke with the family, sold my holdings, the money would still come from beer. I would not be willing to have my wife ashamed of the source of her support."

"I suppose not." Mabel's hand shook as she poured cream into her coffee.

Rolfe sweetened his for the third time. "We'd better get this settled, I think, before either of us gets hurt. Lots of the men in the Army drink beer—you can't say the war is being fought by the country's drunks, can you, Mabel?"

She didn't care, she loathed liquor and she loathed men who drank, Mabel reiterated. "Maybe your father didn't come home silly, night after night. Maybe he didn't let his wife support him, while he earned just enough money to pay for drinks. I don't care whether it's beer or whiskey, or—or spirits of ammonia, I'll have nothing to do with liquor in any form!"

He touched her slim wrist lightly. "Don't yell. I'd like to wring your father's neck, but that wouldn't make you happy, would it? Poor little girl . . . your mother—I met your mother once. . . . Tell me this, Mabel: would you marry a poor man? One without a steady income, so that you'd have to work, say for the first five years of marriage?"

Mabel thought, *Lord, how I hate my job! Five more years of it and I'll lose my freshness and then he'd want me to start in and have babies. Mama married a poor man and look at her now.*

"I think the man should have enough so that the girl can stop working," stipulated Mabel. "I couldn't keep house and go to business, too. Money isn't everything, but it does make life smoother."

"Suppose the man has an income from a brewery?"

For a moment the dream she had cherished seemed within her grasp. Rolfe Bentley had fifteen thousand a year, she had been told. With that amount coming in, as Mama always put it, a girl could stay home from work, have a nice apartment, pretty clothes, entertain for her husband and his brother officers home on leave. She was so tired of her job, of counting pennies, of always wanting the nice things and of being able to afford only the substitutes. Marriage without an adequate income would mean no escape. Men, Mama had said so often, could be beasts and one never knew until too late.

The image of Mama's tired, restless face replaced the dream. How had she ever for one moment considered marrying a man whose money had been made in beer? Poor Mama, doubtless some of the dollars that should have gone to her had been paid over bars for Rolfe's family's beer. His people were comfortable, they lived in luxury on the money taken from weak, selfish men like Papa.

A wave of affection for her mother, a desire to protect her, to make up to her for a lifetime of disappointment, rose like a warm tide in Mabel's heart. It was bad enough for a woman to have her husband a slave to drink, without also losing her daughter to the very forces that had helped to send him to destruction. When she thought of everything, the idea of marrying Rolfe Bentley was like insulting Mama.

Mabel forced her gaze upward to meet the Lieutenant's blue eyes. "I couldn't. It's blood money. Mama would never get over it."

She waited numbly while Rolfe paid the cashier, a fat, jovial woman who had a mug of beer on her desk, and begged off from dancing when they reached the street. They were good friends, she assured Rolfe, they had a date for the next day, but if he didn't mind she'd like to go home. It was early, so his evening wouldn't be spoiled.

They were both silent in the taxi and at the door of the house he shook hands, not offering to kiss her.

"So long," he said lightly and she responded mechanically, "So long."

In the hall Sarah came to meet her, her face so ravaged by weeping that Mabel's first thought was that Ginger must have died.

"Ginger wouldn't let me stay with her!" Tears choked Sarah's harsh voice. "She hates the sight of me, because of the baby. Mabel, she *wanted* a boy!"

Before Mabel could answer, Sarah's mood altered swiftly, anger thrusting aside grief. "Your father came home and I sent him packing!" she stormed. "I've stood everything from him, all my life, but when he turns my children against me, I'm through. He can never enter this house again."

Chapter Fifteen

THEY would have to do something about Leidy before summer vacation set in for the elementary schools, Ida Ferris said at Sunday breakfast. "One more week and she'll be racing the streets from morning till night. Unless we make plans. She ought to go to camp."

Frank did not answer, but Ida knew the futility of the suggestion. Years ago, when Leidy had been a baby, the little daughter of one of Frank's business acquaintances had drowned at a children's summer camp. The usually pliable Frank had rejected camps, of all kinds, from that day forward and Ida had no hope of persuading him to change his mind.

Leidy had her own ideas about her vacation. She wanted to go to the playground, three blocks from the house. All the kids were going—they had classes in sewing and painting, Leidy urged.

Most of the playground teachers were Jewish and fully one-third of the children were colored, with a large enrollment of Jewish, too, Ida confided to Frank, when Leidy had reluctantly departed for Sunday school. "What chance has an ordinary American white child in such a set-up?"

"There aren't enough ordinary American white children as you so delicately express it, to keep a playground going," Frank informed her. "Doesn't it ever occur to you why there are so many colored and so many Jewish and of course so many Catholic children? Those families have kids in dozen lots. We quit with one."

Ida reminded him that had been his idea, that she herself thought two children an ideal number. "Of course people like us can't compete with the irresponsible who marry at nineteen or twenty and have a baby every year. But I don't intend to have my child trampled on by the horde, just because she's in the minority."

Leidy stood a mighty fair chance of having a Jewish cousin some day, Frank suggested. He lowered his voice, for although he and Ida were on the screened back porch, one never could be sure how far a voice might carry. "Ceil will be having children, I suppose. By the way, does anyone ever write to her?"

The entire clan had written her about Fern Eustice running off on her commencement night to marry Jim Kotoski, Ida said. "I wrote her myself that Ginger had joined her husband in Tennessee and that Mabel is living at that woman's club, downtown. Mabel swears she won't ever come home as long as her father lives."

"More comfortable for him, I guess," Frank commented. "Ceil still in Texas?"

Ida said yes, according to the last letter Dora had received. "They have a house and Cecil's constant fear is that a colonel will want it for his own family. She's also worried about Tag going overseas, but there's nothing definite about that, yet."

Ida turned to the newspapers, read the war headlines at a gallop. "Do you think Ceil's children would look Jewish, Frank?" she inquired. "She's—well, undiluted English and Dutch stock and he is so good-looking, with his mother a Gentile and all."

You couldn't tell, Frank assured her. Cecil's baby might be a throw-back and turn out the living image of a rabbi. "That is, if she has a boy."

"If she has any sense, she'll pray for a girl." Ida turned the radio dial. "A girl can change her name. Tag should have done it before he married Ceil." Ida handed the radio program to her husband. "Look and see what station has that Jewish comedian; the girls at the plant say his dialect is a scream."

The next afternoon Frank left the bus at the stop opposite the large playground he had passed for years without a second glance. He was a good hour ahead of his usual time and Mrs. Holdfast would not be delayed if he detoured long enough to see what lay beyond the high, wire fence. Public playgrounds had not been part of his education in the grades; the uptown city streets, where the family had lived, had been safe for youngsters after school. Trees and lawns had lined either side of the wide expanse of asphalt and if the neighbors suffered from the noise accompanying baseball and football games, and the incessant roller skating, why presumably they had suffered in silence for the sake of their own children's pleasure.

He had moved to the suburbs to give Leidy space for play, Frank reflected, peering through the wide-mesh fence. Since gasoline rationing, traffic had declined somewhat, but still presented a hazard. However, with yards of their own and no dearth of vacant lots, the modern kid seemed to have a violent aversion to playing within sight of his home. He'd do anything, go anywhere, to escape sight and sound of parental supervision. Yet the playground, to which children flocked, was supervised by a staff who imposed regulations and saw to it that they were observed. He must ask Ida what she made of it, Frank decided; perhaps the books she read might have the explanation.

A sign on the gate—folded back to permit entrance—said that the playground was open from three to six o'clock on week days, from nine till six on Saturdays, and closed all day Sunday. The vacation schedule was posted as from nine till five-thirty o'clock, six days a week.

"Used to be they closed at five o'clock on week days, and noons,

Saturday," volunteered a cracked voice. "They changed, on account of so many defense workers asking 'em to keep their kids."

Surprised, Frank perceived a bench faced toward him on the other side of the wire. A little, wrinkled, old woman sat there, placidly knitting. Her back to the playground, she was evidently more interested in the street than in the children. A heap of khaki-colored wool filled the lap of her cotton house dress and wisps of white hair, looking like strands of wool, too, straggled from the knot pinned high on her head.

"I just thought I'd look around," Frank said.

"Ain't it wonderful, all they do for the kids these days?" his new acquaintance demanded. "In my time we played when we could, between helping with the housework, running errands, and like that. Play's a system now and yet more kids are running wild and getting into trouble than when I went to school. You know why?"

Frank walked through the gates, half turned. Over his shoulder he mumbled hastily. "Sorry, I haven't much time."

The sound of the cracked voice followed him. "All the trouble started in the last war. When our men took to marrying French women. My son came home with a French wife."

Frank began to walk faster.

"The French haven't any morals, never did have," the old woman shouted after him. "We never got back to our plain, God-fearing ways, after the boys came home the last time."

The competitive screams of children guided Frank to the wading pool. Youngsters paddled happily in the shallow, concrete basin, or sat on the rim, admiring the contorted images of their feet in the water. Beyond them older children played in the swings and a game of soft ball was in progress in a far corner, boys and girls on each team. There were a good many colored children, Frank noticed and they seemed to stick together in groups of three or four, although that might be his fancy.

He strolled over to a long, saw-horse table, about which a crowd of children clustered. A girl, scarcely taller than the oldest child, was cutting a picture from a magazine. She paused, looked at Frank and said, "Hi!" But her dark eyes, appraising him, demanded identification.

"I'm a visitor," he told her. "My little girl wants to use the playground during vacation. We live over on Maple Avenue."

The girl handed her magazine to the child standing next to her. "Anna is to cut one picture, then you may each choose—and no arguments. I'll be back in a few moments."

She came around the table and Frank saw that she wore denim slacks and a white, short-sleeved blouse. Her hair was a thick, dark mass. She radiated vitality and energy and her manner was unaffected and frank.

"I'm Norma Steiner," she said, smiling. "On duty from three to six. When vacation starts we'll have another girl. Perhaps two. Does your daughter come often? Perhaps I know her."

Leidy might have been to the playground, Frank returned, but as far as he knew she had never spent much time there. It was lonely for her at home, their housekeeper didn't have the gift for handling children. "My wife works, so in one way or another our daughter is left pretty much to herself." He repeated that he had dropped in to look around, since Leidy had been so enthusiastic over the vacation attractions.

"You want to know if the swings and other apparatus are safe and what precautions are taken against accidents," Miss Steiner said.

Frank nodded. "Exactly."

"And whether the sanitary arrangements are good, and if we war against the older children bullying the little ones."

Frank said, "Yes."

"You're also curious—or anxious—to find out whether your daughter will meet children socially acceptable to your wife and you. She won't." Miss Steiner, who had been watching the table, suddenly called out to the group intent on the magazines. "Louis is to do the pasting today. It's his turn."

He didn't expect Leidy to make social connections, Frank was protesting in irritated resentment. "But don't you think it natural for a parent to want to know something of the children with whom his child plays? Especially when she is a little girl? It's not snobbish, it's American to hope that one's child will go forward, not drop to a lower level."

Miss Steiner shrugged her shoulders, suggested that they tour the playground. The children running past them noticed them no more than if they had been trees; when a youngster crashed head-on into Frank, the lad recovered his breath in a single gulp, scrambled to his feet, and dashed away, neither knowing nor caring what the obstruction had been.

"Children pick up bad habits, unfortunate traits, more readily than they copy desirable behavior," Frank argued, feeling a vague need to justify himself against an unspoken accusation.

The girl beside him smiled down at a youngster in the sand pit. "What is desirable behavior?" she challenged. "Isn't it in part the ability to get along well with all kinds of people?"

"Maybe, but—"

"And that means a knowledge of their good qualities, a respect for their contributions to our common life."

It was Frank's turn to shrug. Theories were fine, he agreed, until put to the test. Then they usually deflated like—like a pierced barrage balloon. The simile was supplied him by the sight of a great silver bag floating overhead, a sight that attracted the attention of the children, long indifferent, Miss Steiner said, to airplanes.

"Be honest now, don't you have trouble with the various racial groups here—the coons and the Wops and the Poles and—"

"The Jews," Miss Steiner composedly supplemented.

"All right, the Jews. Don't they look down on each other, make nasty remarks?"

The girl shook her curly, dark mane. "Children fight, of course," she conceded. "They have battles royal over whose turn it is to have a seesaw, or a shower, or a ball. They argue fiercely over their maps and jackstraws and glider models. But they never fight or argue about race. All the trouble we have between Italians, colored, Jews, what have you, comes from the parents." Miss Steiner stamped her moccasined foot. "If I had my way," she said, "all parents would be put down in boiling oil!"

Chapter Sixteen

"PEACE, it's wonderful!" Sally Parks, who with her husband shared the first floor of the old house in Columbia with Cecilia and Tag, fanned herself with an enormous palm-leaf fan. "They let us stay three days at the hotel and three days at the hostess house and so far we've been here three weeks. You don't think Grandma will come home before the end of summer, do you?"

Cecilia laughed. Sally was good-natured, easy-going and, surprisingly, a capable executive, when necessity demanded. That the two girls had found an apartment, following Tag's transfer back to Fort Jackson, was due mainly to Sally's sunny persistence. There was a quality of permanency about her visits to the real estate office, the head of the rent control, and the various other sources to which she had been directed, that suggested she would visit each in turn at the same hour every day for, undoubtedly, the duration. Cecilia accompanied her, but served mainly as witness to the facts of Sally's story—that two more Army wives, with husbands in camp, wished to share housekeeping expenses. Both girls agreed that they had been ready to give up and buy tickets home when, on the last day allowed them at the hostess house, (in return for lending her a much-needed hand, the woman in charge had already stretched the three-day limit to six) the little real estate agent had succumbed.

"Say, I think I've found a place for you," he had greeted the now routine entrance of Cecilia and Sally into his small, untidy office. "My brother's wife's grandmother is going visiting for the rest of the summer and she may rent her place. She lives on the first floor of my brother's house."

Sally was half way to the door. "Where is it?"

She'd do better to wait, the agent cautioned. The old lady was leaving on the one o'clock train and she was easily upset. "Let her get off and then you go see my brother's wife."

Neither Cecilia nor Sally had dared believe that anything would come of it, but they ate their drugstore lunch in a flutter of excitement. By ten minutes after one they were ringing Mrs. Ralston's doorbell and twenty minutes later they had paid their deposit. An extra bedroom on the second floor was included in the rental; Mrs. Ralston, very young, very friendly, explained that it was the room of her grandmother's youngest son and that he had gone into the Navy.

"What I want to know," said Sally to Cecilia as they drove away in Sally's small car, "is, does Grandma know that her first floor is rented?"

Cecilia had her suspicions, too, but the girls agreed it was none of their business. What did matter was that they had possession of a huge living room, with a fireplace, a dining room which they didn't really need, two bedrooms, and an electric kitchen.

The furnishings were old—indeed, the bed in which Cecilia and Tag slept had been part of Grandma's wedding outfit, young Mrs. Ralston assured them. It had a headboard that was almost as high as the ceiling and two great carved urns securely (Cecilia hoped) screwed to the heavy posts. There was a second bed, fully as large, in the room and two enormous beds in Sally and Hal's room, too. Grandma had had a large house and when her health failed and the family insisted she take smaller quarters and relax, she had moved as much of her furniture as she could get into her granddaughter's house.

Cecilia and Sally shared the work, the marketing, the expenses. Both agreed that they were the luckiest wives in town, to have space in which to spread out. Sally's constant fear was that the old lady would return and demand the surrender of her rooms. Old ladies, Sally said gloomily, hated to be away from their own firesides and especially from their own beds.

"Grandma's likely to decide that Mrs. Ralston isn't feeding the cat, or has left a window open as an invitation to a burglar," Sally predicted. "All she needs is a flimsy excuse, to dash back and toss us out."

In the short time she had known her, Cecilia had become very fond of Sally. They had met in the hostess house where visitors to camp were permitted to stay the prescribed time, but where no men, not even husbands, were allowed beyond the lobby.

"Can't I carry up her bags for her?" Tag had begged the manager, when he brought Cecilia there.

Tall, straight, immaculately pressed in his uniform, he had only to look at the manager with his smiling, dark eyes, to win her consent. The sergeant might, she said, carry the bags to the top of the stairs, but no further. And she remained at the foot, implacably watching, until at the top of the stairs he dropped the bags, kissed Cecilia, and ran fluidly down again to the main floor.

"Think no evil, see no evil, is the motto," a gay voice observed from one of the room doorways and Sally Parks had come forward to lend a hand with Cecilia's bags.

The hostess had hesitated—not quite imperceptibly—when she had repeated, "Sergeant and Mrs. Silverstein?" and Sally, too, at first hearing had made that inevitable, little movement of stiffening which Cecilia had grown to expect and still could not wholly ignore. But Sally had been friendly and cheerful without visible effort and Cecilia had had no hesitation in adopting her suggestion that they hunt for a place to which "the boys" could come home on the nights when not detained in camp.

Hal Parks' rank was that of Tag's—top sergeant—but in another outfit and the two had never met. Tag approved warmly of the housekeeping project, as did Hal, but finding the place to live was the responsibility of the Army wife.

It developed, as the two girls had doggedly pressed their search, that two phobias haunted Sally. One was a bitter resentment against the townfolk whom she catologued as "insane over money." Her other fixation was a horror of syphilis. Sally had worked, before her marriage, in a large New York hospital laboratory; her two sisters were registered nurses. She could, she told Cecilia, recognize the symptoms of syphilis at a glance and she meant to be examined every six months as long as she followed Hal from camp to camp.

"It's all very well to say the Army has it licked," she would say, when her husband sought to reassure her, "but the Army doesn't get hold of the cases wandering about town. People like Ceil and me, who go into so many furnished rooms in town, where sanitary conditions are as primitive as the moral levels, can't be too careful."

So when Cecilia, on a tip from the grocery store clerk, took Sally to inspect two bedrooms and a kitchen, it was the bathroom facilities at which Sally balked.

"I could, if necessary, cook meals and wash dishes in the bedroom," she admitted, referring to the peculiar arrangement which placed the kitchen at one end of the larger bedroom, which must also serve as the living room, and the sink in the second bedroom, "but did you count up how many lodgers have to use that one bathroom? The landlady told me how many rooms she has rented and I figure sixteen people as a minimum. Can you imagine waiting in a line of sixteen to get to a bathtub? Or what you'd find there, once you reached it?"

But now for a time their worries were over, Cecilia told herself contentedly, sitting on the steps to wait for the postman. Of course they didn't know how long they would be permitted to live, as Sally said, "practically like normal, human beings," but while it lasted the lull was heavenly sweet. Tag came home almost every night and even when he or Hal were out in the field they could send him cakes, chocolate cakes, drippy, upside-down cakes, any kind of cake to share with the other men and which reached him while they were still fresh and moist.

Sally had gone to the doctor's this late July morning. One drawback to having sisters as trained nurses, Cecilia had concluded, was that one knew too much. Every time Sally had a pain she considered all the possibilities; even when she admitted that it was probably not serious, still she had to ponder the terrifying "perhaps." She would come home today, laughing at herself and bringing something special as a treat for supper, to celebrate her release from tension.

The postman, who moved slowly, turned in at the Ralston path. Mrs. Ralston was also out, and Cecilia was, as so rarely happened, quite alone. She smiled at the postman, whose hair and eyebrows and small mustache, bleached white by the sun, looked artificial, contrasted with his brick-red face.

"Morning—" he handed her a sheaf of letters, dropped a postcard into the Ralston box. "You standing the heat pretty well?"

Cecilia said, "I'm used to it," which was a white lie, because the glare of the sun still made her eyes ache and the temperature in the middle of the day would have unnerved her, except that she forced herself to think of the men engaged in manœuvres under its pitiless flame.

She watched the postman plod wearily across the street and

saw that his shirt was dark with sweat and that he walked like a robot, with no spring in his step.

Three of the letters were for Cecilia, three for Sally. The first Cecilia opened was the insurance policies on her furs—shortage of clerical help had delayed them, the storage firm apologized. The other letters were from her Grandfather Ferris and her Grandmother Warren.

Tobias wrote a gossipy, garrulous missive. Cecilia's Aunt Sarah, he related, had only lately seemed to be on the road to becoming reconciled to what she called the loss of her girls. With Nutmeg in the South with her husband, Fern living on a Kotoski fruit farm, and Mabel turned bachelor girl with three other ardent feminists, poor Sarah had been lonely indeed.

"Until, providentially," Tobias wrote, "your Uncle Lion broke his leg. He can't get anything to drink and Sarah has someone to wait on day and night, so she's really pleased with him. Tray service is essential to your Aunt Sarah's complete happiness, I find."

Little Leidy had been sent to a ranch camp for the summer, the letter continued. Frank had consented, when he learned there were no water sports. Frank had been having some throat trouble, had been sent by his doctor to a specialist who was Jewish and extremely bitter against the refugees. Foreign doctors, the specialist had told Frank, were getting themselves established in practice while the young American doctors were in service. The specialist's two sons, one a doctor, one a dentist, were in the Army.

"Dora has just read this over my shoulder," the neat, fine writing began a new page. "She thinks I should leave it out. This I am not willing to do, partly because I would have to rewrite and partly because I do not feel, as she does, that you shrink from reference to the Jews. The throat man was just like any other father, as I see it, mad because he thought someone was grabbing what belonged to his boys."

Dora was still opposed to the Catholics, the Protestants, and the Jews, Tobias confided, for which the mothers of brides were to blame. Quilty remained the balance wheel of the household, gentle and good. "When I realize that she can barely read and write and that she makes excuses for us all, I wonder whether we wouldn't be better off without learning."

Not that a high school or college diploma guaranteed an education, Tobias amended. The theory now, as Dora had explained it to him, was that a child must not have its ego wounded by failure to pass. They must, at all costs, keep up with their contemporaries. If they reached high school without having learned to add two and two, their pride was supposed to sustain them.

"Whether it will get them jobs, who knows?" inquired the critic of modern education. "Leidy can be sure of having her pride and her diploma when she finishes school, but how in hell will she know whether she has any brains?"

His sister Annabel, he continued, had spent a week with him while Molly and Charlie Cotter had attended a convention in Detroit. "Ida visited her mother from eight till ten one evening, dressed in her best, including hat, gloves, and veil. In fact she was an example of what the well-dressed woman wears when calling formally upon her mother."

Dora had added a postscript to the letter. She felt it to be her duty, she wrote, to let Cecilia know that her grandfather's powers of deflation had not atrophied. One of the young girls in the neighborhood had approached Tobias to sell him tickets to a peach and ice cream supper the Girl Scouts planned. As she waited for him to make change, the girl had tried to keep conversation flowing.

"She said to Father, 'I'm simply mad about peaches,' Dora quoted. 'Aren't you mad about peaches, Mr. Ferris?'

"Father looked at her in that provoking way of his and pondered. 'No,' he decided finally, 'no, I don't think I'm mad about them. But you might say I'm attracted to them.' "

Cecilia, smiling, replaced the letter in its envelope. She would leave her grandmother's letter till after lunch. Half unconsciously she shrank from these communications, sometimes carrying a letter about with her unopened for several days. Whatever Grandmother Warren wrote would be depressing, reproachful and if prophetic, apprehensive and fearful.

Sally returned bringing a jelly roll and the cheerful tidings that she needed more Vitamin A. They had lunch and afterward Sally went upstairs to nap. Cecilia, too, tried to sleep in the big, darkened bedroom, but no rest came to her. She forced herself to lie still for an hour, then bathed and dressed and went out to the porch, in a grateful shade now, to read her grandmother's letter.

Sally came out with a panful of peas to shell, just as Cecilia had finished the third reading. It was Sally's week to get the meals and she bemoaned the sturdiness of the Army appetite. "You'd think in hot weather that the boys would be satisfied with a gelatine salad, wouldn't you?" she said.

"No."

Astonished to have been taken seriously, Sally glanced darkly at the letter in Cecilia's lap. "Bad news?"

Not exactly bad, Cecilia fumbled, but rather upsetting. She clasped her hands about her knees, leaned her dark head against the cracked and veined porch post, painted a salmon tinge. "My grandmother," she said, "is offering me two hundred thousand dollars, if I'll persuade Tag to change his name."

At the other end of the step Sally nearly let the pan of peas slide off her lap. She caught it in time, but her mouth hung open. "Two hundred thousand?" she managed finally. "Why, for that money I'd do anything!"

Cecilia spread out her left hand on the porch floor and seemed to be studying her wedding ring. "That's what you think," she retorted.

She didn't think, she knew, Sally insisted. She sat hugging the pan to her aproned bosom, her face bright with curiosity. "Does your grandmother want to adopt Tag, or something?" she asked.

Grandmother Warren, Cecilia set forth with a disconcerting feeling of unreality as she talked, was making a new will. The two hundred thousand was her own money and separate from her husband's estate. "Grandfather Warren left something to me, I don't know how much, to come to me at Grandmother's death. Nothing can affect that. But Grandmother herself is quite free to leave her money as she pleases."

Sally blinked. "Then she wants Tag to take the name of Warren—is that it?"

"She wants him to take any name that has no connotation of the Hebrew." Cecilia looked steadily at Sally.

The other girl leaned forward and a volley of small, green balls skipped merrily down the steps. "Well, for heaven's sake! I thought you'd lost your last friend. What's wrong with the idea? I call it a darn easy way to make two hundred thousand, don't you?"

"I don't know." Cecilia watched an ant traveling the length of a sun-baked crack.

Sally straightened. She did hope that Cecilia wouldn't be silly enough to wreck her life. Not only could she and Tag be sure of a wonderful nest-egg, but their everyday life would be easier in a hundred ways.

"I've never liked to say anything to you, Ceil, because Hal

and I both think you and Tag are tops. But that last name of his certainly handicaps him—both of you, in fact. You know I had a terrible time explaining you to Mrs. Ralston and she's still jittery for fear her grandmother will come back and find her house had been rented to—to—"

"Jews." Cecilia spoke listlessly. "I know. But everyone likes Tag as soon as they see him, Sally. They don't care what his name is, once they know him."

Plenty of people would refuse to know him, because of his name, Sally declared. "If Tag had a Gentile name, he could go everywhere. It isn't fair to him to be forced to overcome such a handicap."

"You mean it isn't fair for him to have to fight the prejudices of people who condemn him for silly, personal antipathies, before they even meet him," Cecilia countered.

Sally grimaced. The world was like that, no one could fight the world.

"I thought we were," said Cecilia. "I thought we were fighting the world to stamp out prejudice. How far would you say we have come?"

But when Sally had gone indoors to make her Hal's favorite pudding, Cecilia remained propped up against the seamy old post, thinking. Two hundred thousand dollars would buy their dream house after the war, would open the way for Tag to study for a profession, or make it possible for him to choose the business he preferred. *It's not disgraceful to change one's name,* Cecilia thought, *people do it every day for a variety of reasons.* She recollected that Tag's mother's name of Taget had a pleasant sound—he might take the name of his mother's family to which he was surely entitled.

Cecilia closed her eyes. She would be Mrs. Taget. Sergeant and Mrs.—not Hyman, no, it could be Herman—Sergeant and

Mrs. Herman Taget. No more of that involuntary stiffening, the almost imperceptible hesitancy, followed by the delighted surprise that was perhaps the hardest of all to bear.

"Jewish, but nice"—that was what people said about her and Tag. Cecilia knew, for she had overheard them.

She told herself now that changing his name would save Tag heartache, too. He pretended not to notice, he ascribed slights to figments of fancy, he would not, he said, be like the Irish woman who complained that everyone slurred her. But Tag was sensitive. He had been hurt a hundred times as a child, he was often hurt now. Herman Taget would protect Tag, strangers would not pick up that name, turn it about in their minds, and reject it before they came face to face with the smiling, handsome man who owned it.

When Cecilia opened her eyes, the ant was making frantic efforts to extricate himself from the crack into which he had slipped. She plucked a bobby-pin from her hair and applied herself to the rescue. *If we have children,* her thoughts flowed on, *they may be discriminated against. Unless their name should be Taget.* She and Tag were adults, they could take it on the chin, but if a little son came home from school in tears, or shut himself away with a wordless grief—*I couldn't endure it, to see my child hurt. Tag and I have no right to take that chance.* Cecilia watched the ant stagger away and plunge crazily over the edge of the flooring, which was probably a precipice to the ant kingdom.

After dinner that night Sally bore Hal off to the movies, announcing pointedly as they departed that she knew Cecilia and Tag had a lot to talk over.

"Have we?" Tag inquired with interest, pulling his wife down beside him on the high-backed carved sofa, divided, as

Tag gravely observed, like all Gaul, into three parts. The springs sagged in the middle, but the ends, again to quote Tag, were as good as new.

Her head comfortably supported on his shoulder, Cecilia gave him her grandmother's letter to read. "I told Sally, because I wanted to get her reaction."

"She voted 'Aye,' I suppose?"

Cecilia said that two hundred thousand dollars would impress most women. "It's a lot of money."

"Well, pride comes high." Tag's lips brushed her hair.

People changed their names every day, Cecilia argued, it was apparently a fairly simple court procedure. "I don't mean just Jewish people, Tag, but others, too. They shorten long names and alter the spelling and take their mothers' family names—"

"Uh-huh, it's to be Taget, is it?" interposed Tag.

A little confused, Cecilia reddened. "Well, you wouldn't want to grab a name out of a hat, would you, Tag? To be called Taylor Hastings wouldn't mean a thing to you. Whereas your mother's family name is yours by right of inheritance. It's a logical selection, it seems to me."

Tag patted her cheek. "What about my father's family name? Not so hot, eh?"

Laughter bubbled unexpectedly to Cecilia's lips. "You have to sell it twenty times a day, that's the only objection to it," she said. "People like us, when they know us, Tag, but it would be nicer if they liked us when they met us."

His handsome, merry face instantly sobered and something like tragedy shadowed his dark eyes. "You have the hardest part, don't you, my love?"

"Oh, no!" Cecilia put her hand on his lips in swift denial. "Don't ever think that, Tag."

"Oh, yes," Tag corrected. "I know how it is. I have known for some time. Don't think that because I have said nothing, I haven't guessed. Even before we were married, I foresaw how it would be."

Cecilia lied gallantly. "It hasn't mattered, Tag. Look at me—I am the happiest of the happy. No one, nothing, can hurt me, at least not beyond the moment."

"I know how it is," Tag said again. He spoke as if to himself. "When you say you are Mrs. Silverstein . . . then the vicious, the stupid, and the cruel begin to bay you, like hounds. Is it any wonder that I hesitated to let you take this upon yourself? Cecil, how could I let you, so innocent and sweet, sacrifice yourself for me?"

She tried to hush him, her arms about him. "I have not been sacrificed. I was never happy, till I became your wife. Tag, you never talked like this before."

"Nights out in the field, I have blamed myself a thousand times. God! There have been nights when I could think of nothing else." His face, as Cecilia watched him, set in haggard, stern lines that wiped out all its youth. "I learned not to mind it for myself years ago," he said.

Cecilia whispered. "When the boys wouldn't let you play on their ball team."

"Yes. And before that. But now, I have to see you up against the same thing at every turn, watch you placate landladies, persuade strangers—you! Cecil, I have learned, since our marriage: prejudice is a seeping, dark stain, I think, more difficult to fight than hatred—which is powerful and violent and somehow more honest, too."

They had made friends, Cecilia reminded him. "Sally and Hal are really fond of us, Tag."

"Well, they like us, yes. But to their other friends they probably excuse themselves with the assurance that we're quite refined."

Tag drew Cecilia into his arms with a passionate, protecting gesture. "Yes, I could do as your grandmother asks, not for money—we must turn back that horrible bribe—but for you alone, my darling, loyal wife."

Cecilia said against his lips, "Could you do it without regrets?"

He was silent and she pulled herself free, to sit up facing him.

"I thought about it all this afternoon, Tag. And if we should have children—"

"Children!" He frowned. "My God, I didn't think." He got to his feet and stood staring at the fan of peacock feathers in the fireplace.

Cecilia faltered, "They might be discriminated against . . . I don't know. If other children taunted them, I couldn't stand it."

He tramped the length of the room, wheeled and came back to her. "I could stand it. I could teach my son to understand and take it. But I could never explain to him that his father had been a coward."

"Tag! That isn't being fair to yourself. If you do it for the sake of your child—to save him pain—why isn't it the good and right thing to do?"

The deep glow of his smile kindled behind his eyes, his whole face became radiant as Cecilia watched him. "It isn't good and it isn't right, Honey Girl," he said almost gaily, "because no soldier walks out on a fight. He has to see the battle through. This happens to be my war."

He leaned down to tilt Cecilia's troubled face up to meet his gaze. "I've involved the innocent, but I guess that always happens, too," he regretted. "I'm sorry, Ceil."

"I shall never be sorry for anything," Cecilia said, "as long as you kiss me like that."

Chapter Seventeen

"MR. LESSER will see you now," the reception clerk said. She beckoned to a neat, slim girl, seated on a bench beside the water-cooler. "Take Mrs. Silverstein in to Mr. Lesser, please, Martha," the clerk directed.

Cecilia followed the trim figure down an office-lined corridor, halted as she tapped on one of the plate-glass panels.

"Mrs. Silverstein to see you, Mr. Lesser!"

The door closed noiselessly behind her and Cecilia found that she stood in a large, square room, handsomely furnished in quiet good taste. Enormous windows opened to the late summer sunshine, but shaded by adequate awnings, filtered abundant air and light and the street noises sounded broken and indistinct. A vast, dark brown expanse of rug covered the floor; the mellow beige walls set off the walnut bookcases and one or two pictures in wide, brown frames.

At one end of the rug was a large, flat-topped desk. Cecilia moved toward it and a man seated there rose to shake hands. "Mrs. Silverstein? Will you sit down?"

Cecilia took the chair beside his desk. He was smiling at her and the goodness, the compassion, the gentleness, but above all the sheer goodness, in his face touched her spirit like a benediction. She had been nervous, rehearsing what she should say, anxious about her references from the old bank, afraid that her awkwardness, always intensified by any new test, might betray her into some ridiculous situation. For almost the first time in her life, she realized, she had faced the ordeal of meeting a stranger and had felt no trepidation. Harmony and peace, she began to comprehend, filled the big room.

"I have a letter from our board chairman," Mr. Lesser was saying. "He tells me that you are applying for a position in the bank—your husband, I understand, is in the service?"

Cecilia said in her low, clear voice, "My husband is on his way overseas. I came North from his camp to work and to be with my grandmother."

She looked very young and slender in a gray and white print, the jacket and skirt set off by a high-throated white blouse. Her dark hair, caught into a soft, full pompadour in front and the revived page-boy bob in back, anchored a white crocheted calot in some mysterious fashion. "Before my marriage, I worked in the Security Trust Company," she offered, so earnestly that Bruno Lesser laughed outright.

"You don't look exactly toilworn," he admitted, "but even brief experience is helpful."

For a few moments he questioned her; about her marriage, her education, the days at the Security Trust. "You think it better to re-enter banking, since you will not be wholly a novice? Well, perhaps you're right." He would make out a slip for her to give to the reception clerk who would furnish her with the customary forms to fill out, he said, dipping a pen into the handsome bronze inkwell.

But when he had ceased to write he did not dismiss her, but held the slip in his hand, his face so filled with kindness a little turned from her. Cecilia, studying him, did not know whether to call him handsome—perhaps his features were not regular enough for that. He had a tall, lean figure and heavy, white hair emphasized the brownness of his skin.

It did not disconcert her when he turned to meet her scrutiny, but she was unprepared to have him say, "Mrs. Silverstein, you are not—of my race?"

Cecilia shook her head. "No. My husband—"

"Ah, yes." He sighed. "You will find it very difficult... at times—" He broke off abruptly, paused. "Perhaps you have already found it difficult?" he questioned.

To her horror, Cecilia felt the forces within herself give way. The compassion in the beautiful, tragic, brown eyes watching her was like a hand laid upon her heart, unlocking all the pent-up grief and pity she had walled off for the sake of Tag's fierce, brave pride. It seemed to Cecilia that her tears were tearing her apart, yet in truth she wept quietly and the dignity of her sorrow suggested fortitude, rather than desolation.

"I am glad and proud to be his wife." She spoke clearly when she could control her voice. "This is because I haven't cried since—since we said good-by."

Bruno Lesser waited while an airplane, flying low, drowned out all other sound. It passed and he said, "Your husband is a happy and fortunate man."

"We are both happy." Cecilia tried to smile.

That might be, he allowed, but she was young and unkindness was as old as the world. In the final analysis, men had always hurt each other when they forgot to be kind.

"I would not preach tolerance, which seems to me another name for condescension and presupposes faults in those to be tolerated," he said gently. "Nor do I believe in demanding love—that should be the gift of a free will. But simply to be kind—that is not too much to ask of any of us."

Cecilia's wet eyes clung to his and he went on to tell her that he had long thought most of the racial antagonism in the

United States was inherent, ingrained—to some degree, one might say, unconscious.

"You can tell this by the sectional differences. In many places where Catholics were discriminated against fifty years ago, today they are still being called the same names by the descendants of the early baiters—but they work together amicably enough. In other regions, Jews are the victims of prejudices so automatic that actually no one attaches any meaning to the timeworn phrases."

Cecilia nodded. "I have a friend who says 'Damn Jew!' everytime a car driver honks his horn at him—without even stopping to see who's driving the other car."

They both laughed and Bruno Lesser rose. "Try to believe in the power of the individual who is kind," he said, giving Cecilia the slip for the clerk.

On an early September Saturday, when the bank had closed at noon, Cecilia hurried home to help her grandmother dress for Molly Cotter's tea. Molly was giving the party for her mother, Annabel Pinn. It was Annabel's birthday, old Mrs. Warren had learned, and she had asked Cecilia to buy a gift for her to take—a bottle of the fragrant toilet water that Annabel loved.

"Your Grandfather Ferris is invited, too," old Mrs. Warren chattered happily. "I said to Molly over the telephone that he's almost the only old man we know. The world seems so full of old women, widows, and the men are so few."

Her grandmother would have declined the invitation, Cecilia knew, if she had still been living alone. The change in old Mrs. Warren since her granddaughter had rejoined her was remarkable, everyone said. She had recovered her interest in clothes and revived her social activities. Her heart was not good, the doctor urged her to be careful, but even he admitted that to go about and see her friends benefited her.

"I wasn't made to be a recluse," she announced, sitting at her dressing table while Cecilia adjusted a net over the smartly-waved hair and pinned it in place. "I need youth around me, darling."

The lovely, absorbed face above her shoulders seemed intent on the task of arranging the fine, fragile net. Old Mrs. Warren, suddenly aware of the brilliant sunshine, asked worriedly, "What will you do with yourself this afternoon, dearie?"

"Oh—I don't know." Cecilia pushed in a hairpin. "Read, perhaps. Or wash my hair. Maybe I'll take a nap."

She ought to go out, her grandmother protested. "Why don't you go up to the convent and see Sister Mary Agnes? You haven't been to see her since you came home."

"I think I'm tired," Cecilia said.

Well, it was her own fault, there was no need for her to work in a tiresome position that tied her down, her grandmother fretted. "You have an allowance from Tag and you know I'm more than willing to add to it."

Even though I am a Silverstein and my baby, if I have a baby, will be a Silverstein, thought Cecilia. She said aloud, "You're generous and good, Grandma, but I must work. Tag and I plan on building a house after the war."

Old Mrs. Warren regarded her image in the mirror with satisfaction. She liked to look nice and she believed she appeared younger than Annabel Pinn. Probably because Annabel wasn't mistress of her own home. She intended to keep the reins of her home always in her own hands, old Mrs. Warren reminded herself, it was a mistake to become a dependent.

She began to powder her face, innocently proud of her still fine skin. Cecilia must stay with her, never again would she face the dreariness of life without her granddaughter. *I won't worry,* old Mrs. Warren decided firmly. *With Tag overseas, anything may happen. Not that I want him to be killed—*

"I wish you'd call up Ida Ferris, after I've started," old Mrs. Warren said. "Tell her they want her to keep Leidy at home, till this evening at least. Mrs. Cotter's afraid the child will burst in upon her mother during the lunch and upset all the arrangements."

Ida, now on the swing shift, answered the telephone and seemed sociably inclined. Cecilia sounded limp, Ida commented; was her bank job too much of a strain? No? Then what was the matter? "I don't suppose there's any use asking if Junior is on his way?"

"Good gracious, I thought even a trained nurse needed more evidence." Cecilia was flustered.

Ida yelped in rising excitement. "Don't tell me I'm right?"

"I don't know." Cecilia hesitated. "I can't be sure. Tag was worried when he left, but we just don't know."

That was right up her alley, Ida announced, taking charge even at long range. "I'll tell you exactly what to do. You march straight up to Rinnell Memorial and have them give you the rabbit test. Oh, laugh if you want to, but don't be silly. Ceil, listen—it's infallible, if they use rabbits."

A belated spell of hot, dry weather served to remind every one whom Cecilia met to ask, "Was it as hot as this down South?" but they scarcely waited to hear her reply. They all asked questions nervously, feverishly, with no real interest in the answers. It seemed to her that apprehension and unhappiness touched every small life, whether for a loved one in the service, or for some hidden cause.

Cecilia herself let the work at the bank absorb her days and at night she wrote long letters to Tag. Mail came from him with fair regularity and surprising swiftness. He was stationed in Africa and for the first time in her life she discovered that continent on the globe. For the rest, she went obediently, almost indifferently, to dine with her Grandfather Ferris and her Aunt Dora, or with Uncle Frank and Aunt Ida, or more reluctantly, with poor Aunt Sarah and that strange, meek silent man who was Uncle Lion.

"I wish I had died years ago," Sarah said over and over, "while my girls still loved me. Your mother was more fortunate, Ceil—she never had to lose you."

At first Cecilia protested that her mother would not have lost her. "And how I wish I had her with me now, Aunt Sarah."

"Your marriage would have broken her heart," Sarah declared. "It's a mercy the poor woman was spared that trial."

Uncle Lion coughed. "Well now, Sarah, I don't think marriage necessarily breaks up the tie between a girl and her mother," he ventured. "It's natural for a girl to marry."

"You forget that Ceil married a Jew." Sarah sent an apologetic smile toward Cecilia. "Of course Tag is a fine boy and all that, but your mother would have felt terrible. I know how I feel about Fern." When Cecilia was a mother herself, Sarah added, she could better understand.

When she went to her Uncle Frank's a night or two later, Cecilia found that Molly Cotter and her husband had been invited for dinner together with Molly and Ida's mother. Although Annabel Pinn was Cecilia's great-aunt, she saw her at such long intervals that the old lady was almost a stranger to her.

Charlie Cotter looked morose and had little to say, unless directly addressed. Cecilia wondered why so many of these older men created the impression of dark heaviness, a smoldering resentment they made no effort to mend. She contrasted Tag's sweetness, his gay spirits, his gentle courtesy, with the brooding sulkiness of these men and wondered how much they had altered since their own young years.

"Bright, cheerful atmosphere at dinner, eh what?" suggested Ida as she and Cecilia did the dishes together. She had thought to enjoy a peaceful meal, with Leidy at a schoolmate's house, Ida went on—"Her grandmother always turns her into a show-off"—but there was a difference between peace and the tomb.

Cecilia absently dried a silver fork. "Did I imagine it, or is Cousin Charlie depressed? He wasn't always this way, was he?"

He had never been a ray of sunshine, Ida admitted, but he had been known to smile. "The trouble is tonight that he didn't want to come. My sister had to drag him here. He hates being in the same fold with his wife's family."

Charlie and Frank got along like the proverbial cat and dog, Ida attested, they were not alike in any way and if they had not married sisters would have avoided each other on any pretext. "Tonight there's a swarm of gnats hovering over Charlie—he hates going anywhere with Mother because she takes Molly's attention from him; he can't bear to eat the salt of Frank, and he's furious at me because I go to business and Molly doesn't."

Orphans were lucky, said Ida, there should be a law that only those without parents could marry. "That's one reason you and Tag are happy, Ceil."

"Oh, no!" Cecilia was shocked, but she remembered that Tag's parents had faced opposition to their marriage, that her father and mother had been unhappy because of parental disapproval. "I don't think it's easy to be a woman, Aunt Ida," she said. "Perhaps it's never natural for a mother to let go."

In the living room, after the dishes were finished, they found Frank and Charlie listening glumly to a news commentator and

Annabel and Molly playing dominoes on the card table which would later be used for bridge. One of the news dispatches from South America had caught Charlie's interest. His firm, he had mentioned, was planning to open a branch in Brazil, after the war.

"But by George, we fumble the good neighbor policy so constantly that I won't be surprised if every country down there turns on us," he grumbled, as Frank dialed another station. "You know what I heard today? Guess what the Catholics have been doing?"

Instantly a constrained silence enveloped them, a gulf that widened with each moment ticked off by the electric table clock. Cecilia cast desperately about in her mind for words, gasped. "Please, it's quite all right."

"Well, we forget—you seem just like us, dear," Molly soothed, which did not exactly put her embarrassed husband at his ease.

"Go ahead, Cousin Charlie," Cecilia encouraged. "What were you going to say? Tag and I often talk about the Catholics, you know."

Red-faced, Charlie stirred uneasily in his chair. It wasn't terribly important, just an instance. "One of the men I lunch with, he's a great church worker, was telling me that the Methodists, or the Baptists—or was it the Presbyterians?—have been sending missionaries down to South America, quite a lot of them."

The Catholic Church, Charlie continued, had lodged a protest with the United States government, claiming that the South American countries were not unchurched and needed no missionaries. "And yet, according to this man, the Catholics are sending down their missionaries in droves. Do you call that fair?"

He had forgotten embarrassment in the earnestness of his indignation, his jaw was tense, his eyes bright. He had swung round to face Cecilia who sat to his right in a high-backed Windsor chair. The dark wood was an effective foil for her long, slim body in a green crêpe frock and her hands, lying loosely in her lap, looked very white.

"I'm only interested in the justness of the thing," Charlie said. "Do you think it's fair?"

Cecilia drew a deep breath. "No, if it's true, it isn't fair," she conceded, her dark eyes glancing at the intent, listening faces turned toward her. "But what I don't understand," she told them, "is why any church in the United States thinks it necessary to go outside this country to teach the Christian gospel. None of us has yet learned it, here at home."

Sometimes in the afternoon, after the bank had closed, Cecilia stopped in at the *Bulletin* office to wait for Dora. They liked to have dinner together downtown and occasionally Trudy Spinelli joined them. She was at her desk one afternoon when Cecilia made her way to the cluttered little corner space, but Dora was not in sight.

Trudy interrupted the middle-aged man seated beside her desk, to speak to Cecilia. "Miss Ferris will be right down. She's in the composing room—knows you're coming."

Cecilia took her aunt's chair and looked respectfully at the litter of proofs and typed pages on the desk and in the wire baskets. Dora's half-smoked cigarette still smoldered in a glass ash tray. The murmur of voices at Trudy's desk suddenly became distinct as the man, his back to Cecilia, began to spell a name.

"V-e-n-i-t-o," he spelled, leaning down nearsightedly to follow the flying pencil. "Got it? That's right. And say, I just want to tell you, that isn't a Wop name."

Trudy answered politely. "It isn't?"

"No. I thought I'd better tell you because everyone thinks it's Italian and you might have a prejudice against Italian names. This man my daughter's marrying is no more a Wop than I am. We'd like her marriage played up a little—it means a lot to a girl."

He finally professed himself satisfied and disappeared into the elevator, as Dora stepped off. She beamed at Cecilia, frowned at the photograph of the bride Trudy presented to her.

"It's Mrs. Lorenzo Venito to be," Trudy explained. "And Venito isn't an Italian name, in case you are allergic to Italian names."

All the damn fools in the city eventually landed at the society desk, Dora grunted. "Mind waiting a bit, Ceil? I'm committed to a phone call, but only till five-thirty. Lord, Trudy, why didn't we have sense enough to change over to some of the nice alphabet civil service jobs? Or even a well-ordered home for the insane, where the inmates would be labeled as patients and not our steady readers?"

Trudy Spinelli shrugged slim shoulders. "You said that nothing would hire you to work in the alphabets, or a large insurance company, or any place where the help's regimented," she reminded her superior.

Well, to be sure, there was the bell, Dora mused thoughtfully, she knew she couldn't endure the bell.

"What bell?" Cecilia, who had been scanning the headlines of the last edition, put her paper aside.

Dora said, her mouth sober, her eyes twinkling. "They ring a bell in those places at half-past ten. That's the signal for you to rise up and er—attend to—er things."

"Imagine going to the bathroom with a little group of five or six thousand," Trudy shuddered.

It wasn't quite as bad as that, Dora interposed, she believed they staggered the employees. "But at that everyone in the building must know your destination, once the march begins. The tramp tramp, would drive me mad."

Cecilia, pondering, became more confused. "But look, Aunt Dora," she hesitated, "suppose when the bell rings you don't have to—and later you do have to—what happens then?"

"Look!" Dora mimicked. "You're supposed to lead a regular life in a big organization. If the ten-thirty bell means nothing to you, you're just out of luck."

"You could learn, I think," Trudy said hopefully. "Didn't someone teach dogs psychology by ringing a little bell?"

Dora retorted that the average person was not as bright as the average dog. "Taking the average reader of the *Bulletin* as the norm. Anyway, now you know why I cling to newspaper work where the only bells are the telephones and those in our heads." She lit a cigarette, put on her reading glasses, and picked up a proof.

Trudy said to Cecilia in a low voice, "What do you hear from your husband?"

Tag was well, the mail was going through wonderfully, Cecilia answered, glowing at the mention of his name. He had described the altar set up for a field mass; he carried the St. Christopher medal she had given him.

"How do you manage about church? I mean before he went over. I've often wondered." She had no problem, Trudy admitted cheerfully, neither she or her husband ever went to church.

"I went with Tag to his and he went with me to mine, whenever we could," Cecilia said simply. "But the Post has the right idea. I told Tag I didn't see why civilians don't manage their churches the same way."

One building served all creeds at the Post, Cecilia explained. The Catholic chaplain said masses Sunday morning, followed by the Protestant chaplain. The Jewish service was held Saturday. The altars differed, but that was all, Cecilia said. She had seen so many small towns and villages, before her marriage, in which perhaps half a dozen separate churches struggled to keep alive. "Why, one place where Grandma and I went for the summer, there were five churches—Catholic, Presbyterian, Methodist, and two denominations of Baptist, and not enough people in the town to fill one church. Why couldn't they all use one building?"

Dora pushed her papers aside. "Why couldn't they use one building?" she repeated. "I will tell you. Down at Fort Jackson there's no Ladies' Aid or Sodality. That's why they have harmony and peace. You get a congregation of men and they worship the Lord and are content. But women take their religion hard."

Cecilia laughed and Trudy smiled in sympathy.

"But I don't believe the harmony down at camp goes beyond the church doors," that dark-eyed cynic announced. "I'll bet the minute church is over, someone calls someone else a damyank."

They did rule the Northerners into the black sheep group, Cecilia admitted; they were all regarded as foreigners and either pitied or condemned. "At least they don't make a distinction between Gentiles and Jews—their suspicions are based on geographical grounds."

The phone on Dora's desk clicked, she lifted the handset. Cecilia noiselessly retreated to the chair beside Trudy's desk.

"Well, now look," Trudy argued in a low tone, "the way I see it, it's nature. We're not intended to like everybody. You said yourself your husband doesn't care for Jewish girls. My God, everyone has likes and dislikes."

The tapping of scattered typewriters sounded in the almost deserted city room. Stale tobacco smoke hung in the air, a stray breeze ruffled loose papers without lifting them from a wire basket. Cecilia watched Trudy light a fresh cigarette.

"I've thought a lot about it," Cecilia said, her thin, young face sober. "It may be natural to dislike some people, but it isn't natural to dislike them before you, as an individual, have a reason. Girls have said to me, 'How can you stand it to live with a Jew—they're all so noisy and aggressive and grubby.' Then, when they saw Tag, who is none of those things, they'd say, 'Why, you'd never take him to be Jewish would you?' "

Cecilia's level gaze swung to Dora, back again to Trudy. "Once I said to Tag, God forgive me, that as a little girl I had lived with my grandmother in an apartment where the landlord was a Jew and wouldn't make any repairs. And Tag said it was funny, but he had known Polish, Greek, and Italian landlords who wouldn't make repairs."

"I know!" Trudy sat up with a jerk. "Read the crime stories. All the murders are committed by Italians, I've been told. But if I said all burglars are white, Protestant Americans, can you hear the row?"

Dora had finished with her phone call. She scribbled a note on her pad. "Ceil, doesn't your good, solid ancestry have any meaning for you?" she asked abruptly. "Aren't you proud of your forebears?"

"In a way, yes." Cecilia considered. Somewhere close at hand a city clock struck the half-hour. "I think it's like this, Aunt Dory: I reverence the courage, the intelligence, the self-sacrifice, and integrity of my ancestors and they lay an obligation on me to develop my character in turn. But those traits are human—not racial. You may find them in a Gentile or in a Jew. Oh, Auntie, it is so simple and we make it so complicated; each of us will be judged by God as an individual soul. Why do we insist on passing judgments on the mass?"

Ginger Steel, en route to the Pacific Coast, stopped over for a day with her mother. She dashed in upon her Grandfather Ferris, who as usual was totally unprepared for her or her conversation. For Ginger's attention was not for her mother or for her sisters' affairs, but only for the question of Cecilia's pregnancy.

"You see, Grandfather," Ginger, sitting on the arm of Tobias' easy chair, patted his cheek affectionately, "some women can't be sure. And Cecil is that type. Naturally it's important for her to know."

"Have you been to see your sister Fern, Nutmeg?" Tobias inquired hastily. He settled Paris, tucked in like a squirrel at the back of the chair, more comfortably.

She had telephoned Fern at the fruit farm, Ginger answered, but a woman who couldn't speak English had said that Fern was over on the next farm, picking grapes.

"How'd you get all that straight, if the woman couldn't speak English?" demanded Tobias, and his grandchild, after the immemorial way of grandchildren, begged him not to be so tiresome.

"Aunt Ida told Cecil about the rabbit test," Ginger resumed. "It's supposed to be infallible. I don't exactly understand the details myself—"

Tobias intervened. Never mind the details, he suggested, how about the result? "She going to have a baby?"

"That's the whole trouble—I wish you wouldn't hurry me so," Ginger complained. "Ceil couldn't take the tests. She has to wait. They were out of rabbits."

"My good godfrey!" The startled Tobias leaped in sudden convulsion and Paris squawked. "Don't tell me there's a shortage of rabbits! Are they rationed? I thought there would always be rabbits."

Well, the hospital was out of them and they couldn't give the tests, Ginger affirmed with some resentment. Cecilia was to be notified, the delay wouldn't be long, Aunt Ida had said. "I'd love to know how they do it," Ginger mused dreamily. "Doctors must lead fascinating lives."

Tobias walked with her to the bus stop and on his way home detoured to the butcher's in search of lamb chops. Lamb, Quilty had instructed him, had become more plentiful since restored to the rationed meats. "Anything that's rationed there is more of," Quilty had observed in the voice of experience.

The doors of the butcher shop screened an interior comparatively dim in contrast to the glare of the late afternoon sun outside. Tobias blinked, adjusting his eyes to the change of light. When he finally succeeded in focusing, he found himself staring at a neat row of tawny, furred rabbits, laid out pathetically in the glass case backed by frosty, white refrigerating pipes. The bunnies rested stiffly on their backs, interiors gaping, hind legs tied together. Tobias, as if hypnotized, stared unbelievingly, until the round face of the genial, stout butcher popped into view.

"Yes, sir! Like a nice Belgian hare today? Fine eating—these just came in this morning."

He was a little disconcerted when his customer brought a clenched fist down on the top of the case.

"My good godfrey, man, don't mention rabbits to me!" Tobias shouted.

The tests were positive, Cecilia was going to have a baby, Dora told him a few days later. Cecilia was delighted and hopeful that she would have a son exactly like Tag in every way.

"She said there wasn't a single alteration she'd ask for," Dora reported, "and if Tag only realized it, that's the most wonderful compliment any husband can have from his wife."

Tobias, at rest with his cat, his pipe, and the Sunday newspapers, stole an uneasy glance at his daughter. She looked "different," he reflected—yes, she was too much dressed up for Sunday morning. The awful conviction smote him that she must be going to church.

"You going out?" he ventured.

To church, Dora acquiesced, confirming his suspicions. "And, since I have no husband, you're going with me. What? Oh, certainly women go to church alone, but the effect is neater when they're escorted. Besides, you ought to go to church now and then when it is neither Easter nor Christmas."

They were going, she informed Tobias, to St. John's, to hear a young rector, the son of a friend of his sister, Annabel Pinn. "I promised Aunt Annabel we'd hear him if he ever preached in our neighborhood."

"I can't go through all that getting up and kneeling down," Tobias protested. "My bones can't take it this fall."

He always complained that his bones stiffened through the long Presbyterian service, Dora reminded him. "You'll have to change your shirt, Father. And I'll brush the cat hairs off you. We start at quarter of."

Defeated, he managed to fire the final shot. "If you're fixing to wear that new hat you brought home this week, you don't need me to take you to church; you need a seeing-eye dog," Tobias said.

The rather small, notably historic church of St. John attracted a number of tourists at every service. Tobias could identify the majority of these since they made it a point to sit almost belligerently erect throughout the service, refusing to stand or kneel with the congregation. Presumably Episcopalians were few among the tourists, Tobias thought, his shrewd old eyes fixed on a pew ahead of him as the body of worshippers rose for the processional. The pew was occupied by a family group, father, mother, two young daughters, and a teen-age son, and they remained as if glued in their seats.

"Would it compromise 'em, if they stood up?" Tobias whispered to Dora. "Or do they figure out the Cross is a heathen symbol?"

Dora said "Sh" and Tobias subsided for the reading of the first lesson. But during the anthem, when he could remain seated, he studied the bulletin and presently he nudged his daughter. "Dora! Here, read this—that paragraph—" he indicated the fine print.

Dora read: "Services of intercession for all men in the armed forces will be conducted every day in the week, except Tuesday and Saturday, at 12:10 P.M."

"What do the armed forces do on Tuesday and Saturday?" whispered Tobias. "Trust in the Lord?"

She smiled, bit her lip. "Hush!"

Hymns, to Tobias, consisted of words alone. He could not follow the simplest tune, but like so many of the tone-deaf he loved to match his voice against the power of the organ. The thing he liked best about the Episcopalians, he was fond of stating, was their custom of singing a hymn straight through. Whether there were three verses or seven, they sang them all, never skipping to save time or breath. Today Tobias roared his way happily through "The Church of God a kingdom is," so absorbed in the hymnal that he did not see when a slight, gray-haired, black-robed figure took his place in the carved pulpit. Tobias, looking up as he closed his book, was surprised to find the rector serenely surveying his audience.

"In the name of God the Father, God the Son, and God the Holy Ghost—"

They sat down and Dora whispered that Aunt Annabel had mentioned Mr. Pomeroy's excellent diction. He was—Dora consulted the bulletin—rector of St. James-the-Less, a church in one of the suburban towns.

The text caught Tobias' attention, already beginning to wander.

" 'Let us consider one another,' " the clear, grave voice read, "... from Paul's Epistle to the Hebrews, the tenth chapter and twenty-fourth verse. 'And let us consider one another to provoke unto love and to good works.' "

The sermon that followed, exhorting men to "think like Christ, forgive like Christ, and love like Christ ... to love like Christ will be the most difficult...." merited approval, Tobias decided, on the grounds that the preacher had sense enough to use simple arguments and words. In reality the faultless English, spoken in a voice trained by years of effort, was part of a complex whole that nevertheless was gentle and sincere.

"Let us consider one another ..."

The September sunlight streamed through the upper sections of the stained glass windows, splashed the hats and gowns of the women worshippers with patches of purple and red. In the stalls a white-robed choir boy moved restlessly, outside the church a single piece of fire apparatus clattered past, its bell clanging dolefully.

"Let us consider one another ..."

After this I'm going to see if Quilty won't do up my shirts, Tobias thought without rancor. *I haven't had a decent collar since the hand laundry sold out to that bunch of damn kykes.*

(5)